*What's in store for this set of tall, rich, Italian
and handsome Rinucci brothers?
Love, marriage and a family reunited!*

# The Rinuccis:
# Carlo, Ruggiero
# & Francesco

Lucy Gordon triumphs again—this RITA®
award-winning author's popular Rinucci Italian
men are just irresistible!

# The Rinuccis: Carlo, Ruggiero & Francesco

LUCY GORDON

All the characters in this book have no existence outside the imagination of the author, and have no relation whatsoever to anyone bearing the same name or names. They are not even distantly inspired by any individual known or unknown to the author, and all the incidents are pure invention.

First published in Great Britain 2012
by Mills & Boon, an imprint of Harlequin (UK) Limited,
Eton House, 18-24 Paradise Road, Richmond, Surrey TW9 1SR

THE RINUCCIS: CARLO, RUGGIERO & FRANCESCO
© by Harlequin Enterprises II B.V./S.à.r.l 2012

*The Italian's Wife by Sunset, The Mediterranean Rebel's Bride* and *The Millionaire Tycoon's English Rose* were first published in Great Britain by Harlequin (UK) Limited in separate, single volumes.

*The Italian's Wife by Sunset* © Lucy Gordon 2007
*The Mediterranean Rebel's Bride* © Lucy Gordon 2007
*The Millionaire Tycoon's English Rose* © Lucy Gordon 2007

ISBN: 978 0 263 89675 6

05-0112

Printed and bound in Spain
by Blackprint CPI, Barcelona

# THE ITALIAN'S WIFE BY SUNSET

BY
LUCY GORDON

**Lucy Gordon** cut her writing teeth on magazine journalism, interviewing many of the world's most interesting men, including Warren Beatty, Richard Chamberlain, Sir Roger Moore, Sir Alec Guinness and Sir John Gielgud. She also camped out with lions in Africa and had many other unusual experiences which have often provided the background for her books. She is married to a Venetian, whom she met while on holiday in Venice. They got engaged within two days. Two of her books have won the Romance Writers of America RITA® award, *Song of the Lorelei* in 1990, and *His Brother's Child* in 1998, in the Best Traditional Romance category.

You can visit her website at www.lucy-gordon.com.

# CHAPTER ONE

THE picture on the computer screen seemed to fill the room with humour and good cheer. It showed a young man of strikingly attractive looks, fair, shaggy hair, dark blue glowing eyes and a smile that hinted at mischief.

'Oh, wow!' Jackie sighed. 'Just look at him!'

Della chuckled indulgently. Her secretary was young and easily moved by male beauty. She, herself, tried to be more detached.

'He's not bad,' she conceded.

'Not bad?' Jackie echoed, scandalised. 'He's a dream.'

'But I need more than a pretty face. I need a man who really knows his stuff, preferably one who's already made a name for himself.'

'Della, this is a TV series you're producing. It matters how he looks.'

'Yes, it matters that he looks like a serious expert and not a mere boy. Carlo Rinucci can't be more than about twenty-five.'

'According to his data he's thirty,' Jackie said, thumbing through papers. 'And he has a big reputation in ruins and bones and things like that.'

'But he's Italian. I can't have him fronting an English television series.'

'Some of which will be based in Italy. Besides, it says here that he speaks perfect English, and you've said yourself that you have to sell the series internationally if it's to make any money.'

This was true. In the world of television Della was a big shot, with her own production company and a brilliant reputation. Her programmes were in great demand. Even so, she had to consider the practicalities.

She studied Carlo Rinucci's face again, and had to admit that he had a lot going for him. He wasn't merely handsome. His grin had a touch of delightful wickedness, as though he'd discovered a secret hidden from the rest of the world.

'I had an uncle once,' Jackie said. 'He was a travelling salesman with a girl in every town and a line in flattery that would charm the birds off the trees. And no matter what he did everyone forgave him, just for the sake of his smile. Dad used to say Uncle Joe hadn't just eaten the Apple of Life, he'd gone to live in the tree.'

'And you think he's the same?' Della mused, scrutinising Carlo's laughing face.

'I'd take a bet on it.'

Privately Della agreed, but she kept that thought to herself. Her hard-won caution was warning her not to go overboard for this young man just because he looked good. Very good. Marvellous.

His resumé was certainly impressive. George Franklin, her assistant, who was helping to research this series, had e-mailed her.

Don't be misled by his youth. Carlo Rinucci is the up-and-coming man in his field. He's done some impressive work and written a couple of books that have attracted attention. His opinions are often unorthodox, but his work is sound.

He'd added a few notes about Carlo Rinucci's current project at Pompeii, the little town just south of Naples, buried long ago in the lava of the erupting volcano Vesuvius, and he'd finished with the words: *Believe me, he's worth investigating.*

'Worth investigating,' Della murmured.

'I'll investigate him for you,' Jackie said eagerly. 'I could get the next plane to Naples, look him over and report back.'

'Nice try,' Della said, amused.

'You mean you've already bagged him for yourself?'

'I mean,' Della said severely, 'that I shall consider all the options in a serious and practical way, make my evaluation, and decide what is best for the programme.'

'That's what I said. You've bagged him for yourself.'

Della laughed and dropped her formal tone.

'Well, there has to be some advantage in being the boss,' she said.

'No kidding! If you use him the ratings will go through the roof. Every country will want to buy the programme. You'll have a great reputation.'

'Some people think I already have a reputation,' Della said in mock offence.

'Not like the one you'll have if he's working for you.'

'So you think I should hire him to make my name for me? Thanks a lot, but I don't need help from him or any other pretty boy getting through life on his charm.'

'You don't know that he's char—'

'Just look at the time! You should be going home.'

Jackie departed, but not without one final lingering look at the computer screen.

'Behave yourself,' Della commanded, laughing. 'He's not that gorgeous.'

'Oh, yes, he is,' Jackie sighed as she retreated and closed the door.

For Della there was no journey to and from work, as she ran her business from her own home—a houseboat moored on the Thames, near Chelsea. She treasured it, not only for its own sake, but also as a symbol of the distance she'd travelled since the day she'd started out with almost nothing.

Now that it was six o'clock her working day hadn't ended, merely moved into a new phase—making calls to the other side of the world in different time zones. She kicked off her shoes and settled down.

Carlo Rinucci's face was still on the screen, but she refused to allow him to distract her. She reached out for the mouse, ready to click him into cyberspace, but her hand paused of its own accord.

Right from the start she'd insisted that the presenter for her series about places of great historical events must be someone with an impressive academic name.

'I don't want a handsome talking head who's going to reveal himself as a dumb cluck the minute he doesn't have a script,' she'd said. 'In fact, I'll expect him to write a lot of the script.'

She'd reviewed a host of possibilities, both male and female, all serious people with impressive reputations. One woman had aroused great hopes, but in the audition she became pompous. One man had seemed a real possibility—in his forties, elegant, serious, yet attractively suave—until he stood in front of a camera and became tongue-tied.

'I'll bet you're never lost for words,' she said, addressing the screen. 'Just looking at you, I know that. You can talk the hind legs off a donkey, which probably helped you get some of those fine-sounding qualifications.'

Then she stopped and stared. She could have sworn he'd winked at her.

'Enough of that,' she reproved him sternly. 'I know your kind. My second husband was just like you. Talk about charm! The trouble was, charm was all Gerry had—unless you include a genius for spending other people's money.'

She poured herself a drink and leaned back, contemplating the face with reluctant pleasure.

'Am I being unreasonable?' she asked him. 'Am I against you just because other people are for you? I know I'm a bit contrary. At least, folk claim that I am. They say I'm difficult, awkward, stubborn—and that's just my friends talking. But I've got a good life. I have a career that gives me all I want, and I'm immune to male attraction—well, sort of immune. Most of the time. You do nothing for me. Nothing at all.'

But he didn't believe her. She could see that in his face.

She gazed at him. He gazed back. What came next hovered inevitably in the air between them.

'So I guess,' she said slowly, 'there's no reason why I can't set up a meeting and look you over.'


'This place looks as though a bomb had hit it,' Hope Rinucci observed.

She was surveying her home: first the main room, then the dining room, then the terrace overlooking the Bay of Naples with a distant view of Vesuvius.

'Two bombs,' she added, viewing the disarray.

But she did not speak with disapproval, more like satisfaction. The previous evening there had been a party, and in Hope's opinion a party that didn't leave the surroundings looking shattered was no party at all.

By that standard last night had been a triumphant success.

Ruggiero, one of her younger sons, came into the room very carefully, and immediately sat down.

'It was a great night,' he said faintly.

'It was indeed,' she said at once. 'We had so much to cele-brate. Francesco's new job. Primo and Olympia, with Olympia's parents over from England, and the news that she's going to have a baby. And then Luke and Minnie saying that they're going to have a baby, too.'

'And then there's Carlo,' Ruggiero mused, naming his twin. 'Mamma, did you ever work out which of those three young ladies was actually his girlfriend?'

'Not exactly,' she said, taking him a black coffee, which he received gratefully. 'They all seemed to arrive together. If only Justin and Evie could have been here as well. But she is so heavily pregnant with the twins that I can understand her not wanting to travel. She promised to bring them to see us as soon as possible after they arrive.'

'So we can have another party,' Ruggiero said. 'Perhaps by then Carlo will have managed to divide himself into three.'

'Do you know which lady he went home with?'

'I didn't see him leave, but I have the impression that they all went together,' Ruggiero said enviously. '*Mio dio*, but he's a brave man!'

'Who's a brave man?' Francesco asked, coming carefully into the room.

Hope smiled and poured another coffee.

'Carlo,' she said. 'He brought three young ladies last night. Didn't you see?'

'He didn't notice anything but that exotic redhead,' Ruggiero said. 'Where did you find her?'

Francesco thought for a minute before saying, 'She found me—I think.'

'We were wondering which of his dates Carlo took home to his apartment,' Ruggiero said.

'He didn't go back there,' Francesco observed.

'How can you possibly know that?' Hope asked.

'Because he's here.'

Francesco pointed to a large sofa facing the window. Leaning over the back, the others saw a young man stretched out, blissfully asleep. He was in the clothes he'd worn the previous night, his shirt open at the throat, revealing smooth, tanned skin. Everything about him radiated sensual contentment.

'Hey!' Ruggiero prodded him rudely.

'Mmm?'

His twin prodded him again, and Carlo's eyes opened.

It was a source of intense irritation to his brothers that Carlo didn't awake bleary-eyed and vague, like normal people. Even after sleeping off a night of indulgence he was instantly alert, bright-eyed and at his best. As Ruggiero had once remarked, it was enough to make anyone want to commit murder.

'Hallo,' he said, sitting up and yawning.

'What are you doing there?' Ruggiero demanded, incensed.

'What's wrong with my being here? Ah, coffee! Lovely! Thanks, Mamma.'

'Take no notice of this pair,' Hope advised him. 'They're jealous.'

'Three,' Ruggiero mourned. 'He had three, and he slept on the sofa.'

'The trouble is that three is too many,' Carlo said philosophically. 'One is ideal, two is manageable if you're feeling adventurous, but anything more is a just a problem. Besides, I wasn't at my best by the end of the evening, so I played safe, called a taxi for the ladies and went to sleep.'

'I hope you paid their fares in advance,' Hope said.

'Of course I did,' Carlo said, faintly shocked. 'You brought me up properly.'

Francesco was aghast.

'Of all the spineless, feeble—'

'I know, I know.' Carlo sighed. 'I feel very ashamed.'

'And you call yourself a Rinucci?' Ruggiero said.

'That's enough,' Hope reproved them. 'Carlo behaved like a gentleman.'

'He behaved like a wimp,' Francesco growled.

'True,' Carlo agreed. 'But there can be great benefits to being a wimp. It makes the ladies *think* you're a perfect gentleman, and then, when next time comes—'

He drained his coffee, kissed his mother on the cheek, and escaped before his brothers vented their indignation on him.

The Hotel Vallini was the best Naples had to offer. It stood halfway up a hill, looking down on the city, with a superb view across the bay.

Standing on her balcony, Della kept quite still, regarding Vesuvius, where it loomed through the heat haze. There was nowhere in Naples to escape the sight of the great volcano, with its combination of threat and mystery. Its huge eruption nearly two thousand years ago, burying Pompeii in one day, had become such a legend that it was the first site Della had chosen when she was planning her series.

The three-hour flight had left her feeling tired and sticky. It had been a relief to step under a cool shower, wash away the dust, then dress in fresh clothes. The look she'd chosen was neat and unshowy, almost to the point of austerity: black linen pants, and a white blouse whose plainness didn't disguise its expensive cut.

Businesslike, she told herself. Which was true, but only partly. The outfit might have been designed to show off her tall, slim figure, with its small, elegant breasts and neat behind. Just how much satisfaction this gave her was her own secret.

Her face told a subtly different story, the full mouth having a touch of voluptuousness that was at variance with her chic outline. Her rich, light brown hair was sometimes pulled back in severe lines, but today she'd let it fall about her face in gentle curves, emphasising the sensuality of her face.

The contrast between this and the plain way she dressed caused a lot of enjoyable confusion among her male acquaintances. And she didn't mind that at all.

She had told nobody that she was coming, preferring to take her quarry unawares. She didn't even know that Carlo Rinucci would be at Pompeii today, only that he was working on a project that concerned the place, investigating new theories.

She hurried downstairs. It was early afternoon, and just time enough to get out there and form the impressions that would help her when she went into action next day.

Taking a taxi to the railway station, she bought a ticket for the Circumvesuviana, the light railway that ran between Naples and Pompeii, taking about half an hour. For most of that time she sat gazing out of the window at Vesuvius, dominating the landscape, growing ever nearer.

From the station it was a short walk to the Porta Marina, the city gate to Pompeii, where she purchased a ticket and entered the ruined city.

The first thing that struck her was the comparative quiet. Tourists thronged the dead streets, yet their noise did not rise above a gentle murmur, and when she turned aside into an empty yard she found herself almost in silence.

After the bustle of her normal life the peace was delightful. Slowly she turned around, looking at the ancient stones, letting the quiet seep into her.

'Come here! Do you hear me? *Come here at once.*'

The shriek rent the atmosphere, and the next moment she saw why. A boy of about twelve was running through the ruins, hopping nimbly over stones, hotly pursued by a middle-aged woman who was trying to run and shout at the same time.

'Come here!' she called in English.

The youngster made the mistake of looking back, which distracted him enough for Della to step into his path and grab him.

'Lemme go!' he gasped, struggling.

'Sorry, no can do,' she said, friendly but implacable.

'Thank you,' puffed the teacher, catching up. 'Mickey, you stop that. Come back to the rest of the class.'

'But it's boring,' the boy wailed. 'I hate history.'

'We're on a school trip,' the woman explained. 'The chance of a lifetime. I'd have been thrilled to go to Italy when I was at school, but they're all the same, these kids. Ungrateful little so-and-sos!'

'It's boring,' repeated the boy sullenly.

The two women looked at each other sympathetically. Quick as a flash the lad took his chance to dart away again, and managed to get out of sight around a corner. By the time they followed he'd found another corner and vanished again.

'Oh heavens! My class!' wailed the teacher.

'You go back to them while I find him,' Della said.

It was easier said than done. The boy appeared to have vanished into the stones. Della ran from street to street without seeing him.

At last she saw two men standing by a large hole in the ground, evidently considering the contents seriously. The younger man looked as though he'd just been working in the earth. Through his sleeveless vest she could see the glisten of sweat on strong, young muscles, and he was breathing hard.

In desperation she hailed them.

'Did a boy in a red shirt run past? He's a pupil escaping from a school party and his teacher is frantic.'

'I didn't see anyone,' the older man remarked. 'What about you, Carlo?'

Before she could react to the name the young man with his

back to her turned, smiling. It was the face she'd come to see, handsome, merry, relaxed.

'I haven't noticed—' he began to say, but broke off to cry, *'There!'*

The boy had appeared through an arch and started running across the street. Carlo Rinucci darted after him, dodging back and forth through archways. The boy's scowl vanished, replaced by a smile. Carlo grinned back, and it soon became a game.

Then the other children appeared, a dozen of them, hurling themselves into the game with delight.

'Oh, dear!' sighed the teacher.

'Leave them to it,' Della advised. 'I'm Della Hadley, by the way.'

'Hilda Preston. I'm supposed to be in charge of that lot. What am I going to do now?'

'I don't think you need to do anything,' Della said, amused. 'He's doing it all.'

It was true. The youngsters had crowded around the young man, and by some mysterious magic he had calmed them down, and was now leading them back to the teacher.

Like the Pied Piper, Della thought, considering him with her head on one side.

'OK, that's enough,' he said, approaching. 'Cool it, kids.'

'Whatever do you think you're doing?' Hilda demanded of the youngsters. 'You know I told you to stay close to me.'

'But it's boring,' complained the boy who'd made a run for it.

'I don't care if it is,' she snapped, goaded into honesty. 'I've brought you here to get some culture, and that's what you're going to get.'

Della heard a soft choke nearby, and turned to see Carlo fighting back laughter. Since she was doing the same herself, a moment of perfect understanding flashed between them. They both put their hands over their mouths at the same moment.

Predictably, the word *culture* had caused the pupils to emit groans of dismay. Some howled to heaven, others clutched their stomachs. One joker even rolled on the ground.

'Now she's done it,' Carlo muttered to Della. 'The forbidden word—one that should never be spoken, save in a terrified whisper. And she said it out loud.'

'What word is that?'

He looked wildly around, to be sure nobody was listening, before saying in a ghostly voice, 'Culture.'

'Oh, yes, I see.' She nodded knowingly.

'You'd think a modern schoolteacher would know better. Does she do that often?'

'I don't know—I'm not—' she began, realising that he thought she was one of the school party.

'Never mind,' he said. 'It's time for a rescue operation.' Raising his voice, he said, 'You can all calm down, because this place has nothing to do with culture. This place is about people dying.' For good measure he added, *'Horribly!'*

Hilda was aghast. 'He mustn't say things like that. They're just children.'

'Children love gore and horror,' Della pointed out.

'It's about nightmares,' Carlo went on, 'and the greatest catastrophe the world has ever known. Thousands of people, living their ordinary lives, when there was an ominous rumble in the distance and Vesuvius erupted, engulfing the town. People died in the middle of fights, of meals—thousands of them, frozen in one place for nearly two thousand years.'

He had them now. Everyone was listening.

'Is it true they've got the dead bodies in the museum?' someone asked, with relish.

'Not the actual bodies,' Carlo said, in the tone of a man

making a reluctant admission, and there was a groan of disappointment.

Bloodthirsty little tykes, Della thought, amused. But he's right about them.

'They were trapped and died in the lava,' Carlo continued, 'and when they were excavated, centuries later, the bodies had perished, leaving holes in the lava of the exact shapes. So the bodies could be reconstructed in plaster.'

'And can we see them?'

'Yes, you can see them.'

A sigh of blissful content showed that his audience was with him. He began to expand on the subject, making it vibrantly alive. He spoke fluently, in barely accented English, with an actor's sense of the dramatic. Suddenly the streets were populated with heroes and villains, beautiful heroines, going about their daily business, then running hopelessly for their lives.

Della seized the chance to study him in action. It went against the grain to give him top marks, but she had to admit that he ticked every box. The looks she'd admired on the screen were enhanced by the fact that his hair needed a trim, and hung in shaggy curls about his face.

He looked like Jack the Lad—a brawny roustabout without a thought in his head beyond the next beer, the next girl, or the next night spent living it up. What he didn't look like was an academic with a swathe of degrees, one of them in philosophy.

'History isn't about culture,' he finally reassured them. 'It's about people living and dying, loving and hating—just like us. Now, go with your teachers and behave yourself, or I'll drown you in lava.'

A cheer showed that this threat was much appreciated.

'Thank you,' Hilda said. 'You really do have a gift with children.'

He grinned, his teeth gleaming against the light tan of his face.

'I'm just a born show-off,' he laughed.

That was true, Della mused. In fact, he was exactly what she needed.

Hilda thanked her and turned to shepherd the children away. Carlo looked at her in surprise.

'Aren't you with them?' he asked.

'No, I just happened along,' she said.

'And found yourself in the middle of it, huh?'

They both laughed.

'That poor woman,' Della said. 'Whoever sent her here on a culture trip should have known better.'

He put out his hand.

'My name is Carlo Rinucci.'

'Yes, I—' She was about to say that she knew who he was, but hastily changed it to, 'I'm Della Hadley.'

'It is a great pleasure to meet you, *signorina*—or should that be *signora*?'

'Technically, yes. I'm divorced.'

He gave her a gentle, disarming smile, still holding her hand.

'I'm so glad,' he said.

Watch it, warned a voice in her head. He plays this game too well.

'Hey, Carlo,' called the other man, 'are you going to give the *signora* her hand back, or shall we put it in the museum with the others?'

She snatched her hand back, suddenly self-conscious. Carlo, she noticed, wasn't self-conscious at all. He just gave a grin that he clearly knew would always win him goodwill.

'I forgot about Antonio,' he admitted.

'Don't mind me,' Antonio said genially. 'I've just been doing the work while you do your party tricks.'

'Why don't we finish for the day?' Carlo said. 'Time's getting on, and Signora Hadley wants a coffee.'

'Yes, I want one desperately,' she said, discovering it to be true.

'Then let's go.' He looked her in the eye and said significantly, 'We've lost too much time already.'

# CHAPTER TWO

DELLA waited while he showered at top speed, then emerged casually dressed in a white short-sleeved shirt and fawn trousers. Even in this simple attire he looked as though he could afford the world, and she guessed that he'd had a privileged upbringing.

'Let's get that coffee,' Carlo said.

But when they reached the self-service cafeteria they both stopped dead. The place was packed with tourists, all yelling with raucous good cheer.

'I think not,' he said firmly.

He didn't wait for her answer, but simply took her hand and walked away, adding, 'I know lots of better places.'

But then, abruptly, he stopped.

'Where are my manners?' he demanded, striking himself on the forehead. 'I didn't ask if you wanted to go into that place. Shall we turn back?'

'Don't you dare,' she said at once.

He grinned, nodding, and they went on in perfect accord.

His car was just what she would have expected—an elegant sports two-seater in dashing red—and, also as she would have expected, he ushered her into it with a flourish. His whole body was a clever combination of different effects. Built like a hunk, yet he moved with subtlety and grace. His hands on the steering wheel held her attention, lying there lightly, barely touching, yet controlling the powerful machine effortlessly.

Della's mind was reeling.

Just what I need, she thought. He's ideal—for the programme. Handsome, charming, never at a loss for words—*he* won't suddenly become tongue-tied in front of a camera, or anywhere else. The perfect— She paused in her thoughts and tried to remember that she was a television producer. 'The perfect *product*. Yes, that's it.

She felt better once she'd settled that with herself.

'Do you live around here?' Carlo asked.

'No, I'm just visiting. I'm staying at the Vallini in Naples.'

'Are you planning to stay long?'

'I—haven't quite decided,' she said carefully.

He swung onto the coast road and they drove with the sea on their left, glittering in the late-afternoon sun. Naples lay ahead, but when they reached halfway he turned off into a tiny seaside village. Della could see fishing boats tied up at the water's edge, and cobbled streets stretching away between old houses.

He parked the car and made his way confidently to a small restaurant. As soon as they entered a man behind the counter yelled joyfully, *'E, Carlo!'*

*'Berto!'* he yelled back cheerfully, and guided Della to a table by a small window.

Berto came hurrying over with coffee, which he contrived to pour while chattering and giving Della quick, appraising glances.

I'll bet they see him in here with a new companion every week, she thought, with an inner chuckle.

The coffee was delicious, and she began to relax for the first time since she'd awoken that morning.

'It was so good to get off that plane,' she said, giving herself a little shake.

'You just arrived from England?'

'You could tell because I'm speaking English, right?'

'It's a bit more than that. My mother is English, and there's something in your voice that sounds a little like her.'

'That explains a lot about you, too.'

'Such as what?' he asked curiously.

'You speak English with barely an accent.'

He laughed. 'That was Mamma's doing. We all had to speak her language perfectly, or else.'

'All? You have plenty of brothers and sisters?'

'Just brothers. There are six of us, related in various ways.'

'Various?' She frowned. 'I thought you just said you were brothers.'

'Some of us are brothers, some of us are "sort of" brothers. When Mamma married Poppa she already had two sons, plus a stepson and an adopted son. Then they had two more.'

'Six Rinucci brothers?' she mused.

'It doesn't bear thinking about, does it?' he said solemnly. 'It's just terrible.'

His droll manner made her chuckle, and he went on, 'Even the most Italian of us are part English, but some are more English than others. The differences get blurred. Poppa says we're all the devil's spawn anyway, so what does it matter?'

'It sounds like a lovely, big, happy family.' She sighed enviously.

'I suppose it is,' he said, seeming to consider. 'We fight a lot, but we always make up.'

'And you'd always be there for each other. That's the nicest thing.'

'You said that like an only child,' he observed, regarding her with interest.

'Is it that obvious?' she asked.

'It is to someone who has many siblings.'

'I must admit that I really envy you that,' she said. 'Tell me some more about your brothers. You don't fight all the time, surely?'

'On and off. Mamma's first husband was English, but his first wife had been Italian—a Rinucci. Primo is the son of that marriage, so he's half-Italian, half-English. Luke, the adopted son of that marriage is all English. Are you with me?'

'Struggling, but still there. Keep going.'

'Primo and Luke have always traded insults, but that means nothing. It's practically a way of communicating—especially while they were in love with the same woman.'

'Ouch!'

'Luckily that didn't last very long. Primo married her, and Luke found someone else, and now their wives keep them in order, just as wives should.'

'Oh, really?' she said ironically.

'No, really. Any man who's grown up in this country knows that when the wife speaks the husband stands to attention— if he's wise. Well, it's what my father does, anyway.'

'And when your turn comes you'll choose a woman who knows how to keep you in order?'

'No, my mother will choose her,' he assured her solemnly. 'She's set her heart on six daughters-in-law, and so far she's only achieved three. Every time a new woman enters the house I'll swear she checks her for suitability and ticks off a list. When she finds the right one I'll get my orders.'

'And you'll obey?' she teased.

His answering grin was rich with life, an invitation to join him in adventure.

'That's a while off yet,' he said contentedly. 'I'm in no rush.'

'Life's good, so why spoil it with a wife?'

'I wouldn't exactly put it like that,' he said uneasily.

'Yes, you would,' she said at once. 'Not out loud, perhaps. But deep inside, where you think I can't hear.'

His answer was unexpected.

'I wouldn't bet against your being able to hear anything I was thinking.'

Then he looked disconcerted, as though he had surprised even himself with the words, and his laugh had a touch of awkwardness that affected her strangely.

Berto came to their table to tell them that the day's catch of clams was excellent, and that *spaghetti alle vongole* could be rustled up in a moment.

'Clam pasta,' Carlo translated.

'Sounds lovely.'

'Wine?' Berto queried.

Carlo eyed her questioningly, and she hastened to say, 'I leave everything to you.'

He rattled off several names that Della didn't recognise, and Berto bustled away.

'I took the liberty of ordering a few other things as well,' Carlo explained.

'That's fine. I wouldn't have known what to ask for.'

His eyes gleamed. 'Playing the tactful card, huh?'

'I'm a newcomer here. I listen to the expert.'

Berto returned with white wine. When he had poured it and gone, Carlo said, 'So, you reckon you can see right through me?'

'No, *you* said I could. Not me.'

'I have to admit that you got one or two things right.'

'Let's see how well I manage on the rest. I know Italian men often stay at home longer than others, but I don't think that you do, because Mamma's eagle eye might prove—shall we say, inhibiting?'

'That's as good a word as any,' he conceded cautiously.

'You've got a handy little bachelor apartment where you take the girls you can't take home because they wouldn't tick any of Mamma's "suitability" boxes, and that's just fine by you—'

*'Basta!'* He stopped her with a pleading voice. 'Enough, enough! How did you learn all that?'

'Easy. I just took one look at you.'

'Obviously I don't have any secrets,' he said ruefully.

'Well, perhaps I was a little unfair on you.'

'No, you weren't. I deserved it all. In fact, I'm worse. My mother would certainly say so.'

She chuckled. 'Then think of me as a second mother.'

'Not in a million years,' he said softly.

His eyes, gliding significantly over her, made his meaning plain beyond words, and suddenly she was aware that she looked several years younger than her age, that her figure was ultra-slim and firm, thanks to hours in the gym, that her eyes were large and lustrous and her complexion flawless.

Every detail of her body might have been designed to elicit a man's admiration. She knew it, and at this moment she was passionately glad of it.

It might be fun.

*He* was certainly fun.

Berto arrived with clam pasta, breaking the mood—which was a relief, since she hadn't decided where she wanted this to go. But a moment ago there had been no choice to make. What had happened?

He was watching her face as she ate, relishing her enjoyment.

'Good?'

'Good,' she confirmed. 'I love Italian food, but I don't get much chance to eat it.'

'You've never been here before?'

'I had a holiday in Italy once, but mostly I depend on Italian restaurants near my home.'

'Where do you live?'

'In London, on a houseboat moored on the Thames.'

'You live on the water? That's great. Tell me about it.'

At this point she should have talked about her serious day-to-day life, with its emphasis on work, and the occasional visit from her grown up son. Instead, unaccountably, Della found herself describing the river at dawn, when the first light caught the ripples and the banks emerged from the shadows.

'Sometimes it feels really strange,' she mused. 'I'm right there, in the heart of a great city, yet it's so quiet on the river just before everywhere comes alive. It's as though the world belongs to me alone, just for a little while. But you have to catch the moment because it vanishes so quickly. The light grows and the magic dies.'

'I know what you mean,' he murmured.

'You've been there?'

'No, I—I meant something else. Later. Tell me some more about yourself. What sort of work do you do?'

'I'm in television,' she said vaguely.

'You're a star—your face on every screen?'

'No, I'm strictly behind the scenes.'

'Ah, you're one of those terrifyingly efficient production assistants who gets everyone scurrying about.'

'I've been told I can be terrifying,' she admitted. 'And people have been known to scurry around when I want them to.'

'Maybe that's why I thought you were a schoolteacher?'

'You've got quite a way with youngsters yourself.'

But he dismissed the suggestion with a gesture of his hand.

'I'd be a terrible teacher. I could never keep discipline. They'd all see through me and know that I was just one of the kids at heart.'

'You had them hanging on your every word.'

'That's because I'm crazy about my subject and I want everyone else to be crazy, too. I believe it can make me a bit of a bore.'

'Sure, I'm sitting here fainting with boredom. Tell me about your subject.'

'Archaeology. No, don't say it—' He interrupted himself quickly. 'I don't look like an archaeologist, more like a hippie—'

'I was thinking a hobo myself,' she said mischievously. 'Someone not very respectable, anyway.'

'Thank you. I take that as a compliment. I'm not respectable. I don't pretend to be. Who needs it?'

'Nobody, as long as you know your stuff—and you obviously do.'

Carlo grinned. 'Why? Because I kept a few youngsters quiet? That's the easy part, being a showman. It's not what really counts.'

She'd actually been thinking of his string of qualifications, but remembered in time that she wasn't supposed to know about them.

'What does really count?' she asked, fascinated.

That was all he needed. Words poured from him. Some she understood, some were above her head, but what was crystal-clear was his devotion, amounting to a love affair, to ancient times and other worlds.

All his life he'd had soaring ambitions, hating the thought of being earthbound.

'I used to play truant at school,' he recalled, 'and my teachers all predicted I'd come to a bad end because I was bound to fail my exams. But I fooled 'em. I used to sit up the night before, memorising everything just long enough to pass with honours.' He sighed with happy recollection. 'Lord, but that made them mad!'

She couldn't help laughing at the sight of him, transformed back into that rebellious schoolboy.

'I couldn't face anything nine-to-five,' he said. 'Not at school, not at work. The beauty of being in my line is that you get to fly.'

'And you really have to fly,' she teased. 'I guess when you get near the earth you crash.'

'Right. That's why I could never be a teacher, or a museum administrator. I might have to—' He looked desperate.

'Might have to what?' she asked through her laughter.

He glanced over his shoulder and spoke with a lowered voice. *'Wear a collar and tie.'*

He sat back with the air of one who had described unimaginable horrors. Della nodded in sympathy.

'But doesn't it ever get depressing?' she asked. 'Spending so much time surrounded by death, especially in Pompeii—all those people, petrified in the positions they died in nearly two thousand years ago?'

'But they're not dead,' he said, almost fiercely. 'Not to me. They're still speaking, and I'm listening because they have so much to say.'

'But hasn't it all been said? I mean, they finished excavating that place years ago. What more is there?'

He almost tore his hair.

'They didn't finish excavating. They barely started. I'm working on a whole undiscovered area—'

He stopped, and seemed to calm himself down by force of will.

'I'm sorry. Once I get started there's no stopping me. I told you I'm a bore.'

'I wasn't bored,' she said truthfully. 'Not a bit.'

In truth, she was fascinated. A fire was flaming within him and she wanted to see more, know more.

'Go on,' she urged.

Then he was away again, words pouring out in a vivid, passionate stream so that she caught the sense even of the bits she didn't understand. After a while she stopped trying to follow too closely. It didn't matter. What mattered was that he could make her see visions through his own eyes. It was like being taken on a journey into the heart of the man, and it was exhilarating.

'You've let your food get cold,' he said at last.

At some point they had passed onto the next course, and it had lain uneaten on both their plates while he took her on a journey to the stars.

'I forgot about it,' she said, feeling slightly stunned.

'So did I,' he admitted.

The voice of caution, which normally ruled her life, whispered, *A practised charmer*, but the warning floated away, unheeded. Something more was happening—something that would make her get up and leave now, if she had any sense.

But she didn't want to be sensible. She wanted to go on enjoying this foolish magic, as crazy as a teenager. No matter how it ended. She would relish every moment.

Carlo watched her without seeming to. It was becoming important to him to 'capture' her in his mind, as though by doing so he could fit her into some niche where he would know what to make of her. Luckily the hours stretched ahead, full of time to get to know her better.

Then, out of the corner of his eye, Carlo saw an acquaintance come into the restaurant, and he cursed silently. The man was well-meaning but long-winded, and if he didn't act fast his evening would be in ruins.

'I'll be back in a moment,' he said hurriedly, leaving the table.

His worst fears were fulfilled. His friend greeted him with bonhomie, and a determination to join him at all costs. Carlo just managed to head him off at the pass, and finally made his way back to the table, determined on escape.

Della was talking on her cellphone as he approached, and he heard her say, 'It's lovely to talk to you, darling.'

It wasn't so much the word that troubled him as the soft adoration in her voice, the glow in her eyes.

For pity's sake, he chided himself. You've only known her a few hours. What do you care who she calls darling?

He wished he knew the answer.

She was laughing, her face alight with affection.

'I've got to go now. I'll call you again soon. Bye, darling.' She hung up.

A moment later Carlo reached the table, showing no sign that he'd heard the call or even knew she'd made one.

'Perhaps we should move on?' he said.

She nodded. She had seen him talking urgently with a man, blocking his way so that he could not disturb them.

Outside, he took her hand and headed for the car, but then stopped suddenly, as though something had struck him.

'No—wait! The time's just right.'

'Right for what?'

'I'll show you.'

He turned and began to lead her in the opposite direction. Gradually the houses fell away and they were going towards the shore, reaching the road that ran beside it and crossing over onto the beach.

'Look,' he said.

The tide had gone out, leaving the fishing boats lying lopsided on the wet sand. Water lay in the ridges and the tiny pools, and the last rays of the setting sun had turned it deep red.

She gazed, awestruck, at so much dramatic beauty before finally breathing, 'It's magic.'

'Yes, it is. Not everyone sees it, but I thought you would

because of what you told me about dawn on the Thames. To some people it's just wet sand and a few boats. If you see them by day they're old and shabby. But like this—'

He stopped, almost as if hoping that she would finish his thought.

'Another world,' she said. 'A special world that only appears for a short time.'

She thought he gave a little sigh of pleasure.

'Just a short time,' he agreed. 'Soon it will be dark, and the special world will vanish.'

'But it'll return tomorrow.'

'It may not. It isn't always like this, only when everything is right. It's like you said: you have to be ready to catch the moment before it vanishes.'

He was leading her out in the direction of the sea, leaving the conventional safety of the land behind, taking her into an unfamiliar world.

'Wait,' she said. 'Let me take off my shoes before they get wet.'

She did so, shoving them into her capacious shoulder bag. He removed his own and she grabbed them, putting them, too, into the bag, and taking his hand again.

Not speaking, they walked towards the horizon, until the shallow water just covered their feet.

'This is when it's at its best,' he said quietly.

The setting sun covered the beach and the film of water with blazing red in all directions, so that they might have been standing in a fire. It drenched them with its mysterious violent light.

Carlo looked at her, smiling, and she braced herself, knowing that this was exactly the right moment for a skilled charmer to kiss her, and that he, who clearly knew all the moves, would be bound to make this one. But then she saw that there was something awkward, almost shy, about his smile. While she was trying to puzzle it out, he raised her hand and rubbed the back of it against his cheek.

She stared, too dumbfounded to react. According to the script he should have kissed her, and if he'd done so she would have known how to 'place' him. But the closest he came was to press his lips gently where his cheek had touched a moment earlier. And when she met his eyes she saw that he was as disconcerted as she.

The next moment the light changed. Something brilliant faded. And it was over.

'It's gone,' she said, disappointed.

'It's gone for now,' he agreed. 'But there are other things. Let's go.'

As twilight fell Carlo drove along the coast until they reached the outskirts of Naples.

'Shall I take you to your hotel?' he asked.

'Yes, please. I need to talk to you where we won't be disturbed.'

She knew she couldn't put the moment off any longer. Something had started to happen, and if it were to flower she must be honest with him first.

As they went up in the elevator at the Vallini she was planning how she would explain that their meeting had not been an accident. Such was his good nature that she had no fears about his reaction.

The last of the light faded as they entered her room and shut the door. Before she could reach for the switch she felt his arms go around her, drawing her close, fitting her head against his shoulder.

At once she relaxed. This was what she'd wanted for at least the last hour. Why deny it? It was undignified to have fallen so easily into the trap, especially as she had seen it from a distance, but that was what had happened.

But the trap wasn't the one she'd armed herself against. A glib tongue and an easy manner—those she could cope with. But the uncertainty in his eyes when they'd met hers had caught her unawares

It was the worst moment for her cellphone to buzz. Groaning, Carlo released her, and she turned away, walking to the window as she reached into her purse. Taking out the phone, she discovered a text message.

'Shall we have champagne?' came Carlo's voice from behind her.

She hadn't realised that he was so close, and jumped sharply enough to drop the phone.

'Sorry,' he said. 'I'll get it for you. It went under that chair.'

He dropped to his knees and reached for it. Then, as he drew it out, Della saw his smile fade. In silence he handed it to her. Her blood ran cold as she saw the words on the illuminated screen.

Have you tracked Rinucci down yet? George

Looking up, she saw Carlo standing back, regarding her. On the surface his good humour seemed unruffled, but she could see the distance in his eyes.

'You came to "track me down"?' he asked coolly.

She sighed. 'Yes, I did come here looking for you.'

'What did I do to merit that?'

'If you'd let me explain in my own way—'

'Just tell me.' His voice was ominously quiet.

'You're ideal for a television show I'm planning. I've got my own production company, and I'm setting up a series about places of great dramatic events in history. I need a frontman, and someone told me you'd be ideal.'

'So you came down to audition me?'

'Not exactly that,' she said uneasily.

'How would you describe it?'

'I wanted to meet you, and—and—'

'And get me to jump through some hoops to see if I was up to your standard? And I obliged, didn't I? I jumped through them all, and then some!'

'Carlo, please—all right, I should have told you before.'

'You sure as hell should.'

'But I couldn't predict what was going to happen. When I saw you with those kids, you were so perfect for my purpose that I couldn't believe my luck—'

'Perfect for your purpose?' he echoed, in a soft, angry voice. 'Yes, it's all been about your purpose, hasn't it? You pulled the strings and I danced.'

'Is it so terrible that I wanted to consider you for a job?'

'Not at all, if you'd been up-front. It's the thought of you peering at me from behind a mask that I can't stand. All the time we've been together I thought—well, never mind what I thought. Just tell me this. Did you plan every single detail?'

'Of course not. How could I? You know that things happened that nobody could have planned.'

'Do I? I'm not sure what I understand any more. I know that you've been clever—subtle enough for an Italian. I congratulate you. It was a masterly performance.'

'It wasn't all a performance,' she said swiftly.

'You know, I think I'd rather believe that it was. It makes things simpler. I was a fool, but at least I found out before any real harm was done.'

'Carlo, please—if you'd just listen to me—'

'I've done enough of that,' he said, in a deceptively

affable tone. 'Let's call it a day. You'd better text George back and tell him that you tracked me down and I said to hell with you. Goodbye.'

He was gone, closing the door behind him.

She wanted to scream with frustration and hurl the phone against the door. Instead she turned out the light and went onto the balcony. From there she could see Carlo's car, parked in front of the hotel, then Carlo himself, hurtling out of the front door and leaping into the driver's seat.

She drew back in case he looked up and saw her, but he only sat for a long moment, hunched behind the wheel, brooding. When at last he roused himself, it was to give the wheel a sharp thump that made the horn blast. After his ironic restraint the sudden spurt of temper was startling.

Then he fired the engine, swung out of the forecourt and vanished down the road. He hadn't once looked up at Della's window.

# CHAPTER THREE

AT SEVENTEEN she might have wept into her pillow. At thirty-seven she lay staring into the darkness, sad but composed, before finally nodding off.

She even managed a prosaic, unromantic night's sleep. But next morning Della awoke early and the memories came flooding back, bringing regretful thoughts.

It would have been nice, she thought. We could have been fond of each other for a while, before he found someone his own age. But, oh boy, did I ever make a mess of it! If there were a prize for handling things as badly as possible, I'd win the gold. I should have known better than to hide the truth, but I wasn't thinking straight.

At this point she found herself smiling wistfully.

But had any woman ever thought straight in his company? She doubted it. Not guilty on the grounds of impaired judgment. She'd wanted to make the moment last, and she had never thought how it would seem to him.

What now? Return to Pompeii and try to find him? After all, he's ideal for the programme.

Nuts to that! She just wanted an excuse to see him again. He was like a light coming on and then going out too soon. But what was done was done. She'd just chalk it up to experience and leave Naples today.

It was a relief to have made up her mind. Jumping out of bed, she stripped and headed for the shower, running it very cold to infuse herself with common sense. She was just drying off when there was a knock on the door.

'Who is it?'

'Room Service.'

She hadn't ordered anything, but perhaps this was courtesy of the hotel. Huddling on a silk dressing gown, she opened the door.

Outside stood a tall man, dressed as a waiter. That was all she could tell, as he was holding the tray high, balanced on the fingers of one hand, at just the right angle to conceal his face.

'*Scusi, signora.*'

He seemed to glide into the room, contriving to keep his features hidden as he headed for the little table by the window and set down the tray.

Della's heart began to dance. He might hide his face, but his hair was unmistakable. Instinctively she pulled together the edges of her thin dressing gown, conscious of how inadequately the silk covered her.

'Orange juice,' he said, turning to her with a flourish. 'Fruit? Cereal?'

'So you're not still angry with me?' she asked, laughing.

'No, I got over my sulk fairly quickly. Forgive me?'

It was so good to see Carlo standing there that she forgot everything else and opened her arms to him. He took two swift steps across the room, and the next moment she was enfolded in an embrace that threatened to crush the breath out of her.

'I was afraid you'd have packed your bags and left last night,' he said between kisses.

'I was afraid I'd never see you again. I'm sorry. I never meant it to happen the way it did—it just sort of—'

'It doesn't matter. It was my fault for making a fuss about nothing.'

'I always meant to tell you, but things just happened, and I lost track of what I was supposed to be thinking—'

'Yes,' he said with meaning. 'Me too.'

He kissed her again before she could speak, moving his mouth hungrily over hers, pressing her body close against his own. Now she could feel everything she had suspected yesterday, the hard, lean length of him, muscular, sensuously graceful, thrilling.

But it was dangerous to hold him like this when she was nearly naked. The gossamer delicacy of her gown was no protection against the excitement she could sense in him, nor against her own excitement, rising equally fast. Nearly naked wasn't enough. Only complete nakedness would do, for herself and him.

There was an increasingly urgent sense of purpose in the movements of his hands, and her answering desire threatened to overwhelm her. She wanted this. She wanted *him*.

It was the very power of that wanting that made her take fright. Twenty-four hours ago she hadn't met this man. Now she was indulging fantasies of fierce passion, desire with no limits. She must stop this now. She forced herself to tense against him, drawing her head back a little so that he could see her shake it from side to side.

'No—Carlo—please—'

'Della—' His voice was edgy, and it seemed as though he couldn't stop.

'Please—wait—'

She felt his body trembling against hers with the effort of his own restraint, and at last he was still. Now he would think her a tease. But when she looked into his eyes she saw only understanding.

'You're right,' he whispered.

'It's just that—'

'I know—I know—not—not yet.'

He spoke raggedly, but he was in command of himself. Della only wished she could say the same about her own body, which was raging out of control, defying her wise words. She pulled herself free, grabbed some clothes, and vanished into the bathroom.

When she emerged, safely dressed, he had discarded his waiter's jacket and was sitting at the table by the window, pouring her coffee. He seemed calm, with no sign of his recent agitation—except that she thought his hand shook a little.

'Here's food,' he said, indicating rolls and honey. 'But if you need something more substantial I'll buy you a big lunch after we've been to Pompeii.'

'We're going back there?'

'Just for an hour, while I give my team their instructions. Then we'll have the rest of the day free.'

His manner was demure while he served her, as if their moment of blazing physical awareness had never been. But then she glanced up to find him watching her, and it was there in his eyes, memory and, more than that, an anticipation amounting to certainty.

'I'm sorry for what happened,' she said again. 'I was going to tell you last night, but—' She made a helpless gesture.

'It was mostly my fault,' he said, shaking his head. 'I just talked about myself all the time, which is a fault of mine. Mamma always says if I'd shut up now and then I might learn something.'

'But you've never taken her advice long enough to find out if she's right,' Della chuckled.

He grinned. 'You really do sound just like her. Besides, I know now that she *was* right. Today you're going to do all the talking, and I won't say a single word.'

'Hmm!' she said sceptically.

He looked alarmed. 'You understand me too well.'

'In that case we have nothing left to say to each other.'

'Why?'

'Well, isn't that every man's nightmare? A woman who understands him?'

'I'm getting more scared of you every minute.'

'Then you'd better steer well clear of me. If I call the airport now there's bound to be a plane back to London today.'

At once his hand closed over hers, imprisoning it gently but firmly.

'I never run away from danger,' he said lightly. 'How about you?'

There was a moment's hesitation, because something told her that never in her life had she met a danger like this. Then, 'Me neither,' she said.

'Good. In that case...' He paused significantly.

'In that case—?'

'In that case I suggest we hurry up and finish our breakfast.'

She choked into her coffee. She had always been a sucker for a man who could make her laugh.

At Pompeii, his team was waiting for him in the canteen. A brief time in his company had made her more sharply aware of things she had overlooked before, and now she saw at once how the young women in the group brightened as soon as he appeared, and flashed him their best smiles.

She couldn't blame them. There was a life-enhancing quality to him that brought the sun out, and made it natural to smile.

Della lingered only a short while as he talked to them in Italian, which she couldn't understand, then wandered away to the museum.

Here she found what she was looking for—the plaster casts of the bodies that had lain trapped in their last positions for nearly two thousand years. There was a man who'd fallen on the stairs and never risen again, and another man who'd known the end was coming and curled up in resignation, waiting for the ash to engulf him. Further on, a mother tried vainly to shelter her children.

But it was the lovers who held her the longest. After so many centuries it was still heartbreaking to see the man and woman, stretching out in a vain attempt to reach each other before death swamped them.

'There's such a little distance between their hands,' she murmured.

'Yes, they nearly managed it,' said Carlo beside her.

She didn't know how long he'd been there, and wondered if he'd been watching as she wandered among the 'bodies'.

'And now they'll never reach each other,' she said. 'Trapped for ever with a might-have-been.'

'There's nothing sadder than what might have been,' he agreed. 'That's why I prefer these.'

He led her to another glass case where there were two forms, a man and a woman, nestled against each other.

'They knew death was coming,' Carlo said, 'but as long as they could meet it in each other's arms they weren't afraid.'

'Maybe,' she said slowly.

'You don't believe that?'

'I wonder if you're stretching imagination too far. You can't really know that they weren't afraid.'

'Can't I? Look at them.'

Della drew nearer and studied the two figures. Their faces were blurred, but she could see that all their attention was for each other, not the oncoming lava. And their bodies were mysteriously relaxed, almost contented.

'You're right,' she said softly. 'While they had each other there was nothing to fear—not even death.'

How would it feel to be like that? she wondered. Two marriages had left her ignorant of that all-or-nothing feeling. What she had known of men had left her cautious, and suddenly it occurred to her that she was deprived.

'Are you ready to go?' he asked.

He drove back to the little fishing village where they had eaten the day before. Now the tide was in, the boats were out, and the atmosphere was completely different. This was another world from that sleepy somnolence, as he proved by taking her to the market, where the stalls were brightly coloured and mostly sold an array of fresh meat and vegetables.

The ones that didn't offered a dazzling variety of handmade silk.

'The area is known for it,' Carlo explained. 'And it's better than anything you'll find in the fashionable shops in Milan.'

As he spoke he was holding up scarves and blouses against her.

'Not these,' he said, tossing a couple aside. 'Not your colour.'

'Isn't it?' she asked, slightly nettled. She had liked both of them.

'No, this is better.' He held up a blouse with a dark blue mottled pattern and considered it against her. 'This one,' he told the woman running the stall.

'Hey, let me check the size,' Della protested.

'No need,' the woman chuckled. 'He always gets the size right.'

'Thank you,' Carlo said hastily, handing over cash and hurrying her away.

'You've got a nerve, buying me clothes without so much as a by-your-leave,' she said.

'You don't have to thank me.'

'I wasn't. I was saying you're as cheeky as a load of monkeys.'

'Slander. All slander.'

To Della's mischievous delight he had definitely reddened.

'So you always get the size right, just by looking?' she mused. 'I mean, always as in *always*?'

'Let's have something to eat,' he said hastily, taking her arm and steering her into a side street where they found a small café.

There he settled her with coffee and a glass of *prosecco*, the white sparkling wine, so light as to be almost a cordial, that Italians loved to drink.

'So now,' he said, 'do what I wouldn't let you do yesterday, and tell me all about yourself. I know you've been married—'

'I married when I was sixteen—and pregnant. Neither of us was old enough to know what we were doing, and when he fled in the first few months I guess I couldn't blame him.'

'I blame him,' he said at once. 'If you do something, you take responsibility for it.'

'Oh, you sound so very old and wise, but how "responsible" were you at seventeen?'

'Perhaps we'd better not go into that,' he said, grinning. 'But he shouldn't have simply have walked out and left you with a baby.'

'Don't feel sorry for me. I wasn't abandoned in a one-room hovel without a penny. We were living with my parents, so I had a comfortable home and someone to take care of me. In fact, I don't think my parents were sorry to see the back of him.'

'Did they give him a nudge?

'He says they did. I'll never really know, but I'm sure it would have happened anyway. It's all for the best. I wouldn't want to be married to the man he is now.'

'Still irresponsible?'

'Worse. Dull.'

'Heaven help us! So you're still in touch?'

'He lives in Scotland. Sol—that's Solomon, our son— visits him. He's there now.'

Light dawned.

'Was Sol the one you were talking to on the phone last night?'

'That's right.'

So there was no other man in her life, he thought, making urgent calculations: her son might be twelve, if she'd been so young at his birth. He was almost dizzy with relief.

'What made you go into television?' he asked, when he'd inwardly calmed down.

'Through my second husband and his brother.'

'Second—? You're married?' he demanded, descending into turmoil again.

'No, it didn't work out, and there was another divorce. I guess I'm just a rotten picker. Gerry ran off leaving a lot of debts, which I had to work to pay. The one good thing he did for me was to introduce me to his brother, Brian, who was a television producer. Brian offered me a job as his secretary, taught me everything he knew, and I loved it—the people I met, the things it was possible to do, the buzz of ideas going on all the time. Brian loaned me some money to start up for myself, and he recommended me everywhere.'

'So now you're a big-shot,' he said lightly. 'Dominating the schedules, winning all the awards—'

'Shut up,' she said, punching his arm playfully.

'You're not going to tell me you've never won an award, are you?'

His eyes warned her that he knew more than he was letting on.

'The odd little gong here and there,' she said vaguely.

'You're not the only one who knows how to use the internet, you know. You won the Golden World prize for the best documentary of the year—'

'You've really been doing your detective work, haven't you?'

'Sure—and, to show you how clever I am, I know how to use a telephone as well.'

'No kidding?'

'I made a few calls last night and spoke to someone who knows your work and admires it.'

He didn't add that his friend had known nothing about her personal life. It had been a frustrating call.

'He mentioned a big new project you were gearing up for, but he didn't know any details. He just said glumly, "I suppose the rest of us can give up for the next year, while she walks off with everything in sight."'

'You've been checking up on me with a vengeance,' she said, laughing at him with her head on one side.

'Which makes us quits, since you came to look me over.'

'You were recommended to me so strongly and by so many people that I started to get a bit cross with you. I must admit that I half hoped to find that you were useless. But you were quite the reverse, and that made me even more annoyed.'

'So you've reluctantly decided to offer me a job? How about I make it easy for you and refuse?'

'Don't jump to conclusions before you know everything. I'm doing eight hour-long episodes, each one concentrating on a place where a notable event happened. I don't just need a frontman, but someone who's an archaeologist and a historian in his own right, who will have some authority.'

'You mean they're all going to be things like Pompeii?'

'One of them will be underwater.'

'Don't tell me—let me guess. *Titanic*.'

'No, the *Titanic* has been done to death. But she had two sister ships, and one of them, the *Britannic*, also sank. It was used as a hospital ship in the First World War, but it went down after only three months—probably because it hit a mine. The odd thing was that after *Titanic* went down *Britannic* was partly redesigned, to make her safer, yet she sank even faster. She's in the Aegean Sea, and there's still a lot to be learned about her fate.'

To her surprise he grew pale.

'And you want me to go down there and—?' he asked in a faint voice. 'Sorry, but that's not my area of expertise.'

'Of course not. I'll have professional divers—although you could make a trip down if you wanted to.'

'No, thank you,' he said at once.

'Not even out of curiosity?'

'Nope.'

'But why?'

'Because I'm chicken,' he said frankly. 'I'll climb any height you want, descend into any cave, but when it comes to diving in deep water—not a hope. It's my nightmare.'

'That's quite an admission,' she said, enchanted by this frankness.

He smiled, looking slightly red.

'It's better for me to admit it than wait for you to find out. So, that's that. You'll have to get somebody else.'

'Don't be silly. You'll do the frontman stuff from dry land.'

'Is that a promise? Because otherwise I'm out of here.' He edged a few inches away.

'Will you stop?' she asked, laughing.

'I just don't want misunderstandings,' he said, giving up the performance and coming closer again. 'I'm a dyed-in-the-wool coward, and don't you forget it.'

'Yeah, right. You're a coward.'

'We're all cowards about something,' he said, suddenly serious.

'I guess that's true.'

'So what's your fatal weakness?' he asked unexpectedly.

'Oh—' she said vaguely, 'I have a dozen.'

'But none you're prepared to share with me?'

'I have too much sense of self-preservation.'

'Is that how you see me? A danger that you need to be armed against?'

Looking at him, smiling and gentle, gilded by the sun that streamed through the windows, she knew he was the biggest danger she had ever faced. But she would not arm herself against him. Even if she'd wanted to, it would have been pointless.

But she kept a teasing note in her voice to say, 'Hell will freeze over before I flatter your vanity by answering that.'

'So the answer would flatter me?' he teased back.

'My lips are sealed.'

'They are now,' he said, and swiftly laid his mouth over hers.

It was the briefest possible kiss, over almost before it had begun, and then he'd risen to go to the counter, leaving her shaken. Lightly as his lips had touched hers, she seemed to still feel them there when he had moved away.

But when he returned, with more coffee, he made no mention of what had happened, leaving her free to get her bearings in peace.

'What about the third ship?' he asked.

'I beg your pardon?' she said stupidly.

'You said the *Titanic* had two sister ships. What happened to the other one?'

'She sailed for twenty-four years before being taken out of service. Nothing dramatic there. I'm still researching other places, although I've half decided to cover the battlefield of Waterloo. I'd got a file of ideas, but none of them are quite what I'm looking for.'

'You can't go by what you see in a file. You need to visit these places. I know of a few around here—it would mean going south, maybe as far as Sicily. We could set off at once.'

She looked at him. 'You mean—?'

'We'd be on the road for about a week, if you can spare the time.'

'But can you spare it? Your work at Pompeii—'

'My team know what I expect of them. They can do without me for a few days, and I'll keep in touch.'

She was silent, torn by temptation. To be alone with him, cocooned from the real world, free to indulge the feelings that were taking her over: it was like looking at a vision of heaven.

'I could call my secretary and tell her I'll be a while coming home,' she said slowly.

'Drink your coffee and let's get out of here,' he said.

On the drive to the hotel Della sat in happy contentment. She was crazy to be doing this with a man she'd known only a day, yet she had no doubts. Everything in her yearned towards him.

She knew that by agreeing to go she'd answered an unspoken question. They wanted each other in every way. Their minds were happily in tune, but right now that was secondary to the physical attraction that was clamouring for release. She wouldn't have agreed to this trip if she wasn't prepared to make love with him. He knew it, and she knew that he did, and he knew that she knew. The knowledge lay between them, brilliant and enticing, colouring every word and thought.

When they reached her hotel she half expected him to come upstairs with her and take her into his arms at once. She would not have protested. But she was charmed by the delicacy with which he bade her goodbye in the foyer, after first greeting several people who hailed him by name.

'I know too many people here,' he said. 'It's like being under a spotlight, and that's—not what we want.'

'No,' she said.

'Tonight I have to visit my mother and explain that I'll be away a few days. I'll see you early tomorrow.'

He gave a nervous look at the receptionist, who was smiling at him, and departed without kissing Della.

# CHAPTER FOUR

CARLO was there next morning, before she had quite finished her breakfast, spreading the map before her, and explaining that Italy was divided into regions—'As England is divided into counties'.

'I thought we'd head for the region of Calabria,' he said. 'It's here, where the shape of the land becomes a boot. Calabria is the ankle and the toe, eternally poised to kick the island of Sicily. There are some little mountain villages full of history in Calabria that I think you'd like. After that—well, we'll see.'

'Yes,' she murmured. 'We'll see.'

They left half an hour later, heading back down the coast road they'd travelled the day before. But soon the familiar scenery was behind them. The further south they went the more conscious she became that Italy had been one country for barely a hundred and thirty years. Before that it had been a collection of independent kingdoms and provinces, and even now the extreme north and south seemed to be united only in name.

Calabria was like another world—so different that it was sometimes known as the real Italy, Carlo told her. In contrast to the sophistication of the elegant northern regions, here there was wildness, even savagery in the countryside. The mountains were higher than anywhere else, their sides dotted with medieval towns.

At last they were climbing, going so high up a mountain road that she hardly dared to look, and finishing in a small, ancient village, with cobblestones and one inn. As he brought the car to a halt Carlo gave her a questioning smile, which she returned, nodding.

'What is this place called?' she asked.

'I didn't notice. It's so tiny it may not even have a name.'

That made everything perfect—an unknown place, set apart from the rest of the world, where they would find each other.

A cheerful man in shirtsleeves appeared as they entered. In answer to Carlo's query, he confirmed that he had two vacant rooms, one large, one small.

'The small for me, the large one for the lady,' Carlo said.

A perfect gentleman, she thought, charmed by his refusal to take her for granted, even after the understanding that had passed between them.

Their doors were immediately opposite, on a tiny landing, so that she gained a brief glimpse of his bedroom with its single bed, so different from the huge double one in her own room.

They were the only guests. Donato, the proprietor, said that his wife would cook whatever they liked, so they dined on macaroni and beans in tomato soup, pickled veal, sausage with raisins, and *cuccidatta*—cookies filled with figs, nuts and raisins—washed down with the full bodied wines of the area.

They talked very little, because their table soon became the focus of attention. Every few minutes one of Donato's two pretty daughters would appear, to ask if there was anything else they wanted. Before leaving they would give the handsome Carlo a lingering look.

Della choked back her laughter while he buried his face in his hands.

'I expect this happens everywhere you go,' she said.

'What do I say to that? If I agree I sound like a conceited jerk.'

'And if you disagree it wouldn't be true.'

'Can we drop the subject?' he asked through gritted teeth.

'I've been watching the girls giving you the glad eye everywhere we go. Some of them are being hopeful, of course, but some look as if they're trying to remind you of something.'

He had the grace to blush, but said nothing for a while. When he finally spoke it was in a different voice.

'That was another life,' he said quietly. 'Too many passing ships—but that was just it. They all passed on their way, leaving no trace *here*.' He laid his hand over his heart.

Then he refilled her glass, and didn't look at her as he asked, 'What about you?'

'Two husbands, a child and a career,' she reminded him. 'I've had no time for distractions.'

'I'm glad,' he said quietly.

There was no mistaking his meaning. She met his eyes and nodded.

Soon after that they rose and went slowly upstairs. At his door he paused, half turning, waiting for her to make the next move. She put out her hand to him.

'Come,' she whispered.

He came to her slowly, as if unable to believe what was happening. She took hold of him, drawing him into her room and closing the door behind him, not putting on the light. With the curtains drawn back at the tall windows the moonlight came softly in, holding them in its glow while they stood, entranced.

His fingertips brushed her cheek softly, and it was the sweetest feeling she had ever known. She wanted him now with her whole body. Every inch of her was eager for him to hurry, to take her to the next moment of passion, and from there to the next.

Yet, contrarily, she wanted to prolong the leisurely tension of this moment, enjoying it to the full before it dissolved into urgency. He seemed to want the same, because he laid his lips over hers with a gentleness that suggested he was in no hurry. She leaned against him and felt his fingers in her hair, while his mouth explored hers slowly.

She relaxed into the kiss, letting it invade her subtly, then offering it back with all of herself. She began to explore his body, finding it just as it had been in her dreams: hard, strong, and all hers. He wanted her more than he could bear, and that knowledge was the sweetest aphrodisiac.

Neither knew who first began to undress the other, but her fingers were working on his buttons just as he was doing the same for her. Every moment there was some new revelation— smooth skin, a seductive curve—all managed in leisurely fashion until suddenly the delay became unbearable and they started to hurry. The hurry became urgency, and they had reached the bed before they'd quite finished undressing each other. There was barely time to strip off the last garments.

As passion mounted she became less aware of his gentleness and more aware of his vigour. For her sake he'd restrained himself until the last moment, but now he was beyond even his own control, and he held her in a strong grip as he moved over her, claimed her totally.

She had lived without lovemaking long enough to find the experience unfamiliar, but even as distant memories returned she knew that nothing had ever been like this. No other man had held her with such urgency and reverence combined, or taken her as deeply, satisfyingly, powerfully. It was like being reborn, or born for the first time.

Nothing had ever been like it before, and nothing would ever be like it after him. She knew that even then.

When their moment came he looked into her eyes, seeking complicity as well as union. Two of them became one, then two again, but not the same two. Now she was a part of him, as he was a part of her, and would always be. And that had never been true before.

He slept first, like any healthy animal whose senses had been satiated. For a while Della lay still, enjoying the weight of his head against her breasts, the gentle pleasure of running her fingers through his hair, the warmth of his breath against her skin.

The whole sensation was unbearably sweet; so unbearable that after a while she slid away from under him and left the bed. She could not think straight while his warm, loving body was nestled against hers.

She went to the window and stood looking out into the darkness, not thinking, letting her feelings have their way with her. But eventually she managed to order her thoughts.

I suppose I'm crazy, but so what? I love him, and I'll always love him, but it won't last. We'll have this little time together, then go our separate ways—because that's what has to happen. He'll tire of me and find someone else, and that's fine. The only heart broken will be mine. And that's fine, too.

But when she awoke next morning all thoughts of broken hearts were far away. She opened her eyes to find Carlo propped on his elbows, looking down at her.

He was almost smiling, but there was also a question in his eyes, and with a sense of incredulity she realised that he was apprehensive. Last night he had been a confident lover, seducing her with practised skill. This morning he was unsure of himself.

Slowly she raised a hand and let her fingers drift down his cheek.

'Hallo,' she whispered, smiling.

He got the message, his face brightened, and the next moment he'd seized her into his arms, crushing her in an exuberant hug, laughing with something that sounded almost like relief.

'No regrets?' he whispered.

'No regrets.'

'You don't want to turn back?'

He might have meant on their journey, but she understood his true meaning. They'd started on another journey, to an unknown destination. She'd made her mind up before this, but after a night of joy in his arms nothing would have held her back. Wherever the road led, she was ready and eager for it.

As they left the hotel he saw her giving yearning looks at his car.

'If you were a gentleman you'd offer to let me drive,' Della sighed,

It was comical how swiftly the ardent lover vanished, replaced by a man guarding his treasure like a lion defending its young.

'An Italian car on Italian roads?' he said, aghast.

'I've driven in France,' she told him. 'So I have an international licence, and I'm used to driving on the wrong side of the road.'

He glared. 'It's the English who drive on the wrong side of the road. And this is my *new* car. Forget it. I'm not that much of a gentleman.'

'I was afraid of that,' she said sorrowfully.

'Get in—the *passenger* seat.'

She assumed a robot voice to say croakily, 'I obey!' That made him grin, but he didn't yield. Not yet.

He headed the car down the hill and drove for an hour, before pulling up in a quiet country lane and demanding to see her international licence, which he examined with all the punctilious care of a beaurocrat.

'It's a clean licence,' she pointed out. 'It says that I'm absolutely safe to drive on continental roads.'

'It says nothing of the kind,' he growled. 'It simply says you haven't been caught out yet.'

'You're not very gallant.'

'No man is gallant where his new car is concerned. This licence doesn't mean anything. The English give them out like confetti. That's how little road sense they have.'

'Or I might have forged it,' she offered helpfully.

He gave her a dark look and got out of the car.

'Five minutes,' he said. 'That's all.'

He instructed her in the vehicle's finer points and they set off. Five minutes became ten, then half an hour. She was instantly at home in the lovely vehicle, for fast, expensive cars were her secret weakness. In England she didn't even own a car, since life in central London made it impractical, so this was a treat that seldom came her way, and she made the most of it, feeling her sedate, respectable side falling away with every mile.

Even Carlo had to admit that she was a natural driver. He might groan all he pleased, but she could sense him relaxing beside her as her skill became increasingly clear.

'Well, I suppose you're not too bad,' he said at last.

'Thank you,' she said wryly.

'All right—you're much better than I expected, and I'm sorry I doubted you.' Then he ruined the effect by saying, 'But let's stop for lunch while my nerves can stand it.'

She chuckled, and pulled into an inn that had appeared just ahead.

After lunch he reclaimed the driver's seat, and as they continued south he explained about Badolato, their next destination.

'It's near the coast. I know it pretty well because I've been researching the Holy Grail.'

'Here? But surely the Grail is—?' she stopped.

'That's the point. Nobody knows where it is—or even what it was. But supposedly the Knights Templar used Badolato as a base, and they brought the Grail to the town for a while. Some people say it's still there, hidden.'

'You believe that?'

'I believe it's a very curious place. There are thirteen churches for a population of three and a half thousand, and the purity of the spring water is legendary. People come from miles around to fill up on it. They come to swim, too. It has its own beach down below, and the town is just above. In fact, there it is.'

She looked up and saw a medieval village rising steeply on the hillside in the distance.

'I called ahead to the hotel where I normally stay,' he said.

'I hope you booked only one room this time?'

He grinned. 'Yes, I did.'

Then she saw the beach.

'It's perfect!' she breathed. 'I've never seen such white sand or such blue sea—no, not blue. It's practically violet.'

'That's a common trick of the light, especially this late in the afternoon. Shall we stop?'

'Oh, yes, please. I'm dying for a swim.'

She felt sticky after the drive. Luckily the Badolato Marina was geared for bathers, and they were able to secure a hut. A run down the beach, a plunge into the surf, and all practical cares fell away as though the sea had washed them to oblivion.

She had discovered his body in the darkness, and knew the feel of every inch, but seeing it in sunlight was a new pleasure. She felt a guilty, almost voyeuristic pleasure in watching him as he plunged in and out of the water. It was like finding valuable treasure and securing it for her private enjoyment.

'What is it?' he asked, finally noticing her standing back and regarding him.

'I'm just appreciating the view, thinking my thoughts.'

'Tell me about those thoughts.'

She laid a hand on his chest, letting her fingers walk down a few inches.

'Those kind of thoughts,' she said.

'Don't do that,' he said in a shaking voice.

She withdrew her hand and stood, giving him a challenging look, with her head on one side.

'And don't do that either,' he begged. 'This is a public place.'

She laughed, having fun. But suddenly she became aware that the light had faded and the air was rapidly growing colder. It had happened all in a moment.

'Come on,' he said.

Grabbing her hand, he dashed for the shore, while the sky darkened still, and growled until it exploded into a bang that almost deafened her. They changed in a hurry and reached the car as the first lightning flashed. She managed to get there first, and opened the driver's door.

'It's better if I drive—' he started to say.

'Get in.'

He had to move fast, and then they were swinging out of the car park and up the hill. At once Della knew the task was harder than she'd reckoned. The road seemed to wind and wind, and it took all her attention to stay steady. Then the rain came crashing down about them, making the journey even more hair-raising.

Luckily it was only a brief drive, and within a few minutes they'd reached Badolato.

'Turn left just there,' Carlo said in a grim voice. 'Then right.'

She did so, and drew up outside a modest but comfortable-looking hotel.

Carlo threw her a sulphurous look, but said nothing until she had switched off the engine. Then he exploded.

'*You stupid woman!*'

'I'm sorry,' she said.

'What on earth came over you? Do you think driving up a steep, winding road in a thunderstorm is—is—?' He became speechless.

'I honestly don't know what came over me. It's so unlike me to go mad like that. I'm usually so sensible.'

'Sensible! Hah! More like five years old. Did I say something funny?' he added sharply, because Della's lips had twisted into a smile.

'Well, I'm a lot more than five years old,' she said wryly. 'Carlo, I'm truly sorry for going crazy like that, but nothing happened. There isn't a scratch on your car.'

'Be damned to the car!' he roared. 'Do you think that's what—?'

'And I didn't hurt anyone else.'

'We're lucky we didn't meet anything coming down the hill.'

'Hey, I'm a good driver.'

'You're a blithering idiot,' he snapped, not mincing matters. 'I've seen children with more sense. You—you—'

He jerked her roughly into his arms and held her close in a grip of iron. She could hardly breathe, but she could feel, with relief, that what drove him was no longer rage but a kind of hair-tearing distraction.

'You could have been killed,' he said in a muffled voice against her neck. 'And don't give me that nonsense about being a good driver. You're not as good as that—d'you hear?'

He drew back, holding her face between his hands so that she could see his eyes, dark with something that was almost desperation.

'Don't you ever dare give me a fright like that again,' he said fiercely. '*Mio dio!*'

She was still partly in the grip of the wild mood that had

seized her, and it was being driven higher by the lightning that flashed through the window, the thunder that almost seemed to be in the car with them. But most potent of all was the way he was trembling, as conflicting feelings raged within him.

'If you ever dare do that again—' he said hoarsely.

'Yes—what—?'

'Come here.'

'Tell me what'll happen if I do it again,' she whispered provocatively.

*I said come here.*

So she did. She did everything he wanted, laughing and singing within herself, so that her spirit soared and everywhere the world was full of joy.

'I'm in love with you. You know that, don't you?'

'Hush!'

'Why? Aren't I allowed to say it?'

'Carlo, be sensible—'

'Not in a million years.'

'But three days—'

'Three days, three hours, three minutes. What does it matter? It was always there, wasn't it? As soon as I saw you there at Pompeii, when I heard you laughing—'

'When I saw you clowning around for those kids—'

'Is that why you love me? Because I can make you laugh?'

'Hey, cheeky! I didn't say I loved you.'

'But you do, don't you? Let me hear you say it—please, Della.'

'Hmm!'

'Say it, please. Don't tease me.'

'Be patient. Three days is too soon.'

'Say it.'

'Too soon…'

* * *

They spent the day in Badolato, with Della making notes and buying up all the local books she could find. When evening came they ate in their room, preferring to hide from the rest of the world. But tonight only half her attention was for Carlo. What she had seen today had fired her imagination.

'It's promising,' she said, flicking through her notes. 'If I can only find a few more like this.'

'Come and have a shower,' he urged. 'It's time we were thinking of bed.'

'Yes, but don't you see—?'

'We can talk in the shower,' he said, beginning to undress her.

But in the shower there were other distractions, and by the time they had lathered and rinsed each other the conversation was no further advanced.

'This is supposed to be a working trip,' she murmured when they were lying naked in bed.

'We've spent all day working,' he complained, brushing one finger over the swell of her breast.

'But I haven't got enough for the series,' she said, trying not to let her voice shake from the tremors going through her.

'What are you looking for?' he asked. 'Do you just want tragic places, like Pompeii and the sunken liner, or dramatic, mysterious places like this?'

His own voice shook on the final words, because her hand had found him, the fingers caressing him softly in a way that made it hard for him to concentrate.

'But what else is there?' she asked.

'Cheerful places.'

'Are there any?'

'Don't you know your own country's history? What about The Field of the Cloth of Gold?'

She frowned. 'Wasn't that—?'

'If you wanted to be pompous you could call it the first great summit conference, but actually it was just a jumbo jolly.'

'A jumbo jolly?' She chuckled. 'I like that.'

'Four hundred years ago King Henry VIII of England and Francis I of France, plus their courts, met in a field outside Calais. They put up huge tents made of silk, satin and gold, and had a party that was so extravagant that the locals celebrate it to this day.'

He slid further down in the bed beside her, stroking the inside of her thigh in a way that made it hard to remember that she was supposed to be working. She tried to apply her mind.

'I thought you said it was a summit conference,' she gasped.

'Officially it was about forging an alliance,' he murmured against her warm skin, 'but actually it was jousting by day, and wine, women and song in the evening. Francis and Henry were young men in their twenties, who still knew how to have fun. It went on for three weeks.'

'Three weeks—?'

'Then they had a wrestling match, and Henry landed flat on his royal ass. After that he decided it was time to go home.'

'Very wise,' she said in a daze. 'You know what I think?'

'What?'

She reached for him. 'I think, to hell with Henry VIII.'

From there they drove further south, to the toe of Italy, from where they took the ferry to Sicily. They spent a day in Palermo, where Carlo underwent a transformation worthy of a sci-fi plot. The playboy disappeared, and in his place was the academic, enthused by being in one of his favourite places, eager to make her see it through his eyes. But for once he forgot to tailor his words to his audience.

'What are you looking at?' he asked once, seeing her staring into the sky above.

'Trying to follow a word you're saying,' she said plaintively. 'It's all up there, above my head.'

'Sorry, I'll make it simpler.'

'You'll have to when you're writing a script—but forget it for now. Can't you talk anything but that serious stuff?'

'I was auditioning,' he said, sounding hurt.

'Don't call me, I'll call you,' she chuckled. 'But I have something different to say.'

He looked mischievously into her eyes. 'What would that be?'

'Something you don't need words for.'

He took her hand. 'Let's go.'

After that they more or less abandoned the idea of work. They spent the days exploring the scenery, the evenings over softly lit dinners, and the nights in tiny hillside hotels with nothing to think of but each other. It became indistinguishable from a holiday, and that was how she told herself to think of it—a perfect time, separate from the real world, to be looked back on later with nostalgia but no regret.

She took a hundred photographs, to last her through the years, and congratulated herself on being sensible.

'It's been a few days. Have I known you long enough yet to love you?'

'You're a very impatient man.'

'I always was. When I want something I want it now. And I want you. Don't you feel the same?'

'Yes—'

'Then can't you say that you love me? Not just want, but love.'

'Be patient. It all seems so unreal.'

'Loving you is the only reality. I've never loved any woman before. I mean that. Casual infatuations don't count against what I feel now. I was waiting for you, for my Della—because you've always been mine, even before we met—*my* Della, the only woman my heart will ever love, from this time on. Tell me that you believe me.'

'I do believe you. I can feel your heart beneath my hand now.'

'It's all yours, now and for ever.'

'Hush, don't talk about for ever. It's too far away.'

'No, it's here and now, and it always will be. Tell me that you love me—'

'Not yet—not yet—'

'Say it—say it—'

# CHAPTER FIVE

DELLA sometimes wondered if the dream would have gone on for ever if blunt reality hadn't dumped itself on them.

'That was my brother Ruggiero,' Carlo said reluctantly, as he finished a call on his cellphone. 'Reminding me that he and I have a birthday in a few days, and there's going to be a family party. If I'm not there, I'm a dead man.'

Reluctantly they turned back, took the ferry across the Strait of Messina, and headed north. On the way Della called the Vallini and booked a room.

It was nearly eight in the evening before Carlo dropped her at the door.

'I must look into my apartment,' he said, 'pick up any mail, call my mother, then shower and make myself presentable. On second thoughts, reverse those two. I'll call her when I'm presentable.'

'But on the phone she can't tell if you're clean and tidy or not.'

He grinned. 'You don't know my mother. I'll be back in an hour.'

He kissed her briefly and departed. As the porter carried her bags upstairs she tried to be sensible. Their perfect time together was over. Now she would do as she had always assured herself, and return to the real world.

But not just now. It could wait another night.

Standing at her window, she could just make out the sight of his car vanishing down the road. So much for common sense, she told herself wryly. But she'd be strong tomorrow. Or perhaps the day after.

As they'd travelled she had purchased some extra garments to supplement the meagre supply she'd brought from England, but now she had nothing that was not rumpled. She unpacked, trying to find something for that evening, but it was useless.

A knock on the door interrupted her musings. Wondering if Carlo could have returned, she hurried to open it.

It wasn't Carlo who stood there, but a heavily built young man, beefily handsome, with a winning smile.

'Sol!' she cried in delight, opening her arms to her beloved son.

'Hallo!' he said, enveloping her in a huge hug and swinging her around while he kicked the door shut behind him.

'What are you doing here?' she asked at last, standing back to survey him with pleasure.

'I came to see you. You've been away much longer than you said.'

'Yes, well—something came up—all sorts of new ideas that I thought I should investigate.' She had an uneasy suspicion that she was floundering, and finished hastily, 'But I explained all this to you on the phone.'

'Yes, you talked about a few extra days, but you were supposed to return to Naples yesterday. In fact, you originally said you'd be back in London last week.'

'How is your father these days?' she asked quickly.

'Making a fool of himself with a new girlfriend. I was definitely in the way, so I went home and called Sally.'

'Sally?' She frowned. 'I thought she was called Gina?'

'No, Gina was the one before.'

'I can't keep track. So Sally's the latest?'

'*Was* the latest. It was never going to last long and—' he gave a casual shrug, 'it didn't. So, since I had a few days free, I thought I'd like to spend some time with my mother, and I came to Naples to find you.' He sighed forlornly. 'Only you weren't here.'

'Don't you give me that abandoned orphan voice,' she said, trying not to laugh.

'Then don't you try to change the subject.' He stood back and eyed her mischievously. 'Come on—tell me. What have you been up to?'

'Oi, cheeky!' she said, poking him gently in the ribs and hoping she didn't sound too self-conscious. 'I've spent a few days with Signor Rinucci, to assess him for the programme.'

'You don't usually have to go to these lengths to audition someone.'

'This is different. He's not just going to be the frontman. He's an archaeologist and a historian, with a big reputation, and he's been showing me several new sites.'

'I can't wait to meet him,' Sol declared, with a touch of irony that she tried to ignore.

'He'll be here in an hour. We can all have dinner together—'

'Ah, well—I've actually made a few plans…'

'You've got a new girl already? That's fast work, even for you.'

'I met her on the plane—she's scared of flying, so naturally I—'

'Naturally,' she agreed, chuckling.

He glanced at the open suitcase on her bed, and something seemed to strike him.

'Did you bring enough clothes for your jaunt?'

'I was just thinking that I need to buy something new in the boutique downstairs.'

'Great idea,' he said heartily. 'Let's go.'

She'd been his mother long enough to be cynical, and had the reward of seeing her darkest suspicions realised when the boutique turned out to be unisex, and he headed for an array of dazzling male Italian fashions.

Della smiled, and observed him with pride. After all, what were mothers for?

'You should try this,' he said, belatedly remembering her and indicating a black cocktail dress of heartbreaking elegance.

But the price tag made her blanch.

'I don't think—'

'Aw, c'mon. So it's a bit pricey? So what? This is Italy's greatest designer, and you'll look wonderful in it. I'll boast to everyone we meet—hey, that's my mum!'

'And it'll make your purchases look thrifty by comparison,' she teased.

'I'm shocked by your suspicions. You cut me to the heart.'

'Hmm! All right—I'll try it on.'

Rather annoyingly, the dress was perfect, and she longed to see Carlo's eyes when he saw her in it.

'Was I right, or was I right?' Sol demanded as she paraded around the shop.

'You were right, but—'

'But it kills you to admit it,' he said, giving her the grin she adored.

It was a constant surprise to her that this son of a boring, commonplace father could be so well endowed with charm. She knew his faults. He was selfish, cocky, and thought his looks and appeal meant the world was his. If the world didn't offer, he would reach out and take, paying his debt in smiles.

But they had been companions in misfortune almost since the

day of his birth. Whatever had happened, he'd been there, with his cheeky grin and his hopeful, 'C'mon, Mum, it's not so bad.'

There had been times when his resilience and his ability to make her laugh had been her chief strength. She'd clung to him—perhaps too much, she sometimes thought. But he'd always been there for her, and now nothing was too good for him.

'Oh, come here!' she said, flinging her arms wide. 'Don't ask me why I love you. I suppose there's a reason.'

Carlo got through everything there was to do in his apartment in double-quick time, sorting through the mail and ruthlessly tossing most of it aside as junk. He called his mother to let her know he was back, and promised to be at the villa punctually the following evening.

'I shall have a lady with me,' he said cautiously.

'Well, it's about time,' Hope Rinucci replied robustly.

That startled him. This wasn't the first woman he'd taken home, so he could only assume that something in his tone had alerted Hope to the fact that this guest was different. She was the one.

He hung up, thinking affectionately that the man who could bottle a mother's instinct and market it would be a millionaire in no time.

Having showered, he drove back to the Vallini, looking forward to the evening ahead. They had just spent over a week living closely together, but after little more than an hour away from her he found that the need to see her again was almost unbearable. At the hotel he parked the car and ran into the foyer, like a man seeking his only hope on earth.

The way to the elevators took him past the hotel boutique. He stopped, checked by a sight that sent a chill through him.

Della was there, wearing a stylish black cocktail dress that she was showing off to an extremely good-looking young man who looked to be in his early twenties. He was watching her with his head on one side, and they were laughing at each other. As Carlo stared, feeling as though something had turned him to stone, Della opened her arms wide. The young man did the same, and they embraced each other in a giant hug.

He heard her say, 'Don't ask me why I love you. I suppose there's a reason.'

Carlo wanted to do a thousand things at once—to run away and hide, pretend that this had never happened, and then perhaps the clock would turn back to before he'd seen her in the arms of another man. But he also wanted to race up to them and pull them apart. He wanted to punch the man to the ground, then turn on Della and accuse her, with terrible bitterness, of breaking his heart. He wanted to do all the violent things that were not in his nature.

But he did none of them. Instead, almost without realising that he was moving, he went to stand in front of them. It was the young man who saw him first.

'Hey, I think your friend's here,' he said cheerfully.

Della looked up, smiling, but making no effort to disentangle herself from the embrace.

'Hallo, darling,' she said. 'You haven't met my son, have you?'

Carlo clenched his hands. Her son! Who did she think she was kidding?

'Very funny,' he said coldly. 'How old were you when you had him? Six?'

The young man roared with laughter, making Carlo dream of murder.

'It's your own fault for looking so young,' he told her.

She chuckled and disengaged herself.

'I was sixteen when Sol was born,' she told Carlo. 'I told you that once before.'

'Yes, but—' Carlo fell silent.

'And he's twenty-one now,' she finished. 'He looks older because he's built like an ox.'

Sol grinned at this description and extended his hand. Dazed, Carlo shook it.

'We had no idea you were coming,' he said, appalled at how stupid the words sounded. But stupid was exactly how he felt.

'No, I thought I'd drop in and pay my old lady an unexpected visit,' Sol said cheerfully. 'I thought she'd only be here for a couple of days. When she didn't return I decided to come and see what mischief she was up to.' His ribald glance made it clear that he'd already formed his own opinion.

Carlo decided that he could dislike Sol very much if he put his mind to it. But he forced himself to say politely, 'I hope you'll stay long enough to visit my family? We're having dinner with them tomorrow night, and of course you must join us.'

'Love to. Fine—I'll be off now.' He kissed Della's cheek. 'I'm in the room opposite yours. See ya! Oh—yes…' He seemed to become aware that the staff were nervously eyeing his new shirt.

'It's all right,' she told them. 'You can put it on my bill.'

'Bless you,' Sol said fervently. 'Actually, I found a few other—'

'Put them *all* on my bill,' she said, amused and resigned. 'Now, be off—before I end up in the Poor House.'

'Thanks!'

Halfway to the door, he stopped. 'Um…'

'What *now?*'

'I hadn't realised what an expensive place this is—' He broke off significantly.

'You've got a new credit card,' she reminded him.

'Ye-es, but—'

'You can't have hit the limit already. Even you.'

His response was a helpless shrug, topped off by his best winning smile. Carlo watched him closely.

'Here,' Della said, reaching into her bag and producing a handful of cash. 'I'll call the card company and underwrite a new limit.'

'Thanks, Mum. Bye!'

He vanished.

'I'll be with you in a moment,' Della said, and went into the changing room.

After a moment she emerged in her street clothes, paid her bill, and gave her room number for the dress to be delivered.

'And the other things, for the young man?' the assistant asked.

'Oh, yes—deliver them to me, too.'

A brief glance at the paperwork showed Carlo that she had spent about ten times as much on Sol as on herself.

They left the boutique and headed for the coffee bar next door. Carlo seemed thoughtful, and she guessed that he now had a lot to think about.

'Does that dress really suit me?' she asked. 'Or did Sol merely say so to get me to pay for his stuff?'

'Why would he bother?' Carlo asked wryly. 'He knew you were a soft touch, whatever he said.'

'Well, of course. Don't be fooled by the fact that he looks grown-up. He's only twenty-one, and has only just left college. Who's going to pay his bills if I don't?'

'He could get a job and start paying his own way,' Carlo suggested.

'He will, but he had to visit his father first.'

'Fair enough. But does it occur to him to curb his extravagance for your sake?'

'Why should he? When he sees me book into one of the most expensive hotels in Naples he probably reckons I can afford a few shirts.'

He shrugged. It was a fair point, but he still didn't like it.

'Does his father help?' he asked after a while.

'His father has three other children by various mothers—the first one born barely a year after we broke up.'

'So you've always worked to support Sol?'

'I'm his mother.'

'And some woman is always going to have to be,' he pointed out, with a touch of grouchiness.

'What a rotten thing to say!' she flared. 'It's not like you.'

It was true, making him annoyed with himself.

'Ignore me,' he said, trying to laugh. 'I just got a nasty shock when I first saw you together. I thought you had another guy. He looks older than he is.'

'Twenty-one—I swear it. And I'm thirty-seven,' she said lightly. 'Thirty-seven!'

'Why do you say it like that? As though you were announcing the crack of doom?'

'We've never talked about my age before.'

'Why should we? There were always more interesting things to do.'

'But sooner or later you had to know that I was middle-aged—'

'Middle-aged? Rubbish!' he said, with a sharp, explosive annoyance that was rare with him. 'Thirty-seven is nothing.'

'I suppose it may seem so, if you're only thirty.'

Suddenly his face softened.

'You're a remarkably silly woman—do you know that?' he asked tenderly.

'I've known it ever since I met you.'

'And just what does that mean?'

'A sensible woman would have taken one look at you and fled before you turned her whole life upside down.'

'So why didn't you?' he asked curiously.

'Maybe I didn't mind having my life turned upside down? Maybe I wanted it? I might even have said to myself that it didn't matter what happened later, because what we'd had would be worth it.'

He frowned. 'But what do you think is going to happen later?'

'I don't know, but I'm not looking too far into the future. There'll be some sadness there somewhere—'

'You don't know that—'

'Yes, I do, because there's always sadness.'

'Then we'll face it together.'

'I mean after that,' she said slowly. 'When it's over.'

He stared at her. 'You're talking about leaving me, aren't you?'

'Or you leaving me.'

'*Dio mio!* You're planning our break-up.'

'I'm not planning it—just trying to be realistic. Seven years is quite a gap, and I know I should have told you before—'

'Perhaps,' he murmured. 'But I wonder exactly when would have been the right moment.'

As he spoke he raised his head, looking at her directly, invoking a hundred memories.

When *should* she have told him? When they'd lain together in the closeness that was life and death in the same moment? When they'd walked in the dusk, arms entwined, their thoughts on the night ahead? When they'd awoken together in the mornings, sleepy and content?

He didn't speak, but nor did he need to. The questions were there, unanswerable, like a knife twisting in her heart.

'We didn't have to talk about it,' he said, more gently, 'because it doesn't matter. It can't touch us.'

'But it has to touch us.'

'Why? I knew you were older—'

'Just a little. Not that much older. And, darling, you

can't pretend it didn't give you a shock. There was a moment back there when you were looking from Sol to me as if you were stunned.'

He stared at her, wondering how two people who loved each other so much could misunderstand each other so deeply. What she said was true. He had been totally stunned, reeling like a man who'd received a shattering blow.

But it wasn't her age. It had been the moment when he'd seen her in Sol's arms and thought she'd betrayed him. The extent of his pain had caught him off-guard, almost winding him. Nothing else had ever hurt so much. Nothing else would ever do so again.

It had confronted him with the full truth of his love, of the absolute necessity of his being with her and only her as long as they both lived. He'd thought himself already certain, but for a moment it had been as if she'd been snatched away from him, and he'd stared into a horrifying abyss.

And she thought he was worried about a trifle like her age.

'It's true,' she urged. 'You need to think about it.'

'I'm not listening to this,' he said impatiently. 'You're talking nonsense.'

'All right.' She made a placating gesture. 'Let it go.'

His eyes flashed anger. 'Don't humour me.'

'I just don't want to waste time arguing.'

'And I don't want you brooding over it to yourself.'

'But it's not just going to vanish—not unless I suddenly lose seven years.'

'Will you stop talking like that?' he begged. 'Thirty-seven is nothing these days. It doesn't have to bother us unless we let it.'

'Are you going to wish it away?' she asked fondly.

He shook his head. 'I'll never wish you other than you are.'

'But one day—you might.'

His response to that was to pull her close and kiss her.

There were faint cheers from other customers in the little café, for lovers were always popular.

As they drew apart she smiled and sighed, letting it go at that. Now time must pass while he took in the full enormity of what he'd discovered. Already she guessed that he was beginning to understand, which was why he'd moved to silence her. Then he would realise that a permanent love was impossible, but together they would enjoy their time together while they worked on the series. It all made perfect sense, and one day perhaps it would no longer hurt so much.

The spent that evening, as they had spent others recently: dining in her room before going to bed. Over the food and wine he told her more about his family, preparing her for the next evening.

'Justin and Evie won't be there, because they live in England and Evie's heavily pregnant with twins. But Primo and Olympia will be there, and so will Luke and Minnie, down from Rome for a couple of days.'

He tactfully forbore to mention that he'd had a call from Luke, his adopted brother, now living with Minnie 'in a state of fatuous bliss', according to his brother Primo. But since Primo himself had lowered his prickly defences for the sake of the divine Olympia, he was, as Ruggiero had tartly remarked, hardly in a position to talk.

'The women are in cahoots,' Luke had warned Carlo darkly. 'So don't say you haven't been warned.'

Carlo had laughed. There was something about a family conspiracy to unite him with Della that filled him with pleasure. If only they knew how little need there was for them to nudge him into matrimony.

The thought of having Sol as a stepson made him pause, but only briefly. He would just have to put up with the young man whom he'd mentally stigmatised as 'that selfish oaf'.

He found, though, that Della was stubbornly resistant to any suggestion that her darling might not be perfect.

'What's he going to do about getting a job?' he asked mildly.

'He'll get one,' she said, a little too quickly. 'But I'm not going to hound him when he's only just left college.'

'Well, having a degree will help.'

'Actually, he doesn't have a degree,' she admitted reluctantly. 'He failed his finals.'

Carlo bit back a tart remark about that not coming as any surprise, and merely said mildly, 'But he can sit them again.'

'He doesn't think it's worth it. He says it'll be more use to look around and see a bit of the world, find out what really suits him.'

Carlo had heard this argument from lazy dead-beats too often to argue with it now. He merely observed, 'I had a job even when I was in college. There was a dig just outside town and during the vacations I slaved for hours every day, grubbing away in the earth.'

'But that's different,' she objected. 'You were doing a job you loved, making a step in your career, making contacts—'

'At the time it just felt like breaking my back so that the whole financial burden didn't fall on my parents.'

'Well, maybe that's why he won't go back to college—to save me another year's fees.'

Her face had a mulish look he hadn't seen before, and a sudden sense of danger made him pull back. Sol could lead them into discord, and he wouldn't let that happen.

There was a new intensity in his lovemaking that night, as though he were reminding her of how good it could be between them. He had always been a patient lover, giving her all the time she needed to reach her moment. Now his consideration for her was endless, and the gentleness of his kisses as he lay with her, teasing her to fulfilment, almost made her weep.

'My love…' he murmured. 'My love for ever…'

How could she refuse a man who could make her feel like this? How could she break his heart and her own?

'Look at me,' he urged.

He had said it before. He always wanted to meet her eyes when the pleasure overtook them. But tonight it was almost a command, as if he knew the dangerous path her thoughts were taking and wanted to summon her back to him.

'Look at me,' he said again.

She did so, and found her gaze held by his as the joy mounted unbearably until they were swept away together.

One of the many reasons she loved him was that when it was over he stayed with her in both body and spirit, not turning away, but resting his head against her until he slept. It was a habit that made her feel valued as nothing else had ever done.

Tonight was no different—except that first he propped himself up on one elbow, looking down on her with worshipful eyes, as though in this way he could hold her to him. In the dim light she could just see that he was smiling.

'I guess this would be a good time to talk about getting married,' he said softly.

# CHAPTER SIX

MARRIED.

The word shocked her. In her wildest moments she'd never thought of marriage. A short affair, perhaps a long affair, but not for one moment had she thought of him committing to her publicly for life.

'What did you say?' she whispered.

'I want to marry you. Why do you look like that? It can't come as a surprise.'

'It does—a little.'

'When people feel about each other as we do it has to be marriage. You're the one. I've known that from the first. Are you saying that I'm not the one for you?'

'You know better than that,' she said, touching his face gently. 'You're my love, my only love—now and for ever—'

'Good. That's settled then. We'll tell everyone tomorrow.'

'No,' she said quickly. 'That's too soon.'

'But it's a party, a big family gathering. What could be better than telling them there's going to be an addition to the family?'

'Well, this may seem a trifle to you, but actually I haven't said yes.'

'Then say it and stop wasting time,' he said lightly.

It would have been so easy to speak the word he longed to

hear and her heart longed to give—especially now. He'd chosen his moment perfectly, for what woman could turn away from a man who had just loved her with such fire and tenderness? Della knew that she couldn't make herself do that—not now, anyway.

'Let's not delay,' he urged. 'We know all we need to—'

'Darling, we know hardly anything about each other.'

'We know we love each other. What else is there?'

'In a perfect world, nothing. But, my dearest love, we're not living in a fantasy,' she pleaded. 'We're grown-up people in the real world, with real lives.'

'Are you talking that nonsense about your age again? We're the same age. We were the same age from the moment me met and loved each other, and we will always be the same. Why are you smiling?'

'I love listening when you say things like that.'

'But you think they're just fancy words? Is that it?'

It was partly true, but she didn't want to admit as much just yet.

'What will it take to convince you?' Carlo asked, moving closer in a way that suggested he was preparing for battle.

'I don't know. I expect you'll think of something. You know me so well.'

'Not as well as I'm going to. Why don't we—?'

A muffled crash from the corridor outside made him tense and look up, muttering a soft curse as they heard laughter that sounded familiar.

'He did say he was in the room facing yours, didn't he?' Carlo sighed.

'Yes, but I hadn't expected him back so soon.'

A female giggle reached them.

'There's the explanation,' Carlo said. 'He didn't waste any time, did he?'

'Don't tell me you weren't the same at twenty-one.'

'Ah, well—never mind that. Hey, where are you going?' For Della was getting up and pulling on her robe.

'He might want to talk to me,' she explained.

'You mean he'll want to find out if I'm still here.' Carlo groaned, climbing reluctantly out of bed and wishing Sol to perdition.

As Carlo had expected, Sol strolled in casually, ready to make himself at home, but his eyes were alert, taking in the sight of his mother in a dressing gown, and Carlo in the day clothes he had hastily resumed.

Della felt blushingly self conscious. She and Sol had never discussed her male friends, but there had been no need. He had never before discovered her in such a compromising position.

'Just checking that you're all right,' he told Della.

'I'm fine, darling,' she assured him. 'But haven't you left your friend on her own?'

'Yes, I must go back to her now I've said goodnight to you.'

*Now you've found out what you wanted to know,* Carlo thought.

Aloud, he said, 'She's welcome to join us at the party tomorrow night.'

'Yes, that would be nice,' Sol said easily, rather as though he were conferring a favour.

'Did you have a good evening?' Della asked.

'Fine, thanks. Although she's an expensive little filly. So many shops stay open late in this town, and she seems to think that I'm made of money.'

'I wonder how she got that idea?' Carlo observed, to nobody in particular.

'But you managed?' Della said quickly.

'Yes—except that we came back in a cab, and I don't have quite enough to pay the fare…'

'All right,' she said, taking some money from her bag. 'Go and give him this.'

From the corridor outside came a girl's voice, calling, *'Solly—'*

'Coming, sweetheart,' he called back. Then something seemed to strike him, and he tried to return the money to Della. 'Mum, I can't leave her alone. Would you mind—?'

'Yes, she would,' Carlo said crossly. 'Your mother's not going to get dressed just to save you a journey downstairs. Do it yourself.'

'Hey, who are you to—?'

'Don't waste my time arguing,' Carlo said, seizing his shoulders and turning Sol to face the door. 'Go down there and pay the fare. Or else—'

'Carlo—' Della was plucking at his arm. 'There's no need—'

'I think there's every need. Go downstairs, Sol. *Now!*'

'Look here—'

*'Clear off!'*

Thrusting him out into the corridor, Carlo locked the door behind him and stood with his back to it, daring Della to object.

'You're not going to defend his behaviour, are you?' he asked.

'No, but—'

'Expecting you to go down there to run his errands? I don't think so. What's so funny?'

Della controlled her laughter long enough to say, 'But I was only going to call Reception, ask them to pay and put it on my bill. I had no intention of going downstairs.'

Carlo's face showed his chagrin.

'I suppose I made a clown of myself?' he groaned.

'No, of course not. I think it's wonderful of you to defend me. Sometimes Sol does go a bit too far.'

'Only sometimes?'

'All right, I've spoilt him. But for a long time it was just the two of us. Still, I guess I've got to learn to let go. He'll make a success of his life and he won't need me any more.'

Carlo could have told her that she was worrying about nothing, since Sol had no intension of releasing her from his demands. But he didn't want to discuss it now. It was better to take her into his arms and forget the world.

Toni Rinucci was waiting for his wife in the doorway of their room.

'I hope you're ready to come to bed now,' he said, as she reached the top of the stairs. 'You've been working all day, and tomorrow you'll be working again, if I know you.'

'Of course. Our sons have a birthday, and naturally I wish to celebrate. This will be a special birthday.'

'You say that every year.'

'But this year is different.'

'You say that every year, too,' he said fondly, beginning to undo her dress at the back.

'Bringing someone like Della Hadley to a family party changes everything.'

'Someone like? You've met her?'

'No, but I have learned how to use the internet. She's a television producer with a big reputation.'

'But surely Carlo told us that? He said she was planning a series and wanted him to be part of it, so he was taking her around to find inspiration.'

'He didn't need to be with her night and day, for over a week. Does that sound like an audition?' Hope demanded with a touch of irony. 'You think he's been sleeping with her to get the job?'

'Perhaps he hasn't been sleeping with her?' Toni suggested mildly, but backed down under his wife's withering look.

'This is Carlo we're talking about,' she reminded him.

'True—I forgot. But surely she can't be very young? Did you find out her age on the net?'

'Not exactly, but it mentioned she began to make her name a full ten years ago, so she must be mid to late thirties. Toni, I just *know* what this woman is like. To have made such a success in a man's world she must be a domineering, pushy careerist, who has contrived to beguile Carlo out of his senses.'

'But all our daughters-in-law are career women,' he protested. 'Evie still does her translating, Olympia practically runs one of Primo's factories here in Naples, and Minnie is a lawyer. Luke even moved to Rome to be near her rather than asking her to come here.'

'Yes, but—' Hope struggled to put into words her instinctive misgivings about this strange woman. 'I don't know— it's just that something tells me that she will bring bad times into this house.'

'Now you are being foolish,' he said fondly.

'I wish I could believe that you are right.'

'Come to bed.'

Myra, Sol's girlfriend, whom Della met next morning, proved to be much as expected: pretty, empty-headed, slightly grasping, but mainly good-natured. She was a native Neapolitan, and greeted the announcement that she was to go to the Villa Rinucci with a wide-eyed delight that said everything about the reputation of the Rinucci family.

As Carlo's car only seated two, a vehicle was sent down from the villa to collect Sol and Myra, which was a relief even to Della. It gave her a chance to talk to Carlo on the drive.

She was wearing the black cocktail dress, and knew she looked her best. Carlo was smarter than she had ever seen him, in a dinner jacket and black bow tie, his shaggy locks actually reduced to some sort of order. He explained this aberration by saying that otherwise his mother would make him sorry he'd been born.

'Don't tell me you're scared of her?' Della laughed.

'Terrified,' he said cheerfully. 'We all are. We were raised to be under a woman's thumb, never to answer her back, always to let her have the last word—that sort of thing. I come "ready-made hen-pecked". You'll find that very useful.'

Since this was a clear reference to a future marriage, she diplomatically made no direct reply.

'Tell me about your family,' she said.

'You wouldn't be changing the subject, by any chance?' he asked lightly.

'I might be. Maybe a man who's ready-made hen-pecked doesn't appeal to me.'

'You'd prefer to do your own hen-pecking?'

'Any woman would. That way she can ensure that the product is customised to her personal requirements.'

'True. I hadn't thought of that. I suppose reducing him to a state of total subjection is half the fun.'

'Absolutely.'

'In that case, my darling, you may find me a bit of a disappointment. I've been your devoted slave from the start, and I don't think I could manage anything else.'

'But suppose one night you come home disgracefully late and I'm waiting with a rolling pin? Surely you're going to defend yourself?'

'The situation would never arise. If I was out late you'd be with me, and we'd be disgraceful together.'

'You mean you're not going to fight me?' she demanded in mock horror.

'I don't think I'd know how,' he replied meekly. 'I was raised not to stand up to the boss lady.'

'So you won't be my lord and master?'

*'Mio dio, no!'*

'Come, come! Be a man.'

'If that's what "being a man" means, I'll settle for being a mouse—as long as I'm your mouse.'

There was simply no way of answering this lunatic, she thought, her lips twitching. He could make her laugh whenever he pleased, reducing her defences to nothing.

But then he added quietly, 'I've never had much use for the kind of man who feels he has to bully a woman before he can feel manly.'

His answer brought her right back into the danger area from which she'd tried to escape with humour, reminding her that it was his combination of quiet strength and gentleness that she found truly irresistible. The blazing sexual attraction that united them was only a cover. If it should die, the love would live on.

Glancing at his profile as he drove, she saw things she had missed before. The angle emphasised the firmness of his jaw, so intriguingly at odds with the meek character he'd teasingly assumed. It was at odds, too, with his easygoing nature, which she now realised was deceptive. They had never quarrelled beyond small spats that lasted five minutes, and she had almost come to think that he could never quarrel, never be really angry. The contours of his face told a different story, of a man with the self-control and generosity to keep his temper in check. But the temper was there.

The car slowed to let somebody cross ahead of them, and he took advantage of the moment to glance at her. What he saw brought a smile to his face, and she realised with a qualm that it was the smile of a supremely happy lover, full of confidence, with no doubts of his coming victory.

If she could have stopped the car and disillusioned him before his blissful dream grew stronger, she would have done so. But that was impossible, so she merely said, 'Tell me about the people I'm going to meet tonight.'

She was an only child, as both her parents had been. So she had no experience of a large family, and was curious about Carlo's. He'd previously told her about them, making them sound like a big, booming clan who were fun to be with. Now he observed that they would have dominated every part of his life if he'd allowed it.

'That's why I have my own apartment,' he said. 'So has Ruggiero, and so did Primo and Luke before they married. I adore the lot of them, but I need a place where I can behave as badly as I like.'

He spoke of the whole family, but one look at Carlo's mother told Della whose scrutiny he was really avoiding.

As they turned into the courtyard people streamed out of the villa to stand on the terrace, watching the car. Studying them quickly, Della saw a man and woman in their sixties, five younger men and two young women. They were all smiling broadly, and the smiles changed to roars of approval as Carlo waved at them.

'So you came back,' yelled one of the men. 'We thought you'd vanished for ever.'

'You mean we *hoped* he'd vanished for ever.'

More laughter, back-slapping. The man who'd said this bore a definite resemblance to Carlo, and Della guessed that this was his twin, Ruggiero.

Hope and Toni Rinucci came forward, and Della knew that she was under scrutiny. Hope saw everything. Although she did nothing so rude as to stare. Her welcome to Della was courtesy itself, her smile perfect, exactly judged.

And yet there was something missing, some final touch of warmth. Della returned her greeting, said what was proper, but her heart was not engaged any more than Hope's.

She wasn't sure if Carlo had noticed this, for everyone's attention was distracted by the arrival of Sol and Myra, who'd been travelling just behind them.

Della introduced her son, and caught Hope's startled expression at the sight of this grown up young man. After one quick glance at Della her smile became determinedly empty, as though she would die before letting the world know her real feelings.

Myra caused a sensation, being eye-catchingly attired in a dress that was low at the front, lower at the back, and high in the hem. It practically wasn't there at all, Della thought, amused, and what little there was shrieked 'good-time girl'.

More relatives appeared—Toni's brothers and sisters, aunts, cousins—until the whole world seemed to be filled with Rinuccis. Carlo gave her a glance in which helplessness and amusement were mixed, before seizing her hand and plunging in.

Della knew she was under inspection. Everyone behaved perfectly, but there was always that little flicker of interest at the moment of introduction. She became adept at following the unspoken thoughts.

*So this is the woman Carlo's making a big deal about.*

*Not bad looking in that dress—but surely too old for him?*

Once she found Hope's eyes on her, full of anxiety. The older woman lowered her eyelids at once, but the truth could not be concealed.

A few minutes later she sought Della out, placed a glass of champagne in her hand, and said, laughing, 'I've wanted to meet you ever since I learned all about you on the Internet. When Carlo told me he knew a celebrity I was so excited.'

So Hope had been checking up on her, Della thought wryly.

'I must congratulate you on your extraordinary career,' Hope continued. 'It must be so hard to succeed in what is still, after all, a man's world.'

'It is sometimes a struggle, but there are plenty of enjoyable moments,' Della said in an even voice.

'I'm sure it must be very nice to be the one giving orders and having them obeyed,' Hope said. 'It's a pleasure that women seldom experience.'

I'll bet it's a pleasure you've often experienced, Della thought. She was beginning to get Hope's measure. It took one bossy woman to know another.

Dancing had started. Myra twirled by with Ruggiero, which seemed not to trouble Sol at all. He was smooching with another female.

'They all act like that at twenty-one,' Della said defensively.

'Twenty-one? I'd have thought him older.'

'Everyone would,' Carlo said, just behind them. 'It's because he's built like a tank. I was exactly the same, Mamma, and you used to say I'd come to a bad end.'

As he spoke his eyes rested on Della, as if proclaiming to the world that this was the 'end' to which he had come, and he had no complaints.

'Come and dance with me,' he said, drawing her to her feet.

'It will soon be the moment,' Hope said, patting his arm. 'Don't forget.'

'The moment for what?' Della asked, as they danced slowly away.

'The exact moment we were born. Of course she doesn't know the exact moment for Luke and Primo, plus Ruggiero and I have an hour between us, so she goes for the midway point. In ten minutes' time she'll announce that it's exactly thirty-one years since we arrived in the world.'

He gave a sheepish grin.

'It embarrasses the hell out of us, but it makes her happy.'

Sure enough, ten minutes later Hope called for silence, and, standing before a huge birthday cake, made her speech. The twins exchanged glances, each ready to sink, but they said and did everything she wanted, and the rest of the crowd cheered.

'Now I'm thirty-one, and you're only six years older than me,' Carlo told Della when they were together again.

Smiling, she shook her head.

'But I have a birthday next month, and then it'll be seven again. Thirty-eight is only two years from forty, and—'

He silenced her with a finger over her lips. This time his eyes were dark, and he wasn't joking.

'I'm serious about this,' he said. 'You know we have to be together. Nothing else is possible for us.'

'When you talk like that you almost convince me.' She sighed longingly.

'Good, then let's tell everyone now.'

'No!' She clung to him firmly. 'I said *almost*. It's not as easy as you think.'

'It is,' he insisted. 'It's as easy as you want it to be.'

He was holding her close in a waltz. Now he drew her closer still, and laid his mouth over hers. It was the gentlest possible kiss and it surprised her so that she instinctively leaned into it while her body moved to the music.

'I love you,' he whispered.

'I love you,' she murmured back.

'Let me tell them now.'

Before she could answer they were engulfed by a wave of applause. As the music stopped, and he half released her, Della looked around and saw that the guests had made a circle all around them, smiling and clapping heartily.

'I think you've already told them,' she said reproachfully.

'Not in words. It's what they see that matters. Don't be angry with me.'

'I'm not, but—stop smiling at me like that. It isn't fair. You're not to say anything to anyone, you hear?'

'Is that an order?'

'Yes, it is. You said you were going to be my hen-pecked mouse, remember? So be one.'

'Ah, but that's only after the wedding,' he parried quickly. 'Until then I'm allowed an opinion of my own.'

'No, you are not,' she said firmly. 'The Boss Lady says so.'

His lips twitched, and his eyes were full of fun, looking deep into hers in the way he knew melted her.

How unscrupulous could a man be?

'So you be good,' she said, in a voice that was shaking with laughter and passion. 'Or I'll get my rolling pin out.'

For answer, he seized her hands in his, raising them to his lips, kissing the backs, the palms, the fingers.

And everyone saw him do it.

# CHAPTER SEVEN

SOL appeared in Della's room the next morning, looking much the worse for wear.

'Your mother's in the shower,' Carlo said, letting him in. 'How did the rest of your evening go?'

'Nuts to it. Myra just vanished. I didn't even see her to say goodbye.'

Carlo kept a straight face. It was clear now that Myra had gone to the party hoping to snare a Rinucci, and had presumably struck gold. He made a mental note to call his brothers and ask a few carefully worded questions.

'But the car brought you back here safely?' he said, apparently sympathetic.

'When I realised that you two had already left without me—'

'We were being tactful,' Carlo assured him. 'After all, things might have worked out with Myra—or someone else—and then you wouldn't have wanted us around. Coffee?'

Sol slid thankfully into a chair while Carlo filled a cup, then called Room Service and ordered another breakfast.

'So, what's the programme for today?' Sol said, yawning. 'I seem to be at a loose end now.'

'My programme is to spend the day with your mother,'

Carlo said, speaking in an easy manner that didn't quite hide his determination. 'Just the two of us.'

Sol seemed to consider for a moment.

'That was quite a show you and Mum put up last night,' he mused.

'Be very careful what you say,' Carlo told him quietly.

'Yes, but look—just how seriously can you—? Aw, c'mon, people think we're almost the same age. How am I going to tell the world, "This is my dad"?'

'You leave me to worry about that. If you give your mother any trouble, you'll have me to deal with.'

'What do you mean, trouble? I have a terrific relationship with her.'

'Yes, you take, and she gives—and gives, and gives. I don't entirely blame you for that. I was the same at your age, selfish and greedy, but I was luckier than you. I had a twin who was as jealous of me as I was of him, plus several older brothers ready to thump the nonsense out of both of us. There was also my father, to look out for my mother. Della's had nobody—until now.'

But Sol was holding an ace, and he played it.

'If *you* give *me* any trouble, you'll have Mum to deal with,' he said.

He spoke with a touch of defiance, but it was only a small touch because he'd seen something in Carlo's eyes that most people never saw, and it made him careful.

'You could be right,' Carlo said thoughtfully.

'So we understand each other?'

Carlo gave him a brilliant grin that would have chilled the blood of anyone more perceptive than Sol.

'I understand you perfectly,' he said. 'And in time you'll understand me.'

A knock at the door announced the arrival of the extra

breakfast, and by the time Della emerged from the shower Sol was concentrating on food.

'Don't question him,' Carlo said genially. 'He had a bad night.'

Della hugged her son. 'Poor darling. What are you going to do now?'

'We're going to spend the day together,' Carlo said. 'You and I need to go back to Pompeii, to start making a plan of action, and Sol's dying to come with us and hear all about it.'

The beaming smile Della turned on him effectively shut off Sol's protests.

'Sol, that's wonderful. You're really interested?'

'Of course,' he said bravely. 'I can't wait to see—everything.'

'I'll meet you both downstairs in an hour,' Carlo said, departing.

He used the hour hiring a car large enough to take the three of them. When they emerged from the elevator he hurried forward.

'I've had a call from someone who wants to discuss progress on the dig,' he told Della. 'He's waiting for me at Pompeii now, but he can't stay long so we have to get moving.'

'Oh, but—Sol wanted to do a little shopping first—'

'No time. Sorry. Let's go.'

Before anyone could argue they were in the car and on their way. Della was a little surprised, but she supposed he needed to see how the work had progressed in his absence. And she appreciated the way he made Sol sit beside himself, and talked to him throughout the journey about the fascinating tasks that awaited them.

Not that Sol seemed to appreciate this as he should. She couldn't see his face, but she could read his back view without trouble, and her lips twitched.

'You're wicked,' she murmured to Carlo, when they had parked the car and were walking to the site.

'Just wait,' he said, grinning. 'The best is yet to come.'

His team greeted him with riotous cheer, then welcomed Sol warmly. He brightened up when Lea, a young woman in brief shorts and top, smiled at him and said, 'Have you come to help us? There's so much digging to be done. Just look at me.'

He did so. Perspiration had caused Lea's long, elegant legs to shine and her top to cling to her.

'I guess I wouldn't mind helping out,' he said, and found a trowel in his hand before the words were finished.

Carlo put his arm around Della's shoulder.

'You and I should go and consider the rest. We need to have serious business discussions.'

As he drew her away Della couldn't resist one glance over her shoulder.

'No,' Carlo said firmly, tightening his arm. 'He's all right.'

'He'll get fed up in ten minutes.'

'You do Lea an injustice. An hour at least. Forget him. From now on you belong to me.'

There was only one proper answer to this chauvinistic statement: to point out that as a modern, liberated woman she belonged to no man, and he must respect that. It must have been a moment of weakness that made her rub her cheek against the back of his hand on her shoulder, and say, 'That sounds lovely.'

They had no chance to spend the morning alone. First Carlo had to talk with the colleague who had asked him to be there early. Then he had to take the reins back into his own hands, and she listened with interest as he gave his instructions, contriving not to make them seem like orders, and generally had everything his own way by the exercise of charm.

It was an impressive performance, and it inspired her to map out this segment of the series.

They had lunch with Sol, who was hot and bothered, and not in the best of tempers.

'A strong lad like you,' she teased him.

'It's not that,' he said. 'It's just that it's boring.'

'Surely not?' Carlo said. 'My friends are very pleased with you. In fact, if you want a job they'd be glad to—'

'I don't think that's quite me,' Sol said hastily. 'I don't see myself as an archaeologist.'

'No, it takes brains,' Della teased.

'I've got brains,' he said, offended.

'Not according to your exam results,' she reminded him.

'I've told you, there was a mistake.'

'Then go back to college and take your exams again,' Carlo urged.

Sol made a face.

Renato, one of Carlo's colleagues, happened to pass at that moment, and greeted Della cheerfully. Leaning over to talk to him, she turned her back on the other two, giving Carlo the chance to say quietly to Sol, 'Then think of something else. But think of it quickly before you feel my boot in your rear. Your life is not going to be one long holiday at your mother's expense. Is that clear?'

Sol glared, but said no more. Seeing that he was thinking the situation through, Carlo left him to it.

Renato sat down to chat, and the conversation became general. Then he touched on some mysterious point relating to the dig, and within seconds he and Carlo had their heads together.

Sol took the chance to say to his mother, 'I suppose I could always go back to college.'

'I wish you would,' she said eagerly.

'What about the cost?'

'Hang the cost, if it helps your future.'

'Then perhaps I'll go home and get it organised. I think I've gone off Naples.'

Della adored her son, but the thought of a little more time alone with Carlo was more than she could resist.

'That's a good idea, darling.'

'What's a good idea?' Carlo asked, seeming to become aware of them again.

'Sol's going back to college for another year.'

'That's great.'

Sol flashed a brief glance at Carlo. Della saw it, also the bland expression that Carlo returned, and some part of the truth came to her.

'Did I imagine that?' she demanded of him as they returned to the dig, walking a few feet behind the other two.

'Imagine what?'

'You know what,' she said suspiciously. 'Don't you give me that innocent expression when I know you're as tricky as a sackful of monkeys.'

'Well, you know me better than anyone else.'

'You fixed it, didn't you?' she accused. 'You've been pulling strings all day. First of all you bored him to death—'

'Then I made him do some hard work. Are you mad at me?'

She opened her mouth to tell him that he had no right to interfere between her and Sol, but then a new thought occurred to her.

'No,' she conceded thoughtfully. 'I ought to be, but I've been trying to get him to return to college ever since his results came through.'

'You've been trying? But I thought you'd bought his line about looking around?'

'I pretend to believe a lot of the nonsense Sol talks because I have no choice. What did you do that I can't?'

'Scared him with the alternative,' Carlo said, grinning. 'He's a grown man. It's time he did something decisive instead of always running to Mamma. He'll be better for it, I promise you.'

'I know.'

'Come on, let's get back to town and make the arrangements before he changes his mind.'

That evening they treated Sol to the best dinner in Naples, and drove him to the airport early next day. On the drive back, Carlo said casually, 'Now we'll clear your things out of the hotel and take them home.'

'Home?'

'*Our* home.'

'I haven't said I'm moving in with you.'

'*I'm* saying it, so quit arguing.'

'And this man calls himself a hen-pecked mouse,' she observed, to no one in particular.

'I promise when we lock that door behind us I'll be as docile as you like.'

'Once you've got your own way, huh?'

'That's about the size of it,' he said outrageously.

His home was a compact bachelor apartment, three storeys up in a condominium. On two sides were large windows, looking out onto the sea and the volcano. While she was rejoicing in the view Carlo took gentle hold of her from behind.

'It seems ages since I made love to you,' he murmured.

'Shouldn't we be getting to work?'

'Everything in good time…'

After their lovemaking she assuaged her conscience about neglecting business by spending an hour sending e-mails and making calls. Then she mapped out some more plans for the series, and when Carlo awoke they worked together for an hour.

It was fascinating to see him don a new personality—serious, dedicated, knowledgeable. She'd briefly glimpsed this 'professor' before, but the change was so startling that it was almost like meeting a different man each time.

But then he would catch her eye, and she'd realise that the other Carlo hadn't gone away. He was merely biding his time. As was she.

In the afternoon they drove out to Pompeii and strolled through together, discussing camera angles and working out a script. Inevitably they ended in the museum where, after looking around for a while, Della returned to her favourite figures, the lovers curled up in each other's arms. Carlo stood close by, watching her intently, as though he could read something in her manner.

'It's such total love,' she murmured. 'Completely yielding, reducing everything else to nothing.'

He nodded.

'You wonder how they could really ignore the lava closing in on them,' he said. 'But of course they could—as long as they had each other.'

'"How do I love thee?"' Della murmured. '"Let me count the ways."'

'What was that?' He looked at her intently.

'It's a poem, one of my favourites, written by a woman. She lists all the different ways that she loves her husband, and finishes, "If God choose, I shall but love thee better after death." Elizabeth Barrett Browning lived nearly two thousand years after this couple, but she knew the same thing that they knew.'

'What all lovers know,' Carlo said. 'When you meet the woman you want to marry—that you know you *must* marry— then it's to death and beyond. If it's not like that, it isn't real.'

He was watching her in a way that suddenly made her heart pound, waiting for an answer she couldn't give.

'But this *is* real,' he persisted. 'I've known that from the start. Tell me that you've known, too. Tell me that you love me.'

It was a plea, not an order.

'You know that I love you,' she said.

He took her hand, turning it over to kiss the palm.

'How do you love me?' he asked with a touch of humour. 'Can you count the ways?'

'I'd better not,' she said tenderly. 'You're quite conceited enough already.'

But he shook his head.

'Not where you're concerned. You do as you like with me, but that's all right, as long as you love me.'

'I could never begin to tell you how much I love you.'

He contrived to put both arms around her, leaning his head down so that his forehead rested against hers.

'I think you might try,' he murmured. 'It's the only thing I want from you—no, not the only thing. There is something else—but you know that. We can talk about it later.'

'Yes, later,' she said.

He was drawing her closer to the decision she dreaded facing.

'Any time will do,' he replied softly. 'Because I know you won't refuse me the thing I want most on earth. It's what you want, too, isn't it? You've made me wait for your answer, but—'

'Darling—'

'I know, I know. I said I wouldn't hurry you, and that's what I'm doing. I'll try not to.'

'But you can't help it,' she said, trying to tease him out of the dangerous mood. 'You're much too used to having your own way.'

'That's true,' he said, his eyes glinting. 'I like to have what I want, and what I want is—'

'Hush!' She laid her fingertips over his mouth. 'Not here. Not now.'

'As my lady pleases.'

The entrance of a party of schoolchildren made them pull apart and hurry away.

For the rest of the day he was relaxed and happy, content simply to be with her. Sometimes she would look up to find him smiling, at peace with the world.

And yet it was that which made her uneasy. Clearly he had no worries—like a man completely sure of her answer. The doubts that tormented her seemed not to trouble him. She wished that she could dismiss those doubts so easily.

Soon she must have a sensible talk with him, beginning, *I'm far too old for you—*

But that wouldn't be the end, she reassured herself. Marriage was impossible, but they could stay together while they made the series—perhaps for a year. By then he would realise that she was too old for him, and things would come to a natural conclusion.

It was bliss to live with Carlo, to wake up with him, to be with him every moment and go to sleep in his arms, without having to wait for his arrival, bid him goodbye or worry about anyone else.

The only awkward note came one night when they dined at the villa. Luke and Primo had returned home, but Francesco was still there, also Ruggiero, who had brought Myra.

'It was Mamma's idea,' he murmured to Della.

'So I would have supposed,' she murmured back, amused by Hope's none-too-subtle way of reminding her that the trail led back from Myra to her grown son.

Not a word was said. Hope was too clever to press the point, and her manner to Della could not be faulted. She treated her as a guest of honour, and let it be known in a thousand little ways that if this was her darling son's choice she was prepared to accept her.

Everyone except Myra was relieved when the evening was over. Della returned Hope's implacable smile with one that she hoped was equally resolute, and sagged as soon as she got into the car.

'Even I find them a bit overwhelming,' Carlo said sympathetically.

They didn't discuss the matter again until they were ready for bed, when she breathed out, saying, 'Your mother doesn't like me, and she's never going to.'

'It's just a passing phase because she knows you're the one and only. Nobody else has mattered like you. Wait until Sol finds his one and only.' Carlo chuckled at the thought. 'You'll be exactly the same.'

'Thank goodness he's too young for that. The college has agreed to take him back, so I'm washing my hands of him.'

'I'm glad to hear it. Or I would be if I believed it.'

Later she was to remember those remarks with irony. For now she was glad to let everything float away as she snuggled down in bed with him.

They made love sleepily, enjoying taking their time. The languorous pleasure seemed to hold her captive, making everything part of the same dream, a dream in which the world was simple.

'Say yes,' Carlo whispered. 'Say you'll marry me—it's so easy.'

He was right. It was so easy. The word hovered on the tip of her tongue. In another moment it would be said and the decision made. So easy—

Her phone rang, breaking the spell.

'If that's Sol I'll wring his neck,' Carlo growled.

And it was Sol, sounding desperate.

'Mum, is that you?'

'Yes, it's me. Sol, whatever is the matter?'

'Gina just came to see me.'

'Gina? Oh, yes—she was the one before Sally, wasn't she? How is she?'

'Mum, she's pregnant.'

Della sat up in bed. 'She's what?'

'She's pregnant. She's going to have a baby. She says it's mine.'

'Do you think it is?'

'Well—yes, probably. We were very intense for a while, and I don't think she'd have had much chance to—you know—'

'I get the picture.'

'Mum, what can I do? She says she wants to have it.'

'Good for her.'

'It's not. It's a disaster.' His voice rose to a wail. 'I'm gonna be a daddy.'

'Sol, for heaven's sake calm down.'

'How can I calm down? It's terrible.'

'We'll manage something.'

'Will you come and talk some sense into her?'

'Not the way you mean. I'll come and offer her my help and support.'

'Oh, yeah? So that she can make you a granny? Is that what you want?'

'What does it matter what I—? What did you say?'

'I said she's going to make you a grandmother. Are you going to support her in that? Mum? Mum, are you still there?'

'Yes,' she said slowly. 'I'm here. Sol, I'll call you back.'

'When are you coming home?'

'Soon. Goodbye, darling. I can't talk now.'

She hung up and sat there, not moving, sensing the world shift on its axis. Just a few words, yet nothing was the same. Nothing would ever be the same again.

She was going to be a grandmother.

'What is it, *cara*?' Carlo asked, startled by the sight of her face.

A grandmother.

'Della, whatever's the matter? What did Sol have to say?'

She remembered her own grandmother, a grey-haired elderly lady.

'*Cara*, you're scaring me. Tell me what's happened.'

She was going to be a grandmother.

'Della, for pity's sake—are you laughing?'

'Yes, I think I am,' she gasped. 'Oh, dear, I must have been mad. Well, I came down to earth in time.' She was shaking with bitter laughter.

'I haven't the faintest idea what you're talking about.' He tried to speak lightly, but there was a nameless dread growing inside him.

'I'm not sure I really know myself,' she said, forcing herself to quieten down before she was overtaken by hysterics. 'I've been living in fantasy land—it's been like a kind of madness, and I didn't want it to end. But it had to. Now it has.'

She began to laugh again, a kind of gasping moan that drove him half wild.

'Stop it,' he said, seizing her shoulders and dropping down beside her. When she didn't stop he gave her a little shake. 'Stop that!' he said, in a voice that sounded suddenly afraid.

'It's all right,' she said, ceasing abruptly. 'My head's clear again now.'

'For the love of heaven, will you tell me what's happened? Is Sol in some sort of trouble?'

'Yes. I've got to go back to England and help him.'

'Then we must get married first. I don't want you going

back until you're wearing my ring. Don't shake your head. You were about to say yes—you know you were.'

'Yes, I was. Because I was mad. But now I'm sane again. My darling, I can't marry you. Not now or ever.'

# CHAPTER EIGHT

FOR a moment Carlo didn't speak, refusing to allow her words to alarm him.

'You still haven't told me what's happened,' he pointed out. 'What did Sol tell you?'

'He's got a girl pregnant. I'm going to be a grandmother in a few months. What's so funny?'

A roar of laughter had burst from him, but he controlled it quickly, his eyes on her face.

'I'm sorry, *cara*, I can't help it. If there's one young man in the world I'd have thought would land in that kind of trouble, it's Sol. Don't tell me you're surprised. I suppose he called you to sort it out for him?'

'Carlo, did you hear what I said? I'm going to be a grandmother.'

'But why make such a tragedy of it? What are you saying? That you're going to go grey-haired and wrinkled in the next five minutes? Or are you planning to get a walking stick?'

'Don't laugh at me.'

'But it is laughable the way you make a fuss about trifles.'

'I'm going to be a granny.'

'So what? You haven't changed. You're still you—the same

person you were five minutes ago. You haven't suddenly become eighty just because of this.'

'I've moved up a generation,' she said stubbornly.

'Then I'm coming with you,' he said cheerfully. 'We'll buy two walking sticks and hobble along together. Now, come back to bed. The night isn't over, and Sol's problem has given me some interesting ideas.'

He tried to draw her down between the sheets again, but she resisted.

'Will you try to be sensible?'

'What for? What did being sensible ever do for anyone?'

She loved him in this mood, but this time she couldn't yield to him. It was too serious.

'I wish you'd listen,' she said. As she spoke she fended him off, which made him stop and stare at her, puzzled.

'I've said that you're still *you*,' he said. 'The woman I love, and will love all my days. None of this makes any difference.'

But she shook her head helplessly.

'It does.'

'But why? You haven't aged by so much as a second.'

'Haven't I? I've suddenly *seen* myself aging.'

'Because of a word? Because that's all "grandmother" is— a word.' He tried again to take her into his arms. '*Cara*, don't give in to fancies. None of this matters to us.'

He didn't understand, she realised. His words were logical, but they had no effect on the chill of fear in her heart.

'No, it's more than a word.' She sighed. 'It's a thought with a picture attached. You saw that picture yourself—grey-haired, wrinkled, walking stick. And it's made me face up to something that in my heart I've always known.'

She took his face between her hands, trying to find the courage for what had to come next.

'I fooled myself that it could work between us,' she said at last. 'What we have is lovely, and I didn't want to spoil it. I still don't. We can have everything we want—except marriage.'

He frowned, and the light died from his eyes.

'What kind of everything do you have in mind?'

'It'll take months to make the programme, and we can have that time together. Afterwards—we'll see what happens.'

There was a silence before he said, in a strange voice she'd never heard before, 'Afterwards you think I'll act like a spoilt brat who's had his fun, dumps the woman, and goes onto the next thing? That's your opinion of me? Do you even realise that you've insulted me?'

'I don't intend to insult you. I just think we should take life as it comes and not make too many demands on the future.'

He pulled away from her and got to his feet.

'No,' he said harshly. 'What you think is that I'm not sufficiently adult to make a commitment. That's what this is really about, isn't it? Behind all this "too old" talk, what you're really saying is that I'm too young—not up to standard? Why can't you be honest about it, Della?'

'Because that's not what I mean,' she cried passionately.

'Isn't it? Della, I'm thirty-one, not twenty-one. A man of thirty-one is usually reckoned mature enough to make his own decisions, and you'd see that too if you didn't have this fixation about being older. I may look like a kid to you, but nobody else would say so.'

'A man of thirty-one is still young, but I'm on the verge of middle age,' she said fiercely. 'You may not want to face it, but I have to.'

'That's a damned fool argument and you know it. Perhaps it's just a cover for something uglier?'

'What do you mean?'

'I think you decided you needed me just so long and no longer.'

Both his eyes and his voice were cold.

'Have you been stringing me along? Making a fool of me just to get material for your programme?' he demanded.

'That's nonsense. If all I wanted was research, I've got people to do it for me.'

'But not as we've done. Living it. Feeling it. And why not have a nice little vacation at the same time? He looks promising, so let's pick him up and try him out. If he succeeds as a toy-boy he may even succeed as a presenter—'

'Don't you dare say such a thing,' she flashed. 'There was nothing even remotely like that in my mind.'

'From where I'm standing, that's what it looks like.'

'I never thought of you as a toy-boy—'

'You thought of me as someone to be used—someone you could treat as a kid. I should have learned my lesson that first day, when you didn't tell me the truth about why you were in Naples. I thought I'd met the woman of my dreams, and all the time you were sizing me up, assessing whether I fitted the slot. I had my warning, but like an idiot I ignored it because— well, never mind.'

He turned and moved away from her, as though he needed to put space between them.

'You were going to keep me around for just so long, then end it when it suited you,' he said over his shoulder. 'It was nothing but a game to you.'

'I thought it was only a game to *you*,' she said wretchedly. 'It ought to have been.'

'"Ought to have been"?' he echoed, aghast. 'What the hell does that mean?'

'In the beginning—' She stopped, for emotion was making it hard for her to speak.

'Yes?' he said remorselessly.

'At the start I thought it was just a fling, for both of us. It had to be for me, and honestly I thought you were just passing the time. Carlo, be honest. Women have come and gone in your life, haven't they?'

'Yes,' he said bleakly. 'Too many. But none of them meant anything compared to you. You've always been different. I tried to make you understand that, but obviously I didn't do a very good job.'

'I thought I'd be just another of them. What we had was lovely, but I knew it couldn't last. I thought, Why shouldn't we enjoy ourselves for a while? I truly believed you'd be the one to end it. I didn't think your feelings would get that much involved.'

'You treated me as something that had no feelings at all,' he said harshly. 'But I didn't stick to the script, did I? I fell deeply in love with you and wanted to marry you.'

Suddenly he began to laugh, but not with amusement. It had a bitter sound. 'Oh, boy! What a joke! How you must have loved that one!'

'I swear you're wrong. Carlo, listen to me. I love you more than I ever thought I could love any man, and I've tried to believe it's possible for things to work out for us. Now I know they can't.'

'I've told you I don't give a damn about your age. It doesn't matter.'

'But it'll matter later. That seven years is going to stretch. I'll be forty-five while you're still in your thirties. Then fifty. Fifty is a big milestone, and I'll pass it years before you do. You'll be in your prime and I'll be having face-lifts and injections.'

'Don't you dare,' he said at once. 'I want you as you are.'

'Darling, when I'm fifty we won't be together—'

'Stop that talk. In a hundred years we'll still be together.'

One minute they were quarrelling, the next he was laying out their future as though nothing had happened. She wanted to laugh and cry at the same time. His refusal to see the barrier between them made her love him more, but the effort of making him understand tore her apart.

'Maybe we will be together longer than I thought,' she conceded. 'I'm not saying we should separate immediately—'

'Just when the programme's complete. I'll have my uses until then.'

'No, it can be as long as you like. I won't marry you, but I'll live with you.'

'How?' he demanded. 'When the series is over we'll be working in different countries. Or are you planning to give up your career and follow me about the world?'

'I can't do that, but—'

'Or am I supposed to abandon my career and live in your shadow?'

'Of course not. But we could still find ways to be together as often as we can manage.'

'A weekend here, a weekend there,' he said bitingly. 'Until one day I turn up a day early and you won't look up from your computer because I don't fit into the schedule—'

'Or the day *I* arrive early and find you with some sexy little thing who's got all the youth I no longer have—'

*'Don't say any more!'*

'Why not?' she cried. 'You're bound to face the truth one day. Why not now? It'll happen, and I won't blame you because it'll be right and natural. Can't you see that that's the only way we can love each other—to be ready to let go when the time comes?'

'And if I don't want to let go?' he demanded fiercely.

'Then we'll stay together as long as you want.'

'You're so sure I'll be the one to break us up, that *I'll* betray *you*,' he raged. 'You think my love is worth so much less than yours?'

'No, I've never thought that. But those seven years matter. I know you don't think so now, but one day you'll see it.'

'You mean, give me enough time and I'll learn to agree with you?' he said, with a touch of a sneer.

'When you see me getting old before you, getting lined before you, losing my strength while you still have all yours—then—'

'Then *what*?'

She forced herself to say it.

'Then you'll realise what a mistake you've made. But there'll still be time to escape.'

'Your opinion of me is really down there in the dust, isn't it?' he asked quietly. 'All this time I thought we loved each other. But you were humouring me, treating me like a child to be indulged.'

She tried to deny it, but the words wouldn't come. Dreadful as it sounded, might this be true, even a little? She'd taken it on herself to make all the decisions in their relationship, without telling him.

On the first day she'd concealed her real purpose in being there, and then she'd concealed her age, always telling herself that she was doing it 'for the best'. Wasn't that what mothers did? Perhaps she'd had no right?

Suddenly he began to speak more gently.

'Listen to me, Della. I'm asking for more than your love. I want everything about you—the whole of your heart and mind and your body—for the rest of your life. I want to know that you trust me enough to commit to me, instead of arranging things for an easy escape.'

'An escape for *you*—'

Her answer roused his anger again.

'Oh, no—that's the gloss you've put on it, but it's your pride you're protecting. If I prove as shabby as your expectations—well, you've arranged it that way, haven't you?'

'I'm only leaving the door open for you—'

'No, you're practically pushing me through it,' he raged. 'It looks generous, but it's actually a form of control. *You* say how long we'll last, *you* arrange the conditions of the break-up—my God, you've even written the scene! You come back suddenly and find me in the arms of a luscious beauty. What then, Della? Do I stutter something like, *You weren't meant to find out this way?*'

'Don't,' she whispered.

'Or how about, *Della, there's something I've been meaning to tell you.* Yes, I think that would be better. Or haven't you written my lines yet?'

He drew a long, shaky breath before continuing.

'But our love—or what I thought of as our love—isn't some damned programme you're planning, where you can cut and edit and rewrite until it's just what you want.'

She was silent, stricken to the heart by this judgement—so cruel, yet so alarmingly near the nerve.

He came close and laid his hands on her shoulders. He was in command of himself now.

'I meant what I said, Della. It has to be marriage and total commitment—or nothing. I'm not asking you to give up your career. Just relocate. You can produce your programmes from here as well as London. But I want you for my wife—not a glorified girlfriend with an escape clause, who treats me like an idiot. I want to know you trust me to be a husband, not an inferior to be guarded against because he's bound to let you down.'

'That's a terrible way to put it,' she said, aghast.

'It's how I see it.'

'Carlo, all you see is what you want. You once told me of how you go after things you've set your heart on. But you don't know the reality of marriage, and I do. I've endured two, and I know how feelings die. Not all in a moment, but inch by inch: the little irritations that loom large when they happen for the thousandth time, the moments of boredom, the times you want to bang your head against the wall, the unending day-after-dayness of it. You have no idea—'

'And neither do most people who marry,' he interrupted her. 'Follow your argument and nobody would ever get married. But they do it anyway, because they love each other enough to take the risk. And because it's how they show their trust in each other. If you don't trust me enough to marry me, then we have no future together—not even the few months you've allocated me.'

'What do you mean?' she asked, searching his face.

'I want your promise now, or it's finished. When you go to England, don't bother coming back.'

She gasped. 'You don't mean that.'

'I do mean it. You've been playing with me, and it stops here. Before you leave I want us to tell my family that we're going to be married. Mamma's expecting the announcement anyway, and we'll leave her planning the wedding.'

'My darling, I can't do that.'

He drew back, looking at her coldly.

'Of course you can't. The answer was always going to be no, wasn't it? It was no from the very first moment. It was no when everyone saw us together at the party and knew that I worshipped you. You saw what they were thinking—what *I* was thinking—and you let us all think it. You could have told me the truth at any time, and you chose not to.'

'No,' she whispered, horrified. 'It wasn't like that.'

'Wasn't it? Look me in the eye and tell me honestly. Was there ever one second when you really meant to marry me?'

'Carlo—'

'*Answer me!*'

'I don't really know what I meant. I always knew that I ought to refuse, but—'

'But it would have been inconvenient. Isn't that it?'

'No, I just couldn't bear to. It was lovely, and I wanted it to last. Sometimes I deluded myself that it might even be possible. I didn't want to admit that it couldn't happen, so I put it off and put it off.'

'Very convenient,' he said softly. 'The truth is that you made a fool of me.'

'I swear I didn't.'

'Then prove it. For the last time—will you give me the commitment I want? Because if not we have nothing more to say to each other.'

Her temper rose. 'Are you giving me an ultimatum?'

'I suppose I am.'

'Don't do that, Carlo. I won't be bullied, and certainly not into marriage.'

'I suppose that's my answer,' he said softly.

'It has to be.'

'All those nights you lay in my arms and whispered to me—all those dreams you let me indulge—you knew I was living in a fool's paradise, and you left me there because it was more convenient that way.'

'It could never last. You can't see that now because you want me—'

'Della, I am not a little kid to be protected. Don't insult me.'

'All right,' she said, tortured by this scene, unable to endure more. 'Maybe you were right when you said I'm trying to protect myself, so that I don't have to be around to see the disillusion come into your eyes. I don't want to know the moment when you ask yourself how the hell you could have done anything so stupid. I don't want to see you avert your eyes so that you don't have to look at what's happening to me. I don't want to watch you treading on eggshells because you're trying to be kind.'

There was an expression on Carlo's face that she had never seen before, and it frightened her. It was close to contempt.

'At last,' he said. 'The truth.'

'It's one truth.' She sighed in near despair. 'But there are so many different truths in this. Don't just look at that one—please, Carlo.'

His mouth twisted.

'Are you sure there's any other truth but that?' he asked, in a deadly cold voice.

After a long time she said, in a defeated voice, 'I don't know. Maybe there isn't.'

He seemed to consider this dispassionately, before reaching for the pair of trousers that he'd tossed onto the floor last night in his haste, pulling on a shirt and walking out of the door.

For some time she sat without moving, listening for his return. She couldn't believe that he'd really left her like this. It wasn't like him.

But as the minutes passed, with no sound of his footsteps, she was forced to recognise the truth. He would not return and she had mistaken him, seeing only his sweet temper and laughing disposition, missing the steely core that had made him fight her with a touch of cruelty.

She'd been prepared for his pain, but not for his rage and scorn.

'That's the getting of wisdom,' she thought wryly. 'We neither of us knew or understood the other well. It's better as it is.'

After a while she forced herself to rise, call the airport, and book a seat on the afternoon flight to London. Then she set about packing her things, leaving out the clothes she would wear to travel while she showered.

It was finished. He would stay away until she'd left, and then she would never see him again. She said it over and over, trying to make herself believe it, accept it.

Lost in her sad thoughts, covered by cascading water, she failed to hear the bathroom door open, and had no idea that anyone was there until she turned off the water and opened the shower door. The shock caused her to slip, and she would have fallen if his arm hadn't shot out and curled around her waist, holding her firmly.

He reached up for a towel, then carried her back into the bedroom, still holding her with one arm, set her on her feet and began to dry her. He didn't speak. Nor did she expect him to. His face showed too much sadness for words.

When he'd finished she tried to take the towel, to cover herself, but he tossed it away and drew her against his chest. He hadn't bothered to do up his shirt, and the feel of his bare skin came as a shock, as though she'd never felt it before.

And in a sense that was true. In the last hour they had moved into a new world where everything was unfamiliar— everything for the first time, everything for the last time.

He drew her down on the bed and removed the rest of his clothes so that they were naked together. She tried to protest that this wasn't a good idea, but he simply laid his face between her breasts, his eyes closed. Unable to stop herself, she clasped her hands tenderly behind his head. Whatever came later, she would have this.

He began to kiss her everywhere, murmuring softly as he did so. Bittersweet pleasure and happiness warred within her. It was the last time, but the joy of the moment was there, hot and fierce, driving out any other thought. She would love him now, and afterwards she would survive somehow.

His lovemaking was like never before, yet still the culmination of all the other times. He drew on everything he'd learned about her to increase her pleasure, calling up a storm of memories with each movement, prolonging the moments while her tension rose and she wanted to cry out for her release. But he made her wait, reminding her of how she loved this, how long the years ahead would be without the warmth of his love, asking whether she could live without it.

The answer terrified her. But she had made her decision, and she wouldn't let him suspect that her heart was already breaking.

'Don't go,' he whispered. 'Stay with me.'

Before she could answer he entered her, moving against her with passion and tenderness until she wanted to weep. As her climax came she clung to him, looking up into his face, filled with love and fear.

Their parting was a kind of death, and brutal reality was still there, waiting, remorseless.

'Stay with me,' he whispered again. But even as he said the words he saw the desperation in her face, not what he was searching for.

'It's changed nothing, has it?' he asked bleakly.

'Nothing. I'm sorry.'

He rose and left the room without looking at her. After that there was nothing to do but get dressed and prepare to leave.

'I'll take you to the airport,' he said when she joined him.

'There's no need. I'll take a taxi.'

'I'll take you to the airport,' he repeated obstinately.

The journey was a surreal experience. They travelled mostly in silence, and when they spoke it was about mundane matters—her ticket, her luggage.

At Naples Airport he came inside with her, watching as she checked in her luggage.

'I'm a bit late for the plane,' she said, looking anxiously at the board. 'I should go.'

'Yes, you'll have to hurry. By the way—about the series—of course I can't be in it.'

'I suppose not.'

'But you'll find another frontman,' he said coolly. 'They're ten a penny.'

Then, without warning, he broke.

'I can't stay angry with you,' he whispered. 'Della, for pity's sake, forget everything—forget what I've said—what you've said. None of it matters. Let's put all this behind us and love each other as we did before.'

She shook her head violently.

'I'll always love you,' she said. 'But it was only a dream—'

'And you can let it go just like that? Did it mean so little to you?'

'Don't,' she said, closing her eyes. 'You'll never know what it meant to me. But we can't build a life on it, and one day you'll know I was right.'

He grasped her hand so hard that it hurt.

'But you're not right. You're taking us to disaster and you can't see it. Della, I'll beg you one last time—don't do this to us both.'

*'This is the final call...'*

'No,' he said fiercely, taking hold of her. 'I won't let you go. You're staying with me.'

She didn't answer in words, just shook her head in dumb misery, and at last he released her with a gesture of despair. She walked through the gate, meaning to go on without looking back. But at the last minute she had to know if he was still there, and turned slowly.

The crowd was building up, other faces passing in front of his. But she could just make him out, watching her until the very last moment, motionless, like a man whose life was ebbing away, until the crowd moved again and she could no longer see him.

# CHAPTER NINE

DELLA took off from Naples in sunshine and landed in England in pouring rain. The perfect comment on her situation, she thought, if you were of a dramatic turn of mind.

Sol was at the airport, relieved that she had arrived to sort out his problems.

'Good to have you back, Mum,' he said, hugging her.

They'd had this conversation before, and her next line was, *It's lovely to be back, darling.*

But this time the words wouldn't come, and she was glad to hurry to the waiting taxi.

As they reached the houseboat Sol said, 'I've done some cleaning up, so that it's perfect for you.'

'*You've* done some cleaning up?' she queried.

'Jackie helped me a bit,' he conceded.

'Hmm!'

The place was spotless, which convinced her that this was mostly her secretary's work, but she let the subject drop. Sol was on his best behaviour—carrying her bags into the bedroom, telling her to sit down, making her coffee.

'The situation must be pretty bad to make you such a perfect gentleman,' she said, slightly amused despite her unhappiness.

'I just don't know what to think. What am I going to do with a baby?'

'I thought the idea was for me to arrange everything?'

'You're wonderful.' He kissed her cheek.

'Sure I am,' she said wryly.

With such domestic diversions she was able to fend off reality for a while. Even when she went to bed and lay thinking of Carlo she fell mercifully asleep within a few minutes. She began to think she might be let off lightly.

She discovered otherwise the following morning, when she awoke at dawn and went on deck to watch the sun come up over the river. It was a mistake. She found herself reliving the day they'd met when she'd told Carlo about this scene.

'You have to catch the moment because it vanishes so quickly.'

She'd said that, meaning the magic of dawn on the water, not knowing how perfectly the words would apply to their brief time together. The moment had come and gone, vanishing for ever, uncaught.

Now the memory would always be there, waiting for her with every dawn.

She went quickly back inside.

Nobody in the Rinucci family thought it strange that Della should need to return to England for a while. It took time for it to dawn on them that she wasn't coming back. Carlo did not encourage questions. Only to Hope did he go as far as to say, 'It could never have worked, Mamma, and we both knew it. Our careers wouldn't have fitted together.'

'Your careers?' Hope echoed, disbelieving.

'Of course,' he said lightly. 'That was always going to be a problem.'

'Can't you tell me the truth, my son?'

He sighed and gave up the pretence. 'It was the age-gap. She made so much of it that—it was really an excuse. She didn't want me.'

'*She* rejected *you*? Rubbish!'

He managed to laugh at that.

'Unbelievable, isn't it?' he asked with a hint of teasing. 'There's actually a woman in the world who thinks I'm not up to standard.'

'Well, she must be the only one,' Hope declared, staunchly loyal. 'She's mad, and you're better off without her.'

'Yes, Mamma, if you say so.'

'Don't you take that tone with me,' she snapped.

'What tone?'

'Meek and mild. I know what it means.'

It meant that inwardly he had vanished to a place nobody could reach. Carlo, so soft-spoken and easygoing on the surface, had another self that he visited rarely and only he knew about.

Hope glared at her son, furious with him, with Della, with the world that had dared allow her darling to be hurt.

That night she confided in her husband.

'But it's what you wanted,' Toni protested. 'You never thought she was good enough for him.'

'But I meant *him* to reject *her*,' Hope said, outraged.

'He was never going to do that,' said Toni, who saw more than he said.

As if to allay their fears, Carlo began to spend more time at the villa, often staying overnight, sometimes bringing female company, but always sending the ladies away in taxis. He seemed to become his old self, laughing, flirting, always ready for a party. And the more he enjoyed himself, the more Hope's fears grew.

Once she asked him, 'Have you heard from her?'

'Not a word. What is there to say?'

'That project you were working on—?'

'Nothing will come of that now.'

'I thought—if it caused you to see each other again, then maybe…' She trailed off, not sure what she'd hoped for, but ready to accept anything that would make him happy.

'Mamma, there's no point in talking about it. It's over. Let's forget it.'

'Will *you* forget, my son?' Hope asked pointedly.

He smiled faintly and shook his head.

'No, I never will. But that's because I'm under a special kind of curse. Forgetfulness would be a blessing, but I'll never have it, and I just have to accept that.'

Hope nodded. She, too, knew about that curse. She never spoke of it, but now she wondered if her youngest child had suspected her secret. Part of her still thought of him as the baby of the family, but now she saw that this man had a painful wisdom that he, too, kept to himself.

'*Can* you accept it?' she asked quietly.

'I can manage. And I'm damned if I'll make everyone else suffer by going around in a black cloud. We've got a lot of good news coming in this family. Justin's twins, for a start.'

'You're right,' she said. 'And yet…' She paused as she came to something that was hard to say.

'What is it?'

'I see you empty and hurting inside, and I wonder how much of it is my fault.'

'How can any of it be your fault?'

'I didn't welcome her as perhaps I might have done,' she forced herself to say. 'She wasn't what I wanted for you. Oh, I said and did all the right things. But she knew I was forcing myself, to conceal a lack of warmth inside. My son, did I drive her away and ruin your life?'

'Of course not,' he said, honestly puzzled. 'Mamma, you don't know how it was between us. Nobody could have driven her away from me—not if she didn't want to go. We had our world, and it was everything. Except that I spoiled it by—' there was a faint tremor in his voice '—by not being the man she wanted.'

'But—?'

'Try to understand this, and then never let us speak of it again. It wasn't your fault, or anyone else's except mine. In her eyes I just don't measure up. That's all there is to it.'

She understood. He was telling her, gently, that even she was irrelevant when set against his love. His eyes were kind, softening the hint of rejection, but she had no doubt that he meant it.

For a moment she hated Della with a ferocity that shocked her. All this might have been hers, and she'd tossed it away, breaking his heart, abandoning him in an endless desert.

But the man he had become understood even this, and said quietly, 'Don't hate her, Mamma. For my sake.'

'Very well, I won't. In fact, I think you should go to England. Whatever is wrong between you put it right—if that's the only thing that will make you happy.'

It was a bad thing to say. Carlo's face was hard and set.

'Go after her?' he echoed. 'Beg from a woman who's turned me down as not up to standard? What do you think I am?'

'My dear, don't let your pride get in the way.'

He shrugged and made a wry face.

'Let a man keep his pride. It matters.'

'Well, can't I help? If I talked to her—'

She stopped before the anger that flashed in his eyes.

'Never even *think* of such a thing. Not even for a moment. Do you hear me, Mamma?'

'Yes,' she faltered. 'I won't do anything you don't want.'

For a moment she had glimpsed the fierce will inside him, and it had almost frightened her.

Carlo softened and put his arm about her.

'Forgive me for speaking to you so,' he said contritely. 'But you mustn't interfere. You can't help this situation.'

'Then what *can* help it?' she cried.

'Nothing,' he said quietly. 'Nothing at all.'

Della's first job was to visit the flower shop where Gina worked. There, she saw a pretty, tired-looking girl of about nineteen.

'Can I help you, madam?' Gina asked, but no sooner had she spoken than her eyes closed and she swayed.

Della caught her and guided her to a chair.

'The same thing used to happen to me,' she said sympathetically.

She looked up as the shop's manageress bustled out.

'I'll take her home,' she said, in a voice that brooked no argument. 'I'm her aunt.'

Gina lived in a couple of rooms a few streets away. Recognising a stronger personality, she made no protest as Della called a cab and took her away.

The rooms were much as Della had expected—shabby and basic, but clean and cared for. Having urged Gina to a sofa, she made a pot of tea and sat down beside her while they both drank.

'I'm Sol's mother,' she said. 'I came to see how you were.'

'Did he send you?' Gina asked, with an eagerness in her voice that touched Della's heart.

'No, I'm afraid not. I wouldn't hope for too much from Sol, if I were you.'

'I know. He doesn't want anything to do with the baby.'

'What about you?'

'I want it,' Gina said eagerly. 'I'm going to have my baby, no matter what anyone says.'

Della hadn't expected to like the girl, but she found herself drawn to her instinctively, and this remark drew her even closer.

'Good for you,' she said.

'Do you mean that? You didn't come here to tell me to—? I know Sol hates the idea—'

'Forget Sol. He has nothing to say about this. He's very immature, I'm afraid.'

'Yes, he gets bored easily,' Gina admitted. 'I know he's fed up with me.'

'Some men are like that,' Della said quietly. 'But not all of them. There are men in the world you can rely on, who want to stay with you for ever and face everything side by side.'

'Are you all right?' Gina asked suddenly.

'Yes, of course. Why do you ask?'

'Your voice trailed off suddenly, and you just stared into space.'

'Did I? I didn't realise.' She added quickly, 'Tell me about your family.'

'My mother's dead, my dad's remarried, and they don't really want to know. My mother's mother is still alive, but Dad quarrelled with her when Mum died. He said she kept interfering, and wouldn't let her visit us.'

'Then you're going to need some help, and that's why I'm here.'

She took over, arranging to pay the girl an allowance, and practically ordering her to leave work with a firmness that afterwards made her blush to recall. Luckily Gina recognised the good will behind the ruthless organisation, and was only too ready to do as she was told.

Della went home feeling happier, although slightly shocked at herself.

Bossy, she thought as she looked out at the lights on the

river that night. I arrange things for people without asking how they feel.

And I never saw it until now, she added wryly to herself.

The year was moving on, and the work at Pompeii was coming to an end. Now Carlo was there at all hours, going back to his apartment to sleep, then rising early to get to work next morning. One afternoon he looked up to find Ruggiero staring at him with a baffled expression on his face.

'What is it?' Carlo asked.

'I'm trying to recognise you. What have you done to your hair?'

'Cut it off,' Carlo said, rubbing his scalp self-consciously.

'But why so short?'

'It was an accident,' Carlo said defensively. 'I spilt some goo on one side and it wouldn't wash out, so I had to cut it off, and then I had to cut off the other side, too.'

'And you did it yourself, by the look of it.'

'I was in a hurry.'

'So that's why you haven't been home for ages. You can't face Mamma.'

'Not at all. I just don't want to give her a fright. I thought I'd let it grow a bit first.'

'Get your things and come with me.'

'Where?'

'First to a barber, so that he can make you look human again. Then your apartment, so that you can shower and get presentable. Then we'll have a night out. You look like a man with an urgent need to get drunk.'

'Let's go.'

Many hours later, as the Villa Rinucci was preparing to close down for the night, Toni suddenly grew still and cocked his head towards the door. 'Can I hear singing?'

They both listened, and Hope said with wry amusement, 'I think it's *meant* to be singing, anyway.'

The next moment their twin sons appeared in the doorway, supporting each other.

'Good evening,' Ruggiero declaimed tipsily.

'Who's that with you?' Hope demanded, staring. 'Good grief!'

'It really is Carlo,' Ruggiero said. 'Although it doesn't look like him.'

'You didn't drive home like this?' Hope demanded, aghast.

'No, we took a cab,' he said, adding as an afterthought, 'Both ways.'

'So you went out knowing that you were going to get disgustingly drunk?' Toni enquired with mild interest.

'That was our intention,' Ruggiero agreed.

'Well, you might have taken me with you.'

'Next time, Poppa, I promise.'

'Stop talking nonsense,' Hope said, trying to sound stern. 'Sit down before you fall down.'

They made it at far as the sofa before Carlo collapsed and lay sprawling, his shirt open at the throat, his head thrown back, dead to the world.

Hope regarded him for a moment, trying to see the perfect picture of a happy playboy, as had happened so often before. But her mind went back to the night not so long ago when he'd slept on this very sofa after a party. That had been a man living life to the full. This was a man seeking oblivion.

Looking up, she saw the same memory in Ruggiero's eyes. A silent question passed between them, and he shook his head.

In early December the weather became much colder, and sometimes Della could barely make out the river through the rain.

She began to look forward to Christmas, when she would see Sol again and hear how his time at college was progressing.

She had become good friends with Gina, accompanying her to the clinic whenever she could, and helping her become reconciled with her grandmother. Now she had gone to spend Christmas with the old lady, and Della was alone.

She made a point of going out in the evenings. In this way she could tell herself that she was dating again, and had put Carlo behind her, but the truth was that her 'dates' were usually with men who were dealing with her professionally. Often there were four in the party.

One night in December she came home to find a light on in the boat.

'What are you doing here?' she asked, as she boarded and Sol appeared. 'Don't tell me you've been thrown out?'

'No, no—it's not as bad as that,' he said, in a soothing tone that made her heart sink. 'They just suggested that I come home for Christmas a few days early, to cool off.'

'Off from what?'

'Well, a group of us made merry. Only we had a bit too much and it turned into a fight, and—well, the police were called—'

His shrug implied that it was all a storm in a teacup, and he topped it off with a sheepish smile, designed to charm her out of making a fuss. It had worked so often before, but now she saw him through different coloured lights. He was no longer a boy but a grown man, always seeking the easy way.

'I think I'd better call the head of your college—'

'But I've told you what happened—'

'Yes, and he'll tell me what really happened. Don't take me for a fool, Sol.'

His look of surprise said clearly enough that this hadn't been a problem before. Her eyes warned him not speak.

'You'd better go to bed now, and tomorrow I'll let you know where you stand with me. Right now I'm not sure.'

This time he actually gaped.

When he'd gone to bed she sat up, brooding.

She knew that since returning to college Sol had continued to be extravagant, despite his good resolutions, but she guessed that now things were even worse. He'd accepted it as normal when she'd taken responsibility for his child. She had spoiled him all his life, damaging him in the process.

And only one person had seen it.

Carlo had known how to deal with Sol. He hadn't got heavy. He'd simply been quietly implacable, and the young man had backed down in the face of authority.

I wish he was here now, she thought. I could do with his advice.

Next day she made the call and learned the worst.

'The principal says you're a big disappointment,' she told Sol later. 'A lurid social life, and doing as little work as possible. That's it! I'm cutting off your funding. You get a job, and from now on you support yourself.'

'But I'm good for nothing,' he said, trying to charm her again.

'That's the truest thing you ever said. But even good-for-nothings can work. Get a job as a road-sweeper if you have to, *but get a job*.'

'Hey, Mum, don't give me orders. I'm not a kid.'

'As long as you're living off me, you *are* a kid. You want to be a man—earn a living.'

He gulped.

They entered into edgy negotiations. Now he had to take her seriously, as though something warned him that she'd really changed. His master stroke was to go out and get a job delivering parcels, then work himself into the ground.

He returned home triumphantly one evening, with his first wage packet.

'I haven't even opened it,' he told her virtuously.

'Good,' she said, whipping it out of his hand. 'I had a phone call today from the bank behind your credit card. Your payments are overdue. This will come in very handy.'

'But can't you—?'

'No,' she said remorselessly. 'I can't.'

Caution born of self-preservation kept him silent, and sent him back to work hard enough to make her reconsider. She relented up to a point, and when the New Year began he returned to college to 'make a new start'.

Della didn't allow herself to hope for too much, but she felt a mild sense of triumph. Sol was treating her with a cautious respect that was new, and for that she knew she had Carlo to thank.

She sent him a silent message of gratitude, wondering where he was and what he was doing. Did he ever think of her. And, if so, how?

Evie's twins had been born in late November. Carlo had entered the villa to find his mother on the phone, his father dancing a little jig of joy, and Ruggiero grinning.

He'd mouthed, 'Boy and a girl,' to Carlo.

'I'm so relieved,' Hope said, hanging up. 'The birth was a few days late and I was getting worried. And poor Justin was tearing his hair out.'

'*Justin?*' everyone cried sceptically.

Justin Dane, Hope's first son, parted from her at birth, had reappeared in their lives three years ago. In time he'd grown close to his family, but it had been hard at first, for he'd been marked by the harsh way life had treated him. He was a grim, taciturn man, who'd developed a protective shell designed to fend off human contact.

Evie's love had warmed him, so that these days he was more relaxed, and had learned how to be happy. Even so, the thought of him revealing strong emotion made the three men hoot with laughter.

'Tearing his hair out?' Ruggiero teased.

'In a manner of speaking,' Hope said. 'He says little, but I can tell.'

She and Toni departed early next morning, stayed away three days, and returned with a hundred photographs.

'Evie looks happy,' Ruggiero observed, studying the pictures.

He'd had a soft spot for Evie ever since her first visit. She was mad about motorbikes, and he'd been just about to buy a share in a bike factory, and they'd each recognised a kindred spirit in the other.

'When do we get to meet them?' Carlo asked, studying the pictures.

'They're coming for Christmas,' Hope said.

Christmas was the time the Rinuccis gathered in force. Primo and Luke returned with their wives, Francesco came over from America, Ruggiero produced a new girlfriend. And Justin and Evie came over from England with their baby twins, accompanied by Justin's fifteen-year-old-son Mark, from his first marriage.

It was he who'd brought Evie and Justin together, when she'd been a temporary language teacher at his school and he'd been her star pupil, with a propensity for playing truant. He was fascinated by languages, especially Italian, which he'd learned from her, and he loved his visits to Italy, seizing the chance to brush up not only his Italian but also on the Neapolitan dialect.

Carlo found him one day, deep in a newspaper article about Pompeii.

'Can you understand it?' Carlo asked, grinning.

'Enough to know it's about you,' Mark said.

But Carlo shook his head. 'No, it's about the site. I added a few opinions, but a good archaeologist never lets himself become the story.'

'Aren't you going to do a whole series?'

'No, that fell through,' Carlo said hastily.

'But Evie said—'

'What do you think about Pompeii?' Carlo interrupted him with a touch of desperation. 'Would you like to come and see it? I'm making my final visit tomorrow.'

Next day they drove out to Pompeii together. Mark was an ideal pupil, wide-eyed, eager, drinking everything in, responding intelligently. Carlo began in much the same way as he'd done with the schoolchildren, the day he'd met Della, and Mark enjoyed the performance. But then he said, 'But it's much more than that, isn't it?'

'Much more,' Carlo said, recognising a kindred spirit with pleasure.

He showed the boy around the whole place, talking to him as to a fellow academic, and introducing him to the team, who were finally packing up to depart. Mark was enthralled by the museum, especially the plaster figures. He lingered over the mother sheltering her children.

'How do you get on with Evie?' Carlo asked curiously.

'She's great,' Mark said at once. 'Dad's ever so much nicer now he's got her.' He giggled suddenly. 'The night we were waiting in the hospital he said he wanted us to have a talk, "man to man".'

'Heaven help us!' Carlo said with feeling.

'Yes, I thought it would be awful, but he just wanted to talk about Evie. He said when my turn came I shouldn't be in a hurry, because a man had to wait for the right person, even if he waited for years and years.'

'Justin said a thing like that?' Carlo queried, trying to imagine this from his taciturn half brother.

'Well, the twins were being born,' Mark said, as though this was a complete explanation. And Carlo thought perhaps it was.

He left Mark talking to Antonio, one of his team, and moved quietly away, brooding on the unexpected words that he'd just heard.

Even Justin had found the secret that had eluded himself.

He walked, without looking where he was going, and came inevitably to the place where the lovers still clung together—as they had done on that far-off day when he and Della had seen them for the first time; as they had still been when they were together here for the last time, when everything had seemed most perfect between them.

Nothing had changed. The lovers lay as they had done for nearly two thousand years, dead to the world but alive to each other for all eternity.

For all eternity. That was what he'd wanted, what he'd been so sure of. And he'd been wrong. He hadn't understood her for a moment.

*How do I love thee…?*

He could never have answered that. There were no words for how he had loved her.

*Let me count the ways.*

For him the ways were too many to count. For her they were too few to bother with. They had run out, leaving nothingness behind.

'I'll be going now,' said a voice nearby.

'What?' He came back to himself with a start.

'I'm on my way,' Antonio said. 'Are you all right?'

'Yes, I'm fine—fine.'

'The job's done. There's nothing to stay for.'

'No, there's nothing to stay for.'

# CHAPTER TEN

IT WAS Hope who suggested to Evie that they might invite Carlo to accompany them back to England.

'He's a good influence on Mark,' she said. 'That boy's getting really interested in all sorts of serious things.'

'Yes, he's a budding intellectual,' Evie said, smiling. 'We'd love to have Carlo.'

If Carlo was suspicious of his mother's motives he kept his thoughts to himself, and agreed to the visit with every sign of pleasure. Evie afterwards said that she didn't know how she would have managed without him, as she was poorly on the flight home, and it was Carlo who took charge of the twins. This had a knock-on effect on Mark, who decided that, since his hero was happy looking after babies, it obviously wasn't unmanly after all.

On the second day of the visit Evie answered the phone briefly, then covered the receiver to say to Carlo, 'Your fame has preceded you. Will you do a live TV show tonight? They've heard you're here, and they need an expert to talk about some new discovery.'

She named the discovery, a brilliant one by a fellow archaeologist, which had left Carlo full of envy. He accepted eagerly, and that night he arrived at the studio ready to talk. The discussion grew animated. One of the other speakers was jealous and dismissive. Carlo was up in arms, defending a man he admired. A good time was had by all.

The producer was ecstatic.

'It doesn't often get so lively,' he enthused. 'Hey, weren't you going to do that series for Della? What happened?'

'We couldn't dovetail our schedules,' Carlo said, trying to calm the frisson that went through him at the sound of her name.

'What a shame! Everything she touches now turns to gold. She's up for yet another award in a week or two. The rumour is that she'll get it.'

'I'm sure she will,' Carlo replied, not quite knowing what he said. 'Excuse me, I have to be going.'

The visit passed pleasantly. Once Justin invited Carlo to lunch at a restaurant near his offices in London, and they talked about their mutual parent. It was the details of babyhood and childhood that seemed to fascinate him, as though he was trying to imagine a time with his mother that he'd never known. Carlo's warm heart was touched, and he did his best to fulfil Justin's hopes. By the time they reached the liqueurs they were good friends, and both inwardly groaned when there was an interruption.

'Carlo, let me introduce Alan Forest,' Justin said. 'A valued business colleague.'

Forest was a chunky middle-aged man, with a bluff, outgoing manner.

'I saw you on television the other night,' he said. 'Great stuff.'

He burbled on, impossible to interrupt. It became clear to Carlo that he had a great deal of money and, since his wife had left him the previous year, very little else. With too much time on his hands he indulged a variety of hobbies—one of which was archaeology, although his interest was amateur—and he spouted a good deal of nonsense. Carlo grinned and indulged him.

'Now, I want you and your family to be my guests tomorrow night,' Forest declared expansively. 'I've got a table for a very glamorous occasion, but unexpectedly I find myself alone.'

Since they were both too polite to say that this wasn't surprising, they merely smiled, while seeking for a reply that would get them out of the unwanted invitation.

'It's a televsion awards ceremony,' Forest burbled on. 'And it's taking place at a hotel that I own, so they have to give me a table. It's the biggest "do" of the year. Not to be missed.'

'You're very kind, but we're busy—' Justin began.

'I think not,' Carlo interrupted him swiftly. 'I'm sure we have no plans for tomorrow night.'

Understanding what was expected of him, Justin hastily backtracked, and within a short time they were engaged for the next evening.

'I think you've taken leave of your senses,' Justin observed in the car afterwards.

'Oh, yes,' Carlo said quietly. 'That happened a long time ago.'

Della didn't recognise him at first. It was late at night and she was half asleep in front of the television. Through the sleepy haze she heard a man's voice saying, 'Far too much has been made of…sense of proportion—'

Then another man began to talk, and she felt disorientated because the voice was Carlo's but the appearance wasn't. She blinked, forcing herself to focus, and realised that it really was him but, with his shaggy locks cut off, almost unrecognisable.

His boyish looks had owed a lot to the neglect of his hair, she realised. With most of it gone, he seemed like someone else, serious, intense, and learned. She didn't understand a word he was saying, beyond the fact that he was defending a recent discovery against those who would dismiss it. He was fierce and angry, almost contemptuous.

It was strange to see him as never before, and yet to recognise him. This wasn't the young man who'd loved her passionately through the long, hot nights, and laughed with her through the sunny days. This man was stern, controlled, radiating a conviction that the world must take him on his own terms or not at all. Her heart ached as she watched him.

At any moment he would smile, and it would be the smile she loved, that had brightened the world. But suddenly the programme was over, and he hadn't smiled once.

She discovered that she was leaning forward, her whole body tense, shaking. She wanted to reach out and touch him, but he wasn't there. He never really had been there. He would never be there again, and the tears were pouring down her face.

She tried to put him out of her mind and concentrate on the coming award ceremony. She decided to wear the elegant black cocktail dress she'd bought in Italy, and when it was on she knew she looked her best. She'd lost weight in the last few weeks, and had the figure of a girl, which the tight black dress emphasised. Her make-up was skilled and professional. This was going to be her big night.

And she would make the most of it, she decided. For professional triumph was the only satisfaction she would know for the rest of her life.

Her 'date' was her assistant, George Franklin, who had earned tonight almost as much as she had.

'The word on the grapevine is that you've won,' he told her, as they reached their table and he pulled out a chair for her.

'Go on with you,' she chided, trying to not to hope for too much. 'I'll bet we've all been told that.'

He grinned, and she thought how different he looked in a dinner jacket. Normally she saw him only in jeans and old sweaters, but now, shaved and almost elegant, he looked reasonably attractive, carrying his fifty years lightly.

The ceremony began. Factual programmes were dealt with first, and in half an hour the announcer was proclaiming, 'Now the award for the best documentary series. The contenders are—'

He read out five names, and the screen showed five brief extracts from the programmes.

'And the winner is—Della Hadley for *The Past is the Future*.'

She was a popular choice, and the applause swelled as she approached the stage. There she delivered a brief acceptance speech and departed quickly, to more applause. As she went back down the room lights flashed, blinding her, and when she'd blinked and recovered she found herself looking straight at the one person she'd thought never to meet again.

People were pushing past in each direction, but neither of them noticed. The world had stopped, leaving them on an island.

'Congratulations,' he said, seeming to speak from a distance.

'I—thank you.' He didn't say any more, but stood looking at her with something in his eyes that she didn't want to see. It saddened her too much. 'I didn't expect to see you here,' she said, for something to say.

'I was invited at the last minute. You're looking well.'

'So are you,' she said. 'But I wouldn't have recognised you if I hadn't seen you on the box the other night.'

'You saw that?'

'You slaughtered the opposition. I couldn't follow a word, but I understood that much.' She gave an awkward laugh. 'I was right about you. You're a natural on television.'

'Thank you,' he said lamely. After a moment he asked, 'What happened about the series?'

'I'm still doing it, using several different presenters.'

'Will you be going to the same places?'

'Not all of them. I changed some. I've included the wreck of the *Britannic*.'

'You managed to find someone who wasn't chicken, then?'

'Yes, I did.'

Silence.

'I'm glad you're still doing the series,' he said.

'Yes, so am I.'

It was months since their last meeting, and now the air about them seemed to clamour with unspoken thoughts and feelings. But these commonplaces were all that would come.

There was a brief agitation around them as people tried to get past.

'We're in everyone's way,' she said. 'It was nice seeing you again.'

'And you.'

Carlo watched her return to her table, waiting for the moment when she would look back at him. It never came. He saw a middle-aged man rise, put his arm around her and kiss her cheek. So that was her escort, he thought, no doubt chosen for his suitability.

He'd said she was looking well, but the truth was she was looking fantastic: beautiful, glamorous, sexy, every man's dream. After the way she'd claimed to be getting old it was like another rejection hurled at him.

He returned to his own table, where his family were regarding him with curiosity, and Alan Forest with awe.

'You know her?' he asked, wide-eyed.

'We met once briefly.' He was still standing, watching her, willing her to turn and look at him.

'Get her over here—we'll all celebrate together.'

'I'm sure she has her own arrangements,' Carlo said, trying to keep the tension out of his voice.

'Nonsense. We'll have a great time—'

'I don't think we should trouble them,' Evie broke in quickly. 'She's with a party of her own.'

Della was certainly having a night of triumph. People were coming up to congratulate her, kiss her, admire the award. The man with her was regarding her with proprietary pride, and it was clear to Carlo that everyone else saw them as a couple.

As he watched, Della lifted the statuette, so that it glittered in the light, and her crowd of admirers cheered and applauded.

Then she finally turned his way, and for a moment their glances locked. He thought her smile grew broader, her eyes more triumphant, as though she was telling him something.

He understood. She did very well without him. Just as she had always known she would. She had tried to warn him, but in his blind arrogance and stupidity he'd refused to see it.

'I guess you're right,' Alan Forest said, beside him. 'That lady doesn't need us. She's got everything she could ever want in the world.'

'Yes,' Carlo said, almost inaudibly. 'She has.'

He sat down, and after a moment he felt Evie's hand creep into his and give a sympathetic squeeze.

The next day he went home.

The award was the most prestigious there was, and it set the seal on her career. Congratulations poured in, also offers. Now everyone wanted her.

As well as work, she could occupy herself with Gina's pregnancy, but she soon discovered that she was no longer needed. The Christmas visit to the grandmother had been a success, and it wasn't long before Mrs Burton invited Gina to make her home with her.

'I still want you to be part of the baby's life,' Gina explained to Della. 'But—'

'But you want to be with your own family. Of course you do.'

'I'll never forget what you've done for me.'

Her new home was a hundred miles away, just too far for easy visiting.

On the last day of February Della escorted the girl there herself, and it was a happy occasion. Mrs Burton was a vigorous woman in her sixties, prosperous enough to take on the new responsibility, and eager to do so. She and Della established cordial relations, and there was an open invitation to visit.

It had ended well, but as she returned home Della realised that she was more alone than ever.

She reached the houseboat in the middle of a thunderstorm. Rain poured down in torrents, and it was a relief to get inside. Soon she'd dried off and done her best to get warm, but somehow it didn't work. There was a part of her that remained trapped in a chill desert, and no amount of heating could reach it.

She went to look at the statuette, high on a shelf where it could broadcast her achievement, trying to draw comfort from it. But it only reminded her of that night, and his face, tense and drawn. Something was destroying him, just as it was destroying her.

She wondered if he, like her, had an ache in his heart so intense that it was an actual physical pain that went on and on. It had been there for months and she was beginning to wonder if it would ever fade.

But surely she'd made the right decision?

She listened, almost as though expecting a voice to answer her. But the only sound was the drumming of the rain in a bleak universe.

Reaching into a drawer, she took out the folder of pictures from her time in Naples. There were a hundred stills, plus a disk recorded in a camcorder, taken by a friendly passerby. Since returning she'd rarely allowed herself to look at it, but now she slipped it into the machine.

It was like watching strangers. The man and the woman

were totally in love, totally right for each other, rejoicing in that rightness. Nobody watching would have known that her thoughts were far away, planning to leave him. Certainly he hadn't known. There was a defenceless innocence in his manner towards her because he trusted her totally.

And he was wrong, she thought, tears streaming down her face. He shouldn't have trusted her for a moment, because she'd been planning to betray him. He'd never suspected because there wasn't a dishonest bone in his body, and when he found out it had nearly ruined him. Even then he'd wanted her back, and she'd refused because she hadn't one tenth of his courage.

She could hardly bear to look at the blissfully happy young joker before her eyes. He'd gone, replaced by the haggard, distant man she'd seen at the awards. And she had done that to him.

She switched off and sat in the darkness for a long time.

If I go to Naples, he'll know the truth as soon as he sees me. He'll know I can't keep away from him. How can I tell him that, after what happened?

Pride. It mattered, didn't it?

The drumming of the rain seemed to give her the answer. Pride. Emptiness. A lifetime without love. Years of endless, searing misery.

Or the flowering that was there inside her at the thought of seeing him again. It spread, streaming through her veins, taking her over until there was nothing left but joy.

I could tell him that I love him, and that I got it wrong. Maybe there's even a chance we can still find the way. But if not, if it's too late, at least I can tell him that I'm sorry.

While she waited for the flight to be called she sat down for a coffee, and at once her cellphone went. It was Sol.

'Where are you?' he demanded. 'I just got a text saying you were going away for a few days—'

'I'm going to Naples.'

'To see him?'

'No,' she said quickly. She couldn't bear Sol to know the truth just yet. 'I'm still looking over sites—tying up loose ends. I'll be in touch.'

'Yeah. Right. How long will you be gone?'

'I don't know. I have to go now.'

Della was hardly aware of taking her seat, fastening the belt. She was on edge until the plane rose from the ground, and then there was the relief of knowing that the decision was final.

The flight to Naples was three hours. She began to wonder what she would do, having made no plan of action beyond putting up at the Vallini.

I don't even know where he is. He may not be at Pompeii now, or even be in Naples any more.

She tried not to think that she might arrive too late, closing her eyes, fighting the fear. But the thought took hold of her. Her whole life might be haunted by her failure to find him in time. Then a sudden violent lurch brought her back to the present. She opened her eyes to find everyone looking around in alarm.

'Ladies and gentlemen, we are experiencing a little turbulence. Please fasten your seatbelts…'

She hated this, but comforted herself with the thought that it wasn't far now. It was hard to fasten the belt because another lurch made it fly out of her hand.

*You're nearly there now. Concentrate on that thought, and on seeing him again.*

She finally managed to fasten the clasp and sat back, taking deep breaths. She could feel that they were going down, so this was nearly over.

But then she heard the screams begin, and she knew that it wasn't nearly over. The worst was just beginning.

\* \* \*

'So you're off to Egypt?' Hope asked.

'I thought you said Egypt had been done to death?' observed Ruggiero from further down the table, where the three of them were breakfasting on the terrace of the villa.

'It's just a stop on the way,' Carlo said. 'Then Thailand. Then—I forget.'

'You sound as though it doesn't matter,' Hope said, alarmed. 'But in the past when you started a new job you were always lit up inside. Today—you *shrug*. You do that too often, as though nothing mattered any more.'

'You're being fanciful, Mamma. Of course something matters—my new contract with Mr Forest, which will give me freedom to go anywhere and research anything.'

'And it will keep you away for a long time—which is what you really want, isn't it?' she asked shrewdly.

He almost shrugged again, but stopped himself, conscious of his mother's all-seeing eyes. It was true that he'd seized the chance of an alliance with the man he'd met in England. Alan Forest could fund his research, freeing him to travel anywhere for as long as he pleased. But he reasoned that any ambitious archaeologist would have done the same, whatever Hope might imply.

'You're lucky to be able to run away,' Ruggiero remarked.

'I am not running away,' Carlo said sharply.

'Like hell you're not! You even tried to talk Forest out of staying in the Hotel Vallini.'

'Because there are better hotels in Naples,' Carlo said indifferently.

Ruggiero's answer was to make a sound like a chicken clucking.

'I'm going,' Carlo said.

'But you haven't finished your breakfast,' Hope protested.

'I prefer not to listen to the ravings of this person,' Carlo said coolly, jerking his head in his brother's direction.

'I just like a man who's honest with himself,' Ruggiero observed. 'Running to the other side of the world is the reverse of honest.'

'Now, listen, you two,' Carlo said, in the voice of a man exasperated beyond endurance. 'I am not running away. I'm simply not going to spend the rest of my life brooding. It's over. Finished. Della made her decision and that's that. And the more I think of it, the more I realise that she was right. Life goes on.'

Ruggiero drew in his breath. He might or might not have been going to cluck again. It was impossible to say since the look Carlo turned on him effectively froze his blood.

'I'm off,' Carlo said, draining his cup. 'We should have signed that contract two days ago, but better late than never.'

'And after you've gone, when will I see you again?' Hope wanted to know.

'That's in the lap of the gods.' He kissed her cheek and departed.

'He's really changed,' Hope sighed.

'I'll say!' Ruggiero exclaimed with feeling. 'Another moment and he'd have killed me. You know why this is happening suddenly, don't you? It's because he saw her in England.'

'He never talks about that,' Hope said sadly. 'We wouldn't even know if Evie hadn't told us.'

'After that he thought she'd get in touch with him.'

'He said so?'

'No, but he jumped every time his phone went. It was never her.'

'Why didn't he just call her?'

'Mamma, don't you understand him yet? *She* rejected *him*. Very finally. He won't go back to her and beg.'

'But perhaps she called him when you weren't there.'

'No, she never called him.'

'How can you be sure?'

'Because he's going away,' Ruggiero said.

The sight of Alan Forest gave Carlo a shock. He had one arm in a sling, and a black eye.

'Were you mugged?' Carlo asked.

'No, I was on that plane that crashed at the airport a couple of days ago. I expect you saw it on the news. It was a terrible business. Fifteen people dead, several more expected to die.'

'But when you called me to say there'd be a delay in the contract you didn't mention the crash,' Carlo said. 'You just said something had come up.'

'I was out of my mind on sedatives and I just wanted to sleep. They take very good care of you in the Berrotti Hospital. But I'm fine now.'

'Are you sure?' Carlo asked worriedly.

'Believe me, I was one of the lucky ones. But the others—there was even someone I knew—by sight, anyway. That TV producer you talked to at the awards ceremony.'

'What?' Carlo's cup clattered into the saucer.

'Della somebody—'

'*She* was in that crash?' Carlo asked in a tense voice.

'I saw them carry her off on a stretcher, and she wasn't moving. She could be dead by now. Hey! What are you—?'

He was talking to empty air. Carlo had fled.

Afterwards he couldn't remember how he got to the hospital. He was functioning on automatic, blotting out the hideous truth. For two days she'd been lying within a few miles of him—alone, perhaps dying. And he hadn't known.

At the hospital he parked the car in a hurry and hurled himself inside.

'Signora Hadley,' he said fiercely to the young woman receptionist. 'Where is she?'

'Are you a relative, *signore*?'

'No, but I—know her very well.'

'I'm afraid we have strict rules—'

'For the love of God, tell me she's alive,' he said hoarsely. 'Just say that. *Say it!*'

'She's alive,' she said, regarding him in alarm. '*Signore*, please—don't force me to call Security.'

'No—' He ran his hand through his hair. 'There's no need. I just want to know how badly hurt she is—she was in the crash.'

She relented, taking pity on his haggard face sufficient to say, 'Yes, she was on the plane, and she was brought here.'

'And she's still alive? You said so, didn't you?'

'Yes, I did. She's alive, although I must warn you— Perhaps you'd better talk to her son.'

'He's here?'

'We sent for him at once. If you go up to the second floor, you should find him.'

He was gone before she'd finished talking. As he ran, the receptionist's words hammered in his head. '*I must warn you—I must warn you—*'

He shut them out. He was afraid.

He saw Sol as soon as he turned into the corridor, standing at the far end, staring out of the window, so that at first he was unaware of Carlo's approach. Even when he looked up he didn't seem to recognise the man hurrying towards him, his face harsh and desperate.

'How is she?' Carlo demanded.

'My God, it's you!'

Carlo took a step towards him. He was closer to losing control than he'd ever been in his life.

'*How is she?*'

'She's been unconscious since they dragged her off that plane,' Sol declared in a flat voice. 'The doctors talk a lot of guff, but we all know what's going to happen.'

Suddenly his voice shook.

'She's dying, and there's nothing anyone can do.'

# CHAPTER ELEVEN

'THAT can't be true,' Carlo said harshly. 'I don't believe it.'

'Do you think I haven't said that to myself?' Sol demanded. 'When I first got here and found her unconscious I thought she'd wake up at any moment, but she didn't. It goes on and on. The longer she's unconscious the worse it is. They had to operate, but she should have come round by now.'

'Where is she?'

'Behind that door. They sent me out while they did something with the machines. You should see all the things she's attached to.'

He closed his eyes for a moment before he went on,

'They say she took a terrible bang on the head. Even if she does come round we just don't know how she'll be—if she'll recognise anyone, or know who she is—'

Carlo turned away swiftly, lest he betray too much.

'I know the doctors expect her to die at any moment,' Sol continued. 'They don't say so outright, but you can tell from the careful way they phrase things.'

Suddenly he glared at Carlo.

'You took your time getting here, damn you!'

'I came as soon as I heard. That was only half an hour ago.'

154     THE ITALIAN'S WIFE BY SUNSET

'Yeah, like you didn't know she was on her way.' Sol's tone was almost a sneer. 'Why the hell couldn't you leave her alone?'

'What are you talking about?' Carlo demanded harshly. 'I haven't been in touch with her since she left.'

'Don't give me that!' Sol snapped. 'Why was she flying to Naples if not to see you?'

'I don't know.'

'I don't believe you. I phoned her at the airport and she— I don't know— Hell!'

'She told you she was coming to me?'

'No, she denied it. But I knew.'

'What did she say?'

'What does it matter?'

*'What did she say, damn you?'*

Carlo had slammed his shaking hands down on Sol's shoulders, and for a moment looked as though he might be about to throttle him.

'What did she say?' he repeated hoarsely, releasing Sol.

'I can't remember exactly,' the lad said, moving away carefully. 'Something about tying up loose ends—'

'But that could mean anything,' Carlo said, feeling dizzy. 'It could be work. Was there nothing else?'

'Just that she didn't know how long she'd be away—'

Carlo wanted to shake him. Instead he took a step away. It was safer for them both that way.

He felt torn in many directions. He'd longed for Della to return to him, but not at this cost to her. Sooner than see her hurt he would live lonely all his days.

'I didn't know she was coming,' he growled. 'I only heard today that she was on the plane.'

Sol looked at him, his head on one side in an attitude that implied cynicism. Carlo hated him. Then he noticed that the young man's face was pale and haggard, as if something had finally pierced his armour of selfishness. The hatred faded. They both loved the woman who lay beyond the door, fighting for her life, and for her sake he wouldn't quarrel with her son. No matter what.

'I didn't know she was coming,' he repeated. 'If I had, I'd have been at the airport. Nothing would have kept me away. But since she didn't tell me I think you're wrong, and she came to Naples for another reason.'

Sol shrugged.

They both turned sharply as the door opened and a nurse looked out.

'Signor Hadley—'

'Has she come round?' Sol asked tensely.

'I'm afraid not. But you can come in now.'

Sol hurried back into the room. Carlo tried to follow him, but the nurse stopped him.

'I'm sorry, *signore*, but only one person at a time—'

Carlo looked over her shoulder, feeling stunned. The figure on the bed could have been anyone, but his heart knew her at once.

Then the door closed, shutting him out.

He stayed there for the rest of the day, his gaze fixed on the blank wall, trying not to think. His mind pulled this way and that. She had returned to him and they had a future. She was dying and his own life was over with hers.

Then his thoughts would shut off, just in time to stop him going crazy.

When he could stand it no longer he went and opened the door. At once the nurse came to fend him off.

'I'm sorry. You can't—'

'Let him in.' Sol's voice came from the bed. He muttered as Carlo approached, 'Let him see what he did.'

Now he could see her clearly, and it was a nightmare. Her head was swathed in bandages and her eyes were covered.

'What happened to her?' he whispered.

'Her head was injured and we had to operate,' the nurse said. 'And there's some damage to her eyes. Just how bad it is we don't know yet.'

'That's if she lives,' Sol added with soft fury.

Carlo was looking at the machines, with their flashing lights and occasional clicks, measuring her heart-rate, blood pressure, and a dozen other things—too many to take in. A tube, leading to an oxygen machine, was clamped brutally into her mouth.

There were other attachments—one to a blood transfusion, one to a saline drip, one to a painkiller—all connected to her by small cables attached to inserts in her flesh—two in her arm, one in her hand, and one, he winced to notice it, directly into her neck.

If they had been alone there were a million things he wanted to say to her, but now he could only stand and watch, helpless.

A buzzer sounded, and the nurse answered urgently, 'Yes—all right. I'm on my way.'

To the others she said, 'I have to leave for a moment. If her condition changes press that bell.'

She hurried out.

'You look done in,' Carlo said. 'Why don't you go and get yourself some coffee?'

Sol shrugged, lacking the energy for an argument, and slipped out.

Carlo sat beside the bed, not taking his eyes from her. He wanted to speak, but his throat ached too much. If only she would move. But she lay as deathly still as if—his appalled mind found the connection—as if she'd been there for two thousand years.

That thought brought her back to him as she'd been on that

first day, when she'd danced into his life, turning the world upside down so that everything settled back into a different place. Together they had stood looking at the silent lovers, and now the memory broke his heart.

He leaned as close as he dared, whispering so that his breath touched her cheek.

'Do you remember that day? How they held each other? I knew then that one day we would hold each other like that—did you know it, too? Why were you returning to Naples? Was it for me?

'Where are you now? Have you really started on that road where the light beckons at the other end and your memories of the world are fading? Do you know that I'm behind you, calling you back? How can I make you turn to me?

'Do you know that I love you? Wherever you are, whatever has happened to you, whatever the future holds for us, I love you. If you live, I love you. If you—if you die, I shall love you and only you. You'll always be in my heart. We'll never really lose each other, and one day we'll be together again. I don't know where, or how long it will take, but it can never be over for us.

'Until then, I belong to you as totally as I say you belong to me, as finally as though the words had been said before an altar. Nothing could make me more yours than I am at this moment.'

He moved his fingers gently, so that they were beneath hers.

'They say that hearing outlasts the other senses. Is that true? Can you hear me? If only you could let me know! Can't you squeeze my hand, even slightly?'

But she never moved. It was as though she was dead already.

The door opened and a man in a white coat looked in, surprised at the sight of him.

'The nurse was called away,' Carlo said.

'But I haven't seen you here before. Who are you?'

Carlo rose to his feet.

'I am her husband,' he said.

The darkness was everywhere, but it changed quality all the time: sometimes thick and impenetrable, sometimes shot through with coloured flashes. Mixed with the darkness was the hideous noise.

There had been a blow on her head as the plane smashed into the runway. When she'd become half conscious again she'd found that opening her eyes was searingly painful, and given up the attempt. Dazed, she'd lain, listening to the screams around her, shouts, cries for help.

Someone yelled, 'Get that ambulance here quickly.'

Then another voice said, more quietly, 'This one's dead. Who's next?'

A violent jolt sent pain shrieking through her body, and the sounds vanished. Then there was only blackness, hot and swirling about her head.

She recovered consciousness, lost it, regained it, lost it again, until she could no longer tell one state from another. The air grew cooler, voices changed, pain faded, everything became blessedly peaceful. But it was the peace of nothing.

The world grew dim, leaving her in isolation through which presences came and went. Ghosts danced around her—Carlo as he'd been in their happy days, reaching out to take her in his arms and lead her to the new life that had beckoned for them, which she had rejected.

She could see Sol—and somehow Gina was there, but she faded, then Sol faded. Only Carlo was left, and he was running away from her. He knew that she'd come to Naples to find him and he didn't want her any more.

She was tired now. All she had to do was walk on, to a place where she could sleep, but suddenly he was there behind her, calling, pleading, demanding that she turn back because he was her husband.

She tried to think how that had happened, but everything was confusion and at last she knew that it did not matter. He had claimed her, and she was safe.

Sol returned two hours later, looking sheepish.

'I fell asleep in the café,' he said.

'Don't worry about it,' Carlo said. He was feeling in charity with Sol for leaving him alone for so long, even by accident. 'Has there been any change?'

Before Carlo could answer a doctor and nurse came in. After studying the machines the doctor said, 'It's strange how sometimes that happens, very suddenly.'

'What happens?' Carlo asked sharply.

'The vital signs simply start to improve for no apparent reason. It's happening here. Heart-rate, breathing, blood pressure—all better. Good. Let's try disconnecting the breathing machine. If your wife can breathe on her own, that'll be a big step forward.'

Sol looked puzzled at the word 'wife', but after a glance at Carlo's face he said nothing, and both of them stood back while the machine was disconnected.

The tense silence that followed seemed to go on for ever. Then Della's chest heaved, and she was breathing. The nurse smiled, the doctor hissed a soft 'Yes!' and Sol and Carlo thumped each other on the shoulder.

Carlo was the first to stop, turning away and hurrying out of the room, so that nobody should see him weep. He stayed a long time at the window in the corridor, convulsed with silent sobs, trying to bring himself under control.

'Carlo!'

He turned to see his mother, advancing from the far end of

the corridor. She opened her arms to him and he went into them willingly.

'What are you doing here?' he asked huskily.

'Signor Forest called the villa, asking about you. When he told us what had happened I knew everything. How is she?'

'She's very, very ill, Mamma. She's just started to breathe unaided, but it's only the start. She's still unconscious, and she may be blind. I've tried talking to her, telling her that I'm here for her. I hoped it might help her fight.'

'You must be patient, my son. This will take time, so I brought you a bag with some clean clothes and shaving things. I expect you'll be here for a while.' She gave him the bag, adding, 'Call home as often as you can. I want to be kept up to date.'

When she had left he called Alan Forest to explain, apologise, and thank him for talking to Hope.

'No need to say more,' Alan told him kindly. 'I got the picture as soon as you dashed off. Good luck. Maybe we'll work together one day.'

He returned to Della's room find the doctor talking,

'It's looking better, but it's too soon to uncross our fingers. As I expect you know, she's already had a heart attack.'

'No, I didn't know,' Carlo said sharply.

'It happened on the first day. It was mild, but in her condition everything is serious.'

It took two more days for Della to be declared out of danger. The staff were still unwilling to let them both be in the room together, so he and Sol reached a working arrangement under which they took it in turns.

As hour followed hour the machines showed that she was growing stronger, and he tried to think ahead. But he hit a brick wall, unable to imagine what the future held.

It seemed to him the most brutal ill luck that he wasn't there when she finally came round. He came in to find Sol rejoicing, while Della had relapsed into unconsciousness.

'What did she say?' Carlo demanded.

'Not much,' Sol told him. 'I held her hand and told her who I was, and she knew me. Her mind's clear.'

'Did you tell her I was here?'

'No. I'm not sure how much she can take in yet. The doctor said not to put pressure on her.'

It was reasonable, but Carlo's disappointment was bitter.

Sol watched Carlo struggling to come to terms with it, and saw what the effort at self-control did to him. A grudging respect tinged his hostility and he said, 'OK, there's something you'd better see. I had to go through her stuff, and I found this in the hand luggage.' He handed Carlo a thick envelope. 'I guess it tells its own story.'

He left the room quickly, giving Carlo no chance to reply.

The envelope contained photographs. Letting them spill onto the bed, Carlo saw his own face a hundred times, either alone or with her. They had all been taken during their first glorious week together, and she had brought them with her, in her hand luggage. Perhaps she had even looked at them during the flight.

She had been coming back to him. Nothing else could account for this.

But his first leap of delight was overtaken by another feeling as he studied the pictures. They showed him to himself in a new light. Here was a man clearly in love, but equally clearly driven by possessiveness. He'd made jokes about being her slave, but his hands had always been holding her tightly, as though fearing to free her to make her own decisions.

How often had he pressed her to do what he wanted? How

often had she begged for more time? In the end he'd suffocated her, driving her to flee. It was his fault that she was lying here.

He sat beside her, watching her face, silently pleading with her to wake up and speak to him. Because more than anything in the world he wanted to tell her that he was sorry.

He stayed with Della for the next few hours, talking, praying that she could hear him, but when his stint was over she had still given no sign. At last Sol came in.

'Anything?'

'No.' He pointed to the envelope. 'Thanks.'

'Did it tell you what you wanted to know?'

'It told me a lot more than I wanted to know. I think I even know why she didn't call me before coming out here.'

'Well, the two of you can sort it out next time she wakes up. OK—my turn.'

Carlo went to the door, but he couldn't resist turning for a last hopeful look at Della.

It took all his self-control to stand there, unknown to her, watching her suffer but unable to offer her any comfort. He clenched and unclenched his hands, willing her to awaken while he was still here.

'Sol—'

The voice from the bed was so faint that they had to strain to hear it.

'Sol, are you there?' Della reached out as she spoke, grasping frantically at the air.

'I'm here,' he said quickly, taking her hand and returning to the chair by the bed. 'Just as I was last time.'

'I thought you'd gone.'

'No, I'll be here as long as you want me.'

'I'm just being silly. I'm sorry. I get these funny ideas.'

'What kind of ideas?'

'Just fancies. I imagined—'

Sol looked over his shoulder. Silently Carlo mouthed, *Tell her.*

'There's something I've got to tell you,' Sol said, turning back to Della. 'Carlo's been here. He heard about what happened and he's worried about you.'

Carlo waited for her to smile, to call for him, but instead she was suddenly frantic.

'You haven't let him in here?' she cried in a cracked voice. 'Promise me that you haven't.'

'Mum—'

'You won't let him in here, will you?'

'But I thought you still—'

'Thought I what?'

'You know,' he said, uneasy and embarrassed.

'Still love him?'

'Yeah. That.'

In the doorway Carlo tensed, waiting for her answer. The silence seemed to go on for ever.

'Of course I love him,' Della said softly. 'And I always will. But it's too late. I couldn't bear him to see me like this. You haven't let him in, have you?'

Faced with her mounting agitation Sol had no choice but to say, 'No, I swear I haven't.' He saw Carlo's hands raised in protest and gave him a desperate shrug as if to say, What else could I do?

'He mustn't see me.' Della's voice rose to a cry. 'Promise me—promise me—'

'I promise—Mum, I promise. But I think you're wrong. The guy loves you, for Pete's sake.'

'He loved me as I was then, but he's never seen me like this, and I don't want him to.'

Carlo had recovered enough to mouth, *Makes no difference.*

'Maybe it wouldn't make any difference,' Sol recited obediently.

'That's what he'd say,' Della murmured. 'And he'd mean it, because he's kind and generous, but I couldn't put such a burden on him. It wouldn't be fair.'

'Maybe love isn't fair,' Sol replied, repeating Carlo's silent message.

'It isn't. If it were—if love was fair—I could find a way not to love him so much. I've tried not to—I thought I could forget—be strong—but he's always there. No, it's not fair—'

Sol looked up again, expecting some direction, but Carlo was leaning against the wall, his face distorted, his hands hanging helplessly by his sides. It was as if Della last words had knocked the strength out of him.

'Perhaps you don't really want him to go?' Sol suggested, dragging some inspiration from inside himself.

'That's very clever of you, darling. It's true, I don't want to lose what we had, but I can only keep it now by letting it go and remembering.'

'Let me bring him here,' Sol urged.

'No—no! You mustn't do that. Sol, I'm trusting you. I can trust you, can't I? You wouldn't deceive me about this?'

'No, I— Of course you can trust me, Mum.'

'Don't you see why I could never let Carlo see me this way? I want him to remember me as I was the last time he saw me.' Her lips curved in a sudden smile. 'It was the awards night. I was dressed to kill and I know I looked good—you saw the tape—my best ever. He was there, and he saw me. I'll never look as good as that again. But it doesn't matter because he'll never know. He'll remember me as I was that night, and that's what I want.'

'But think of all your life—' Sol began to argue.

'I can manage if I know he's all right. What I couldn't bear is to tie him down when he should be flying.'

'Flying?'

'On the first day he told me about his ambitions, how he wanted to do something that could send him soaring. No nine-to-five job or collar and tie for him. That's what I want for him, too. I couldn't bear to be the one to take it away.'

'Can you really live on memories for ever?' Sol asked.

Again she smiled—an incredible smile, breathtaking in its happiness.

'I have the very best memories,' she said softly.

After that there was silence. When Sol looked at the door again, Carlo had gone.

# CHAPTER TWELVE

DOWN the side of the hospital ran a narrow street, lined with small shops and cafés, some with outside tables. At one of them sat Carlo, drinking coffee, staring fiercely at the floor.

'Well, look who's here!'

He looked up to see Ruggiero pulling out chairs for Hope and himself. His brother called the waiter and ordered *prosecco* all round.

'Is that her window up there?' Hope asked, pointing to the hospital.

'That's right. The third one along. How did you know I was here?'

'We've been spying on you, of course,' Ruggiero said. 'What else?'

'Why aren't you with her?' Hope demanded. 'That's where you belong.'

'So I thought,' he said heavily. 'But I was wrong. She doesn't want to see me. The mere idea upsets her.'

'Because she no longer loves you?'

'Because she thinks I won't want her now she's injured.'

'Perhaps she's right?' Hope said carefully. 'She'll be a heavy responsibility.'

His eyes flashed. 'Do you think I'm afraid of that?'

Hope looked at him thoughtfully for a moment.

'No,' she said at last. 'I don't think so.'

'But *she* does.'

'Then you must convince her otherwise. It should be easy, since she loves you so much. After all, she came back to find you.'

'Yes, I think she did. But the crash has changed everything—not for me, but for her.'

'Nonsense. She still wants you. Nothing has changed,' Hope said robustly. 'Your mother says so, and your mother is always right.'

He gave a faint smile, but looked at her curiously. 'At one time you were against her.'

'In those days I was a stupid woman. I didn't understand her, but most of all I didn't understand you. I see more clearly now.'

She saw Carlo glance up at the window, to where a young man stood, signalling to him.

'Sol,' he explained.

'You two have become friends?' Ruggiero demanded sceptically.

'Not quite that, but we're managing to work together. He's not so bad.' He rose and kissed her cheek. 'Thank you, Mamma, for everything.'

'Give Della my love.'

He found Sol in the corridor, agitated.

'Now we're in the soup,' he said. 'Why did you tell that doctor that you were her husband?'

'What's happened?'

'He told her about it, didn't he? Only she didn't know, and she asked me a lot of questions, and now she's all worked up and I don't know what to do.'

'But I do. Stay here, and don't come in.'

He found the doctor beside Della's bed, trying to soothe her. 'Please leave,' Carlo said.

'*Signore*, I don't know who you are, but I cannot allow—'

'I am her husband and I tell you to leave.'

The doctor departed quickly. There was something about Carlo that he didn't want to argue with.

Carlo paid him no attention. He'd heard Della's horrified gasp and he dropped down beside the bed, taking her hands in his and kissing them.

'No, don't struggle,' he said. 'Or we'll both get tangled up in your machines. Hush, be still.'

Either his voice or the feel of his hands seemed to get through to her, and at last she lay quiet.

'Is it you?' she whispered.

'Who else should it be? Della, my love—my love—'

She grew still, knowing she should fight this, but also knowing that she had no strength left to fight. She had come to the end, and he was there, waiting for her.

Then she felt the sensation that had haunted her dreams: the gentle pressure of his head against her, so that her hands moved instinctively to enfold and caress him possessively. It wasn't what she'd meant to do, but the choice was no longer hers. As her fingers clasped him she felt him move a little closer, as though seeking a long-lost refuge.

'Do you think you could keep me away?' he whispered. 'You never could and you never will. Don't try to leave me again, my darling. I couldn't bear it.'

'But look at me,' she said huskily. 'I'm crippled and half blind—or maybe completely blind—'

He raised his head, looking down at what he could see of her wan face, half covered in bandages.

'It doesn't matter,' he said, 'as long as we love each other.'

'But—'

'No.' He laid a gentle finger over her lips. 'No more words. They only get in the way.'

This time they held each other in silence for a long time.

'You told them you were my husband?' she said after a while.

'Yes, because I am. I won't let anyone deny me—not even you. Only tell me this. Why did you come back?'

'To find you. I should never have gone away, and I wanted to tell you that. Even if you didn't want me any more—'

'Hush,' he said, silencing her mouth tenderly with his own. 'I could never stop wanting you. If you knew how hard I've hoped that you came back for me. When I saw the pictures I dared to let myself believe, but I needed to hear you say it.'

'Even now that I'm like this?'

'I see no difference in you,' he said simply. 'Except that you are hurt, and need me at last.'

Before such total commitment there was nothing for her to say. She began to weep, the tears pouring out from under the bandages until he kissed them away.

From then they had to be patient as Della progressed by slow inches. Painful life returned to her leg, the bandages were removed from her head, although not from her eyes, and her hair began to grow again.

'It isn't grey, is it?' she asked Carlo anxiously.

'No, it's not grey,' he said, laughing. 'It's fair and soft, in little tight curls, like a shorn lamb. You'll start a new fashion.'

'I can't bear not knowing what I look like. How long before they remove these bandages?'

'Be patient until— Hey what are you doing?'

He moved to stop her, but Della was too fast, taking the edge of the bandage, lifting it just a little, then dropping it at once.

'What is it?' he asked, full of dread. 'My darling, don't panic—'

'I think I can see,' she said breathlessly. 'My right eye is fuzzy, but I can make out shapes and colours. *I'm going to see.*'

They flung themselves into each other's arms and stayed that way for a while, unable to speak. Then Della, inspired by sudden determination, raised her hands to her head. But Carlo caught them.

'No, *cara*. We'll ask the doctor before we do anything rash.'

'But he'll just tell me to be patient, and I'm tired of that.'

'One step at a time.'

'I'm sorry,' she said grumpily, resting her head on his shoulder. 'But I'm fed up. I'm fed up with being here, with not being able to move properly, with not knowing what's happening. *I'm fed up.*'

He laughed, caressing her.

'I can see you're going to be a handful to look after.'

'You won't have to look after me.'

'Yes, I will. As soon as you can leave here I'm taking you home, to nurse you until you're well enough for us to be married.'

A noise outside made them pull apart. It was the doctor.

'I can see,' Della told him at once. 'Just out of one eye, but I can.'

'In that case, let's have a look.'

They held their breath as he removed the bandages. Della blinked rapidly.

'I've got the right one back,' she said joyfully. 'It's getting clearer all the time.'

'And the left?'

'Nothing.'

'Well, we may be able to do something about that later.'

'Just one eye makes all the difference,' she said fervently.

The doctor asked some more questions, and went away looking pleased.

'It's so good to see you again,' she said, meaning it. 'I

thought I never would.' She blinked again. 'It's getting better all the time. I'll be able to work again.'

'Will you wait until the rest of you has recovered?' He was almost tearing his hair.

'Sorry. I can't help it.'

Seeing that she was on a high of delight, he gave up trying to calm her down and joined in her pleasure. His own heart was rejoicing at her happiness, content to forget the future in the first good news they'd had.

Sol arrived, already exulting.

'I met the doctor on the way in,' he said, producing a bottle of champagne, 'and turned back to get this.'

They drank it out of paper cups, toasting each other cheerfully, until Della said, 'Darling, it's wonderful that you're here, but now I'm so much better I want you to go home. Your exams must be coming up soon.'

He nodded. 'And I really must pass them this time,' he said. 'I've got to get a job and start sending Gina money. Her grandmother says I can visit them as soon as the baby's born.'

'You've been in touch?'

'I found Mrs Burton's phone number in your things, and—well, I thought I should do something. It's my kid, after all.'

'Good for you,' Carlo said.

Next day he drove Sol to the airport. Now on easy terms, they had a coffee while they waited for the flight to be called.

'You know,' Sol said, considering, 'you didn't handle it very cleverly last year.'

'Handle what?' Carlo asked.

'Everything. "Marry me now or it's all off." I ask you!'

'She told you about that?' Carlo asked, horrified.

'No, of course not. She told Jackie, her secretary. They're friendly.'

'And Jackie told you?'

'Nah, I was eavesdropping.'

'Why didn't I think of that?'

'Dunno. Usually you assume the worst of me on instinct—'

'Maybe I don't any more. A lot of things have changed. Go on with what you were saying.'

'Mum's as stubborn as a mule. Give her an ultimatum and she's off in the other direction. You should have played along with her.'

'Settled for an affair because she thought I was too young?'

'That was just talk,' Sol declared, with the wisdom of twenty-one. 'Once she'd got used to living with you she'd have seen that you were right. When the time came to leave she wouldn't have been able to. You'd have been married by now.'

The truth of this was so blindingly obvious that Carlo nearly burst out laughing.

'If anyone had told me that I'd be sitting here taking advice from you,' he murmured, 'I'd never have believed them.'

At the gate he clapped Sol on the shoulder.

'Good luck,' he said. 'See you again soon.'

It was Hope who took over the arrangements for the day Della left hospital. When she heard that Carlo planned to take her to his apartment she vetoed the idea without hesitation.

'That place is on the third floor, and quite unsuitable,' she declared.

'There is an elevator, Mamma,' Carlo observed, but he spoke mildly, for he could see where Hope was leading, and it pleased him.

'No arguments,' she said with finality. 'I have decided. She's coming home with us. It's all settled.'

Della had a demonstration of exactly what it meant to be Hope Rinucci when it came to persuading the hospital to let her go early. At first the doctor was dubious, but Hope swept him off to the villa, showed him the ground-floor rooms that were being prepared for the invalid, and emphasised that there would always be people there to care for her.

'She will never be alone in the house,' Hope insisted. 'Not for one moment, even when the nurse has left—for of course I will hire a nurse at the start.'

Della began to see how alike Carlo and his mother were. The same quiet forcefulness was present in both of them.

On the day she left hospital the doctor took Carlo aside.

'There are things you need to know, *signore*. She's better, but her health has been seriously impaired, and it always will be. She had a heart attack immediately after the crash, and she'll always be vulnerable to another one. If you're thinking of having children—'

'No,' Carlo said at once. 'I won't do anything that means the smallest risk for her.'

'Good. Hopefully that will prolong her life.'

'But not by much,' Carlo said quietly. 'Is that what you mean?'

'With the greatest care she could have another twenty years. But she'll always be frail, and it might be less.'

'Whatever it is, it'll still be more than I feared.'

'I'm glad you're a realist, *signore*. You're going to need to be.'

Carlo travelled in the ambulance with her. At the villa she was greeted by Toni and Hope, Ruggiero, Primo and Olympia, and with flowers and messages of goodwill from the others of her new family who could not be there.

They had prepared a home for her, with a room for herself—so well equipped that she might still have been in hospital—a room next door for the nurse, and one nearby for Carlo.

At first they left her alone, knowing that she would need rest more than anything, and she slept for two days before waking to feel better than for a long time.

Now Carlo was with her all the time, even when the nurse was tending her. He watched everything the nurse did, and learned. It was he who got her back on her feet and held her as she struggled to walk again. From a sedentary life she progressed to a walking stick, first clasping him with her free hand, then without him.

'You're improving fast,' he told her. 'At this rate we can start planning the wedding.'

She sat down, gasping slightly from the effort she had made.

'Are you really sure you still want to go ahead?' she asked. 'It's such an undertaking—'

'You mean you don't think you can face a lifetime with me?' he asked wickedly.

'You know what I mean. The cost to you will be much greater now.'

'I can't believe that we're still arguing about this. We settled it long ago. In my heart you are already my wife. Now you will become my wife in the eyes of the world. That's it. Final. End of subject.'

'You don't give me any choice?'

'It's taken you so long to realise that?' he asked, with a touch of his old humour.

'But one day—' Della stopped, silenced by the look he gave her.

She'd been going to say that she wouldn't tie him down. He could divorce her whenever he liked.

'No,' he said firmly, following her meaning as if by telepathy. 'Never say that. *Never!*' He kissed her, then spoke more gently.

'It would be treating me like a boy, one who can't make his own decisions, and we've been down that path before. When we marry it must be for real—and for ever.'

'But I can't give you children,' she reminded him.

'Then we must love each other all the more.'

They spent many evenings on the terrace, looking out at the night, wrapped in each other's arms, talking endlessly, discovering each other's minds. She began to realise how little they had talked in the old days, when their fierce passion had left no time for talk. Now he sometimes seemed afraid to touch her for fear of doing harm.

'I'm not breakable,' she told him once, when he had broken off a kiss by sheer will-power. 'We could go into my room and—'

To calm his nerves he took refuge in clowning. 'Make love before our wedding night?' he asked, in mock horror. 'I'm shocked. Shocked!'

'Well, perhaps it's best that you know the truth about me,' she said, matching his mood.

He seized her wandering hand and spoke in a shaking voice.

'Will you stop, please? How much self-control do you think I have?'

'I'm having fun finding out.'

He gave her a hunted look that made her burst out laughing. He joined her, while still gripping her hand out of sheer self-preservation. They made so much noise that Hope came out to see what the commotion was. But beneath the laughter Della saw the seriousness of the man who would never risk her safety, whatever it cost him. And it *did* cost him, she knew. There were evenings when he parted from her abruptly, lest his strength of will collapse, for his desire for her was as great as ever. She loved him for that, too. But most of all she loved him for what she discovered in his mind, in the long talks they had in the semi-darkness.

Now she could tell him about the path she'd travelled as she lay, unconscious, in hospital.

'Everything was scary, dark and confusing. But then I heard

you talking to me, telling me that everything would be all right because you were my husband, and you'd look after me.'

'So why did you try to keep me away when you woke up?'

'Because when I came back to reality everything changed. I knew it had been a wonderful dream, and that I had to be sensible.'

'Being sensible has always been our curse,' he observed. 'It's time you stopped that bad habit.'

'I promise never to be sensible again.'

Sometimes she stared anxiously into the mirror, worried that her ordeal might have aged her faster. Her face was thinner, and there were scars around her left eye, which the nurse assured her would fade to thin lines. But to her relief there was no sign of premature grey hair.

'Not like me,' Carlo told her one day. 'Look.'

Incredibly, the first signs of grey had started to appear at the side of his head. She examined them, wondering if suffering had done this to him.

'You'll have to treat me carefully now I'm getting decrepit,' he told her mischievously.

'Don't let him fool you, daughter,' Toni said. 'The Rinuccis always go grey early. It's just a family trait.'

'Spoilsport.' Carlo grinned. 'I was going to make the most of it.'

Toni winked at Della. 'When your name's Rinucci it'll happen to you, too.'

'I didn't think it worked like that,' she said, chuckling.

'You don't believe me? Try being married to this one, and it'll put ten years on you.'

Everyone laughed, and Della felt the world become a brighter place—partly, she thought, because Toni had called her daughter.

Gradually she saw that her looks had changed, but not in the way she'd feared. Her hair, which had merely curved gracefully before, now decided to curl, so that it was easier to wear it much shorter.

'You look like a pretty little elf,' Sol informed her.

'Cheek.'

'No, it's nice.'

And Carlo thought so, too.

Sol was visiting, armed with photos of his newly-born son. He'd gained his degree—not brilliantly, but well enough to escape censure—and had a job lined up for when he returned to England.

Hope was thrilled with the child.

'Our first great-grandson,' she said.

'But, Mamma,' Carlo began to protest, 'he's not— I mean—'

'Are you saying that Della isn't one of us?' Hope demanded.

'Yes, she is. But—'

'Then this baby is also one of us,' Hope said firmly, thus settling the matter for all time.

When Della was well enough to move around almost normally Carlo vanished one day, and returned in the evening with the news that he had taken a job in a local museum. He explained that he would only need to go in on three days a week, which would give him time for his own projects at home, but it was still the kind of conventional employment that he would once have spurned, and Della and Hope were both loud in their dismay.

'What are you thinking of?' Hope asked him when they were alone.

'Money,' he said simply. 'I haven't worked for months and my cash is running out.'

'You've been giving us too much—we can take less—'

'I know that having Della here is expensive, and I won't let that expense fall on you.'

'As though Poppa and I minded—'

'But I mind,' he said, in the quiet, firm voice that was usual with him these days. 'I'm taking this job.'

'For how long?'

He shrugged cheerfully.

'But what about expeditions?'

'I can't risk leaving Della. When she's stronger we might manage some short trips together, but we'll see how it works out.'

Hope said no more. She saw this dazzling son of hers, the most talented, the most brilliant, giving up his chance of an outstanding future. And yet he was happy. Because he'd found something that meant more to him.

At one time she would have blamed Della, but she knew better now.

It was Della herself who brought up the subject, finding Hope alone that evening.

'You must hate me,' she said slowly.

Hope spoke gently. 'I have no reason to hate you. Never think that.'

'You didn't want me to marry him, and you have even more reason now. I'm tying him down, taking up his time when he should be working at his career.'

'Once I would have thought so, too. But now I know that what he's doing is more valuable to him than any career. Before, everything was easy for him—too easy. Then he had to fight for you, and it made a man of him. Don't try to stop him. Take what he offers. Because in doing that you'll be giving him the kind of love that he most needs.'

On the night before the wedding Hope found Carlo sitting alone under a lamp in the garden.

'What are you reading, my son?' She took the book from his hands. 'English poetry? You?'

'The sonnets of Elizabeth Barrett Browning,' he said, showing her the one that had held his attention. 'I found them through Della.'

'"*How do I love thee?*"' Hope read. '"*Let me count the ways.*"'

'Look at the last line,' Carlo said. 'I've read it so often—' He whispered the words. '"*And if God choose, I shall but love thee better after death.*"'

'Do you think of that very much?' Hope asked, sitting beside him.

'All the time. Twenty years, if we're very lucky. Perhaps fifteen—or less.'

'And then you'll be left alone, with no children and nothing but memories,' Hope said sadly. 'But at least you'll still be young enough to—well—'

'No,' he said at once. 'I won't marry again.'

'My dear boy, you can't know that now.'

'Yes, I can,' he said slowly. 'You'd be amazed at how far and how well I can see ahead. It's as though a mist has cleared, and I can follow the road to the end. I see it all, and I know where I'm going.'

She didn't want to ask the next question, but she needed to know the answer.

'And when you get there? How will you bear it without her?'

'But I won't be without her,' he said quietly. 'She'll always be with me, still loving me, as I'll always love her. Don't worry about me, Mamma. She'll never really leave me.'

His eyes were shining, and she had to look away. The next moment his arm was about her shoulder and he was hugging her.

'Hey, come on,' he said in a rallying voice. 'Don't cry. Everything's all right. Tomorrow's my wedding day. I'm marrying the woman I love, and I'm the happiest man in the world.'

Next day, the women in the family gathered to adorn Della in her ivory lace wedding gown, then to escort her to the main room, where the rest of the family was waiting. Only Carlo and Ruggiero were missing, having gone ahead to the church.

Sol was there to give her away. As he helped her out of the car she threw away her stick, not needing it now. Waiting for her at the altar was the man who valued her higher than anything else in life.

Sol smiled and offered his arm. She took it, and together they made their way down the aisle to Carlo. As she grew closer she could make out his expression of expectant joy.

Her heart began to speak to him in silent words.

I love you because from the first moment you accepted me wholeheartedly, asking for nothing except that I should be yours, and by valuing me you showed me how to value myself.

I love you because you taught me how to feel love, when I thought I'd never know.

I love you because you showed me that a man's heart can be deeper and more powerful than I had dreamed possible. And then you gave that heart to me, renewing my life, for however long that life may be.

*'And, if God choose, I shall but love thee better after death.'*

* * * * *

# THE MEDITERRANEAN
# REBEL'S BRIDE

BY
LUCY GORDON

# CHAPTER ONE

'I, CARLO, take you, Della, to be my wife. I promise to be true to you in good times and in bad, in sickness and in health. I will love you and honour you all the days of my life.'

On a bright summer day in Naples, Carlo Rinucci uttered these words in the Church of All Saints and Angels. He spoke with his eyes fixed on the bride he had fought so hard to win, and behind him a quiet murmur went round the congregation.

His best man and twin brother, Ruggiero, stood quietly, waiting for the service to be over. This wedding was an unsettling experience for him.

For thirty-one years the twins had squabbled, enjoyed themselves together in various over-indulgent ways, played truant, chased girls. Though not identical, they were alike in their conviction that the race went to the swift and life was meant to be fun—and they had always acted as they were: handsome young bachelors with the world at their feet.

Now here was Carlo, dedicating himself, with quiet gravity, to a woman of frail health, seven years his senior, and doing so with the air of a man who had finally come to the place his heart desired.

Ruggiero played his part at the church perfectly, performed all his duties, then went home to the reception at the Villa

Rinucci to eat and drink, flirt, and cope with the usual hearty wedding jokes,

All the Rinucci brothers were handsome, but Ruggiero had something else—the kind of outstanding looks that made him a target at weddings. A ripple would go around the female guests, combining fascination and a mysterious sense of outrage, as though no man who looked like that had any right to be on the loose.

It had been his trademark all his life: looks and charm, both with a slightly fierce edge that turned heads. He knew what was said of him, that he could have any woman he wanted, and although he enjoyed the joke he accepted it as his due.

Any woman he wanted.

Except one.

'Only you and Francesco left now,' someone said. 'I guess your mother's making plans.'

He laughed, saying, 'They won't get me.'

'You say that at every wedding,' observed his brother Luke, who was passing.

'*You* used to say it at every wedding,' Ruggiero reminded him. 'The difference is that I've held out. I'm a shining example.'

Luke paused long enough to wave to Minnie, his wife of two years, who waved back between sips of champagne.

'Just beware,' he said to Ruggiero, 'lest one day the shining example wakes up to find he's a lonely old man. Coming, *cara*.'

Ruggiero grinned, accepting this as just one of those things brothers felt obliged to say at weddings, and returned to his duties, flirting with a shy young woman until she laughed and began to enjoy herself.

When it was time for the speeches he did an excellent job, even if he said so himself—which he did. He was rewarded with looks of gratitude from Carlo and Della, and a smile of fond approval from his mother.

'You're a wonderful best man,' she said afterwards.

'Against all your expectations?' he teased.

'The only thing that surprises me,' Hope informed him, 'is that you don't have some over-painted young hussy clinging to your arm.'

'I didn't want any distractions when I had a job to do,' he explained blandly.

'Hmm!'

'Don't be so cynical, Mamma.'

'Don't be—? I have six sons, and you're surprised that I'm cynical?'

He grinned, and glided away to attend to the needs of a Rinucci great-aunt.

'Be fair to him,' Evie said, appearing at Hope's side.

She was the wife of Justin, Hope's eldest son. Before their marriage she'd been a natural rebel, caring only for her motorbike. Happy marriage and the birth of twins had softened some of Evie's glittering edge, but had done nothing to dull the gleam of humour in her eyes.

'It's reasonable for Ruggiero to want to concentrate on his duties,' she said now.

'Reasonable?' Hope echoed. 'This is Ruggiero we're talking about.'

'I take your point,' Evie said with a laugh.

'When was he ever reasonable about anything? Working, playing, eating, drinking, hussies—everything over the top.'

'Surely his girlfriends aren't all hussies?'

'He doesn't let me meet most of them. That's how I know.' Hope sighed fondly. 'Evie, it's such a pity you can't split yourself in two—one for Justin and one for Ruggiero.'

'Maybe I wouldn't suit Ruggiero.'

'You're bound to. You're as crazy about motorbikes as he is.'

'Is it true that he actually owns a firm that makes them?'

'Half-owns.'

'Maybe I should go and talk to him,' Evie said, laughing, and sauntered away.

It was later that evening when she caught up with Ruggiero. The guests had gone, and those family members who were staying at the villa had settled into small groups to enjoy a good natter. Justin was deep in conversation with his mother, and Evie found Ruggiero on the terrace, looking out over the lights of Naples gleaming against the darkness. With a sigh of relief she threw herself into a chair and kicked off her shoes.

'Weddings are exhausting,' she said.

He nodded. 'And there's another party tomorrow night. Mamma's never happier than when planning a big get-together. I'm going to spend the day peacefully testing a bike.'

'Ah, yes—tell me about your factory.'

He poured her a glass of wine, and sat on the low wall.

'I found the place on its last legs a couple of years ago. I knew Piero Fantone—the owner—slightly, and I bought in. Things have gone well. Our bread and butter is the standard bikes that "normal" people buy, but the specials are the racing bikes that only the "crazies" want. We've started winning races. Now we're bringing out new racing bike, and I'm testing it tomorrow.'

'The fastest, hottest, most fearsome bike in the country,' Evie declaimed theatrically.

'Do you mind?' he said at once, in mock offence. 'In the *world*.'

'I'm sorry. But aren't there professional testers? Does the boss have to risk his neck—?' She broke off and struck her forehead. 'Oh, of course! Stupid of me. You *want* to risk your neck. Otherwise, where's the fun?'

'You've got it.' He grinned. 'Evie, you're the only woman I know who'd understand that. You should come and watch tomorrow.'

'I'd love to.' She sipped her wine and said mischievously, 'People have been talking about you all day.'

'I know. It's a bachelor's fate at a wedding.' He assumed a twittery voice of the kind he'd heard so often that day. '"He'll be next. Just wait and see."'

'Was that why you didn't bring a date?' she asked, chuckling.

'One reason. My mother complains about the girls I bring home, and when I don't bring one she complains even more.'

'I gather they're real eye-openers?'

He made a wry face, and she became serious to say, 'I guess you're a long way from finding what Carlo has.'

'I think there are very few men who find what Carlo has. Or what you and Justin have.'

She was silent, watching him sympathetically.

After a while he added, 'And thank you for not saying, *Don't worry, your turn will come.*'

'Don't you think it will?' she asked, struck by the sudden quiet heaviness in his voice.

'Maybe. Or maybe it came and went.'

Evie was silent, astonished. She had always sensed that there was more to her brother-in-law than the rough, hard-living man he was on the surface, but this was the first time he'd offered so much as a hint of a more reflective inner self.

Cautiously, so not to scare him off, she said, 'Can you be sure that it's gone finally?'

'Quite sure. Since I know hardly anything about her. She was English, her name was Sapphire, and we had two weeks together. That's all.'

But it wasn't all, she could tell. During those weeks something had happened to him that had been like an earthquake.

'Do you want to talk about it?' she asked.

'I met her in London about two-and-a-half years ago. I was

visiting friends, but they suddenly had a family crisis, so I left
them to it and explored London on my own. We met in the
bar of my hotel. She was there to meet a friend who didn't
show up, we got talking and—that was it.'

'What was she like?'

'Like something from another world. So insubstantial that
I was almost afraid to touch her. I knew her for two weeks,
and then she vanished.'

'Vanished? Where?'

'I've no idea. I never saw her again. Perhaps she was
nothing but a mad hallucination?'

Evie was astonished. Who would have thought the hard-
headed Ruggiero could talk in this way? She wondered if he
even realised what he'd revealed. He was looking into the
distance, his eyes fixed on some inner world. She held her
breath, willing him to go on.

But instead he made a sound that was part-grunt, part-
nervous laugh, seeming to draw himself back from the brink.

'Hey, what the hell?' he said edgily. 'These things happen.
Easy come, easy go.'

'But I don't think it was easy,' Evie urged. 'I think she
meant more to you than that.'

He shrugged. 'It was a holiday romance. How much do
they ever mean?'

'Ruggiero—'

'Do you want to come with me tomorrow or not?'

'Yes, of course. But—'

'Fine. Be ready to leave early in the morning.'

He bid her goodnight and hurried to his room, despising
himself for making a cowardly escape, but unable to help it.
Much more of that conversation and he would have gone mad.

He stripped off his clothes and got under the shower,
hoping to wash away the day. But nothing could banish the

thoughts that had troubled him from the moment he'd arrived at the church with Carlo.

Carlo, the twin barely an hour younger than himself, who'd shared with him all the riotous pleasures of youth, now transformed into a man lit by a powerful inner joy. And the sight had thrown him off balance because it had called up a voice he'd thought he'd silenced long ago.

*'Forget the rest of the world—there's only our world— what more do we need?'*

Memories started to crowd in. She was as he'd first seen her, in a glittering tight red dress, low enough in front to show her exquisite bosom, high enough on the thigh to show off her endless legs. It was the attire of a woman who could attract men without trouble, who enjoyed attracting them and had no scruples about doing so as often as she pleased.

Within a few hours of their meeting he'd held her, naked, in his arms. Everything about her had been breathtaking—her body, the whisper of her voice, her laughter.

Other pictures crowded in: a day out together at the funfair, doing childish things. They'd sat together in a photo booth, arms entwined, heads leaning against each other, while the machine's lights flashed. A moment later two pictures had appeared in the dish, and they had taken one each.

'Sapphire,' he murmured.

It was the only name she had ever told him. She'd kept her last name a secret, and even that had been part of her magic.

Magic. He'd resisted the idea, considering himself a prosaic man and proud of it. But Sapphire had burned with erotic power, dazzling him and luring him into a furnace from which he'd emerged reborn.

She'd been an adventurous lover, who hadn't tamely waited for him in the bed but had come after him eagerly, appearing in the shower and sliding her arms around him as water laved them. How many times had he seen her shadow outside the frosted glass, then felt her beside him?

The last memory was one from which he still shied away. They'd made love in the afternoon and she'd left him in the evening, promising to return in the morning. He'd lain awake that night, vowing to bring things to a head the next day.

But the next day there had been no sign of her.

He'd waited and waited, but she hadn't appeared. One day had become two, then three.

He had never seen her again.

Now he stood in the shower, his eyes closed, keeping out the world. But at last he opened them and switched off the water.

Then he tensed.

She was there, just outside the shower, her shadow outlined on the glass. She was waiting for him.

He moved fast, hurling himself against the glass so hard that he nearly broke it, reaching out, trying to find her.

But his hands touched only air. There was nobody there. She had been an illusion as, perhaps, she had always been. He stood there alone, shaking with the ferocity of his memories.

He dried himself mechanically, trying to force himself to be calm. It shamed him to be out of control.

That was the mantra he'd lived by since the day she'd vanished into thin air. Control. Never let anyone suspect the turmoil of joy and misery that had destroyed and remade him.

He'd returned to Italy, apparently the same man as before. If his rambunctious hard living had been a little forced, his manner more emphatic, nobody had seemed to notice. He had kept his memories a secret, sharing them with nobody in the world—until tonight.

With Evie he'd come closer to confiding than with anyone else, ever. But he wasn't a man who easily discussed feelings, or even knew what his own feelings were much of the time. So he'd gone just so far before retreating into silence.

Today, at his brother's wedding, he'd sensed that Carlo had found a secret door and gone through it, closing it behind him.

For him the door had stood half-open, but then it had brutally slammed shut in his face, leaving him stranded in a desolate place.

All around him the villa was hushed for the night. It was packed to the rafters with people—many of whom loved each other, some of whom loved him. In the midst of them he felt lonelier than ever before in his life.

The flight from London had been delayed, and by the time Polly landed at Naples she was feeling thoroughly frazzled. The extra time had given her more chance to think about what she was doing and regret that she had ever agreed to do it.

There was a long queue to get through Passport Control, and she yawned, trying to be patient. A large mirror stretched the length of the wall, providing an unwelcome opportunity to anyone who could bear to look at themselves after a flight. For herself, she would gladly have done without it. There was nothing in her appearance that pleased her.

It was wickedly unjust that, equipped with much the same physical attributes as her cousin Freda, she had turned out so differently. Freda had been tall, slender, willowy—a beauty who'd walked with floating grace. Polly was also tall and slender, but her movements suggested efficiency rather than elegance.

'And just as well,' she'd tartly remarked once. 'I'm a nurse. Who wants a nurse drifting beautifully into the ward when they need a bedpan? I run, and then I run somewhere else, because someone's hit the alarm button. And when I've finished I don't recline gorgeously on a satin couch. I collapse in an exhausted huddle.'

Freda, who'd been listening to this outburst with amusement, had given a lazy chuckle.

'You describe it so cleverly, darling. I think you're wonderful. I couldn't do what you do.'

That had been Freda's way—always ready with the right words, even if they'd meant nothing to her. Polly, prosaic to her fingertips, had seen that slow, luxurious smile melt strong men, luring them on with the hint of mystery.

To her there had been no mystery. Freda had done and said whatever would soften her audience. It had brought her a multitude of admirers and a rich husband.

Polly had even watched helplessly as a boyfriend of her own had been enticed away from her, without a backward look. Nor had she blamed him. She hadn't even blamed Freda. It would have been like resenting the sun for shining.

Freda's heart-shaped face had been beautiful. Polly, with roughly the same shape, just missed beauty by the vital millionth of an inch. Freda's hair had been luxuriously blonde. Polly was also fair, and could probably have had the same rich shade if she'd worked on it. But life as a senior nurse in a busy hospital left her neither time nor cash to indulge her hair. She kept it clean and wore it long, her one concession to vanity.

Trapped in the slow-moving queue, she had plenty of time to consider the matter and come to the usual depressing conclusions.

'I look like I've been left out in the rain by someone who's forgotten. But is that so strange, after the way I've spent the last year?'

At last she was out, and searching for a taxi to take her to the cheap hotel she'd booked on-line, which was all she could afford. It was basic, but clean and comfortable, with friendly service. Judging it too late now to start her search, she dined in the tiny garden restaurant off the best spaghetti she'd ever tasted. Afterwards she showered and stretched out on the bed, gazing at the snapshot she'd taken from her purse.

It was a small picture, taken in a machine, and it showed Freda, gorgeous as always, sitting with a young man in his late twenties. He had dark hair that curled slightly, a lean face and a stubborn mouth. Freda was leaning against him, and his arm was about her in a gesture of possessiveness. His cheek rested on her head, and although he was half smiling at the camera it was clear that the rest of the world barely existed for him.

Polly studied him, trying to decide why, despite his air of joy, there was a kind of fierceness about him that defied analysis. He seemed to be uttering a silent warning that Freda belonged to him, and he would defend his ownership with his last breath.

But it hadn't worked out like that. He had lost her for ever. And soon he would know it finally.

For a long time Polly lay looking at the ceiling, musing.

What am I doing here? I don't really want to see Ruggiero Rinucci, and I'm sure he doesn't want to see me.

Maybe I should have written to him first? But I don't have his exact address. Besides, some things are better face to face. Plus, men are such cowards that if he knew why I was coming he'd probably vanish. Oh, heavens, how did I get into this?

On the edge of Naples stood La Pista Grande, a large winding track that was the scene of many motorbike races.

Here, too, the firm of Fantone & Rinucci tested their motorbikes, with Ruggiero insisting on doing all tests personally, and taking every machine to the limit.

'If it doesn't half kill him he thinks there's something wrong with it,' one of the mechanics had remarked admiringly, and when Ruggiero was on the track as many as possible of the workforce turned out to watch, cheer and take bets on his survival.

He arrived next morning with Evie, gave her some technical paperwork about the bike and showed her to the best place in the stands, just where the track curved three times in a short space, so that briefly he would be riding straight for her before turning into another sharp bend.

'If I break my neck, it'll likely be just there,' he said, indicating the mechanics who were also there. 'That's why they gather in this spot—hoping.'

Evie laughed. There was a sprinkling of women among the mechanics, and she doubted if they'd come hoping for an accident. More likely it was connected to the sight of Ruggiero in tight black leather gear that emphasised every taut line of his tall, lean but muscular figure.

He gave a harsh grin and departed, leaving Evie to get to her seat in the front row. As she was settling she became aware of a young woman standing a few feet away. She was slim, with long fair hair and a slightly nervous manner. She gave a brief smile and sat down, looking rather as though she hoped to avoid notice.

'Are you from the factory?' Evie asked pleasantly.

'No—you?'

'No, I just came to see Ruggiero. He's my brother-in-law.'

After exchanging a few more words, the stranger smiled absently and seemed disinclined to talk further. Evie took out the paperwork and plunged happily into facts and figures about sequential electronic fuel injection, adjustable preload and eccentric chain adjuster, totally absorbed until the testing was about to begin. Then she looked at the young woman and realised that she sat like stone, motionless, her eyes fixed on the track as though something vital depended on what she saw there.

Ruggiero kept his grin in place as he walked towards the two men who were holding the bike. He used the grin as a kind of visor behind which he could hide. Today the effort was greater than usual, because he'd had little sleep. His thoughts about Sapphire had been destructive. Once conjured up, she'd refused to depart, haunting him all night until he fell into an uneasy sleep and awoke after one hour, not at all refreshed.

The sensible course would have been to delay the test until another day, but he couldn't bring himself to admit that he didn't feel up to it. Besides, he refused to give in to fancies. Sapphire could be banished if he were only resolute.

He pulled on the black helmet that enveloped his head completely, blotting out his identity and turning him into a cross between a spider and a spaceman. A kick and the engine roared into life. Another kick and he was turning out onto the track.

He took the first circuit at a mere ninety miles an hour—a moderate speed—leaning into the turn so deeply that his knee nearly touched the ground. Then he shot ahead, going faster and faster, until the machine reached a hundred and fifty— the extreme of its ability. But he knew that beyond the official limit there was always a little extra, and he urged it on, demanding just that bit more, and then more, because if he went fast enough he might outrun the ghost that pursued him.

Yet she was there, just behind him, warning him that flight was impossible. She was there inside his helmet, telling him that she would always be with him.

But she was also ahead of him, on the track, her long fair hair fanned into a halo by the wind—waiting for him.

Suddenly all the pictures ran together, so that he could no longer see ahead. Only half knowing what he did, he turned the front wheel, desperate to avoid the apparition that might or might not be there. The next moment he was flying through the air, to land with a brutal force that knocked the breath out of him and sent the world whirling into chaos.

# CHAPTER TWO

FREDA had known little about Ruggiero except that his family lived in the Villa Rinucci, and Polly would have gone there on the morning after her arrival but for the chance of the hotel receptionist leaving open a Naples newspaper with a picture of Ruggiero just visible. Knowing no Italian, she'd asked the man to translate the piece, and found a description of Carlo's wedding, with some background about the family, including a mention of the motorbike firm. She had decided to go there first, and the receptionist had called a taxi and given the driver the name of the firm.

At the factory the language problem had cropped up again, but after a certain amount of misunderstanding she'd discovered that Signor Rinucci was at the racetrack today. She'd taken the taxi on to the track, glad of the chance to observe him unseen. The place was closed to the public, but she'd arrived just as some employees of the firm were being allowed to enter through a side door, and by mingling with them she'd managed to slip inside.

As soon as she'd reached the stands she had seen him, showing a young woman to a seat in the front row. Polly had held back, wondering what place the woman held in his life.

Suddenly he'd grinned, and something cold, almost wolfish about it had made her shiver. Then he'd departed and she'd been able to move down to the front row. The young woman had smiled at her.

'Are you from the factory?'

'No,' Polly said cautiously. 'You?'

'No, I just came to see Ruggiero. He's my brother-in-law.'

'You mean,' she asked in alarm, 'he's married to your sister?'

'No, I'm married to his brother.' She chuckled. 'I can't see Ruggiero ever getting married. He enjoys a wide choice of women without tying himself down.'

Polly sighed with relief. A wife or girlfriend would have made her mission much harder. She settled down to watch as Ruggiero, in the distance, mounted the fearsome looking bike, started up, gathered speed, then took off like a rocket.

Lap after lap she watched him with fierce intensity, admiring his ease in the face of danger. The track twisted and turned like a snake, so that he'd no sooner taken a bend, leaning far over to one side, than he had to swiftly straighten up and swing deep in the other direction, then back again, and again. Every move was performed with careless grace and no sense of strain.

In one place the twisting of the track brought him directly ahead, so that for a stunning moment he was heading right for her. Then he leaned deep into a terrifyingly sharp bend and was gone, vanishing into the distance, while the black visor still seemed to hang in the air before her.

Then a strange thing happened.

For no apparent reason she felt a sense of dread begin to invade her. Her brain was on red alert, saying that something was badly wrong. She knew nothing about bikes, but much about troubled minds, and every instinct told her that this man was labouring under a burden and fast reaching his limit.

She stood up, pressing against the rail, frowning as her brain tried to understand what her instincts could sense. He was right ahead again. Coming straight for her until he swung into the bend.

But it was as though he leaned in too deep and couldn't get out. The next moment the front wheel twisted, jerking the machine into a scissor-like movement that sent him flying through the air.

All around there were shouts of horror, but Polly was galvanised into action. She was first over the barrier, racing across the track, dodging the lethally spinning wheels of the bike, lying on its side, and throwing herself down by Ruggiero.

'Don't move,' she said, unsure whether he could hear her.

'Hey—' Piero Fantone had caught up and tried to pull her away.

'I'm a nurse,' she said, struggling free. 'Get an ambulance.'

'*Ambulanza!*' Piero bawled, and turned back to her.

Ruggiero gasped and made a movement. Through the dark plastic of the visor Polly saw him open his eyes, saw the stunned look in them before they closed again.

'Did he break anything?' Piero demanded.

She ran her hands lightly over Ruggiero.

'I don't think so. But I'll know better when some of this leather is removed. We need to get him inside.'

'We keep a stretcher here. It's on its way.'

From behind the visor a voice growled words she didn't understand, but the gist of them was clear to Piero, from his urgent voice and attempts to restrain him. His reward was a stream of Neapolitan words that Polly rightly guessed to be curses.

'He's all right,' Piero said.

'It's certainly reassuring,' she agreed.

Ruggiero began to fight his way up, swinging his arms

wildly so that Polly, kneeling beside him, was knocked off balance. He managed to get onto one knee before keeling over and landing on her as she raised herself. She reached out quickly, supporting him as he collapsed against her, his head thrown back. For a moment she thought his eyes opened and closed again, but it was hard to be sure.

'We should take off his helmet,' she said, laying him gently back onto the ground.

Piero gently eased the helmet off, and now she could see Ruggiero clearly for the first time. It was the face in the photograph with Freda, but older, thinner, his hair disordered and damp with sweat, making him look vulnerable—something she guessed was rare for him. His eyes remained closed, but she saw his lips move.

'What's he saying?' Piero asked.

'I can't tell.' Polly leaned forward, putting her ear close. She felt the warmth of his breath against her cheek and heard a whispered name that made her tense and look at him sharply.

*'Sapphire!'*

'What did he say?' Piero asked.

'I—I didn't catch it. Oh, good—there's the stretcher. Let's get him inside.'

She backed away as several men lifted him and began the journey back across the track. Polly stood watching, frozen with shock, until Evie put an arm around her.

'Are you all right?'

'Yes,' she said in a dazed voice. 'Yes, I'm fine.'

'Come on—let's follow them.'

His head was full of darkness, spinning at top speed, like an endless circle. In the centre of it was her face, smiling provocatively, as so often in their time together. But then the picture changed and he saw her as she'd been at the track, standing there, luring him on until he crashed.

But then she'd appeared beside him, taking him up in her arms, pulling open his clothes, speaking words of comfort. He'd groaned, reaching out to her, and she had vanished.

He opened his eyes to find himself lying on a leather couch, with Evie beside him.

'Steady,' she said.

'Where is she?'

'Who?'

'*Her*. She was standing there—I saw her—where is she? Ouch!'

'Don't move. You had a bad fall.'

'I'm all right,' he croaked, trying to rise. 'I've got to find her.'

'Ruggiero, who are you talking about?' she asked frantically, fearful that his wits were wandering.

'That woman—she was there—'

'Do you mean the one by the track?'

'You saw her?'

'She was in the stand with me. When you crashed she rushed over and helped you.'

He stared at her, scarcely daring to believe what he heard.

'Where is she?'

'I'll fetch her. By the way, she only speaks English.'

'English?' he whispered. His voice rose. '*Did you say she was English?*'

'Yes. Ruggiero, do you think—?'

'Get her here, for pity's sake!' he cried hoarsely.

Evie slipped out.

While he waited Ruggiero tried to stand, but fell back at once, cursing his own weakness. But inwardly he was full of wild hope. It hadn't been imagination. *She* had returned, her arms outstretched to him, as so often in hopeless dreams. Now it was real. At any moment she would walk through that door—

'Here she is,' Evie said from the doorway, standing aside to usher in a young woman.

At first he saw only a tall, slender figure with long fair hair, and his heart leapt. In a movement that afterwards caused him agonies of shame, he reached out an eager hand, said her name. Then the mist cleared and he found himself looking at a face that was gentle and pleasant, but not beautiful—and not the one his heart endlessly sought.

'Hallo,' she said. 'I'm Polly Hanson. I was watching, and I'm a nurse, so I tried to help.'

'Thank you,' he murmured, dazed.

The world was in chaos. He'd thought he'd found Sapphire. Instead, here was this prosaic female whose passing resemblance was just enough to be heartbreaking. Once more Sapphire was only a ghost.

He knew he'd spoken her name—but how loud? Had they heard him? He fell back, passing a hand over his screwed-up eyes, wishing things would become clearer.

'Thank you,' he said again, forcing his eyes to open.

Piero looked in to say, 'The ambulance is here.'

'What damned ambulance?' Ruggiero roared. 'I'm not going to hospital.'

'I think you should,' Polly said. 'You have had a bad accident.'

'I landed on my shoulder.'

'Partly. Your head also took a thump, and I'd like it properly looked at.'

'*Signorina*,' Ruggiero said through gritted teeth, 'I'm grateful for your help, but please understand that you don't give me orders.'

'Well, the ambulance is here now,' she said, riled by his tone.

'Then you can send it away.'

'Signor Rinucci, your head may be injured, and I urgently suggest—'

'You may suggest what you like,' he snapped, 'but I'm not getting into an ambulance, so spare me any more of your interference.'

'Such pleasant manners,' said a voice from the door. 'It must be my son.'

Hope swept into the room.

'Mamma,' Ruggiero said painfully, 'how did you—?'

'Evie called my cellphone,' Hope said, also in English, taking her cue from the others. 'And as I was shopping nearby I had only a little way to come.'

'You just happened to be shopping nearby?' Ruggiero growled.

'Yes, wasn't it a fortunate coincidence?' Hope said smoothly.

'If you believe in coincidences.'

'Be quiet and watch your manners,' his mother said firmly. 'You've now been rude to everyone—'

'He hasn't been rude to me,' Evie observed mildly.

'Give him time. He will.'

'Especially if she mentions an ambulance,' Ruggiero retorted.

They argued. He was obdurate. In the end his mother sighed and gave in. The ambulance was sent away.

'I'll go home and rest,' Ruggiero conceded. 'And I'll be all right for the party tonight.'

'Or you may have passed out completely by then,' Polly said, with the faintest touch of acid in her voice.

Evie hastened to explain Polly's professional qualifications, and what she had done for Ruggiero.

Hope's response was to embrace Polly fervently and declare, 'We are friends for ever. So now I ask you to do one more thing for me. You must come to our party tonight.'

Beside her, Polly sensed rather than felt Ruggiero make a

gesture of protest, and she knew that he didn't want her in his home. He wanted to get rid of her as soon as he could. And she could guess why.

But Hope seemed oblivious. 'Tonight I can thank you properly, and perhaps you'll also be kind enough to—' She gave her son a baleful look.

'Don't worry, I'll keep an eye on him,' Polly said.

'You will not,' Ruggiero snapped.

'Indeed I will,' she riposted at once.

'I won't have it.'

'Try to stop me.'

'That's the spirit,' Hope said, pleased. 'And, Signor Fantone, I commend you for your good sense in having a nurse at the track. I wouldn't have expected it of you.'

Having praised and insulted him in one breath, she turned her attention back to Ruggiero. With relief, Polly realised that for the moment she could avoid explanations. Sooner or later everyone would have to know why she was really here. But not yet.

Hope took charge, arranging for Ruggiero to be helped to her waiting car, and leaving Evie to give Polly a lift to her hotel.

'It's a big family get-together,' Evie explained as they drove. 'The Rinuccis tend to be scattered, but we all returned for Carlo's wedding yesterday. And, since Hope loves giving parties, she's going to have another one tonight, before we all disperse again.'

'Was it really chance that his mother was shopping nearby?'

'Of course not.' Evie chuckled. 'She does it whenever he's testing, and she always makes sure she has her cellphone, so that she can be fetched quickly if something like this happens. Of course he guesses, although he won't admit it, and it makes him grumpy. I'm sorry he was so rude to you. He isn't normally like that.'

'He was feeling bad,' Polly said, unwilling to reveal that there could be another reason for Ruggiero's hostility to her.

A few minutes later Evie dropped Polly at her hotel, promised that someone would fetch her at seven o'clock that evening, and drove off.

In her room, Polly discovered a problem. She had travelled light, wearing jeans and a sweater, and carrying enough basic clothes for a few days, but nothing that would be suitable for a party.

And I'm not turning up looking like a poor relation, she thought. I think I'll prescribe myself some shopping!

Even in that less privileged area, the clothes shops had a cheering air of fashion. A happy hour exploring resulted in a chiffon dress of dappled mauve, blue and silver, with a neck that was low enough to be 'party' and high enough to be fairly modest. The price was absurdly low. Even more absurd were the silver sandals she bought in the market just outside the hotel.

Glamorous cousin Freda, once married to a multimillionaire, would have turned her nose up at such a modest outfit, but Polly was in heaven.

As she dressed that evening she considered her hair, and decided that it would be more tactful to pin it back.

Perhaps I should have done that this afternoon, but I never thought. He might have forgotten her—no, men never forgot Freda.

For a moment she was back by the track, watching him approach, his face unknowable behind the black visor. What had he seen? What had it done to him to bring him so close to death?

It had felt strange to hold him in her arms, the powerful, athletic body slumping helplessly against her. Vulnerability was the last thing she had expected from Freda's description.

'He had enough cocky arrogance to take on the world,' her cousin had said. 'It made me think, *That's for me.*'

'But not for long,' Polly had reminded her quietly. 'Two weeks, and then you dumped him.'

Freda had given an expressive shrug. 'Well, he'd have dumped me pretty soon, I dare say. I knew straight off that he was the love-'em-and-leave-'em kind. That was useful, because it meant he wouldn't give me any trouble afterwards.'

'Plus the fact that you hadn't given him your real name.'

'Sure. I thought Sapphire was rather good—don't you?'

What Polly had thought of her cousin's actions was something she'd kept to herself—especially then, when Freda had been so frail, her once luxurious hair had fallen out and the future had been so cruelly plain.

That conversation came back to her now, reminding her of Ruggiero as she'd seen him first, and then later. Cocky arrogance, she thought. But not always.

He'd said Sapphire's name and reached blindly out to her before he'd controlled himself and pulled back. For him, Sapphire still lived—and that was the one thing Polly had not expected.

A chauffeur-driven car arrived exactly at seven o'clock and swept her out of the city and up the winding road to where the Villa Rinucci sat atop the hill. From a distance she could see the lights blazing, and hear the sounds of a party floating down in the clear air.

Hope came out to greet her eagerly.

'I feel better now you're here,' she said. 'Our family doctor is also a guest, but he'll have to leave soon.'

'I'd better talk to him first,' Polly suggested, and was rewarded with Hope's brilliant smile.

Dr Rossetti was an elderly man who'd been a friend of the family for a long time. He greeted Polly warmly, questioned her about her impressions that afternoon, and nodded.

'He's always been an awkward so-and-so. Now, Carlo—

his twin—if *he* didn't want to do what he was told, he'd get out of it with charm, and it would be ages before you saw how he'd outwitted you. But Ruggiero would just look you in the eye and say, "Shan't!"'

Polly chuckled. 'You mean he doesn't bother with any of that subtlety nonsense?'

'Ruggiero wouldn't recognise subtlety if he met it in the street. His head has a granite exterior which you have to thump hard to make him believe what he doesn't want to believe.'

'And under the exterior?'

'I suspect there's something more interesting. But he keeps it a secret even from his nearest and dearest. In fact, especially from his nearest and dearest. He hates what he calls "prying eyes", so don't make it too clear that you're concerned for him.'

'No, I think I gathered that before,' she said wryly. She glimpsed Ruggiero across the room and added, 'From the way he's moving his left arm I think his shoulder's hurting.'

'Yes—you might find it useful to rub some of this into it,' he said, handing her a tube of a preparation designed to cool inflammation.

'And I'm sure he has concussion.'

'I doubt it's serious, since he seems well able to remember what happened. But he needs an early night. See if you can get him to take a couple of these.' He handed her some tablets.

'They might do his headache some good,' she said, nodding as she recognised them.

'Headache?' the doctor demanded satirically. 'What headache? You don't think he admits to having a headache, do you?'

'Leave him to me,' she said. 'I'm used to dealing with difficult patients.'

They nodded in mutual understanding. Then something

made Polly look up to find Ruggiero watching her, his lips twisted in a smile so wry that it was almost a sneer. Of course he knew they were discussing him, and he wasn't going to make it easy for her.

Then Evie was by her side, taking her to meet the family. Carlo and Della, the newlyweds, had left for their honeymoon, but everyone else was there. While Polly was sorting out the clan in her mind, Hope appeared beside her.

'Let me take you to Ruggiero.'

'Better not,' Polly said. 'If he's expecting me to descend on him like a nanny, that's exactly what I'm not going to do.'

Hope nodded. 'You're a wise woman. Oh, dear! Why do men never listen to wise women?'

'I suppose the other kind are more fun,' Polly said with amusement. 'Let him wait and wonder. I think I should meet some more people, just to show I'm not watching him.'

Hope took her around the room to meet the older, more distant members of the extended Rinucci clan. They all greeted her warmly, and seemed to know that she was there to look after one of their number. They were kind people, and open in their appreciation.

It didn't take long for Polly to understand that they were taking their cue from Hope, who was the centre of the whole family, a charming tyrant, exercising her will so lovingly that it was easy to underestimate her power. Toni's fond eyes followed her everywhere.

After a while Polly became aware of a glass being pressed into her hand. Looking up, she saw Ruggiero, surveying her grimly.

'It's only mineral water,' he said. 'Since I take it you're not allowed to drink on duty?'

'On duty?'

'Don't play dumb with me. You're here to fix your beady

eyes on me in case I go into convulsions. Sorry to disoblige, but I'm having a great time.'

'A man with cracked ribs is never having a great time.'

'Who says I have cracked ribs?'

'You do—every time you touch your left side gingerly. I've seen that gesture before. Often enough to know what it means.'

'And you think you're going to whisk me away to a hospital—?'

'There's no need. If you'll only—'

'Once and for all,' he said, with a touch of savagery, 'there is nothing wrong with me.'

'For pity's sake, what are you trying to prove?'

'That I'm fine—'

'Which you're not—'

'And that I don't need a nanny,' he growled.

'A nanny is just what you *do* need,' she said, coming close to losing her temper. 'In fact I never saw a man who needed it more. No—scrap nanny. Let's say a twenty-four-hour guard, preferably armed with manacles. Even then you'd manage to do something brainless.'

'Then I'm beyond help, and you should abandon me to my fate.'

'Don't tempt me,' she said through gritted teeth.

She waited for a sharp answer, but it didn't come. Looking at him, she saw why. He sat down, slowly and heavily, leaning his head back against the wall. She just stopped the glass falling from his fingers.

'Time to stop pretending,' she said gently.

For a moment Ruggiero didn't answer. He looked as if all the stuffing had been knocked out of him. At last he turned his head slowly, to look at her out of blurred, pain-filled eyes.

'What did you say?'

'I said it's time to go to bed.'

Hope appeared, looking anxious. 'What's happened?'

'Ruggiero has told me he wants to go to bed,' Polly informed her.

'Did I?' he asked.

'Yes,' she said firmly. 'You did.'

He didn't argue, but gave the shrug of a man yielding to superior forces and rose slowly to his feet. Then he swayed, and was forced to rest an arm quickly on Polly's shoulder. She heard him mutter something that she didn't understand, but she guessed it was impolite. Hope gave a signal, and at once Ruggiero's brothers appeared, taking charge of him.

'I'll come and see you when you're in bed,' Polly told him.

He groaned. 'Look, I don't think—'

'I didn't ask what you thought,' she told him quietly. 'I said that's what I'm going to do. Please don't argue with me. It's a waste of time.'

The young men wore broad grins, and the braver among them cheered. Then they caught their mother's eye, and hastily escorted their injured brother to bed.

# CHAPTER THREE

POLLY gave them fifteen minutes before entering Ruggiero's room, where he lay in bed, now dressed in dark brown silk pyjamas. Hope sat beside him.

'That headache's pretty terrible, isn't it?' Polly asked sympathetically.

'You could say that,' he said in a painful whisper.

'This will make it better and give you some sleep.' She opened one hand, showing him a couple of pills, and held up a glass of water in the other.

This time he didn't argue, but struggled up and swallowed the pills, and lay back at once, eyes closed.

'He'll be better in the morning,' Polly assured Hope. 'Why don't you go back to your guests?'

'I don't like to leave him alone.'

'Don't worry—he won't be alone,' Polly said. 'I'm staying here.'

'Are you sure that—?'

Hope checked herself suddenly, and a strange look came over her face. Her children could have told her that it meant Mamma was hatching a plot, but Polly, seeing it for the first time, was merely puzzled.

'Of course you're right,' Hope said. 'I know he's safe with you.'

She gave Polly a peck on the cheek and hurried out. Polly turned out all the lights except one small lamp, and went to the window. From there she could see light as the guests spilled out into the garden. Luckily the double glazing deadened the sound, although she doubted if he would have heard anything for a while even without that.

He stirred, groaning softly, and she returned to the bed.

'It's all right,' she said. 'I'm here. Let it go.'

She could hardly have said what she meant by those words, but he seemed to understand them at once and became quiet. She drew up a chair and sat close to the bed, leaning forward to whisper, 'Let it go. There'll be time later. But for now— let her go.'

He gave no sign of hearing, so she couldn't tell if he'd heard the subtle change she'd made in the words.

One by one Ruggiero's family looked in. Sometimes they spoke to her in whispers; sometimes they merely smiled. Hope opened the door quietly and stood watching Polly by the bed, her eyes fixed on Ruggiero. She waited a long time for Polly to move, then smiled, nodded to herself, and backed out, unseen.

A few minutes later Evie wheeled in a small trolley, laden with party food, plus wine, mineral water, and a pot of tea. Polly drank the tea thankfully. Tonight looked like being a two-pot problem.

Ruggiero lay without moving and she sat beside him, relieved that he seemed calm at last. When she was sure he was resting properly she rose and crossed again to the window. It was now quiet enough for her to risk opening it and looking out to where the last of the guests were drifting into the cars that would take them away, waving goodbye to Hope and her husband Toni.

She was about to draw back when another car drew up. The driver got out and pulled a bag from the back seat, showing it to Hope, who made a gesture of satisfaction.

Then Polly stiffened and leaned out further, frowning as she recognised the bag as her own, and the truth dawned on her. Hope had sent someone to the hotel to bring her things here—and she'd done it without so much as a by-your-leave.

Toni glanced up, saw her, and nudged Hope, who also looked up. In the lamplight Polly saw her smile in a slightly guilty way, and shrug as if to say, What else could I do?

She drew back, closing the window, and a minute later Hope was there at the door, beckoning her into the corridor.

'Don't think badly of me,' she begged, 'but you are so good for Ruggiero I had to make sure he had you looking after him all the time.'

'So you just hi-jacked me?' Polly observed mildly.

'We will make you very welcome here,' Hope promised, avoiding a direct answer. 'You'll be paid, and of course your hotel bill has been taken care of. Please don't be angry with me.'

Her manner was placating, but it was clear that Hope Rinucci had simply taken the shortest route to getting her own way. Polly was more amused than annoyed. For one thing, moving into the villa would be helpful for her mission.

Just down the corridor she heard a door open, and the chauffeur went into the room next to Ruggiero's with her suitcase.

'I think you'll be comfortable here,' Hope said, leading her inside. 'You have only to ask for anything you want.'

After the cramped poverty of the hotel, the luxury of this room was a pleasant change. The double bed looked inviting, and there was extensive wardrobe space and a private bathroom. This was the home of a wealthy family. Ruggiero's own bedroom, though severe and reflecting a masculine taste, was furnished with the finest of everything.

Polly took a quick moment to unpack her few clothes, then changed her party outfit for jeans and flat shoes. For her top she chose a plain white blouse that she hoped would make her look nurse-like. Then she returned to Ruggiero and prepared to settle down for the night.

Hope looked in one last time, and after that the lights went off and the house grew silent. Slowly the hours ticked away, and Polly's eyelids began to droop. It had been a long day, filled with incident, and weariness was catching up with her.

Suddenly her body gave a little jerk and her eyes flew open. She breathed out hard and forced herself to wake up properly. Then she realised that Ruggiero was looking at her. She thought he was smiling faintly, but in the dark it was hard to be sure.

'All right?' he asked.

'Was I asleep long?'

'About ten minutes.'

'I'm sorry.'

'Don't apologise. It's nice to know I'm not the only one who finds things happening that weren't planned.'

He hauled himself up painfully in the bed.

'I think I ate something that disagreed with me—or drank something. Can you help me to the bathroom?'

He put an arm around her shoulder and she steadied him as far as the bathroom door, where he gingerly felt his ribs.

'You may have been right,' he conceded. 'I'm not saying you were, but you might have been. I'll manage from here.'

When he came slowly out she'd remade the bed and put on the small lamp. She reached out to help him but he waved her away.

'I'm feeling a bit more human now my stomach's settled. Ah, that's better.'

He lay down and let her pull the duvet over him.

'How's the pain?' she asked gently.

'My head isn't too bad, but my shoulder and side feel as if they've been bashed with a sledgehammer.'

'It's time for a couple more pills. But they don't mix well with alcohol, so no more drinking until you've stopped taking them.'

'When will that be?'

'When I say,' she told him with quiet authority.

He took them from her, and accepted a glass of water, as docile now as he'd been aggressive before. When he lay back she turned out the lamp again, so that the only light in the room was the soft touch of moonlight.

'There's something different about you,' he said suddenly. 'You've changed your clothes.'

'Yes, I'm here for a few days. I've checked out of my hotel and into the room next door.'

'How did Mamma persuade you to do that?'

'Good heavens—you don't think she asked me first, do you?'

He gave a short bark of laughter that ended in a gasp of pain. 'Of course. I should have remembered Mamma's way. When did you find out?'

'When my things arrived.'

'I'm sorry. Just taking you over like that—what about your holiday?'

'That doesn't matter,' she said hastily. 'Go to sleep now.'

He stared at her for a while before saying vaguely, 'Was it you by the track?'

'Yes, it was me.'

'Are you sure? No—that's stupid—I mean—'

'Who did you think it was?' she risked saying.

'What?'

'I need to know how much you can remember. It'll tell me how serious your concussion is.'

'I did several laps and everything was all right. But then—' He took a long, shaking breath. 'Why did you come onto the track?'

'I didn't.'

'But you did. You were walking straight towards me, and your hair was blowing in the wind. I could have ridden right over you, but you didn't seem to realise that. You were smiling—like the time—'

His breathing was becoming laboured and she went to him quickly, trying to soothe him.

'It wasn't me. Truly. It was the speed that confused you, and that visor. You couldn't have seen anything properly. Just an illusion—someone who wasn't really there.'

'But—she was there,' he whispered. 'I saw her—'

'You couldn't have. It's impossible.'

'How can you be sure?'

'Because—' Suddenly realising that she was straying onto a dangerous path, she checked herself. At this moment she couldn't tell him why she was sure he would never see Sapphire again. The truth would crush him.

'Because if there had been anyone on the track you'd have hit them,' she said.

'You can't hit a ghost,' he said wearily. 'Do you believe in ghosts?'

'Yes,' she murmured, saying it almost against her will. 'I try not to, but sometimes people just won't let go—no matter what you do, they're always with you.'

'So you know that too?'

'Yes,' she said quietly. 'I know that too. Go to sleep now.'

He moved his hand forward and back, then sideways, as though searching for something. She reached out and took his hand, feeling the tension in it.

'It's going to be all right,' she said.

Some corner of his mind—the part of him that argued with everything—wanted to demand how she could be so sure. But the argument retreated before the reassurance of her clasp. His thoughts were confused.

She'd said, 'Please don't argue with me. It's a waste of time,' —talking like his mother. He'd tried to be annoyed, but it had been a relief to have her rescue him from the hole that his pride had dug for him. Hell would freeze over before he admitted that he'd been ready to collapse into bed, but she'd known without being told.

At last the tension began to fade. His eyes closed, his hand relaxed, and he was asleep.

As dawn broke Hope looked in.

'Is he all right?'

'Sleeping like a baby,' Polly assured her.

'Then why don't you go and get some sleep? I'll take over for a while.'

'Thank you.'

In her own room she snuggled blissfully down in the luxurious bed. When she awoke the sun was high in the sky. She stood under the shower, wondering what the day would bring and whether she would get the chance to fulfil her mission.

As she finished dressing she looked at her watch and was shocked to see that it was ten o'clock.

'Hope said to let you sleep,' said Evie, who'd just popped in.

'I'd better go and see my patient.'

'I'll send your breakfast up.'

She paused outside Ruggiero's room, wondering how difficult he would be this morning, and how much he would remember of the night before. She found him watching the door.

'Come in,' he said.

He sounded cautious, and she felt much the same as she approached the bed. Neither was quite sure of the other's mood, and for a moment they looked at each other.

'I apologise,' he said at last.

'For—what?'

'For whatever I did. I don't remember much about last night, but I'm pretty sure I acted unforgivably.'

'You acted like a damned fool,' she said frankly. 'Like a complete and total idiot. I've never seen such blinding stupidity in my whole life.'

'Hey, don't sit on the fence. Tell me what you really think of me.'

That broke the ice, and they shared a grin.

'Yes, I guess I shouldn't have gone clowning around after bumping my head,' he admitted. 'But, hey, it's a tough world. Don't let them see any sign of weakness or the tigers pounce.'

'But they weren't tigers at that track,' she said. 'They were your friends. And perhaps having to impress people all the time is also a sign of weakness.'

He looked alarmed. 'Are you going to psychoanalyse me?'

'That's all for today. I'll save the rest until you're feeling better.'

'I'm all right,' he said in a dispirited voice. 'Except that I don't seem to have any energy.'

'You've probably got a hangover as well as everything else. I want you to stay in bed for a while. Or are you going to fight me about that?'

'No, ma'am. I'm sure you know best.'

She regarded him cynically. 'You must be worse than I thought.'

There was no chance to say more, because Evie appeared with Polly's breakfast, and after that the rest of the family came to say goodbye before returning to their distant homes. Ruggiero greeted them all boisterously, cracked jokes and generally acted the part of a man who was on top of the world. But when it was over his forehead was damp and he was full of tension.

'That was quite a performance,' she said sympathetically.

'Sure—a sign of weakness, like you said.'

'Not this time. You sent them off easier in their minds about you.'

He tried to shrug, but immediately winced, making a face and rubbing his shoulder.

'You should let me look at that.'

She helped him off with the pyjama jacket, revealing a shoulder that looked inflamed.

'I haven't broken anything,' he said, sounding mulish again.

'Will you leave me to make the diagnosis?' she asked lightly. 'As a matter of fact I don't think you *have* broken anything, because otherwise you'd be in a lot more pain than you are. But stop trying to take over.'

'Yes, I'm wasting my time doing that with you.' He sounded resigned.

'That's right,' she told him. 'I've seen off far more trouble-some patients than you.'

'Yeah?'

'Yeah!'

*'Yeah?'*

*'Yeah!'*

She was slowly working on his shoulder, feeling for injury, talking to distract him.

'On the wards they call me Nurse Bossy-Boots. People scurry for cover at my approach.'

'Think you can make me run?'

'Right this minute nothing could make you run. You might manage a stagger, but even then I'd have to hold you up.'

He started to laugh, but ended with a sharp gasp. 'Don't make me laugh,' he begged.

She eased herself behind him, one knee on the bed so that she could reach his shoulder from the best angle. He drew a deep breath of relief, muttering, 'That's better.'

For a while neither of them spoke while she worked on the

shoulder, massaging it until it relaxed, then moved his arm gently in several directions. It was bruised and inflamed, but not dislocated. She finished by rubbing in some of the gel the doctor had left with her.

Studying him professionally, she saw that he was in superb physical condition, lean and muscular, as she would have expected from a man who lived an athletic life, and evenly tanned, as though he swam a good deal under the hot sun.

He carried so little weight that when he leaned forward for her to examine his spine she could easily make out its straight line, and the lines of his ribs.

'It wouldn't hurt you to gain a few pounds,' she observed, flexing her fingers gently against his skin. 'It might give you something to land on.'

'I'd put on weight if I could. I eat like a horse but I stay like this.'

'Lucky you. Lie back.'

She pressed him gently back against the pillows while she felt his ribs at the front.

'A couple of cracks,' she confirmed, 'but you've got off very lightly, considering.'

'You're not going to drag me off to hospital to be strapped up?'

'There's no need. Strapping fixes your ribs, but it can make it harder to breathe. So just be careful how you move and it'll heal naturally.'

The quiet authority in her voice seemed to ease his mind, and she felt him relaxing under her hands.

'Let's put your jacket back on,' she said. 'Then I'll give you a couple more pills.'

He winced as she slid the jacket back over his shoulders, but at last it was done. He accepted the pills with a faint smile, and was soon asleep.

The house was quiet now that the guests had departed, and Hope, Toni and Francesco had travelled to the airport to see off the English party. Polly listened to the silence, which seemed to have an edgy quality, and thought she was being warned that this tranquil time could not last for ever. The moment was approaching.

She slipped next door and found the picture of Freda and the young man she now knew as Ruggiero. She studied his face a while, trying to reconcile its glowing joy with the dour, tense individual he had become. Then she put it in her pocket and returned to sit quietly with him until she heard a car return late in the afternoon.

Hope and Toni came in together, full of gratitude.

'I will stay with my son for a while,' Toni said, 'while you go down for supper.'

Ruggiero was awake but drowsy as Toni slipped into the room.

'All gone?' he asked, yawning.

'Their flight took off on time. How are you feeling?'

'OK, I guess. I seem to be floating.' Suddenly he remembered. 'Poppa, do you know what Mamma did? She practically kidnapped Polly.'

'Don't blame me,' his father said hastily. 'I knew nothing about it until it was too late. You know your mother.'

'But didn't you make some protest?'

'Why? I'm glad you're being properly cared for.'

'I guess she told you what to say,' Ruggiero said with wry amusement. 'You're bullied—you know that?'

'Oh, no,' Toni said seriously. 'Your *mamma* never bullies me. She knows what I need before I know myself, and she makes sure that I have it.'

'There's a difference?'

'Yes,' Toni said simply. 'There's a difference.'

Downstairs the table was spread with a banquet, and Polly found herself treated as an honoured guest. Hope ceremonially poured champagne, clinked glasses, and produced an envelope plump with euros.

'But this is far too much,' Polly gasped. 'I can't take it all.'

'You are worth every penny,' Hope declared. 'Not only for what you are doing for us, but also because you have allowed us to take over your holiday without complaint.'

'That's all right,' Polly said awkwardly. 'It wasn't really a holiday.'

'Do you mean that you have to return to England soon? When are you due back at your job?'

'I don't have a job at the moment.'

'Aha—then you are free to remain as long as you wish. Good. You will stay with us. Now, let us eat.'

Toni joined them after a while, with the news that Ruggiero was sleeping.

'I'll go back fairly soon,' Polly said.

They made it hard for her—treating her like a queen, toasting her with champagne, encouraging her to talk about herself. That was a dangerous subject, and she had to be circumspect, but these were warm-hearted people, taking what they wanted with a charm that threatened to melt her heart.

As soon as possible she brought the conversation back to Ruggiero, explaining about his condition and how she could take care of it.

'He'll be fine if he can be persuaded to rest for a few days,' she finished.

'You can persuade him,' Hope declared. 'You have him eating out of your hand.'

Polly put her head on one side. 'I try to picture him eating out of anyone's hand,' she said whimsically, 'but it's beyond me.'

As they laughed, she added, 'Thank you for a lovely meal. Now I think I'll go upstairs and crack the whip a little. Goodnight.'

She seated herself quietly beside Ruggiero's bed, seeing with satisfaction that he was deeply, contentedly asleep. She waited beside him for a while, dozing gently herself, so that she didn't notice when he awoke, and didn't know that his eyes were open until he murmured, 'Polly.'

'Yes, I'm here. Is something the matter?'

'Yes, in a way. I'm so sorry.'

'Hey, you've already apologised.'

'For being a jerk, but not for—' He broke off, groaning, 'I hit you, didn't I? When you were by me on the track—I seem to remember—'

'You sent me flying,' she said lightly. 'But it was an accident. You didn't mean to do it. You were just flailing around blindly.'

'I do a lot of that, I'm afraid.'

'It wasn't your fault,' she said in a rallying voice. 'Why are you so determined to give yourself a hard time?'

'Perhaps somebody ought to,' he said grimly.

She was touched by this glimpse of humility, so unexpected.

'You're very quiet,' he said. 'Are you sure you don't blame me?'

'Honestly—it's not that.'

'Then what is it? What's the mystery, Polly? And don't try to brush me off, because I've been lying here doing a lot of thinking, and I don't reckon you just happened to be at the track—did you?'

'No,' she admitted. 'It wasn't an accident.' She took a long breath. 'Maybe it's time I told you everything.'

Suddenly the enormity of what she had to tell him came over her. She'd wanted to choose her moment—not have it forced on her like this.

'I meant to tell you earlier,' she said at last. 'But then you were ill so I had to wait.'

'Whatever it is, I think I need to know.'

Switching on the bedside lamp, she reached into her bag and took out the photograph of him with Freda.

'I think this will explain part of it,' she said, handing it to him.

As he stared at the picture she saw a change come over him—but not the one she'd expected. After the first shock he became possessed by dark fury.

'You've been going through my things,' he accused.

'Of course not.'

'You must have done, or you couldn't have this picture.'

'That isn't yours,' she said urgently.

*'Don't lie to me.'*

'I'm not lying. I have one too. Yours is still wherever you keep it.'

He hauled himself up in bed, wincing, so that she reached out to help him. He pushed her away.

'Get off me,' he snapped.

She realised that she should have thought of this, but she hadn't.

He made it painfully over to the chest of drawers on the far side of the room, pulled open the top drawer and reached deep inside. Polly wondered at the swift change in him. There was no trace now of the humility that had briefly touched her heart. His streak of ferocity, never far below the surface, had reasserted itself.

She saw his face change as he drew something out of the drawer and looked at it. She guessed it was the companion picture. Coming slowly back to the bed, he almost fell onto it, breathing hard with the pain. In silence she handed the first photograph back to him. He gazed from one picture to the other, like a man who'd received a stunning blow.

'Where did you get this?' he demanded hoarsely.

'She gave it to me.'

*'She?'*

'My cousin—Freda. She said you went to the funfair together and had the pictures taken in a machine. There were two, and you took one each.'

'Freda?'

'You knew her as Sapphire.'

He turned his head on the pillow, looking at her intently.

'Take your hair down,' he said.

'Surely there's—?'

'Do it.'

A quick movement and it fell about her face. She guessed that the dim light emphasised her likeness to Freda, and was certain of it when he closed his eyes, as if to shut her out.

'That's why I thought you were her,' he said, almost to himself.

'It's not much of a resemblance. She was always the beautiful one.'

He opened his eyes again and studied her. She was sure the contrast between her and his fantasy image struck painfully.

'You said she's your cousin?'

'She *was*,' Polly said softly. 'She's dead now.'

# CHAPTER FOUR

'DEAD,' he whispered. 'No—you didn't say that. I just thought for a moment—'

'She's dead,' Polly repeated softly. 'A few weeks ago.'

He looked away, concealing his face from her, while his fingers moved compulsively on the photograph until it began to crumple.

'Go on,' he said at last, in a voice that seemed to come from a great distance.

'Her real name was Freda Hanson—until she married George Ranley, six years ago.'

He stirred. 'She was married when I knew her?'

'Yes.'

'He made her unhappy? She no longer loved him?'

'I don't think she was ever madly in love with him,' Polly said, choosing her words carefully. 'He's very rich, and—'

'Stop there,' he said quickly. 'If you're trying to tell me that she married for money—don't. She wouldn't—not the girl I knew.'

'But you *didn't* know her,' Polly said gently. 'Don't you realise that she made sure of that? She didn't even tell you her real name. That way you couldn't find her again when she went home.'

'Where was home?'

'In Yorkshire, in the north of England.'

'How much do you know of what happened between her and me?'

'You met in a bar in a London hotel, and you were together for two weeks.'

'You could put it like that,' he said slowly. 'But the truth was so much more. What we had was there from the first moment. I looked at her, and I wanted her so badly that I was afraid it must show. I even thought I might scare her off. But nothing frightened her. She was brave. She went out to meet life—she came to me at once.'

There was an aching wistfulness in his voice that saddened Polly. She knew the truth behind her cousin's 'bravery'. She hadn't had much time to pursue her object. That was the ugly fact, and it was painful to see this blunt, forceful man reduced to misery by her ruthless tactics.

'I remember being surprised that she was English,' Ruggiero continued. 'I thought English women were prim and proper. But not her. She loved me as though I was the only man on earth.'

'Didn't you think it strange that she wouldn't tell you her full name?'

'At the time it almost seemed irrelevant—something that could be sorted out later. What she gave me—I'm not good with words, I couldn't describe it—but it made me a different man. Better.'

There was something almost shocking in the quiet simplicity of the last word. Hesitantly, Polly asked, 'How do you mean, better?'

Slowly he laid his fingers over his heart.

'What's in here has always been just for me,' he said. 'I've kept it that way. A man's safer that way.'

'But why must he always be safe?' she ventured to ask.

'That's what she made me ask myself. It was like becoming someone else—ready to take risks I couldn't take before, glad of it. I even enjoyed her laughing at me. I've never found it easy to be laughed at, but she—well, I'd have accepted anything from her.'

Against her will Polly heard Freda's voice in her head, chuckling.

*'The tougher they are, the more fun it is when they become my slaves.'*

And this was the result—this bleak, desolate man holding onto his belief in her like a drowning man clinging to a raft. What would become of him in a few moments when that comfort was finally snatched away?

'What happened after she left me?' he asked.

Polly took a deep breath.

'She went back to George, and nine months later she had a baby.'

He stared at her. 'Are you saying—?'

'*Your* baby.'

He hauled himself up again, waving her away so that he could sit on the edge of the bed, his back to her.

'How can you be sure it's mine?' he demanded harshly.

'It isn't George's. It couldn't be.'

'But why didn't she tell me? I never concealed where I lived. Why didn't she come to me? She couldn't have thought I'd turn my back on her. She knew how much I— She knew—'

'She didn't want you told.'

'But—'

'She wanted to stay married to George, so she had an affair hoping to get pregnant.'

For a moment he was as still as if he'd been punched over the heart.

'Shut up!' he said at last in a fierce voice. 'Do you know what you're saying about her?'

'Yes,' she said, with a touch of sadness. 'I'm saying that she planned everything.'

'You're saying she was a calculating, cold-hearted bitch?'

'No, I'm not,' she insisted. 'She could be warm and funny and generous. But when she came to London that time she wanted something, and it turned out to be you.'

'You don't know what you're talking about,' he snapped. 'You don't know how it was with us when we were together— how could you understand—?'

She remembered George when he'd learned the truth, wailing pitiably, 'I thought she really loved me.'

The mood hadn't lasted. He'd become vicious and vengeful, but she'd briefly glimpsed the devastation that Freda could cause. She'd been a genius at inspiring love by pretending love, and she'd obviously done it well with both men.

'Did her husband think the child was his?' Ruggiero asked.

'At first, yes. Then he found out by chance that he had a very low sperm count, and he began to doubt. He demanded a test, and when he discovered that he wasn't the father he threw Freda and the baby out of the house.'

'When was this?'

'Almost a year ago.'

'Why didn't she come to me then?'

Because she'd hoped to entice George back, was the truthful answer. But Polly couldn't bring herself to hurt him more, so she softened it.

'She was already growing thin from illness. She said she'd contact you when she got well. But she never did. She came to live with me. I nursed her as best I could, but it was hopeless. She made me promise to find you afterwards—to tell you that you have a son.'

'She's dead,' he murmured. 'Dead—and I wasn't with her.'

In the face of his pain there was nothing she could say.

'Why didn't I know?' he demanded. 'How come I didn't sense it when we were so close?'

Polly was silent, knowing that Freda had never felt close to him.

'You should have found a way to contact me while she was alive,' he insisted.

'I couldn't. She wouldn't tell me where to find you. I didn't even know that you lived in Naples. I found out that and the name of this villa in a letter she wrote me, to be opened when she was dead.'

'I would have looked after her,' he said in a daze.

'She didn't want you to see her. She hated not being beautiful any more.'

'Do you think I'd have cared about that?' he flashed, with a hint of ferocity. 'I wouldn't even have seen it. I *lo*—'

He stopped himself with a sharp breath, like a man pulling back from the brink. His haggard eyes met hers.

'It's too late,' he said, like a man facing the bleak truth for the first time. 'Too late.'

'I'm sorry,' she whispered. She reached for him but he flinched away.

'I want you to go,' he said.

'But—'

'Get out, for pity's sake!' he said in agony.

She rose, reaching out for her copy of the picture, but he took it, saying curtly, 'Leave that.'

At the door she glanced back at him. He was holding both pictures, looking from one to the other as though in this way he might discover a secret. He didn't notice as she left.

Polly understood his need to be alone. She shared it. The conversation had been even harder than she'd expected. She'd been fooled by Freda's 'love-'em-and-leave-'em' description of Ruggiero, thinking he might take the news in that spirit.

Instead, his explosion of emotion had astonished her. Suddenly she saw the chasm yawning at her feet. From the first moment everything about Ruggiero had been a surprise—starting with the discovery that her cousin haunted him. She should have been prepared for tonight, but she'd sensed the danger almost too late.

*'You're saying she was a calculating, cold-hearted bitch?'*

He'd spoken as though the mere thought was outrageous, but it was an exact description of Freda. In the great days of her beauty she would have taken it as a compliment.

'It's such fun to make them sit up and beg,' she'd once trilled. 'You can make a man do anything if you go about it the right way.'

Later, talking about Ruggiero, with his baby in her arms, she'd said, 'He was the best—know what I mean? Well, no—maybe you don't.'

'I certainly don't have your wide experience for making comparisons,' Polly had replied, trying to speak lightly.

'Well, take my word for it. Ruggiero was really something in bed.' She had given a luxurious gurgle. 'Every woman should have an Italian lover. There are things about passion that only they understand.'

There had been no affection in her voice. Freda had taken what she wanted from her lover, then dispensed with him. She'd appreciated his technical skills, but she'd never thought of him as a person.

And in that she'd lost out, Polly realised. Clever as she was, Freda hadn't discovered the things that made Ruggiero truly fascinating: the contrast between the contrived self that he showed to the world and the true self that he hid as though alarmed by it, the mulish stubbornness that collapsed into un-

expected moments of self-deprecating humour. He was in-
triguing because everything about him contradicted everything else. A woman could spend years trying to understand
him, enjoying every moment of the challenge, and Freda
hadn't suspected it.

I've seen it, Polly thought suddenly. But I didn't want to.
Heaven help me, this is no time to be falling into that trap!
I'm just here to do a job.

She'd been clumsy tonight—hinting that his goddess had
had feet of clay, which he hadn't been ready to hear. He'd
loved Sapphire, perhaps without fully realising it until that
moment. If so, it was a cruel discovery made in the cruellest
possible way.

She'd wanted to escape him before—but now she wanted
to be with him, consoling him.

She went out into the corridor, pausing outside his door,
her hand raised to knock. But then she heard a soft, rhythmic
sound coming from inside the room, as though a man was
thumping the wall in rage and misery.

She turned away.

Polly spent the rest of the night sitting up by the window,
thinking of him, alone in his suffering, because that was how
he preferred it. The thought of that appalling bleakness made
her shudder, and her heart reached out to him. But she wasn't
the one he wanted.

At last, as dawn began to break, there was a soft knock at
her door. He was standing there, a cotton robe over his pyjamas.
The anger had gone from his face, leaving only weariness.

'Come in,' she said quietly.

But he didn't move, only looked at her with a kind of
desperation.

'What is it?' she asked. 'Can't I help you?'

'I'm not sure—perhaps I should—'

'Why don't you come in and talk about it?'

He looked at her, feeling himself paralysed by indecision. His self-confidence had drained away without warning, and now he hardly knew how to cope.

He'd dismissed Polly from his sight, but even then he'd known that he must follow her. He resented her, almost hated her, but against his will he was drawn after her. Now he stood on her threshold, fighting an impulse to back off, knowing that if he yielded to it a deep need would make him return.

'Let's talk,' she said gently, taking his arm and drawing him inside.

He sat uneasily on the bed.

'I seem to have a mountain of apologies to make.'

'Never mind,' she told him lightly. 'You've had a big shock.'

'I shouldn't have taken it out on you.'

'It's over. Past. Forget it.'

'Thank you. Polly, did I imagine that whole mad conversation? Did you tell me that Sapphire was dead and I have a son?'

'Yes.'

'And that's why you're here? It wasn't chance that we met?'

'No, I knew you lived in Naples, and I knew about this villa. I'd have come here first, but there was something in the newspaper about your brother's wedding. It mentioned your firm, so I went there and found out about the racetrack. Ruggiero, please believe me—I haven't been spying on you. I stayed here because it gave me a chance to be near you and choose my moment. I wanted to explain before, but you were ill—how could I?'

She made a helpless gesture, and he nodded.

'OK, I understand that. Although it gives me an awkward feeling to remember the curious looks I've seen you giving me.'

'I was a nurse, studying a patient for signs of trouble.'

'And maybe you were also remembering things Sapphire said about me and thinking, *Him?*'

He said the last word with a searing irony that took her breath away.

'I was curious about little Matthew's father,' she said cautiously. 'This last year I've got to love him very much. I can't wait to show him to you.'

His answer shattered her.

'I don't want to see him.'

*'What?'*

'I want nothing to do with him,' he growled. 'Why didn't you leave well alone?'

'Because Matthew is your son, and he needs a family.'

'He has you.'

'I'm not his parent. You are. Don't you even want to *see* him?'

'Is there any reason why I should?' he asked, almost brutally.

'A few hours ago you were saying I should have come here sooner.'

'Yes, when *she* was alive. I could have been with her. But this child is a stranger. I can't feel it's part of me.'

'He was part of *her*,' Polly said quietly. 'Doesn't that mean anything?'

'It might have done if she'd wanted me to know about it.'

'Will you stop talking about "it"?' Polly demanded, becoming annoyed. 'Matthew is a he. He's a baby. He needs love and care—'

'If he's mine, I'll support him.'

'Money?' she snapped. 'Do you really think that's all there is to being a father?'

'I don't feel like a father. This is the best I can do.'

'Then it's not good enough,' she retorted.

'Do you think a father's love can be turned on and off at the press of a switch?' he demanded, equally angry. 'Or any other kind of love?'

'No, of course it can't. But you can turn the love you used

to feel to account now. You can't give your love to her, so give it to the child you share.'

'Share? Did she share him with me? If she hadn't died I'd have known nothing.'

'But she did die, so why not be gentle with her memory? She can't hurt you now.'

'*Can't—?*' He stared at her in sheer outrage before saying, with soft vehemence, 'The dead can hurt you more than the living, because things can't be put right. You can't go back and explain, or apologise, or say the healing words, and the wounds stay open for ever. How can I be gentle with her memory when what she did to me will never end?'

'She gave you a child,' Polly said. 'Whatever she intended, that's what happened. Matthew's alive, and he carries part of you in him.'

He didn't answer for a while, but at last he said, 'Who does he look like?'

She took out a picture and handed it to him. It showed a toddler of eighteen months, with Ruggiero's colouring, dark, sparkling eyes and a brilliant smile.

How could anyone resist this little charmer? she thought. But after a glance he handed it back.

'I can't take him,' he said. 'But of course I'll support him— and I'll support you while you care for him.'

'Excuse me—I'm not looking for a job as a hired nanny.'

'I didn't mean it like that. It wouldn't just be wages; it would be a generous income. You could live comfortably.'

'Oh, really? So you think using cash to avoid your responsibilities is fine as long as the gesture is big enough?'

'I didn't mean—Look, he already knows you. He'd probably rather stay with you.'

'And how about what *I'd* rather? I'm a trained nurse, and I'd like to starting working again.'

She was making it up as she went along. She adored little Matthew, and part of her longed to keep him. If she hadn't liked what she found in Naples she would have left without revealing his existence.

But she did like it. The Rinuccis fitted her inner picture of the perfect family—riotous and colourful, with plenty of love and laughter to go around.

Ruggiero himself would need a little work to improve him, she thought, but in the meantime she would entrust Matthew to Hope and Toni without a qualm. And with all those uncles, aunts and cousins life would be happier for the little boy than in the narrow existence he would find with her.

'How can you reject him?' she demanded, indicating the picture. 'He's your flesh and blood.'

'For Pete's sake,' he snapped. 'You spring this on me and expect me to press a button and have all the right reactions. Just what *is* the right reaction to a son I never knew I had from a woman who didn't even tell me her real name?'

'Don't you feel anything for him?'

'No,' he said after a moment. 'Nothing.'

It wasn't true, she guessed. He was in pain. In trying to numb that, he had numbed every other feeling.

'I'd like you to think about keeping him,' he said. 'On the terms we discussed.'

'We did not discuss anything,' she said, her temper mounting again. 'You laid down your requirements and expected me to fall into line.'

'Just think about it.'

'No!'

'Why the hell not?'

'Because my fiancé would never agree.'

'What?'

'The man I'm engaged to marry doesn't want a child that isn't ours,' she said deliberately.

'You didn't mention an engagement before.'

'There was no need. It's no concern of yours. I came here because little Matthew has a right to his family, but when I've seen him settled I'm returning to my own life.'

He rose. 'I'm going. I need to think about this.'

He moved swiftly towards the door, but when he'd opened it he halted, transfixed.

'Good morning,' said a sweet voice.

Hope was standing there in her dressing gown.

'Mamma, what are you doing here?'

'I came to see why you two are making so much noise. Normally, of course, I wouldn't enquire. It would be indelicate—'

'Mamma!'

'Don't be a prude, my son. It doesn't suit you. Polly, please tell me what has happened.'

'I think Ruggiero had better tell you.'

'If one of you doesn't tell me something soon I shall get cross.'

Ruggiero handed her the picture of Matthew.

'I knew his mother briefly a little more than two years ago in England,' he said, in a flat voice, blank of emotion. 'She never told me about him. Now she's dead.'

'She was my cousin,' Polly supplied. 'She wanted me to find Ruggiero after her death and tell him about his son.'

To her relief, Hope asked no awkward questions. She was entranced by the picture.

'This little man is my grandson?' she asked, in tones of wonder.

Polly gave the exact date of Matthew's birth, and Ruggiero nodded.

'Nine months,' he said briefly.

Hope's eyes were alight with fondness, just as Polly had hoped.

'Such a little darling,' she murmured. 'Where is he now?'

'In England,' Polly told her. 'Some friends of mine are caring for him while I'm here.'

'How soon can we fetch him?'

'*Mamma!*'

'Your son no longer has a mother, but he has a father. Of course he belongs here.'

'I think so too,' Polly said. 'I believe he's a Rinucci. But of course it can be easily established with a test.'

Hope pulled a face. 'No need. If he's one of us I'll know as soon as I hold him in my arms. I'll book the flight to England at once. Polly, you will return here with me, won't you? To help him settle in.'

'Her fiancé may object,' Ruggiero observed.

'He won't,' Polly said hastily. 'Yes, I'll come back for a while.'

Hope cast her a strange look, but said nothing. Wasting no time, she picked up Polly's bedside phone, called the airport, and found a flight to London that afternoon.

By now the light was growing, and the house was waking up around them. Hope bustled away to tell everyone of the plan for today.

'I'm afraid you got taken over again,' Ruggiero said wryly.

'That's all right. I'm glad about this. Hope will love him—'

'Even if I don't? Is that what you mean?'

'You will—in the end. Perhaps you should go now.'

It was a relief when he left. She needed time to work out more details of her 'fiancé'.

He's a doctor called Brian, she decided. And I met him at

the hospital where I used to work. And he's doing a lot of night shifts, so he's hard to get hold of.

She'd invented a fiancé on the spur of the moment, solely to silence Ruggiero in their argument. If she'd stopped to consider first she might not have done it.

But that's me, she thought ruefully. Speak first, think afterwards. I might have come up with something else if I'd had time, or if Ruggiero couldn't annoy me so much that—ah, well. I'm stuck with a 'fiancé' now, so I may as well make use of him.

Today Ruggiero went downstairs for breakfast. Polly found herself sitting next to Toni, who seemed eager to talk to her. She'd seen little of him before, but now she found him a gentle, soft-spoken man, full of joy about his new grandson.

'You won't stay away too long, will you?' he asked anxiously.

'That's up to Hope,' she said. 'She's arranging everything.'

For a moment his eyes rested fondly on his wife.

'Yes,' he said. 'She knows just how to make everything right.'

After breakfast she called the friends caring for Matthew to say she was on her way. Then she went looking for Ruggiero, and found him in the garden, sitting on a fallen log, looking at his clasped hands.

'I've left you some of those pills, but use them sparingly,' she said.

'I probably won't need them. I feel better now I'm up.'

'Good. But don't overdo it.' A sudden suspicion made her add, '*Don't* go back to work.'

'I'll just drop in to talk to my partner. No racing, I promise.'

'Your partner can visit you here.'

'And let him see me looking like an invalid? Forget it.'

'Is there any way to get some sense into you?'

'Nope, so stop wasting your time.'

There was a sulphurous silence. Then he grinned reluctantly.

'Sorry if I give you a hard time.'

But she had his measure by now. 'You're not sorry. That ritual apology is just to shut me up.'

'Well, it's failed, hasn't it? As a matter of interest, has anyone ever actually managed to shut you up?'

'Would I tell you?'

'Not if you were wise.' He grinned again, more warmly this time. 'I promise to be good while you're gone.'

He brightened suddenly.

'You and my mother have a lot in common. The way you took your fiancé's consent for granted was very like her. What's his name, by the way?'

'Brian,' she said quickly. 'And he'll understand about my coming back here. After all, it won't be for long.'

'What did he say when you called to tell him?'

'I haven't done that yet.'

'You'd better hurry if you want him to meet you at the airport.'

'He can't. He's a hospital doctor and he's on night duty at the moment,' she said, repeating the story she'd mapped out. 'I'd better go and get ready.'

Before she could move he reached out and took her hand.

'A moment,' he said. 'I want to ask you a favour.'

But he stopped there, as though it was hard for him to go on.

'What can I do for you?' she asked gently.

His hand tightened on hers.

'When you get home—do you have any more pictures of her?'

'Yes, I have plenty. I'll bring some of them to you.'

'Bring them all. Everything—*please*.'

'There are a lot of blanks to be filled in, aren't there?'

'I used to think I'd have the chance to fill them in one day. I never thought it would be like this, when it's too late to make any difference.'

But it could still make a difference, she thought. It would help him learn to relate to his son, and she would do everything in her power to help that happen.

'You'd better let me go,' she said, wincing slightly.

He seemed to return from a distance, to realise that he was gripping her hand hard. He made an exclamation as he released it and began to rub it between his two hands.

'I think the circulation's started again now,' she said lightly.

'I'm sorry—again. Hell! Why don't I just give you a big apology now, and hopefully it'll cover everything in the future?'

'Well, I'm leaving in a couple of hours,' she said lightly. 'You won't have time to annoy me before then.'

'You underestimate me. Let's go in.'

He helped her to her feet and they walked indoors, briefly in accord.

# CHAPTER FIVE

THEY were to spend two nights in England—the first in Polly's home and the second with Justin and Evie, who were eager to see the new arrival.

During the flight Hope asked about Polly's fiancé, assuming, as Ruggiero had done, that he would meet them. Polly repeated the excuse about 'Brian's' night duty, and Hope seemed to accept it.

Although the matriarch of an Italian family, Hope was English, and she knew the country well.

'How do you come to live in London if you come from Yorkshire?' she asked.

'I was engaged several years ago, but we broke up. I wanted to get away so I came south. Freda joined me when she became ill.'

'And the baby is—how old?'

'Eighteen months.'

'Is he walking?'

'Oh, yes, he's well grown. He took his first tentative step at nine months.'

'So did Ruggiero,' Hope said with satisfaction. 'He and Carlo competed to see who could walk first, and they've been vying with each other ever since.'

They were to collect Matthew the next morning, as it would be too late to do it that day. The light was fading when they arrived in the evening. When they had sent out for a take-away meal, and were sitting together in the tiny kitchen, Hope said gently, 'Why don't you tell me the things you couldn't say in front of Ruggiero?'

Faced with this kindly understanding, Polly explained everything. At the end Hope nodded sadly.

'He said very little when he got home—something about a "holiday romance", but so casually that it seemed to mean nothing. I should have seen through that, but there had been so many—' She made a sad gesture.

'I imagine he was very determined to keep his secrets?' Polly suggested. 'Freda summed him up as "love 'em and leave 'em," and maybe for a man like that...' She hesitated, but Hope understood.

'It would be very difficult to find that he was the one left,' she filled in. 'That must have made it harder for him to cope with. I wonder how much more there was?'

'I don't know—and I'm sure he doesn't,' Polly reflected. 'It was all built on fantasies, because he knew nothing about her—not that she was married, or that she had a secret agenda. He didn't even know her real name. I know how you must feel about her, but please don't hate her.'

'Once I might have done,' Hope admitted. 'But she ended so sadly that I must forgive her. Is this where you lived together?'

'Yes, until just a few weeks ago. Then she went into hospital for the last time.'

'She was beautiful,' Hope said, studying the pictures.

'It was more than just beauty. She had that extra "something" that we'd all like to have. A kind of magic. I think he's been trying to cope by pretending to himself that that it really was just a holiday romance. He might have managed it if I hadn't turned up. Now he has to face what actually happened, and I don't think he knows how.'

'But you'll help him, won't you?' Hope urged. 'You are special to him because of her. You're the only one he can turn to now. I, his mother, say so.'

'I'll do my best. I want things to turn out well for little Matthew.'

'And only for him? Oh, yes—you are engaged to be married, aren't you? I forgot.'

When they had gone to bed Polly lay awake, feeling the little flat full of ghosts. Freda seemed to be here again, chattering feverishly about herself and her conquests, especially Ruggiero.

'He was so strong, Polly, and that makes a man so much more exciting. He'd hold me tight in his arms and love me and love me and love me, all through the night. But he always had energy for more.'

By then her sickness had been far advanced, her beauty gone, and Polly had listened kindly to the tales of triumphs that would never come again.

'He's an athlete, you know,' Freda had purred. 'Likes to live an active life. Well, I could see that as soon as he was naked— all well-developed muscles and not an ounce of fat. Just looking at him, I knew he was made for love.' Then she'd given Polly a sideways glance, with a touch of malice. 'I don't disturb you, talking like that, do I?'

'No,' Polly had said. 'You don't.'

It was true. In those days Ruggiero had had no reality for her. Freda's descriptions had conjured up no pictures.

But things had changed. Now that she'd seen him and held him in her arms the words came alive with vivid meaning.

*I knew he was made for love.*

She sat up sharply, breathing hard, staring into the darkness.

'Nonsense,' she said to herself.

Suddenly it was impossible to sleep. She had to get up and walk restlessly about.

'It's getting to me,' she muttered. 'I need to finish this, come home, get a job, live a normal life—whatever that is— and forget about him.'

It was impossible. She could vividly recall running her fingers over his skin, seeking injuries; a coolly professional action at the time, but one which brought her senses alive in retrospect.

But what affected her even more was the memory of him clasping her hand with painful intensity as he begged for some pictures of the woman he'd loved, and spoke the terrible words 'too late'.

In her mind she heard Hope saying, 'You are special to him,' and was dismayed at the tiny flicker of pleasure she'd felt until Hope had quenched it by adding, 'because of her.'

Special to him, but only because of her, she thought. I guess I'd better remember that, just in case I get any silly ideas.

She lay down again, and, by dint of talking sensibly to herself, finally managed to get to sleep.

Next morning was chaos. Iris, the friend caring for Matthew, called early to say that one of her own children was being whisked to hospital with a broken leg, and she needed to off-load the baby fast.

'Joe will pass your house on the way to the hospital.'

Joe, her husband, turned up half an hour later with Matthew. The toddler, sensing a crisis, was bawling at the top of his voice, drowning out Polly's attempts to introduce Hope, enquire after the injured daughter, and thank him.

Luckily Hope knew all about babies, and picked him up without the slightest fuss or bother. Polly had thought of so many things to say, but nothing was necessary. Hope cooed and smiled—until the noise died suddenly, and grandson and grandmother were left considering each other in silence.

He burped.

A broad smile broke over Hope's face and she laughed in delight. At once he returned the smile, burping again. Hope pulled him tightly against her and dropped her head so that her face was hidden. When she raised it again there were tears on her cheeks.

'My grandson,' she said huskily. 'Oh, yes, he's mine. We knew each other at once.'

As they got ready to leave Hope said, 'Why don't you call your fiancé and invite him to join us tonight at Justin and Evie's place?'

'That's kind of you,' Polly said hastily. 'But I don't think he could get away—'

'But you won't know if you don't ask him. Or you could slip out and see him now. We have a few extra hours, since Matthew is here early, so you could make use of them.'

Polly assented, because she guessed her refusals might start to sound unconvincing. It would give her a couple of hours to do some shopping.

'Have you had a good time?' Hope asked as soon as she arrived home.

'Wonderful, thank you,' she said brightly.

She just about managed to infuse her manner with delight, as befitted a woman who'd seized a few stolen minutes with her lover, but she wasn't enough of an actress to carry it further, so when Hope would ask more questions she gave a little shriek.

'Is that the time? We should be going or we'll be late.'

Soon they were on their way to Justin and Evie's home, and

mercifully Hope dropped the subject. She talked instead about the phone call she'd had with Ruggiero.

'I told him all about his son, how beautiful he is. I said you were out so little Matthew and I were getting to know each other. He sounded very pleased.'

Polly longed to ask if Hope had told Ruggiero that she was meeting Brian, but she didn't dare. Instead she said how much she was looking forward to talking to Evie again, and soon they reached their destination.

After the tense misery of the last year it was wonderful to visit a cheerful home, with a husband and wife who loved each other, their baby twins, and Justin's teenage son. Evie and Hope went into a happy huddle over Matthew, who was all smiles for a while, but then tried to play a rough game with the family puppy, who objected and ran away. The toddler vented his frustration in a screaming fit.

'Just like his father,' Hope observed, picking him up. 'He always roared at the world when it didn't dance to his tune.'

Her eyes met Polly's and the silent message, *And he hasn't changed*, flashed between them.

'You two really understand each other,' Evie said when she and Hope were alone. 'Have you decided on her?'

'I don't know what you mean,' Hope said with an air of innocence.

'Oh, yes, you do,' Evie chuckled. 'You pick out a daughter-in-law and pull strings until you get her.'

'I merely like to ensure the best for my sons,' Hope said.

'And you've decided on Polly. Go on, admit it.'

'She might be the making of him,' Hope agreed. 'But we have to go carefully.'

'Yes, her fiancé might get in the way a little.'

'I don't think so,' Hope mused. 'No, I really don't think so at all.'

\* \* \*

They flew back to Italy the next day. Polly spent the last half hour looking out of the plane window, trying to understand the sudden nervousness that had come over her.

Ruggiero was in her thoughts all the time, but he'd been at a safe distance. Now she would be with him again, and the awareness that had come to her so suddenly, two nights ago, was disturbing her. She wasn't sure what to think, but she'd know when she saw him.

It was just fancy, she tried to reassure herself. I'm a severely practical person. This sort of thing just doesn't happen to me, because I don't let it. I wonder if he'll be at the airport?

He was. He and Toni stood there, waiting as they came out of Customs, Hope carrying the child, and Polly saw Toni's face light up with joy. Then he was running forward, arms outstretched, to embrace his wife and grandson together.

Ruggiero's face remained blank. Nor did he move as Toni and Polly greeted each other pleasantly.

'All this has thrown him for six,' Toni muttered in her ear. 'Since my wife called he hasn't known what to do with himself.'

That could be taken both ways, she thought. It didn't tell her about Ruggiero's true feelings. But then she saw him smiling at her with a hint of relief, as though he'd just been hanging on until she came back. And, despite her efforts to stop it, a spring of pleasure welled up inside her.

They had come in two cars, to ensure enough room for everyone on the return journey.

'You and the baby go with Poppa,' Ruggiero told his mother. 'I'll take Polly.'

The little surge of happiness was there again, irrational and reprehensible, but too strong to be fought. He opened the door for her and made sure she was comfortable before going around to the driver's side. She looked at him, smiling. She couldn't help herself. Something told her that his next words would be momentous.

As Toni's car pulled away Ruggiero turned to her.

'Let them go for the moment,' he said. 'There is something I must say to you first.'

'Yes?'

'You did bring them, didn't you?'

'What?'

'The pictures. You promised faithfully to bring me pictures of Sapphire. Please, Polly, don't tell me you forgot. You don't know how important it is.'

So this was all he wanted—why he'd lit up at the sight of her. The depth of her bitterness warned her how far she'd strayed into danger.

'Please, Polly,' he repeated.

'It's all right. I've brought the pictures.'

With sudden resolution, as though he'd been given a reviving draught of life, he started the car and swung out of the airport.

Well, what did you think was going to happen? Polly thought scathingly. That he was going to forget her and see you? Get real!

On the way home she said, 'Have you been sensible while I was away?'

'No riding. I swear it.'

'Short of that.'

'I dropped in at work for an hour, but I behaved very feebly, and came home early. You'd have been proud of me.'

'How about the pills?'

'Just a couple at night. I'm on the mend.'

When they reached the villa Primo and Olympia were there. Apart from Carlo and Della, away on their honeymoon, they were the only Rinuccis who lived in Naples, so their arrival represented the rest of the family.

At first Polly stayed where Matthew could always see her, lest he grow alarmed. But he was easy in company—a natural charmer, who relished the attention.

Everyone was delighted when Ruggiero dropped down on one knee to look his son in the eye, and received a steady stare in return.

'Buongiorno,' Ruggiero said politely.

'Bon—bon—' he tried to repeat.

Ruggiero repeated the word and the tot responded by yelling, 'Bon, bon, bon!' in tones of delight.

Everyone laughed and clapped.

'His first Italian word,' Hope cried. 'Why don't you sit down and hold him?'

He sat on the sofa, and she helped little Matthew to get up beside him. He peered closely at this new giant, and finally became curious enough to try to climb onto his lap.

'Better not,' Ruggiero said quickly. 'I'm still a bit sore, and I'd be afraid of dropping him.'

It was an entirely reasonable excuse. Surely Polly only imagined that he'd seized the first chance to back off?

He behaved impeccably, regarding the child with apparent interest, smiling in the right places, watching as he was bathed and dressed in the sleepsuit that Polly had brought with her, then put to bed. It was agreed, for the moment, that he should sleep in Polly's room, in a crib that one of the maids had rescued from the attic.

'I suppose you're going to say that was mine?' Ruggiero asked with resigned good humour.

'No, this was Carlo's,' Hope declared triumphantly. 'You managed to set fire to yours.'

Everyone laughed, including Ruggiero, but it seemed to Polly that he was doing everything from a distance, trying not to reveal that this first meeting with his son meant nothing to him.

When Matthew had fallen asleep, Ruggiero said unexpectedly, 'Could you all give us a moment, please?'

Everyone smiled at this sign of fatherly interest, but when the door had closed behind them he said urgently to Polly, 'The photos? Can I have them now?'

'Of course. I unpacked them ready for you.'

She took the two albums from a drawer and handed them to him.

'Thanks,' he said briefly, and departed without a look at the sleeping child.

That night Polly stayed up late in her room, telling herself that she was watching over the little boy, but secretly knowing that she was watching over his father. Opening her window and looking out, she could see the glow from his window next door. There was to be no rest for him tonight.

She imagined him turning the pages, seeing 'Sapphire's' face over and over, feeling fresh pain with every new vision.

Why had she let herself be taken by surprise? Deny it how he would, Sapphire had been the woman he'd loved so passionately that a few days ago the briefest imagined glimpse of her had driven him to madness, almost claiming his life. Perhaps he would have preferred that, now *she* was dead. He was, in effect, a widower, but denied a widower's freedom to mourn openly—denied even the memories of a shared love that might have made his loss bearable.

Suddenly she remembered that Freda's wedding pictures were in the second album. In the hurry and agitation it had slipped her mind, but now she wished she'd remembered and removed them. It was too late, but she might have spared him that.

A quick glance showed that Matthew was still sleeping. She went out into the corridor and knocked softly at Ruggiero's door.

'Come in.' The words came softly.

He was sitting on the bed, his hands clasped between his knees, the wedding pictures open beside him.

'I just came to see if you were all right.'

'I'm fine—fine.'

She sat on the bed beside him.

'No, you're not,' she said gently. 'I've been watching you all evening, and you're like a man stretched on a wheel. Your nerves are at breaking point—even your voice sounds different.'

'Different how?'

'Tense. Hard. Every five minutes you ask yourself if you can survive the next five minutes, and then the next. You smile at people and try to say the right things, but it's taking everything out of you.'

'Am I really as transparent as that?' he asked, with a brief wry smile.

'No, I don't think anyone else has noticed.'

'Just Nurse Bossy-Boots, keeping an eagle eye on the patient?'

Or a woman with a man whose every word and gesture means something, she thought, and longed to be able to say it aloud.

He sighed and squeezed her hand. 'No, it's not just your being a nurse. You see things that nobody else does. Where do you get it from?'

She resisted the impulse to squeeze back, and said, 'In a way it *is* part of being a nurse. You watch people so much that you starting noticing odd details. I don't just mean medical things, but about their lives.' She gave a little chuckle.

'What? Tell me.'

'I got so that when a man brought his wife into the ward I could tell at once how things were between them. I knew which husbands were going to be faithful while their wives were in hospital, and which ones were going to live it up.'

'How?'

'Something in the voice. If he called her "darling" every second word I knew he'd be on the phone to a girlfriend before he left the building. The ones who were going to go home and worry didn't say very much, just looked.'

'You've got us all ticketed, then?'

'Absolutely,' she said, trying to ease the mood by making a joke of it. 'No man can spring a surprise on me. You're all boringly predictable.'

There was one man she hadn't told Ruggiero about—a soldier, who'd brought his wife to the ward and had seemed to think he was on parade, talking at the top of his voice and bullying everyone. But afterwards she'd found him sitting in the corridor, staring into space.

'Boringly predictable' had been a joke, and far from her real thoughts. It was that desperate soldier who'd given her the clue to Ruggiero.

He interrupted her thoughts by saying suddenly, 'Does Brian know how you think?'

'Well, I don't talk to him that way. A woman should keep her secrets.'

'From the man she loves?'

'Especially from the man she loves,' she said firmly.

'And he doesn't suspect?'

'Not if I can help it.'

'Keep the poor fool in blissful ignorance, eh? I guess that runs in the family.'

He said the last words so quietly that she didn't need to respond to them, but their bitterness wasn't lost on her.

'What kind of man is Brian?' he asked suddenly. 'Does he tend to be faithful, or go the other way?'

'I've hardly had time to judge.'

'But with you being so preoccupied this last year—you weren't afraid that he'd stray?'

'I haven't been putting his fidelity to the test,' she said, with perfect truth.

'Is that because you're afraid to try, or because he doesn't have enough spirit to be unfaithful?'

'You make infidelity sound like a virtue?' she said, half laughing.

'Not exactly. But to be as sure of him as you are—he sounds like a suet pudding.'

'I promise you he's not a suet pudding. Brian's lively enough, but he spends long, exhausting days looking after people who need him.'

'And when you get together you talk about test tubes. That must be thrilling.'

She hadn't wanted this discussion, but it was useful. Being close to Ruggiero like this affected her so strongly that she was terrified he would sense it, and Brian was a useful shield. So she played along.

'Anything can be thrilling if you share the same interests,' she mused.

'And that's what you talked about when you saw him yesterday?'

She chuckled. 'I don't think we talked much.'

'But didn't he try to persuade you to stay with him—in between doing whatever you were doing?'

'No, of course not.'

'Of course not? Does he love you or not?'

'He does, but he knew I had to come back for as long as I'm needed here. He understands about putting duty first.'

'Another thing you share?'

'Another thing we share.'

'You told him that you're crazy about him but you had to return to this grumpy so-and-so who'll collapse without you? That *and* test tubes? How did you tear yourself away from such passion?'

'Nurse Bossy-Boots never lets down a patient,' she said primly. 'And passion can be found in the oddest places.'

She found she was enjoying this conversation too much for safety, and hurried to say, 'But I don't think I ought to discuss him any more. He wouldn't like it.'

Ruggiero threw her a grim look. His nerves were stretched from the two tense days he'd spent waiting for her, wondering if he would ever see her again.

He was a man with no gift for self-analysis. He could dismantle an engine both actually and in his head. He even had some faint understanding of others. But to himself he was an almost total mystery.

In the last two days he'd been miserable, thinking of the pictures that Polly might or might not remember to bring back. He'd focused on that because he understood it, but somewhere along the line it had blurred with the fear that she might not return at all.

Arguments had raged in his head. His strong, reliable Nurse Bossy-Boots was a woman of her word. She wouldn't let him down because that wasn't her way. But the ties holding her back were immense—including the man she loved, who might be fed up with waiting and demand to come first in her life.

Perhaps she'd give the pictures to Hope and leave, confident that she'd done her duty?

But she wouldn't have done it, he told himself firmly. She was the one person he could talk to, and she had no right to desert him.

Hope had called him that morning to say they were returning together. He'd breathed again, but even so he'd been shocked by the explosion of relief that had attacked him when she'd appeared at Naples Airport. It had the perverse effect of making him abrupt, even angry with her. And this, too, he did not understand.

CHAPTER SIX

## CHAPTER SIX

HIS EYES WERE on the photographs. Sapphire. Briefly she'd faded, but now she flamed back into his consciousness, as sharp and poignant as ever. He drew in a sharp breath at the sight of her radiant beauty on the day she'd married another man.

'They're lovely pictures, aren't they?' Polly said.

She began to turn the pages. Freda had been at her best on that day: her extravagant beauty flaunted in a glamorous satin creation, George's wedding gift of diamonds on her head, holding in place a veil that stretched to the floor.

There she was with her new husband, looking adoringly into his face because she wanted to be convincing in her role. George had been good for several more diamonds yet.

There she was with her chief bridesmaid, poor cousin Polly, looking horribly out of place in a frilly pink satin dress, her dullness cruelly contrasted with the bride's lustrous looks.

One picture was a close-up of Freda alone, with a soft, sweet smile and a tender expression that had seldom been there in real life. She'd been an accomplished actress, and for this shot she'd managed to banish the gleam of greedy triumph from her eyes. The woman in that picture was enchanting: soft, generous, giving, yielding; everything that she had not been.

'I'm sorry,' she murmured. 'I shouldn't have brought the wedding pictures.'

'Why?' he asked sharply. 'Do you think I'm afraid of them?'

'Perhaps you ought to be. What difference can it make now?'

'Don't say that. I can't rid myself of her just because she's dead. In some ways I feel I've only just met her, and I need to know everything.'

She shook her head, but she didn't say aloud what she was thinking—that 'everything' was precisely what he couldn't endure knowing. Instead she begged, 'Let the past be. It's the future that matters—your future and Matthew's.'

'But the future grows out of the past. What do I do if the past is a blank? I need to find out as much as I can, then maybe—I don't know. Maybe things will be different. If I could see the places where she lived, get some picture of her life in my mind—you could take me back there.'

'Ruggiero, no.'

'But you could. We could go to England tomorrow. We don't have to be away for long—just long enough for me to see where she lived and go around the places she knew—'

She seized his good shoulder, giving him a little shake.

*'It won't bring her back,'* she said fiercely. 'Stop this!'

'I can't,' he said in agony.

Looking at him closely, she saw that he was in the grip of a powerful force that was devouring him. His eyes were full of a terrifying obsession. His hot breath brushing her face might have come from the fires of hell.

'Stop it!' she said. 'Stop it!'

'How?' he asked bleakly. 'Help me, Polly. You're the only friend who can. Nobody else knows—I can't tell anyone— how could I?'

It was true. Hope knew roughly what had happened, but not how deep his pain went. Because he loved his mother he would conceal the worst from her, but it left him with nobody to turn to except Polly.

'All the time you were away,' he went on, 'I kept hoping for a miracle. Somehow I'd get things into perspective and see her clearly—that's what I thought. And when you brought the baby back, I know I was supposed to take one look at him and be overcome with fatherly love.'

'No, that's only in sentimental films,' she said. 'I think what really happened is that you looked at him and thought, Oh, my God!'

'*O, mio dio!*' he agreed. 'Call me a monster if you like, but I feel nothing for my son. Nothing.'

'You're not a monster at all. When you look at him I dare say you don't actually see him, because there's a brick wall built between you, and you can't get past it.'

'Except that she's there too—both of her.'

'Both?'

'The beautiful girl who loved me and transformed my life, and the manipulator who took what she wanted and left me in a desert, without a backward glance. I don't know which one of them is real, and until I know more nothing is ever going to be real.'

'Maybe the reality is a bit of both,' she said, trying to soften it for him.

'Or maybe I'm simply telling myself pretty fairy tales— seeing only what I want to see, blocking my ears to anything that doesn't fit in with my picture: a weak, foolish man who can't bear to face unpleasant facts?'

'Stop being so hard on yourself,' she said fiercely. 'You haven't recovered from the shock yet.'

'I thought I might find some sort of answer in the child's face, but it seems to change all the time. Sometimes her, sometimes me—'

'And sometimes he's just himself, which is how it should be. That poor little boy, carrying the burden of so many expectations.'

'Do you think I don't know that? They're all looking at him to see if he's a true Rinucci—just as they're watching me to see if I'm feeling the right things. So I do what I have to— kneel down, speak to him—so that they don't think how heartless I am. Nobody must guess the truth except you. Without you to hold onto I think I'd go mad.'

She should be sensible and run away now. She'd already had a warning of the perilous path she was treading. But she didn't want to be sensible. She wanted to take the burden from him, even if it led her further down that path and cost her dear.

Polly put her arms around him, letting her forehead rest against his.

'And you *can* hold onto me. I'll help all I can, but not by creating a dream world for you.'

'I don't want that,' he said softly. 'I want to know what she was like in the real world, and only you can tell me.'

'And will telling you help?' she asked. 'Maybe talking about her will only make it worse?'

His eyes burned with his obsession, warning her of the dangerous direction his mind was taking.

'But it might keep her with me,' he whispered feverishly. 'I'm not ready to let go yet.'

'Even of her ghost?'

'If that's all I can have.'

'Haven't you had enough of ghosts?' she asked passionately. 'She's haunted you for over two years, and she nearly killed you. Don't you realise that?'

'Or you did,' he said wryly.

'No, it wasn't me who sent you spinning off the track into what might have been your grave.'

Something in her brain seemed to snap, and for a moment she went mad, her mind following his down the road to destruction.

'That was her,' she said passionately. 'Because she's jealous and possessive and she can't bear to let you go, even though she doesn't want you. That's how she was. If she couldn't have something, she hated anyone else to have it. Her life was taken, so now she—'

Appalled, she checked herself.

'What am I saying?' she choked. 'I'm talking about her as though—almost as if—'

'That's what she's doing to my head, too,' he told her. '*Now* do you understand that there's no escape?'

'There is if you fight it.'

'And if I don't want to fight it? Do you know what happened to me that day at the track? When I saw her standing there in front of me I was glad. I knew she was beckoning me to disaster but I didn't care. I was so full of joy at seeing her after so long. I think I called out to her—'

'Yes,' she said, remembering how he'd lain in her arms afterwards and murmured Sapphire's name.

'I was chasing her across a great distance, but she always evaded me, and then she was gone.'

'And you think if I take you back to her old haunts you'll find her? You won't. That's not where the truth lies.'

'But I have to believe that it's somewhere to be found otherwise I'll go mad.'

'Can't it be enough that she was beautiful?' Polly begged. 'That you had a perfect time together and she left you a son?'

'A chimera,' he murmured. 'Nothing more.'

'That little boy wasn't born from a chimera. He's real, and he's all that's left of her. Ruggiero, please, *please* try to understand. *You can't bring her back.*'

He seemed to relax against her, and for a moment she

thought she'd got through to him. Moving slowly, she reached out to the wedding album and drew it towards her.

'Let me take this,' she said. 'Don't brood over it.'

But his hand clamped over hers. 'Leave it.'

'Ruggiero—'

'I said leave it.'

Before he could reply she heard the shrill of her cellphone from her room.

'I must answer that before it wakes him up,' she said, and hurried out without closing Ruggiero's door.

From the next room he heard her say,

'I called you earlier today, but there was no answer so I assumed you'd gone to the hospital.'

Then he closed his door, resisting the temptation to eavesdrop further.

In her room, Polly moved well away from the cot and spoke softly into the phone.

'Iris, I'm so glad your daughter's all right. I'm sure she'll be home from the hospital soon. And thank you for everything.'

She hung up and returned to Ruggiero.

'Can I come in again?' she asked through the closed door.

'No,' came his voice. 'I won't disturb you any longer. Goodnight, Polly.'

'Goodnight.'

There was nothing to do but turn away, wondering about the opportunity that had been lost.

The next day Ruggiero announced that he was well enough to go work.

'Is he?' Hope immediately asked Polly.

'Yes, *he* is,' Ruggiero declared firmly.

'Yes, he is,' Polly said, speaking like a robot. Then she laughed and said, 'You heard him. I've been told what to say.'

'The idea of *you* taking orders!' Hope scoffed, giving her an admiring look.

'He'll be all right if he's careful,' Polly said.

'Then we're going shopping,' Hope said gleefully. 'I want to celebrate my new grandson.'

'By stripping the shops bare?' Toni enquired with wry amusement.

'Can you think of a better way of celebrating?'

She, Toni and Polly set off, accompanied by Matteo, as he had now become. Hope was in her element, spending money on toddler clothes, toddler toys, toddler food, turning to Polly for advice and sometimes actually taking it.

'You're not offended with me?' she asked Polly anxiously. 'I know you've always given him the best you could afford—'

'I'm not offended. He was growing out of most of his stuff anyway, and who wants to pass up the chance of a shopping trip?'

Cheered by this sign of Polly's good sense, Hope swept her into a dress shop and bought her the basis of a new wardrobe— 'So that I can be really sure you're not offended.'

'But I'm not—'

'Then accept these few things, with my thanks.'

'Don't argue,' Toni begged. 'Let her have her own way, *please*!'

'All right,' Polly said, understanding him correctly. 'For your sake.'

They all laughed.

The family was gathering, all eager to inspect the newest Rinucci. Later that day Luke and Minnie arrived from Rome, while Primo and Olympia made a second visit. Once more Matteo was in his element, holding court. In a very short time Matteo became Matti.

Ruggiero arrived to find Olympia holding the child up

high while they giggled together. He behaved delightfully, kissing his sisters-in-law, joshing his brothers, and later joining in the family amusement at the sight of his father with his grandson on his lap, an adoring slave.

It was a charming scene, but again Polly knew that he was using it as a screen to hide how little he felt for his son. Once she would have blamed him, but now she understood more clearly. Freda's rejection had wounded him as much as her death, perhaps more, and for now the child was merely a reminder of that.

When it was Matti's bedtime Hope came to Polly's room and assisted. When he was in his cot, she leaned down and kissed him.

'*Buona notte,*' she murmured.

Seeing Ruggiero in the doorway, she beckoned him forward.

'Kiss him goodnight,' she urged.

'Better not disturb him now he's sleeping,' he said. 'I think I'll go to bed now, Mamma. Goodnight.'

Polly spent the next day at the villa with Hope and Toni, enjoying the sight of their rapport with Matti. Hope had noticed that Ruggiero wasn't at ease with the child, but it didn't trouble her greatly.

'It will take a little time for him to relax about this,' she said cheerfully. 'But that's all right. I'm not in a hurry to see him vanish back to his apartment.'

'Apartment?' Polly asked, startled. 'I thought he lived here.'

'He does some of the time, but he has his own place in Naples too. All our sons have homes away from us, but they keep their rooms in the villa.'

'But how will he manage on his own with a child?' Polly wondered.

'He can't. Matti will stay with us at first, and live with Ruggiero later, when he's grown up enough to do things for himself.' She added in an under-voice, 'And when my son has grown up enough to be a father.'

'That's not fair,' Polly said at once. 'It's less than a week since he knew she was dead, and he's grieving for her.'

'A woman who treated him like that? Polly, have you told him everything yet?'

'No, he's not ready. He has suspicions, but nothing he can't shake off. How can I give him a clear picture of my cousin without also destroying Matti's mother in Ruggiero's eyes?'

They were both silent. Then Hope patted her hand.

'You will find a way. You are a wise woman, and you have all my trust.'

'And mine,' said Toni, who didn't always allow his wife to speak for him.'

The evening meal was early, with Matti sitting on Toni's lap like a little grandee, lording it over his court. There was no sign of Ruggiero, but as they were all climbing the stairs to put Matti to bed the phone rang. Toni went to answer it, and joined them a few minutes later, saying, 'Ruggiero won't be back tonight. After the time he's had off he says he must work late, so he'll go to his apartment.'

He didn't return the next day, or the one after. Polly became more troubled, haunted by the things he'd said to her the night before he'd left, the glimpse she'd had of a tortured mind. She longed to talk to him again—see into his thoughts, help to rid him of his obsession.

Or maybe I just want him to forget her and think of me, she thought with wry realism. Who am I kidding? Not myself, that's for sure. Freda would be the first person to tell me what I'm really hoping for.

And she did.

That night her cousin came to her, dancing out of the misty darkness.

'Freda? What are you doing here?'

The vision laughed, swirling her glorious hair so that it was like a halo. She was in a long, floaty dress that swirled about her, and all her beauty had returned.

'I'm not Freda any more,' she teased. 'Freda's dead.'

'*You're* dead.'

'No, I'm Sapphire now. Because that's how *he* thinks of me, and you've started to see me through his eyes.'

'Go away,' Polly cried.

'You'd like that, wouldn't you? You want to make him forget me so that you can have him for yourself. But you never will. He's still mine. He loves me, and there's nothing you can do about it—nothing—nothing—nothing—'

She was gone.

Suddenly the darkness vanished, dawn light filled the room, and Polly awoke with a shudder to find herself sitting up in bed.

'It was a dream,' she gasped. 'Only a dream.'

She went to the bathroom to splash water on her eyes. The face in the mirror was so superficially like Sapphire's, yet so cruelly different.

'She's dead,' she told the image firmly. 'She's gone for good.'

'But I haven't,' Sapphire whispered in her mind. 'I'm not dead to him. Why do you think he's vanished? He wants to be alone with me.'

Suddenly the fear was hard and real, driving Polly out into the corridor and into Ruggiero's empty room.

A thorough search confirmed her worst suspicions. The photo albums were missing.

The Palazzo Montelio overlooked the Naples docks. Despite its name it wasn't a palace, but a grandiose edifice, built by a self-important merchant who'd wanted a place where he could keep a constant eye on the boats that provided his wealth. For two centuries his fortunes had flourished, but then declined, so that the building had had to be sold and turned into apartments.

As she made her way slowly up the wide stairs to the second floor Polly wondered again if she was wise to come here. But perhaps it had been inevitable since the moment Hope had called Ruggiero's firm and discovered that was not there.

'Not for the last two days,' she said, looking significantly at Polly. She scribbled something on a scrap of paper. 'That's where he lives.'

So now here she was, about to beard the lion in his lair, ready to face his fury at her temerity in hounding him.

But all he said when he opened the door was, 'What took you so long?'

She'd half expected to discover that he'd been drowning his sorrows, but his voice was sober and his movements steady.

The apartment was an odd mixture of faded grandeur and modernity, with old-fashioned comfortable furniture and a gleaming kitchen. She managed to look around cautiously while he made some English tea, which was unexpectedly good.

Now that she could observe him better, her first favourable impression was changing. If he hadn't been drinking, neither had he been eating or shaving. His dark hair meant that several days' stubble stood out starkly, making his lean face almost cadaverous. Nor had he slept much, if his eyes told a true story.

He looked as if he'd dressed in the first thing he'd been able to find to throw on—old jeans, old shirt, mostly unbuttoned so that she could see the rough, curly hair beneath.

'You knew I was coming?' she said.

'I'd have bet money on it.'

'Well, you're still my patient. I needn't ask how you've managed. I can see that you've been taking proper care of yourself, eating well, getting enough rest, behaving sensibly. I can't think why I bothered.'

That made him laugh, and he winced, holding his side.

'It hurts more than it did,' he admitted.

'And it'll go on hurting for a while. I've brought you some more pills. These won't send you to sleep like the last ones.'

'Thanks. I've been trying some that I bought in a shop, but—' He shrugged, then stopped quickly and rubbed his shoulder.

'Here,' she said, producing the pills. 'Take a couple now, and we'll think about something to eat.'

'I don't have much in the place.'

'Then we'll have to go out. My treat.'

'No, I can't let—'

'I didn't ask you to let me. I just said that's what I'm going to do.'

'Yes, ma'am.' He gave a brief snort of laughter. 'You don't know how good it feels to have you bullying me again.' He added abstractedly, 'Maybe my father was right.'

'About what?'

He'd recalled Toni's words about how Hope anticipated his needs and fulfilled them before he was even aware. The outside world might dismiss it as domination, but Toni had spoken like a man with a happy secret. Ruggiero was about to tell Polly, but backed off, realising that this would lead him into unknown paths where perhaps he couldn't rely on her hand to steady him.

What he did know, beyond doubt, was that if she hadn't arrived when she did he would have sought her out.

'Never mind,' he said hastily. 'Poppa says a lot of strange things.'

'Then you're not his son for nothing,' she mused.

She spoke lightly, but the sight of him worried her. How

long was it since he'd last eaten? She decided to get some food into him fast.

The light was fading as they left the building. Lamps were coming on in the little restaurants along the seafront, and on the boats that came and went in the harbour.

'They're mostly ferries,' he explained, 'linking us with Capri, Ischia and several other islands.'

'That place looks nice,' she said, pointing at a tiny café near the water. A board over the door announced Pesci Di Napoli.

'Fish from Naples,' she announced triumphantly. 'You see, I've actually learned some Italian words. Let's go.'

'Not there,' he said quickly.

'Why? Is there something wrong with it? Is the fish rancid?'

'Of course not. But there are better places—'

*'Ruggiero, mi amico!'*

The bawling, friendly voice stopped them as he was about to hurry her away, and made him turn reluctantly.

'Leo,' he said.

The man standing in the doorway of Pesci Di Napoli beamed and shook his hand so vigorously that Ruggiero winced.

'Leo, this is Signorina Hanson, and she only speaks English.'

'Welcome, *signorina*. Ruggiero, it's too long since we saw you. Come in and have something to eat. We've got fresh clams today, and I know how much you like them.'

There was no escape. Ruggiero smiled and ushered Polly in.

'You know this place well?' she asked, looking at him curiously.

'He owns part of it,' Leo said. 'The profits he makes here he throws away on motorbikes, so that he can have the fun of half killing himself. One day he'll complete the job and we'll all have a good laugh.'

Ruggiero grinned at his friend's jeering irony. The atmosphere was warm and jovial.

And yet he'd tried to steer her away.

Leo led them to a table by the window.

'Spaghetti with clams to start with,' Ruggiero said, 'since that's what Leo's decided. And afterwards—'

He explained the menu to her and they decided on *lasagna napolitana* and coffee. Leo tried to interest them in wine, but she shook her head.

'No alcohol,' she said. 'Not with those pills.'

'I know. You told me days ago.'

When Leo had departed Ruggiero asked, 'Did you rush down here to see if I was drinking myself to death? You needn't have. I've stuck to tea, believe it or not.'

'I do believe it,' she said lightly. 'I know that among your many virtues the greatest is self-control.'

'Are you making fun of me?' he demanded suspiciously.

'Why should you think so?'

'My "many virtues"! You wouldn't say that except ironically.'

She was silent, wondering how far it was wise to push him.

'Don't you have many virtues?' she ventured at last.

'Probably not many that you'd call virtues.'

'Perhaps they cease to be virtues when you carry them to extremes?'

'Such as?'

'Self-control is fine, except when you turn it into an iron cage,' she ventured.

'And you think that's what I do?'

'Yes, because you told me yourself. When we first talked about Sapphire you said that what was in here—' she laid a hand over her heart '—was just for you, because it was safer for a man to keep himself to himself.'

He nodded. 'And she lured me out,' he said in a wondering voice. 'That was one reason that I loved her.' He gave a half smile and tried the word again. 'Love. I wouldn't say it because it made losing her so much worse, but with her I talked about things I'd never spoken of before.'

'*He never shut up,*' said Sapphire grumpily in her head, '*just because I once said, Tell me all about yourself. I mean, it's only a come-on. I always said it to flatter men. But he took it literally.*'

'Then that was something she gave you,' Polly said gently. 'You're better for knowing her. And you'll always have it—unless you slip back to being grim and taciturn.'

'Which I was doing,' he mused. 'Until you took me by the scruff of the neck and yanked me back.'

Averting her head slightly, she made a face. Sapphire enticed. Polly yanked by the scruff of the neck. There it was—the truth about them. But at least it would stop her getting sentimental and foolish.

'Why are you laughing?' he asked.

'Never mind. You wouldn't see the joke. Besides, it's not really funny. Ah, here's Leo with our food.'

She changed the subject, chatting about his parents, and how Matti was ruling the roost, but speaking in a casual way that put no pressure on him.

'He's made himself at home, then?' Ruggiero asked. 'Put his feet up, so to speak, and now he's monarch of all he surveys?'

'That's exactly right—especially with your father. He's Toni's special pet.'

A strange look came over Ruggiero's face.

'Ah, yes,' he murmured. 'At last he's got a grandchild.'

'At last? He already has plenty of them by your brothers, doesn't he?'

'No, they're my mother's grandchildren, not his. Primo was her stepson in her first marriage, Luke was adopted, Justin and Francesco are hers, but not Poppa's. Of course they're all family, and Toni loves them because he has a great heart, but only Carlo and I are his actual sons. Carlo's wife is too frail to risk children, so that just leaves me.'

Suddenly Ruggiero sat back in his chair, transfixed.

'No wonder that little kid has taken Poppa by storm. Why didn't I see it before?'

There were a thousand answers, but the one that warmed Polly's heart was that out of the turmoil of feeling that had invaded Ruggiero in the last few days had come a new and generous understanding of his father.

'I'll give you another reason,' she said, smiling. 'Matti looks like him. We've all been staring into that little face, trying to decide whether he resembles you or his mother, but actually it's Toni.'

'You're right! I should have noticed that.'

'Maybe you need to stand back a bit to see things clearly?' she said, giving the words two meanings.

He nodded. 'Maybe.'

'Eat your food before it gets cold.'

'Yes, Nurse.'

# CHAPTER SEVEN

As THEY ate Polly studied him. He might only have been starving for two days but it looked more like a week. What had happened while he'd been shut up alone with those photographs and his pitifully few memories?

And then she knew why he hadn't wanted to come to this place.

Her cousin was there in her mind again, as she'd been in the last few weeks of her life, giving one of her cruel monologues in a voice that had begun to rasp.

*'He used to talk about how we'd go to Naples together and he'd take me to this little fish restaurant he part-owned. He said he'd show me off to all his friends—as if I wanted to be displayed to a load of fishermen! No, thank you! He thought he was really something, but he didn't have a clue.'*

That was why he hadn't wanted to bring Polly here. In his mind it was reserved for Sapphire. He'd never known that she'd appreciated him only for his skill in bed. When he'd grown sentimental she'd despised him.

Get out, she told the evil imp in her head. You don't deserve him.

But the imp was clever. She changed, becoming beautiful again.

*'And you think you do?'* she jeered. *'Do you think you'll take him from me by mothering him? I know what he wants from a woman, and it isn't that.'*

I'll free him from you, no matter what I have to do.

Sapphire vanished, sulking, as she'd always done when she didn't get her own way easily.

'Are you all right?' Ruggiero asked. 'You went strange all of a sudden.'

'Yes, everything fine. This food is good. Tell me, did you ever go into work?'

'Yes, but after the first day I realised I wasn't ready.'

'And you always meant to come back to your apartment. That's why you took the pictures of Sapphire.'

He avoided answering this directly, but gave her a curious look.

'Do you know that you just called her Sapphire?' he asked. 'It was always Freda before.'

'I didn't realise. Well, it's awkward if we're using different names.'

But that wasn't the reason, she knew. Freda had gone. Only Sapphire existed now. Increasingly she had the feeling that her enemy was taking shape before her, ready for a fight that was inevitable.

'I'm not a very good host,' he said with a faint smile. 'When a man takes a woman for dinner he should talk about her—her eyes, her face…'

'You try that and I'll make you sorry,' she threatened, her eyes gleaming.

'Ah, yes. Brian wouldn't like it.'

'*I* wouldn't like it. I'm here to look after you. Your mother hired me as your nurse, and I'm going to earn my salary.'

'My mother's *paying* you?' he asked, in a voice that sounded surprised and not entirely pleased.

'Certainly. I'm providing a service and she's paying the going rate. Well, more than the going rate, if I'm honest, but that only means I have to be more conscientious about doing my job.' A burst of inspiration made her add, 'Brian's very pleased. Getting married is expensive, and we're neither of us earning much yet, so the longer this job goes on the better he likes it.'

'Even though it takes his heart's desire away from him? Why do you make that face?'

'Why do you say such silly things?'

'Aren't you his heart's desire?'

'I'm English. We don't talk like that. Stop trying to make fun of me.'

'I didn't mean to. It's just that you never seem to come at the top of his list of priorities. He's not exactly burning with passion, is he?'

'I have no complaints,' she replied primly.

'But isn't he bothered by the time we spend together? Why isn't he here, threatening me with dire retribution if I dare lay a hand on you?'

Her lips twitched.

'For three reasons,' she said. 'First, I've assured him that you're an invalid who couldn't lay a hand on a rag doll. Second, if you tried I'd knock you into the middle of next week. And third, I'm getting good money to put up with you.'

Ruggiero joined in her laughter.

'Completely unanswerable,' he conceded. 'So I don't have to feel I'm imposing on your kindness if I ask another favour?'

'What favour?'

'Come back with me now, and fill in some more of the blanks.'

'If I can remember,' she hedged.

'I think you can remember everything, and you must tell me whatever I ask. Promise me that?'

Luckily he didn't wait for her answer, but called Leo and rose to leave.

True to her promise, she tried to pay for the meal. But Ruggiero scowled until she gave up, and they left with his arm around her shoulder.

'You don't mind propping me up, Nurse?' he asked lightly.

'Not at all,' she said, matching his tone. 'I shall put it down as overtime.'

Once in the apartment, he took out the albums and laid them on the table between them.

'Have you spent these last days going through these?' Polly asked gently

'Stupid, isn't it? I turned off the radio and television, made no calls, shut out the world in every way I could so that I could be alone with her. But—' He sighed.

'Ruggiero, don't you realise that I could say anything? How will you know what to believe?'

'Because I trust you,' he said simply.

'But how do you know that you can?'

He shook his head. 'I can't tell you that—just that all my instincts say that you're one of the most honest people I've ever met. I trust you as I'd trust my own family. I'd risk my life on your word.'

It was a crushing responsibility, but if she ducked it she couldn't help him, and that was all that mattered. Nor must he guess how she felt about him. Because that would compromise trust and make her useless. Thank goodness for 'Brian', she thought.

'I'll do my best,' she said. 'I probably knew her better than anyone because I lived with her for years. This picture here—' she flipped back to the beginning '—that's my parents, that's Sapphire's parents, and the two little girls are us. It was a sort of joint birthday party. She was seven and I was eight. My mother died two weeks later in a car accident. 'My dad couldn't cope, so they took me in. It was meant to be temporary, but Dad died a couple of years later, so I stayed on.'

'What did he die of?' Ruggiero asked.

'Pneumonia.'

'I thought doctors could cure that?'

'Mostly, yes. But people still die if they're weak enough to start with. He'd been fading away for a while. He never got over losing Mum.'

After a short silence he said, 'Go on.'

'It was a happy sort of life. There was no money, but we were all fond of each other. People used to say that she was the pretty one and I was the brainy one. Well, she wasn't academic, but she was sharp. All the other kids wanted to be her friend, and I was so proud because she chose me.'

Polly gave a reminiscent chuckle.

'It was a while before it dawned on me that she'd hit on the perfect way of getting me to do her homework.'

His grin lightened the sadness in his face and gave her a moment of happiness.

'I was flattered. I became her willing slave. But she gave full value in return. The others in the gang would have left me out of things. Children don't give you any points for being brainy. But she saw that I was included.'

'How old were you there?' he asked, pointing at the two of them in sequined dresses.

'I was sixteen, she was fifteen, and we're dressed alike because it was the school concert and we did a singing act. I remember that while the rest of us were struggling with teenage acne she was already beautiful. Lord, but we all hated her!'

He frowned. 'You mean the other girls bullied her?'

'Don't make me laugh! We didn't *bully* her. We just seethed helplessly in the background. Mostly she didn't notice, but when she did she loved it. It was a kind of tribute. She knew her own power even then.'

'Her power,' he murmured. 'Yes, I remember that.'

'She had only to snap her fingers and fellers would fall at her feet. It was like a spell she cast—over women, too. You couldn't even hate her when she pinched your boyfriends.'

'Plural?'

'Oh, yes. I used to refuse to take them home because they'd take one look at her and collapse. Then I realised that they'd only tagged along with me hoping to get close to her.'

'But you couldn't blame her for that?'

'Of course not. It was natural to her—like breathing. And in a way I enjoyed it too. She was like a queen, and everyone who knew her was in the magic circle.'

He turned the page and stopped at a picture of the two girls and an awkward-looking young man. He had his arm about Polly's shoulder, but his eyes were on Sapphire. Polly was regarding him with almost a glare.

'Who's that?'

'That was my fiancé,' Polly declared with a touch of tartness. 'And this picture must have been taken at the exact moment he started to have doubts. I was madly in love with him—at least I thought I was. She just—I don't know—smiled at him. And suddenly he was hers.'

'She probably didn't even know she was doing it,' he remarked.

Oh, she knew all right, Polly thought. She didn't even want him. He was too poor to really interest her, but she couldn't bear the sight of a man who hadn't fallen under her spell.

But she and Sapphire had declared a truce for tonight so she only said, 'You're probably right. It hurt a lot at the time, but I don't think she realised.'

'And yet you cared for her when she was ill?'

'I'm a nurse. Looking after people is something you learn to separate from your feelings or opinions.'

'I should have realised that. So what happened to this man? Did you get him back? Is he the one you're engaged to now?'

Polly gave a soft chuckle. 'Heavens, no! Why would I want him after that?'

'You couldn't forgive?'

'It wasn't a question of forgiveness. I just couldn't take him seriously again.'

'You thought, How can I be interested in a man who's shown himself such an idiot?' Ruggiero said lightly.

'Well, I think my so-called "love" was only a juvenile crush, so it died very easily when he fell off his pedestal.'

'How lucky that you found Brian, a man of good sense. How did you meet him, by the way? In the hospital?'

'Yes.'

'Was it love at first sight?'

'No, of course not,' she said sharply.

'Why do you say it like that?'

'I don't believe in love at first sight. It's just a sentimental myth.'

'Maybe it is,' he said thoughtfully. 'Or maybe not.'

He met her eyes, and for a moment the air was full of the things she couldn't say.

*Don't you know by now that it's just a myth? If any man should have learned that, it's you.*

But the words were too cruel to speak.

And in that moment she knew what she was going to do. If a kind lie was needed to make him happy, then she would tell that lie. It might not be the path of virtue, but that mattered less than nothing beside the need to bring him some inner peace.

'The thing was,' Polly said carefully, 'that she attracted so much love that it was easy to envy her without seeing what she didn't have. She knew something was missing—or at least she'd begun to suspect—and I think inside her she was looking for that something. Maybe she found it with you. I hope so.'

'Did I make her happy?' he asked quickly. 'Did she say so?'

'Yes. She said you were different to the others—kinder.'

What she'd actually said was, *'Honestly, Polly, it was so easy it was boring. I mean, he was a hot-blooded Italian. I thought at least he'd give me a run for my money. But he just collapsed at my feet like the others.'*

'Kinder,' he murmured. 'I'm glad. She needed kindness so much.'

'What makes you say that?'

'On the surface she had everything. But there was a vulnerability about her that I'll swear nobody else had seen, and that drew me to her almost more than her beauty.'

*'Men love to think a woman is frail. Just let your voice break a bit, and they fall for it every time. It makes them feel good.'*

'But is it kind to delude them?' Polly had asked.

*'Kind? Is the world kind? Look at what's happening to me. My looks have gone and I'm dying. Is that kind? You have to use anything that works.'*

Kind. Was it that echo that had made her use that word now? It had been chance, but the way he'd seized on it had revealed a new vista.

'You said she might have found what she was looking for with me,' Ruggiero said after a while. 'Did she ever say anything to make you think so?'

'She kept her secrets,' Polly said gently. 'There were things she didn't know how to say. But when she talked about you there was a special note in her voice.'

It had been derision, but he needn't know that.

'Are there any other pictures? From the last year?'

'No, she wouldn't allow that. She wanted to be remembered at her best. This one here is the very last.'

It showed Sapphire holding her child, her cheek resting caressingly against the baby's. The illness had made her thinner, but not yet ravaged her, and she was as beautiful as she had ever been in her life. Ruggiero looked at it for a long time.

'It's late,' Polly said. 'I have to go.'

'Don't go,' he said quickly. 'I have a spare room.' He smiled briefly. 'I'm afraid you might not come back.'

'I'll come back tomorrow if you want me to.'

'No, stay. There's a lot more I want to ask you. And don't worry—you're quite safe. I won't do anything that would bring Brian's wrath down on my head.'

Of course not. Because she wasn't the right woman. She was a lot safer than she wanted to be.

Polly called the villa, spoke to Hope and found, as she'd expected, that Matti was safely in bed.

'Not that it was easy,' Hope complained. 'My husband was playing with him and they were like two babies together. I had to get firm with both of them.'

Polly chuckled. 'All right. I'll leave well alone.'

'You stay there and take care of the other one,' Hope said enigmatically.

'Don't worry. I will.'

Ruggiero showed her the room.

'I've got a shirt if you need something to wear,' he said.

'Thanks, but I have everything I need.' She pointed to her bag.

'But I thought—'

'A good nurse always comes prepared. I could do with some tea.'

'Yes, Nurse.'

She came out a few minutes later to find the tea ready, along with a snack of ham and melon. While they ate she entertained him with tales of the childhood she and Sapphire had shared. It was easier to make her cousin sound sympathetic this way, for in those days her charm had yet to develop its ruthless edge.

Ruggiero laughed at some of the stories and sat contentedly through the rest, sometimes nodding, as if to say that this was what he'd waited to hear.

It was one in the morning before she yawned and said, 'Enough for now.'

'Forgive me for keeping you up so late. And thank you.'

He laid a gentle hand on her arm, nodded, and left her.

Polly put on her pyjamas and got into bed, sitting up and staring into the darkness with her hands clasped around her knees. She had a vague feeling of disappointment that she could not explain.

Sapphire was there in her head—so vivid that Polly could almost see her.

*'Now do you get it?'* she said contemptuously. *'All he wants is the pretty fantasy. Which means he's chosen me.'*

'He needs more time. He'll face the truth later.'

*'How, when you're never going to tell it to him? He doesn't want to hear it. He's not brave enough.'*

'That's true,' Polly agreed sadly.

*'Then I've won.'*

'I guess you have.'

Sapphire gave her luxurious, self-satisfied smile.

'Oh, push off!' Polly said crossly.

Sapphire vanished.

She lay down, listening to the soft sounds of night-time life coming from the harbour until at last she fell asleep.

She was awoken by a hand shaking her gently but urgently. Staring into the gloom, she saw Ruggiero, looking urgently into her face.

'Polly, please wake up.'

She pulled herself up, using him for support, then rubbed her eyes.

'I'll set Brian onto you,' she said through a yawn.

'No need. That's not what I'm here for.'

That was the story of her life. This dangerously attractive man appeared in her room, sitting on her bed, and was she wearing a sexy nightie? No way. She was in austere pyjamas with sensible buttons that came up high. She checked to see if the top button had come undone, but it hadn't. She never had any luck.

'It's all right, you're decent,' he said, seeing the gesture and misunderstanding it. 'Don't worry.'

'I wasn't,' she sighed. 'Ruggiero, what's happened?'

In the darkness she knew that he was glaring.

'Let's say I've finally come to my senses,' he said harshly.

'What—exactly—do you mean?'

'Do you need to ask? Haven't you been waiting for me to let go of the damned fool fantasy and get real?'

He switched on her bedside light and showed her the album that he'd put on the bed before waking her.

'Here,' he said.

The book was open at a large, glossy picture of the bride and groom, standing just outside the church. The photographer had been an expert, and had caught every unappealing detail about the groom—including the fact that he was a good thirty years older than his bride, and at least five stone overweight.

Even that might not have mattered. Many an ugly man had won a woman's heart with love and kindness. But George Ranley's overflowing jowls showed only the greasy self-satisfaction of a man who was selfish, greedy, demanding, suspicious and thoroughly unpleasant.

'Look at her.'

Ruggiero pointed to where the bride was regarding her new husband with a look of adoration. 'Did you ever see so much love in a woman's face?'

'No,' Polly said cautiously.

'For *that thing*?' he asked, pointing contemptuously at George. 'The man's a pig, but she's looking at him like he's a god.'

'Well, it *was* their wedding. A bride is expected to...' Polly's voice faltered.

'It was an act,' he said. 'I wonder what she was really thinking at that moment.'

'Ruggiero—'

'Just as I wonder what she was thinking when she looked at *me* like that,' he finished quietly.

Polly was silent. There was nothing to say. After a while he spoke again, in a voice full of anguish.

'That was the look she wore for me—the look of a woman who's totally besotted with a man. And he believes it while what she's really thinking is that she's got the poor sap just where she wants him.'

Her heart ached. She'd wanted him to see the truth, but now it was happening she couldn't bear the hurt it would cause him.

'I expect he had a lot of money,' Ruggiero mused, almost casually.

'He was a multimillionaire.'

'Those jewels on her head? Real diamonds?'

'Nothing less. George had seized them back from his third wife.'

'Third?'

'Sapphire was the fourth.'

'Go on. Tell me the rest—and don't sugar it.'

'He desperately wanted a son, and none of the other wives

had ever got pregnant. He wouldn't admit that there might be a problem with himself, and kept divorcing them as "use-less".'

'Sapphire—Freda—didn't want to be divorced, so when he was away for a couple of weeks she went to London to find someone who would give her a child that she could pass off as his.'

'So she went cruising the bars, looking for a suitable candidate?' he said bitterly. 'I just happened to be there. How did I come to pull the short straw?'

'Your colouring is the same as George's used to be before he went bald, so he'd have been easier to convince. And when she discovered that you'd soon be leaving England it was a plus.'

He winced. A long time seemed to pass before he asked, in a low voice, 'She never cared for me at all, did she? Be honest, Polly.'

'I don't think she did.'

'I was just useful,' he said slowly, as though spelling it out would help him understand. 'When I'd served my purpose I was surplus to requirements. All that mystery that seemed so exotic and romantic was just an efficient way to make sure I couldn't spoil things by following her.'

'I'm afraid so.'

Suddenly he began to laugh. A cracked, bitter sound that was on the edge of madness. He lay back on the bed and laughed and laughed until Polly became scared for him.

'What's funny?' she asked, leaning over, taking his shoulders.

'I am,' he choked. 'It's a great joke. I'm the funniest idiot who ever tramped the streets hunting for something that didn't exist.'

He held her in return, looking up into her face.

'When she vanished I searched for her high and low. Once I'd watched her walk away, so I reckoned she was within walking distance, and I went to every nearby hotel. I described her a thousand times, but nobody knew her. I didn't shave or take any care of myself, and by the end of the week I must have looked like a down-and-out. I didn't eat, because to eat I'd have had to stop, and I couldn't bear to. Sometimes I didn't go back to the hotel at night.

'Finally I gave up, got blind, roaring drunk and ended up in a police cell. The next morning they threw me out and told me to stop bothering "decent people". After that I came home. But that wasn't the end of it. In my dreams I went on searching for her, always thinking she'd be around the next corner, but she never was. At last I realised that she wasn't anywhere, and the dreams stopped. The strange thing is that since I've known she was dead they've come back again. Sometimes I'm afraid to sleep in case I find myself chasing around corner after corner, always finding nothing.'

He sat up slowly, still holding onto Polly.

'I guess part of me has known the truth from the first moment, but I wouldn't let myself face it. Now I have, and I should be glad. If this is how it really was, then there's nothing for me to grieve about.'

Nothing except the end of an ideal. Neither voiced the thought, but it was there in the air between them.

'I don't understand,' Polly said at last. 'You've been looking at these pictures for days. Why has this happened now?'

'I don't know. As you say, I could have seen the truth in her face at any time. I guess I just wasn't ready before. I ducked and dived, and clung to what I wanted to believe—anything to avoid the reality.'

'But what do you think the reality is?' she asked carefully.

'That I'm a fool who fell victim to a clever woman because he was too stupid and conceited to see through her. She acted as though I were the one she'd spent her life waiting for. The only lover who could satisfy her, the one man who could make her life worth living. *Of course I believed her.* I was wide open for it. She must have seen me coming for miles.'

His voice was harsh with the scorn and derision he poured on himself. The more he'd believed in his dream, the more contempt and loathing he felt for himself now.

Polly couldn't bear it. She pulled him into her arms and held him tightly. He clasped her back, as though she were his only refuge. It wasn't the embrace of a lover, and he seemed completely unconscious of her lightly clad body, but he buried his face against her and she could feel him trembling.

In a sudden passion of tenderness she began to stroke his head. She knew it wasn't wise, but suddenly wisdom seemed an abomination when set beside his need. If this moment cost her the rest of her life she would pay the price gladly.

Ruggiero didn't draw away, which emboldened her to lay her cheek against his hair while her hands caressed his body, but only tentatively, half longing for him to sense her, half fearing it.

For a moment she grew still, waiting for his reaction, her heart thumping. If he would only reach for her—

But he didn't move. His body against hers was heavy and relaxed, his head lying against her shoulder in an attitude of contentment. She dropped her head, letting her lips lie against his hair.

He did not react, and something inside her seemed to hide away, weeping.

'Don't…' she murmured.

'What do you mean?'

'Don't be so hard on yourself.'

'It's better if I am. I've been easy on myself for too long. Now it's time to see things clearly. *Mio dio!* What a coward I've been!'

'You're not a coward. You just needed time. And you made

it. She was holding you trapped. The illusion was turning to poison and it would have destroyed you. Now you're free.'

'Free?' He echoed the word as though trying to understand it. 'Free.'

It had a hollow sound, as though it resonated only bleakly in his heart.

He drew back and looked at her for a moment.

'I needed you,' he said. 'Thank you.'

But you didn't notice I was here, she thought sadly. Not really.

# CHAPTER EIGHT

WHEN Ruggiero had gone Polly dozed fitfully, unable to sleep properly. Even Sapphire didn't manage to storm her way in. She tried, but now something was excluding her.

Polly awoke in the morning, wondering if she'd imagined the night before. But her hand could still feel where he'd gripped it in his as he declared his faith in her, and his need. He'd left immediately after that.

Just a handclasp, but it had left her burningly aware of every detail about him. The things she'd been trying not to think of—the strong, hard feel of him, the warmth of his body when it had lain against hers, all the things a good nurse was supposed to ignore—had all come surging back to her.

I'm not going to let this happen, she tried to tell herself. I'm not.

But it had already happened. It was too late to deceive herself about that. Last night she'd given in to weakness, allowing her tenderness to flare briefly into passion. If he'd responded she would have done all in her power to make him want her, to make love with him.

But he hadn't responded. He hadn't even been aware of the change in her. She tried to be glad about that, but against her will her flesh was reacting to her memories, growing hot, the skin beginning to tingle with need.

But the need wasn't just physical. His heart craved the help that only she could give, and it was her nature to be strong, reaching out to those who were vulnerable. If she'd met Ruggiero at any other time, when his macho mask was securely in place, she might not have seen behind it, and then she would never have been drawn to him.

Now he would always appear to her as she'd seen him first—stunned, troubled, cast adrift by events over which he had no control.

And if Sapphire had really been banished, mightn't there be a vacancy?

*Get real!* she lectured herself. *This hasn't turned you into a beauty, so don't think it.*

But her inner voice lacked conviction, and she hummed to herself in the shower.

She found Ruggiero in the kitchen.

'Come and have some breakfast,' he called, in a voice that was firm and cheerful.

'Fine, I could do with some,' she said, matching his tone. 'Can I help?'

'No, just sit at that table and I'll serve you.'

He watched as she went to the table and looked out at the bright harbour, already busy in the morning sun. He was watching for any sign of consciousness on her part, but there was nothing in her voice or her demeanour.

It had been his imagination. He'd lain in her arms, amazed at the sense of peaceful joy that had stolen over him, taking the consolation she'd offered.

But how much *had* she offered? Had he only imagined the way her hands caressed him, her kiss against his hair? Recently he'd been so plagued by hallucinations that he dreaded to discover this was only another. He'd held still, waiting for her to do or say something that would tell him what to think.

But she'd only said, 'Don't be so hard on yourself.' Kind words, but those of a friend, not a lover.

He'd pulled himself together, swallowing something that felt strangely like disappointment. Now he had to do it again.

'How are you feeling after that disturbed night?' he asked, sitting opposite her at the table.

'A bit confused.'

'That's my fault. I've been giving you a hard time. But no longer. We got everything sorted out, didn't we?'

'I suppose so.'

She spoke cautiously, and he smiled, assuming a firm, efficient voice.

'Don't worry. I've got things in perspective. I don't know what took me so long.'

A faint uneasiness began to stir in Polly's brain. This clear-sightedness was surely what she'd wanted, and yet—

Misunderstanding her worried look, he said, 'It's all right, Polly. It's all over. She's gone. After all, she never actually existed, did she?'

Irrationally she wanted to say, *She existed in your heart,* but she was lost for words. She should be glad of his recovery. Instead she felt a creeping dismay that made no sense.

'Freda existed. Sapphire didn't,' she agreed.

'She was an invention—a role she'd decided to play. But then the curtain came down, the heroine vanished, and the idiot was left alone on the stage, not realising that the performance was over.'

'Don't call yourself names,' she said firmly.

'You're right, it's boring.'

'That wasn't—'

'Did I try your patience very hard?'

She shook her head. 'You had something beautiful and I was taking it away. I don't blame you for wanting to hold onto it.'

'Except that it wasn't beautiful,' he said with a shrug. 'It was stupid and dishonest, and it made me weak. I won't let *that* happen again.'

The way he emphasised 'that' increased her unease.

'There's nothing wrong with a little weakness if it means needing people,' she said. 'Trying to be self-sufficient all the time just leads to trouble.'

'You said something like that to me the first time we met,' he remembered wryly. 'In fact you've always had a pretty poor opinion of me. And you were right. I finally stood outside and got a good look at myself. *Mio Dio!* What a sight! But no more. I've got a job to do, and with your help I'm going to do it.'

'A job?'

'I have to learn to be a father to my son.'

The words should have made her rejoice, but she was struck by the cool efficiency of his manner—as though he were ticking off tasks on a worksheet. His love, once so sweet to him, had been revealed as a con-trick—to be dismissed along with the side of his nature that was capable of those feelings. Now his relationship with his son was the next assignment on the list.

She shivered.

'I'd better start with some toys, hadn't I?' he said. 'What does he like?'

'Cuddly things. I don't know what Italian shops sell.'

'Fine, we'll go shopping. That means a taxi. What a pity my car's still at the villa.'

'Makes no difference. I wouldn't let you drive it.'

'Wouldn't *let* me—?'

'Nope. And wipe that outraged look off your face, because it's wasted on me. You've fallen into the hands of a real bully now.'

'I think I'd already guessed that. All right, a taxi it is.'

In the city centre they found a large toy shop and explored it from top to bottom. Polly's mood soared. The day was bright, the sun high in the sky, and his manner was engaging. Surely she was worrying about nothing?

'Why are you looking at me?' he asked once. 'Wait—let me guess. It's the first time I haven't been scowling at you.'

'I ignore scowls. It's just the first time I've seen you looking cheerful,' she teased.

He grinned and put an arm around her shoulder, moving carefully for he was still sore.

'Let's spend some money,' he said.

This wasn't what she wanted from him, but it was a start. And spending money proved to be as enjoyable as she'd always heard it was.

The toys were dazzling. And an array of magnificent teddy bears rose high on the shelves, making Polly sigh with longing.

'They're so beautifully made it seems almost criminal to give them to a child who'll pull them about,' she mourned.

She selected a fluffy bear with golden fur, about a foot high with large, mournful eyes.

Ruggiero plunged into the important business of explaining his needs to an assistant. Polly couldn't follow the words but she gathered he was doing everything methodically, giving precise specifications—just as if he were ordering spare parts for the factory, she thought.

But he was doing his best, and she appreciated that.

When she saw the collection he'd amassed she stared.

'They're for children developing hand-eye co-ordination,' he explained. 'He can pull this one along behind him, and he also has to fit the shapes into the right holes. With this one he presses buttons with animal pictures, and it makes noises.'

'What kind of noises?'

'Animal noises. Moo and cluck.'

To demonstrate he pressed the cow button and the cow mooed.

'Let me try,' she said, entranced, pressing the chicken button. A horse neighed.

'That's not right,' she said. 'That should be a chicken.'

Ruggiero experimented and the same thing happened. He tried the horse button, and a duck quacked. An assistant bustled over, looking concerned.

'Houston, we have a problem!' Polly intoned.

Commotion followed. The staff took out toy after toy, pressing buttons to see if they made the right noises—which they didn't. The shop was filled with the sounds of a barnyard. Passers by stopped and stared in.

The manager was called. He too pressed buttons, without receiving the right sounds in return.

'It's a new consignment,' he wailed. 'They must all be faulty.'

'Do you have anything of the same kind?' Polly asked.

Luckily a similar toy had just come in, based on wild animals, which turned out to be properly connected. Lions roared like lions, elephants trumpeted like elephants, baboons gibbered. Everyone was happy, if slightly hysterical.

'We'll take this one,' Ruggiero said with relief. 'And these.' He indicated all the other toys that he'd collected.

'Aren't some of them a bit complicated for a toddler?' Polly asked.

'Maybe not. Maybe he's brighter than we all think.'

'Of course he'd bound to be a genius with such a father,' she said caustically, and he smiled.

He then tried to carry them all out of the shop—which was mistake since neither his ribs nor his shoulder were ready.

'We need to call a taxi from the nearest firm,' she said.

'Nonsense. I'll be all right in a minute. We just have to pick one up outside.'

Polly didn't waste time answering this. Instead she turned to an assistant and tried to request him to telephone for a taxi. After some confusion he understood.

'Why didn't you help?' she asked Ruggiero.

'Because I was having too much fun watching you.' He added provocatively, 'You must allow me a few innocent pleasures.'

'I've just remembered I forgot to bring your pills with me,' she observed casually.

His horrified stare was very satisfying. He wasn't the only one who enjoyed innocent pleasures.

When the taxi drew up at the villa Hope came flying out, eager to see them, but even more eager to tell her news.

'Carlo and Della are here,' she said, bursting with excitement. 'Della was a little tired, so they came home early.'

Polly recognised Carlo from his picture in the paper. He was a big man with gentle manners that charmed her. He shook Polly's hand warmly.

'I've wanted to meet you ever since I heard what you did for this one,' he said, inclining his head to his twin. 'Not that I can see why anyone should bother to save his miserable life—'

'Get lost,' Ruggiero said amiably.

'I didn't save his life,' Polly hastened to disclaim.

'The way I heard it you tore onto the track and bore him off to safety. Anyway, I'm grateful. I've kind of got used to having him around, and he has his uses.'

Ruggiero grinned, evidently accepting this manner of talking as normal. Carlo brought forward his wife, his arm protectively about her. She was an elegant woman, with such a slight build that she almost seemed to vanish against him. It was clear that she was several years older than her husband, and her frailty showed in her face, but her eyes were bright and sparkling with life, and she hugged Polly with delight.

'As soon as I heard about you and Matti I made Carlo bring me home,' she said. 'We don't often have a sensation like this.'

'Careful, *cara*,' Carlo said, still with his arm around her.

'I'm all right—stop fussing,' she chided him in an under-voice, but she smiled as she spoke, and he didn't remove his arm.

It was pleasant to watch this pair of lovers. The bond between them was shining, complete, and Carlo's care of his wife seemed to bring him a quiet joy that Polly found moving. Glancing at Ruggiero, she found that his eyes, too, were fixed on them, and there was a sadness in his face that was at variance with his earlier cheerful demeanour.

Then, as if his mind was wide open to her, she saw that he thought this was how it might have been between himself and Sapphire if she'd reached out to him in her illness. Instead she'd waited until she was dead before letting him know, so that she didn't have to be bothered with him. Put like that it was cruel, brutal. But it was the truth, and her heart ached for what it did to him.

Then he caught her eye, and the grin was swiftly back in place.

'A great couple, my brother and his wife,' he said. 'You'll like them.'

But just as she could read his mind, he could read hers, and he hastened to say, 'It's all right. I told you—it's in the past. Where's my son?'

Toni was there with Matti in his arms, pointing to Ruggiero and saying, 'Poppa.' He came to stand a few inches away from Ruggiero, and stood surveying his son, while his son surveyed his own son cautiously. Matti regarded them both with aplomb.

Finally he delivered his opinion, turning and putting an arm about his grandfather's neck, and closing his eyes.

'Now I know where I stand,' Ruggiero said c--
son is bored by me.'

'Try a toy,' Polly suggested, and nudged Matti with the teddy until he opened his eyes. 'Here.'

She put it into his hands. He dropped it on the floor.

'Careful—it's so lovely,' she said, lifting the bear and offering it again.

He tossed it back onto the floor.

'Let's see if I do any better,' Ruggiero said, turning to the bags that contained the toys.

Toni set Matti down on the floor and watched as one toy after another was displayed to him. He immediately chose the trolley, causing Ruggiero to cast a look of triumph at Polly, and began staggering across the floor with it. At the fourth step he sat down and gave a yell of annoyance, then immediately got to his feet again and staggered forward some more. This time he managed five steps before sitting down, and everyone applauded.

*'Un miracolo,'* Toni said in delight. 'What a child!'

Suddenly there was a glad cry, and someone shouted, 'Look who's here.'

The next moment Luke and Minnie came into the room.

Hope ran towards them, arms outstretched. 'You made it!' she cried.

'It's only a hundred and fifty miles to Rome,' Luke said. 'Nothing to a brilliant driver.'

'So you think you're a brilliant driver?' his mother challenged him.

'I meant her,' Luke said, indicating his wife. 'She's a better driver than I am—as she'd be the first to tell you.'

were Primo and Olympia, eager to join the Polly gathered her things and prepared to detained her.

e of your new clothes,' she said. I bought them for you.'

'But that's because they're so fine,' Polly protested. 'And I've been working.'

'Yes, and jeans and sweater were all right for that, but this is different. Now, please go and put on one of the dresses I bought you—the green one, I think.'

Polly hurried upstairs to put on the dress—which, she had to admit, suited her. Hope had an unerring eye for colour and fashion, and the green silk was quietly elegant in a way that suited Polly's gentle looks.

She was glad of it when she returned downstairs and saw that she could hold her own with the prosperous, well-dressed Rinuccis. Even so, she was glad to stay in the background, simply keeping a careful eye on Matti, who was centre-stage, charming everyone, especially Carlo and Della, who hadn't met him before.

A pleasant feeling was beginning to steal over her. This was a family as she had always dreamed of families. With such people there could be no loneliness such as there was in her own life. Matti would be safe and happy with them.

At last they all sat down to eat supper at the big table, and she felt the magic circle enclosing her too. Ruggiero caught her eye across the table, grinned, and embarked on the story of the toyshop. She joined in, making animal noises where necessary, to everyone's delight. In the exchange of witticisms that followed Ruggiero reminded her that she'd once threatened to knock him into the middle of next week.

At this the whole family roared their laughing approval, and Polly was sure she heard some applause. Hope even grasped her hand, saying, 'That settles it. You must marry him and keep him in order.'

Perhaps Polly had drunk a little more wine than usual, or she might not have dared to laugh and say, in a teasing voice, 'I'm not sure I want a man I have to keep in order. It might be boring.'

'Or it might not,' Ruggiero murmured over the rim of his glass. 'Think of the fights we'd have.'

'Non-stop,' she agreed. 'You risking your neck with some tomfool nonsense, me trying to prevent you, you growling, "Stop making a fuss, woman."'

'Then you hitting me over the head—'

'You make it sound irresistible.'

Everyone laughed again, and the joke was allowed to die. But something had changed. Whether by chance or design Hope had mentioned marriage between them, and that word would lodge in everyone's brain. As, perhaps, she had meant it to.

After supper Polly glanced at the clock. It was Matti's bedtime, but nobody wanted to let him go and she relented.

He was giving a performance—going through his new toys, dealing with the 'difficult' ones with a skill that had Ruggiero grinning as triumphantly as though he'd achieved a personal success—as, in a sense, he had.

Matti was at ease with the shapes, pushing one then another into the right holes to loud applause. Ruggiero was looking pleased with himself, and with his son.

He's cracked it, Polly thought. It was going to be so difficult, but then suddenly he found the way to get on Matti's wavelength. Or Matti found the way. Make his father proud of him, that's the secret, and he got there at once. The others all adore him. He really doesn't need me now, and soon it'll be time for me to go.

She felt a pang of dismay, and not only at the thought of leaving Ruggiero. She loved Matti too, but now he was dismissing her as no longer needed. Perhaps he'd inherited that iron-willed trait from his mother? she thought sadly.

In this mood, she was totally unprepared for what happened next.

Matti was playing with the trolley, pushing it back and

forth until suddenly it went over onto its side. He made a grab at it, tried to haul it upright, and failed. A little choke of distress burst from him.

'Never mind,' Ruggiero said. 'I'll do it.'

But Matti didn't seem to hear him. It was as though the tectonic plates of his world had shifted. A minor hiccup that he'd laughed off hours earlier was now a major disaster. His choke turned into a wail, growing louder and louder until it became a scream that went on and on in pitiful agony.

'He's over-tired,' Polly said. 'He doesn't normally stay up this late.'

She had to raise her voice to be heard above the child.

'Shall I try putting him to bed?' Ruggiero asked.

But when he reached out Matti fended him off.

'Mummy!' he screamed. *'Mummy!'*

'It's you he wants,' Ruggiero said.

'No, not me,' Polly said sadly. 'I'm not his mother. Freda was, and she's the one he's crying for.'

She dropped down to one knee, trying to take Matti in her arms, but he lashed out, arms flailing in all directions, until one of them caught her a stinging slap across the face, which made him howl louder.

*'Mummy—Mummy—MUMMEEEE—'*

'Doesn't it help that he knows you?' Ruggiero asked desperately. 'He must be close to you, too.'

'Yes, but he wants his mother, nobody else.'

By now Matti had lain down on the floor, pounding the hard tiles and shrieking, *'Mummy! Mu-mmy! MUMMEEEE—'*

Polly raised him, going to the sofa and sitting down with him on her lap. She was ready to dodge another blow, but there was none this time, and the little boy simply collapsed against her, sobbing in helpless despair.

Polly rocked back and forth, shattered by the suddenness

of his collapse, and frightened by what she felt happening deep inside herself. The child's grief seemed to reach into her, awakening her own, tearing her apart. At last something broke in her, and she too began to weep. She tried to keep control, but the tears streamed down her face, mingling with Matti's tears.

'I'm sorry, darling,' she choked. 'I'm so sorry. I know I'm not the one you want. I know—I know—'

'Mummy,' he wailed softly, his face buried against her.

'I wish I could have kept her alive for you—I did all I could—I did try—but I couldn't—I couldn't—'

She gave up and dropped her head, so that her cheek rested against his hair while anguish welled up inside her and over-flowed. At this moment she no longer remembered the self-centred predator who'd used her beauty without scruple. She saw Freda as she'd been in the last months her beauty gone, her life slipping away, her eyes filled with fear—and she was consumed by love and pity.

The family exchanged appalled looks, and the women began to move closer to where they could reach out and offer comfort. But Ruggiero stopped them with a gesture, and it was he who went to Polly and dropped down on one knee beside her, resting a hand on her arm. He didn't speak, but he stayed like that while she tried vainly to control the violence of her feelings.

'Polly,' he said gently. 'Look at me.'

She shook her head. She didn't want anyone to see her face.

'All right,' he said. 'But let's take him to bed.'

She nodded, unable to speak.

'Come on,' he said, urging her to her feet.

The others stood back as she rose with Matti in her arms and left the room, guided by Ruggiero. Hope gave him a nod of approval as he passed.

When they reached her room he opened the door, standing back while she carried the child in.

'I'm all right,' she choked, sitting down on the bed.

He took a paper handkerchief from a box and used it to dab her face. She pulled herself together by force.

'You're still crying,' he said.

'No, I'm not,' she gasped, through a new bout of sobs.

He didn't answer, but sat beside her, his arms about the woman and child, listening to their mingled weeping, saying nothing, waiting until they were ready, however long it might take.

## CHAPTER NINE

AT LAST Polly's shoulders stopped shaking and she managed to grow calmer.

'I'm all right now,' she said.

He didn't believe for a moment that she was all right. She was pretending because she refused to think of herself. He wondered just how often she did think of herself.

But all he said was, 'Let's put him to bed.'

She looked down at where Matti lay in her arms, calmer, but still weeping quietly, and kissed him.

'Come along, darling.'

'Where do you keep his night things?' Ruggiero asked.

'In that drawer.'

He drew out some clothes and watched while she undressed Matti and changed him.

'Why don't you help me put on his night suit?' she said.

But he shook his head.

'He doesn't want a stranger right now. You're all he has to cling to.'

He pulled back the covers for her as she laid Matti into the cot. He was asleep almost at once.

'And now he's as good as gold,' Ruggiero mused, looking down at him.

'He's always as good as gold,' Polly said quickly. 'That wasn't a tantrum. He was confused and miserable because he's missing his mother, and he screamed at the world because that's all a toddler knows how to do.'

'Not just a toddler,' Ruggiero said. 'Isn't that what I've been doing—screaming at the world? Only I don't have his excuse. I told you, I don't like the sight of myself right now.'

He touched the tiny hand lying outside the cover.

'Maybe he and I can help each other,' he murmured. 'We seem to speak same language after all.'

'I should have seen it coming,' Polly said regretfully. 'So much has happened to the poor little mite—'

'But what about you?' he asked, looking at her.

'I'm all right,' she repeated, but already the tears were sliding down her cheeks again. 'I don't know why—just—suddenly—'

'It was bound to happen. You've had to be strong for a long time, but nobody can be strong for ever.'

'I'm a nurse. Being strong is—is—what I do.'

'Even a nurse is human.'

'I'm used to looking after sick people,' she whispered. 'But when it's someone of your own, for months—I did want to help her—but it was beyond anything I could do. I watched, and tried to make it a little easier for her, but I never did any real good. I couldn't—I couldn't—'

It was happening again. As one wave retreated another engulfed her. She began to pace up and down, weeping, not looking where she was going until she found herself facing the wall and laid her head against it, unable to do anything else.

He was behind her at once, taking gentle hold of her, turning her to face him and putting his arms about her.

'Let it go,' he said. 'Don't fight it.'

She made a vague gesture, almost as if to draw back, but

he tightened his arms and then it seemed natural to let her head fall on his shoulder and give way to the grief she'd barely known that she felt.

She felt him drawing her towards the bed, sitting her down and sitting beside her. She seemed to have no energy left, and no hope—nothing but the misery that had consumed her without warning. She sobbed violently, no longer trying to master it.

Polly sensed that he'd turned his head to lay his cheek against her hair. But he made no other movement until the storm had quietened.

'I want you to tell me everything,' he said gently.

'But I already have. We've talked so much about her.'

'No, we've talked about me,' he said heavily. 'And Sapphire—what she was like, what she did to me. But you haven't told me what it was like for you.'

'That doesn't matter,' she said wildly.

'Do you really believe that? That your suffering doesn't matter? That *you* don't matter? Because that's not how I see it. You've got to tell someone or go crazy—and who should you tell but me, Polly?'

She made an incoherent noise.

'It works both ways,' he urged. 'We each know something nobody else knows, and that can't be brushed aside. Don't hide things any more. Tell me what happened at the end. How did it all come about? How did you find the strength to cope? And don't try to put me off by saying you're a nurse, because that's an excuse, not an answer.'

His insight surprised her.

But something held her silent. This was new territory. To be approached with caution, even a little fear. But his eyes were kind, as though he understood everything that was going through her mind.

'Go on,' he said.

Polly took a shaky breath.

'She was living in Yorkshire, in what George grandly called Ranley Manor, while I lived in south London, near the hospital where I worked. One evening she turned up at my door, holding Matti. George had thrown her out and I was the only close relative she had. That night she only told me that Matti wasn't George's child. The rest came later. At first we were quite happy. She was a good cook, and I ate better than I'd done for ages. Then she told me that she was "a little worried" about a symptom. I knew the truth straight away. I rushed her to the doctor but she'd already delayed too long. We explained that she needed treatment, but not how bad things were. She couldn't have borne to know the worst just then.

'The hospital did everything possible, but it was too late. She wouldn't give up hope. She'd say, "I'm getting better, Pol. I really am." The hardest thing —' She stopped, because the memory that was coming towards her was horrible. She couldn't face it. She could only flee in dread.

'What was the hardest thing?'

'No, it—it doesn't matter.'

'Yes, it does,' he said softly. 'Tell me.'

'Please don't ask me to,' she wept.

'Polly, you've got to deal with it, or it'll fester inside and poison you.'

'I can't—'

'Yes, you can—while I'm keeping you safe.'

He bent his head and kissed her tumbled hair.

'Tell me,' he said. 'Tell me now.'

'She trusted me so much because I was a nurse. She'd say, "I'm all right with you, aren't I, Pol? You're a nurse, you won't let me die." She'd make me keep saying it, because if I said it she knew it was true. *I didn't know what to do*—'

'But you said it, didn't you?' he said sombrely. 'You said what she wanted to hear.'

'I had to,' she said passionately. 'I didn't care if it was true as long as it gave her a little peace, and I lied and lied and lied.'

'Of course. You couldn't have done anything else. Did she believe you?'

'For a while. But in the end she knew, and I could see the fear growing in her eyes. At night she used to sob in my arms. By day she'd put on her bright smile and play with Matti. She was a good mother to him. She liked nothing better than to be with him, playing with him, and when she was too weak to play talking to him. That's why he started talking so soon.'

She drew back a little.

'I've told you the worst of her, but you should know the best too. She was a brilliant mother, and he'll always have that—the knowledge that his mother liked his company best in all the world. That's why her death is so terrible for him. He knows he's lost the loveliest thing he ever had.' She added, almost pleading, 'You should understand that feeling because you feel it too.'

'Not any longer.'

'But for him it's true, and it always will be.'

'What happened at the end?' he asked, not answering her directly.

'She had to go into hospital for the last three weeks. I'd take Matti in, and we'd spend as much time together as we could. When she died I took her back to Yorkshire, to be buried with her parents.'

'And then you came here?'

'Not at first. Matti and I went home, locked the door and stayed there for a couple of weeks. During that time I read the letter that gave me a rough idea where to find you.' A shudder went through her. 'I thought I had everything under control, and then suddenly—'

'It hit you out of the blue,' he said softly. 'When that happens it's terrifying, especially if you're a person who likes to be in control.'

'I guess you could say that about both of us,' she murmured.

'Yes, and it's worse for us because we've got no practice in being helpless,' he said with a touch of grim humour, adding, 'Although I may be learning.'

She gave a choke of laughter

'That's better,' he said, holding her face between his hands. 'No, you're not really laughing, are you? You've borne too much alone, but you're not alone now. I'm here, and I understand you as nobody else does—just as you understand me as nobody else does or ever will. We're a great team.'

She tried to smile, but it came out wonky. The sight touched him painfully, and he drew her closer, kissing her cheeks, her eyes, her lips, thinking of nothing except consoling her.

Polly remained still in his hands, feeling the light touch of his lips with the force of a thunderclap.

'Out of the blue,' he'd said. 'Terrifying—'

His words had been strangely prophetic. There'd been no warning of this, no time to steel herself against temptation and the shock of desire. She could only sit there, helpless in his hands, a prey to the sweetest feelings she had ever known, while he kissed her as if oblivious to what he was doing.

She wasn't sure whether he tilted her face further towards him or whether she raised it herself, but his lips found hers and lay against them. For a moment her breath seemed to stop. There was something almost terrifying about being given something she wanted so much—like being transported to heaven without warning.

He kissed her again and again, while her heart pounded and she tried to think. But thinking was impossible. She wanted to move against him, to fit her head against his shoulder and let her lips caress his. Above all she wanted to entice him to explore her, as she longed to explore him.

Then perhaps they could lie back in each other's arms, neither quite knowing who'd made the first move, side by side, inciting each other to pleasure.

She wanted everything. Not just the love of his body but the love of his heart. And that she couldn't have. He'd offered friendship, but that was all. He was way out of reach and she would be foolish to read anything into this sweet moment. But it was hard when she wanted him so badly, and she could feel herself weakening. In another moment she would hurl caution to the winds and tell him she was his.

And then she would die of shame.

That thought gave her the strength to press her hand against him, making him raise his head and study her face, frowning.

'I'm fine now—honestly,' she said.

'You don't look fine,' he said gently. 'You look as if you're collapsing inside.'

She couldn't answer, only gave him a shaky smile. She tried to speak, to say wise and virtuous words about being sensible and stopping now. But they wouldn't come, and he drew her close again.

This time it was different. As his mouth touched hers again she knew she had no more strength. She could never make herself put a distance between them because she could never make herself want to.

There was a grunt from the cot.

She felt the breath go out of him. He tensed and looked up. The little cry came again.

The moment was over. She rose and went to Matti, not lifting him but leaning over and stroking his cheek until he quietened down.

Ruggiero watched them for a moment, then slipped quietly out of the room without speaking.

Polly awoke to find herself alone and the crib empty. Looking out of the window, she saw Hope and Minnie down in the garden, taking it in turns to spoon breakfast into Matti's mouth.

She was glad of the chance to think. Last night ideas and sensations had chased themselves around her brain in an endless circle that started and finished in the same place—with the feel of his lips on hers.

Out of it all only one thing was clear. Twice she'd come to the edge of betraying herself, and now she must recover lost ground. The chaos inside her must remain her secret.

By the time she went down for breakfast she had her mask securely in place. But it was needless. There was no sign of him.

'There you are,' Hope called, coming in from the garden. She was followed by Minnie, carrying the child.

'I crept in to take him so that you could sleep longer,' she said.

'Yes, I saw you out of the window.'

They settled on the terrace with coffee and rolls. Matti was completely recovered, shouting cheerfully at the top of his voice.

'Are you all right?' Hope wanted to know.

'Yes, I'm sorry for all the commotion.'

'Don't apologise. I just hope Ruggiero looked after you properly.'

'Oh, yes, he did.' After a moment she'd recovered her composure enough to say, 'Is he around?'

'He left for work. He'll be back tonight for supper.'

Glad to get away from her, she thought. It would be embarrassing for them to see each other too soon.

Toni appeared and greeted them. Matti waved his arms and made a sound that might, with a little imagination, be understood as, *'buongiorno'*.

'He's becoming bilingual already,' Toni said in delight.

'When I've gone he'll forget all his English,' Polly said.

'Not in this house,' declared Hope, patting her hand. 'That I would never allow. But you're not going for a long time yet. Don't tell me Brian is causing trouble? Let me talk to him and explain.'

'Oh, no—he's fine about everything.'

'Good, then it's settled. You'll stay a while yet.'

It had a pleasant sound. If only she could be sure that Ruggiero hadn't left early to avoid her.

The suspicion increased that evening, when he was late, arriving halfway through the meal and including her in a general greeting. Afterwards he spent most of his time talking to Luke and Minnie, which was only courteous as they were leaving next day, but Polly couldn't help feeling that there was another reason.

She wondered if she was getting paranoid. It might have been only her fancy that when their eyes happened to meet he looked away quickly. Or it might not.

When it was Matti's bedtime everyone came upstairs. Hope bathed him, but then Toni, who'd been watching with a gentle smile on his face, stepped forward.

'He wants his *nonno* to put him to bed,' he said, speaking English but using the Italian word for grandfather. 'That's right, isn't it?' he asked the tot. 'Because Nonno's your favourite.' In a confiding voice he added to Polly, 'He told me that. Mind you, I think he tells everyone the same.'

'I think he does,' she agreed, laughing.

With practised hands he fitted Matti's nappy onto him, eased him into his night suit and laid him gently into the cot. Hope and Ruggiero were standing just inside the room, watching and enjoying the sight of Toni, completely happy.

'*Buona notte, piccino,*' he said. '*Buona notte .*'

Everyone waited hopefully.

'Say it,' Toni pleaded. 'You managed *buongiorno* this morning.'

Matti merely gurgled.

'Goodnight, my little one,' Toni chuckled.

From his pocket he produced a small furry toy, which he tucked into the bed under Matti's hand.

'He used to say hallo,' Polly observed, smiling. 'It was the first word he managed. Now he says *ciao*!"

'He learns very quickly,' Hope said.

'Of course,' Ruggiero said in mock offence. 'He's my son. What else would you expect?'

He followed his father forward to kiss the child, looked at him for a moment, then left.

Minnie announced that she was going to bed, ready for an early start in the morning. There was a round of 'goodnights' and Ruggiero drifted away with the other men.

At last only Hope was left alone in the room with Polly. She was peering at the little toy that Toni had left there.

'Toni's really happy, isn't he?' Polly observed. 'I don't know when I've seen a man who doted so much on a child.'

Hope nodded. 'And his happiness makes me happy too,' she said. 'Little Matti has a special meaning for him.'

'Yes, Ruggiero told me that only he and Carlo are Toni's sons, and that Carlo is unlikely to have children because of his wife's health.'

'There's time for Ruggiero to have others,' Polly said.

'But will he? What does he tell you? Can he fall in love again?'

'Maybe. Or perhaps he'll have to find another kind of love—more contented but less glorious. And that could be hard. How could you be sure that—? How would you know that the time had come to give up hoping, and try to live without hi—the other person?'

'It's possible,' Hope said, watching her. 'If there has to be a parting, it helps if you know you're doing what is best for him. But be quite certain that all hope is lost. Don't give up without a fight. Now, *cara*, I must go to bed.' She kissed Polly's cheek. 'Don't stay up late.'

Ruggiero was late home again the next evening, and would have missed Matti's bedtime if Polly hadn't unaccountably forgotten all about it. It was Toni who remembered, and asked if they shouldn't be moving.

'There's no rush,' Polly said. 'He seems to be sleeping happily in your arms, so he won't lose anything if he stays up until his father comes home.'

Toni and Hope's eyes met, and a glance of understanding passed between them.

'You're a wise woman,' Hope said.

She didn't expand on this, but the warm approval in her voice was enough to remind Polly of the marriage joke from before, and she become self-conscious. It was clear that the Rinucci family was mounting a take-over bid for her—which would have been delightful if Ruggiero himself had wanted the same. But she was in confusion about what he wanted from her, and even what she wanted from him.

Could she marry him and live as second-best while another woman still held first place? She had a feeling that the question was growing dangerously near.

At last she heard his car arrive and went out to meet him.

'Matti was just complaining that you weren't here to put him to bed,' she called.

'Really? With the rest of you dancing attendance he actually noticed that I was missing?' he asked lightly.

Reinforcements appeared in the shape of Hope, with Toni and Matti behind her.

'At last,' Hope said.

'I've been away from work too long, and I have vital stuff to catch up with,' he said, a tad defensively.

'You have vital work here, with your son,' his mother said firmly. 'Get on with it and stop shilly-shallying.'

'Yes, Mamma. No, Mamma.'

'And don't be cheeky.' She bustled inside before he could answer.

'Will you please tell Mamma that I'm thirty-one, and grown-up now?' Ruggiero demanded wrathfully of his father.

'When you grow up, I'll tell her,' Toni promised. 'Now, take care of your son.'

Polly stayed back while Ruggiero put Matti to bed, watching but not interfering. He did everything properly now, including giving the child a final hug, tucking him up and kissing his cheek.

But she knew that something still hadn't fallen into place. He was like an actor who'd learned the lines and played the role perfectly, but his heart was missing.

She'd expected him to avoid the subject, but when he joined her in the garden later that night he surprised her by going straight to it.

'I'm still making a mess of it,' he said, coming to sit beside her on the porch step and sounding frustrated. 'Why? Tell me.'

'You're being too businesslike,' she said gently. 'And he knows. You can't fool him.'

'There must be a way to get it right.'

'There isn't one right way. There's a dozen. And you can't find them. You have to let them find you. It'll creep up on you, and then suddenly you'll realise that this is what works for you and him.'

He made a wry face, full of self-condemnation.

'That sounds easy, but it just doesn't happen.'

'You're trying too hard—watching yourself all the time to see if you've got it right, watching him to see if he's reacting as you want. Stop ticking boxes and let him show you the way.'

'I was hoping *you'd* show me the way.'

She shook her head. 'He's a much better guide than I am. He's such a warm-hearted little thing. He'll love you if you let him.'

'Maybe that's my problem. I'm no good with love—of any kind. I get confused. Why don't you give up on me? I'm a lost cause.'

*'Basta!'* she said, aiming a mock punch at his good shoulder. 'Enough, all right?'

'We'll make an Italian of you yet.'

'Yeah, sure. *Basta* is my one Italian word, and that's only because Matti has latched onto it. You should try saying it to him. He won't take any notice, any more than you would, but you'll be on each other's wavelength in no time.'

'I'll make a note.'

'Don't make a note,' she said, tearing her hair. 'He's not an item on your works schedule.' She took a deep breath, conscious of him giving her a quizzical look that was unsettling. 'I'll make things go right for you two or die in the attempt.'

He gave a laugh. 'Don't do that. How would I manage without you?'

'You're going to have to one day.'

'Yes, I am, aren't I?' he said, sounding almost as though he'd just discovered it. 'It just seems so natural, you being here—'

Ruggiero shook his head, puzzled at himself.

'I've never relied on anyone before. When I was a little kid, just learning to walk, holding onto an adult, I used to snatch my hand away at the first chance because I had to do it alone. Of course I fell flat more often than not. Carlo was the clever one. He'd hold on until he was quite sure. But I had to kick the world in the teeth to show I didn't need anyone's help.'

'Even then?' she murmured, teasing.

'Even then. But with you it's always felt right. The day we met I was clinging to you for safety, even though I didn't know it.'

'In between pushing me away,' she agreed, smiling.

He grinned. 'I sent you flying with a great clout, didn't I?'

'Yes, I seem to remember you did!'

'And the other night Matti did the same thing. Like father, like son.'

'Not exactly,' she chuckled. 'He got the other side.'

He began to laugh, leaning back against the porch, watching her.

'Why do you put up with us?' he asked.

'I can't think. It must be something to do with that generous salary you're paying me.'

'Yes, that must be it.'

A contented silence fell. Leaning back against the other side of the steps, she met his eyes. Was he remembering the last time they had been alone together—what had happened— what had *nearly* happened?

'By the way,' Polly said, as casually as she could contrive, 'I'm sorry I had that screaming fit. I never meant to weep and wail all over you. I don't often do things like that.'

'Not often enough. You released something that's been building up for the past year, and which needed to be released. I'm glad I was the one there.'

He caught sight of her disbelieving face and said, 'I mean it. I like to pay my debts.'

'You do that in hard cash,' she reminded him. 'And plenty of it. I'm not complaining.'

'Oh, yes, I can't tell you what a good feeling it gives me

to know that I'm contributing to Brian's future comfort. I hope you're spending something on yourself?'

'Nope.'

'None of it?'

'What for? I have all I need.'

'Not a pretty dress or a new pair of shoes?' he asked, scandalised.

'Your mother bought me all those new clothes.'

'A luxurious meal out?'

'Sure, with me fighting my way though an Italian menu and reducing everyone to fits of laughter.'

'You're right—it's a terrible prospect. I shall appoint myself your translator for an evening. I know the perfect place. It's time we had an evening out.'

'I don't think so,' she said, remembering her resolve to be sensible.

'I'm your patient and your employer. I have first call on your time. No argument.'

When she didn't reply he asked, 'Are you angry with me?'

'Why should I be?'

'The night before last I came to the verge of—well, forgetting my manners. All right, a little more than the verge. But for a moment you seemed to need me, and I was glad. I felt close to you. Surely you understand that?'

'Yes, I do, but—'

'But Brian wouldn't, eh? All right, I should have respected that. But you can't seriously be afraid of me.' His voice became teasing. 'I've never seen a woman more capable of punching a man's lights out.'

'Not with your injuries,' she said lightly. 'It would be unprofessional.'

'If I offend you I give you leave to forget my injuries and make me sorry I was born.'

'Who is offended?' came a voice from behind them.

'Nobody, Mamma. Polly and I were just planning a night out tomorrow. It's time she had some fun.'

'Of course. What a splendid idea!'

'You see—it's settled,' Ruggiero told Polly. 'We'll do it tomorrow night, before you can change your mind.'

'I didn't know I'd made up my mind.'

'Mamma made it up for you,' Ruggiero said wickedly. 'She's good at that.'

'She's not the only one,' Polly said wryly. But inside her she was smiling. She would have the rest of her life to be strong.

# CHAPTER TEN

'ARE we going back to that fish restaurant of yours?' Polly asked as they drove down the hill on the following evening.

'No, this is somewhere different. In the old city. You haven't had time to see any of Naples.'

The phrase 'the old city' meant nothing to her, but she soon found out that it was a place of little winding streets with cobblestones. In this part of town there were no pavements, so that traffic and pedestrians fenced with each other in both directions at once.

Polly loved it at first sight. It was dazzling, colourful and vivid, the narrow streets blazing with light even as darkness fell, because the little shops and restaurants stayed open very late.

'This part of Naples is like a world apart,' he told her.

'I like it better than the conventional world,' she said.

'So do I. People seem more at ease here. Let's have some coffee.'

They dived into a tiny coffee bar, where the owner hailed him as a friend and seated them at window table.

'If I'd known we were coming here I'd have worn something more restrained,' Polly said. She was wearing the elegant green gown given to her by Hope. 'I feel overdressed.'

'Don't worry—you'll be fine in the place we're going,' he assured her.

'That's a relief. I never did master the trick of getting these things right. I was always too dull or too bright for the occasion.'

'Why must you always criticise yourself?'

'It comes from having lived a life full of comparisons.'

'Comparisons with her?'

'Yes, I just got used to thinking of myself as the plain one in the pack.' She chuckled suddenly.

'What?'

'I was remembering a lad who said he was madly in love with me and he wanted to shower me with flowers. I thought that was so charming—until they turned out to be buttercups he'd picked in the park. Poor fellow. I was very hard on him, but I wanted roses. Someone had given Sapphire roses the day before, and she was actually offended because they were the wrong kind. I thought that was so cool.'

'The wrong kind?' he asked, askance.

'They were tea roses. He was a bit of an academic, and he explained that flowers had their own meanings, and tea roses were a way of saying that he would always remember her.'

'Tea roses for remembrance?' he echoed, beginning to laugh. 'I thought that was red roses?'

'No, red roses are for passionate love lasting to eternity,' she said in a reciting voice. 'Tea roses are for peaceful remembrance.'

'I've never heard that before.'

'Neither had she, and when he produced a learned tome to prove it I thought she was going to explode. He only lasted one day, but I was so envious. Roses were romantic. Buttercups were prosaic.'

'I don't think so,' he said unexpectedly. 'How can such rich gold be prosaic?'

'But they're so common,' she objected, surprised and charmed by this hint of a poetic streak. 'You can pick buttercups anywhere.'

His next answer startled her even more.

'Is that what makes things beautiful? Rarity? Does something stop being lovely because there are plenty? You're rather like a buttercup yourself.'

'You mean commonplace?'

'I mean made of gold.'

For once she was lost for words. He was looking at her with a question in his eyes.

'I wish I could see into your thoughts at this minute,' he said softly.

'There's never any secret about my thoughts,' she said, trying not to be aware of her heart thumping.

'You know that's not true,' he said, still watching her but speaking quietly, like a man trying to lure a wild bird to come to him without frightening it.

'It's a pretence,' he went on when she didn't reply. 'You accused me of playing the role of father, saying the right words for the wrong reasons. But you're doing the same thing—playing the role of sensible nurse, steady and reliable, with no inner life of her own.'

'Which is how I'm supposed to be—'

'But now I know better. Don't forget that. You've let me see that inner life and you can't drive me out again.'

It was true that she couldn't drive him out, but not in the way he thought.

'All right, you saw inside me,' she said at last. 'So keep my secrets.'

'Against anyone else,' he said at once. 'As long as you don't keep them against me.'

She shook her head, and her long fair hair fell about her

face. He reached out to brush it back and was struck by something in her look. It was vulnerable and nervous, and it startled him into drawing a sharp breath.

She heard the sound, and misunderstood it as one of dismay.

Sapphire, she thought. Say what he might, that ghost was still with them. He'd brushed back the hair and seen the wrong face.

'You're fooling yourself,' she told him bitterly. 'She's not dead. She never will be.'

'I wasn't thinking of her—'

'You were doing more than thinking. You were looking for her—here.' She pointed to her face.

'Polly, I—where are you going?'

To his disbelief she leapt to her feet and rushed out of the little coffee bar, leaving him staring after her, too surprised to move.

'Get after her,' the man at the counter said. 'Pay me later.'

'Thanks, Tino,' he yelled, dashing out into the street and looking this way and that.

But she'd gone. In five seconds flat she'd managed to disappear.

Ruggiero ran, looking into the shops that were still open, but she wasn't there. He turned and ran to the other end of the street, but again he was unlucky.

It was impossible, but she'd completely vanished.

He began to walk, twisting this way and that, exploring side streets, all of them full of song and laughter that seemed to mock his confusion. Then he remembered her cellphone and drew out his own, ready to dial her number.

But he didn't know it. He nearly threw the phone away in disgust.

It was an hour before he walked despondently back to the coffee bar. She had probably returned home, and he would have to call and see if she was there, but there was just one last chance that she might have returned to the place where they'd started.

Even as he went in he knew it was a fruitless search. The bar was almost empty.

'Here's what I owe you,' he said, giving some money to Tino.

Then he realised that Tino was winking, and jerking his head at the corner. Ruggiero looked and saw a young woman with fair hair cropped close, a sleek, elegant head. She turned and gave him an appraising look.

'You—you—' He despised himself for stammering, but he couldn't help it.

She was an elfin creature—pretty, pert, with high cheekbones that he'd never noticed before and a neck that was almost swan-like. As he stood watching, struck to silence, she rose and sauntered past him to the door. One challenging glance over her shoulder, then she was gone.

A moment to get his breath and he was after her, catching her up in the street.

'Where were you?' he demanded, grasping her arm firmly. 'No, don't walk away.'

'Let go of me.'

'And risk you vanishing again? I don't think so. How did you manage to vanish into thin air?'

'I just went in there,' she said, indicating a barber shop right next to the coffee bar. 'It was the one place you never thought to look.'

'But that's a *male* barber's.'

'I know. They thought I was nuts, but I just said I wanted it off—all of it. Nothing fancy.'

'But—is it you?' he was peering at her.

'Yes, it's *me*,' she said, emphasising the last word.

'Do you mean,' he asked in mounting outrage, 'that I've

been worried out of my mind about you and you've been having a haircut? Of all the crazy times to pick—'

'It was the perfect time. I should have done it long ago. You as good as told me that tonight.'

'*I?* I never said a word. Polly, have you been taking something? Because you're talking gibberish.'

'I'm talking about the way you looked at me tonight, trying to find Sapphire.'

He stared. 'Why have you got to drag her into this?'

'Because she's there. I saw it in your face.'

'If you did, you put her there yourself,' he said, becoming really angry. 'Why are you obsessed with her?'

'*I'm* not. You're the one who's haunted.'

'I told you—that's done with.'

'Yes, you keep telling me. Too often. Can you really dismiss a ghost that easily?'

'*I might if you'd let me.*'

She stared, thunderstruck.

'What?' she asked in a whisper.

'Don't you know that? It's a lot more complicated than you've realised.'

'Is it me?' she whispered. 'Is that really what's happening?'

'You bring her into every conversation.'

'Only because you—'

'No, don't push it onto *me*. I've fought my ghost, but yours is still there—and maybe she's harder to fight because she's been there all your life. All those comparisons you've told me about, with you always coming off worst. But why should you think like that? You were the brainy one, she needed you as much as you needed her. Who did who's homework?'

'But she was the one with the beauty and charm and—'

'Give me patience!' he groaned. 'Polly, did anyone ever tell you that you're an FCP?'

'What on earth is an FCP?'

'A Female Chauvinist Pig. You didn't know there was such a thing, did you? Hah! At least I've managed to take you by surprise. If a man implied that a woman should be defined by her looks rather than her brains he'd be condemned up hill and down dale, and probably sued as well. But you've just said exactly that. Polly, it's *nonsense*! You're a wonderful person—bright, funny and beautiful.'

'I'm not beau—'

'Don't say it,' he warned, wagging a finger in mock threat. 'Don't say you're not beautiful or I'll get annoyed.'

'Not in comparison to her—'

'But why must you always compare yourself to *her*?'

He read the answer in her expression and said, almost violently, 'She's not here. There's just you and me. I'm looking at *you*, and I tell you you're gorgeous. Why do you look at me like that?'

'Like what?'

'With that disbelieving expression, as though I was crying to the moon. Oh, to hell with everything!'

He'd grasped her shoulders before she knew what he meant to do, and his lips were on hers before she could protest. His arms were like steel rivets about her, and his lips were fierce and angry as they moved over hers again and again. It was a kiss without tenderness. The kiss of a man tearing down a brick wall to make his point. And it left her physically excited as nothing in her life had ever done before.

She tried to get sufficiently free to embrace him back, but before she could manage it he released her suddenly and stepped well away from her with a growl of fury.

'I'm sorry,' he said hoarsely. 'I'm sorry—I'm sorry. I—promised nothing like that would happen. I didn't mean to break my word, but—' He took a long, shaking breath. 'I guess the truth is I'm a bit of a bully.'

'A—a bully?' she asked, trying not to let her voice shake as much as his own.

'People have to see things my way, and if they don't I'll go to any lengths to make them. It's not nice and it makes me behave badly, but do you get the point now?'

'What—what point?' she stammered, wondering which universe she'd stumbled into.

'That you're beautiful. Did I convince you of that before I forgot my manners?'

For a wild moment she was temped to say no, and let him make the point again, and perhaps again. But common sense, the quality that always seemed to ruin things, intervened.

'I'm convinced,' she said, trying to laugh and failing. 'A practical demonstration is always useful.'

'You're angry with me.'

'No, I'm not.'

'You are. I can hear it in your voice—a terrible edge, as though you're wondering how much more of me you can stand. But don't worry. I'm on my best behaviour from now on.'

He neared her again, while still keeping a safe few inches between them, and she could sense that he was still trembling—almost as much as herself.

'I never really thought you looked like her,' he said, glancing at her shorn head. 'Not after that first mistake. But now—I don't know you at all.'

'Let's go from there.'

'Where to?'

'How about that meal you promised me? I'm starving.'

'It's not far away.'

In the next street they passed a jewellery shop, where something attracted him in the window. He drew her inside and made the proprietor show him the little brooch.

'A buttercup,' he said to Polly.

'Well, I told you they were everywhere. Common as muck.'

'Not this one. This is rare and valuable—perfect for you.'

Then Polly saw that the little flower was made of solid gold, and very expensive.

'I can't take this—' she gasped.

'You must. It might have been made for you.'

He pinned the brooch onto her dress and she realised that it did indeed look perfect, glowing under the lights as though it had were a glamorous flower instead of a prosaic one.

She twisted her head, trying to see her own shoulder, beaming with delight.

He led her to a tiny restaurant where the odours wafting out were delicious and the proprietor greeted him by name.

While they were eating *maccheroni* with Neapolitan ragù sauce Polly began to rub her neck self-consciously.

'What is it?' he asked.

'I must look very weird.'

'Not weird, but it's a little unsettling. And that's because you're a combination of someone I know and someone I've never met before. I'm definitely nervous.'

'So you should be,' she teased. 'I don't know the new-comer myself, so she might spring some surprises on both of us.'

'That'll be nothing compared with what it'll do to Brian.'

So absorbed was she in her new territory that she almost said, Who? But she recollected herself in time.

'He's used to my funny ways,' she said vaguely.

'Oh, he's like that? Ready for anything? A man who can't be surprised, dominant, bestriding the world?'

'Stop it,' she said, laughing.

'You mean he's *not* like that? No, on second thoughts I picture him with glasses and the start of a paunch.'

'There's no need for you to picture him at all,' she said, trying to sound firm.

'But you never talk about him. For a man who's won your passionate love, he doesn't seem to make much impact on you.'

The memory of his kiss seemed to hang in the air between them. She was saved from having to answer by the waiter, bearing wine.

'Lacryma Christi del Vesuvio,' Ruggiero said as he poured it into her glass.

Suddenly she held out her hand across the table.

'Hallo,' she said, 'I'm Penelope. We've only just met.'

Ruggiero shook her hand.

'Indeed we have. So, Polly is short for Penelope?'

'Yes, they wanted to call me Penny when I was a kid. But I didn't like it so I became Polly.'

'I like Penelope,' he said, nodding. 'I learned about her in school: the wife of King Odysseus, who waited for him for twenty years. Penelope the faithful and wise.'

'Phooey—she was a twerp,' Polly said firmly. 'You wouldn't catch me waiting twenty years without even a postcard!'

He was unwise enough to answer this. 'They didn't have postcards in those—' He stopped as he caught her eyes on him, brimming with fun.

'But somehow I end up being wise despite trying not to be,' she said. 'At school it was always me warning the others that their daft pranks would lead to trouble, and then fibbing my head off to rescue them when it happened. I've always longed to be wild and outrageous. I try hard, I really do, but it doesn't come naturally to me. I planned all sorts of careers—actress, fashion designer, international bond saleswoman—anything, as long as I could rule the world.'

'But there are plenty of other people doing that,' he said, grinning as he refilled her glass. 'Be original.'

'Yeah, I make a great doormat.'

'Stop that,' he warned. 'You're talking like an FCP again, and I won't allow it.'

They clinked glasses, sharing their amusement, and for once Sapphire was nowhere.

'Anyway,' she said, glowing with joy at the warmth, the lights, the look in his eyes, and just possibly the wine, 'for tonight I'm just going to be Cinderella at the ball.'

'Is Cinderella ready for the next course?'

They passed on to to Neapolitan *rococo*—a sweet dish that seemed to contain everything from toasted almonds to candied peel of orange, flavoured with cinnamon, nutmeg, cloves. Polly closed her eyes in pure ecstasy.

'That's it,' Ruggiero said, satisfied. 'That's what I wanted to see. Have some more.'

*'Yes, please!'*

Their perfect accord continued until they were drinking coffee and liqueurs, when she happened to say, 'Talking as a nurse again, how are you managing now that you're back at work?'

'There's plenty to do. I'm not very popular at the moment, after wrecking our new prototype.'

'But that wasn't your fault.'

'It wasn't the machine's fault. It was working fine until I lost control. Everyone could see that, but they don't know why. The mechanics have been over everything again and again—but how do I tell them to stop bothering because it was only me seeing things that weren't there? I don't want them thinking I'm off my head, even if I am.'

'I can see that it might be a problem,' she admitted.

'And the next thing will be potential customers drawing back, wondering what's wrong with it.'

'What will you tell them?'

'Nothing. I'll have to demonstrate. It's lucky the rodeo is coming up.'

'Rodeo? With motorbikes?'

'Yes. We call it a rodeo, but actually it's a glorified bikers' meeting. It's a gathering of some of the best speedway riders in Italy, or even the world. We get riders from all over.'

'And they'll ride your machine to glory?' Polly asked.

He didn't answer, but she saw the wry look on his face and the truth hit her.

'Oh, no!' she said explosively. 'Definitely no. You can forget that idea right now.'

'It's what I have to do.'

'After what happened—'

'Especially after what happened. Just let them get the idea that one fall frightened me and the machine will get a bad name.'

'You mean you'll get a bad name,' she accused him. 'They'll say you're chicken.'

'Well, I certainly don't want to hear any clucking behind my back.'

'Let them cluck. You have more important things to consider. If you have one more fall like the last there's no knowing what will happen. How often do you think a man can land on his head without damaging his brains?'

A sulphurous silence.

'Why don't you add the next bit?' he demanded at last.

'What next bit?'

'The bit you're dying to say—*if he had any brains in the first place.*'

'I was being polite,' she said acidly.

'Why bother at this late date?'

It was astonishing how quickly a mood of sweet accord could descend into acrimony.

'Anyway, you've said it for me now,' she said crossly.

'Fine, I'm brainless—so there's nothing to damage. Polly, don't make so much of it. Nothing will happen. I'll be more careful this time.'

'Phooey! You're *never* careful.'

'You don't know that.'

'Anyone who's been acquainted with you for five minutes would know that. Ruggiero, listen to me—you are not going to do this, even if I have to stand in front of the bike to stop you.'

He regarded her sceptically. 'Cinderella didn't last very long, did she?'

'Cinderella never had to deal with a man who deluded himself with macho fantasies and had the common sense of a newt. And that's an insult to newts.'

He laughed at that, and Polly let the subject drop. But only because she planned to return to it at a more propitious time.

When it was time to leave Ruggiero didn't pay, but scribbled a note.

By now Polly was beginning to see a pattern.

'Let me guess,' she said as they left. 'You own half of this place as well. And probably several others.'

'Not half. Maybe a quarter here and there. It keeps me in touch with my friends. What is it?' He'd noticed her frowning.

'I just wondered if there's anything you own the *whole* of,' she mused.

'Not that I recall. Why? Does it matter?'

'You've got a finger in so many pies, but you never risk your entire hand. Is that the answer? That you're reluctant to commit yourself totally? Always keeping something back?'

'Aren't you forgetting that I was willing to commit totally to Sapphire?'

'Were you? Are you so sure?'

'What do you mean by that?'

'I mean that it was never put to the test so you can believe what you like. Be honest, Ruggiero, we'll never know.'

He stopped and stared at her. 'Is that really what you think of me?'

'No, it's what I wonder about you. You blamed Sapphire because she didn't turn to you when she was ill. But maybe—' She checked herself and groaned. 'I did it, didn't I? I raised the ghost. You're right. I do it as often as you. Maybe more.'

Polly closed her eyes and pressed her hands to her forehead. 'Let me go,' she whispered to someone neither of them could see. *'Go away.'*

She turned, and would have started to run, but he grasped her quickly.

'No, I'm not going to lose sight of you again. You might never come back.'

'Perhaps it's better if I don't. My job here is nearly done. Let me go.'

'No,' he said drawing her close.

'Ruggiero,' she said, almost pleading. 'Don't—'

But the formal protest didn't fool him, as she had known it wouldn't. His lips were on hers, silencing her, saying all that needed to be said without words.

There was nothing to do now but banish regrets and yield herself up to the greatest joy she had ever known.

Everywhere the lights were going out, and when he drew her into a corner there was only darkness about them.

'Do you think I'm seeking her now?' he murmured. 'Can't you tell the difference?'

'I don't know.'

'Let her go, Polly. Until *you* drive her out neither of us can.'

He kissed her again and again, as though seeking the one kiss that would speak to her heart.

'Perhaps it can't be done,' she gasped.

'Don't say that,' he begged.

'I'm afraid. Aren't you?'

*'Yes.'*

She returned the kiss so that the impulse came from her and the strength was on her side. She was inexperienced in love, and the reverse was true of him, but now he was following her lead, learning from her, trusting her in love as in everything else.

But she was leading him along a road whose end was obscure to her—a road that might be wrong for both of them.

He guessed it too, for he said, 'You can deal with my ghost but can I deal with yours?'

'Hush.'

'Can Brian?' he growled. 'Does he even *know* that you still spend your life making comparisons? That when he kisses you he holds two women in his arms?'

'Forget him,' she urged.

'As you have?'

'He doesn't belong here now. Nobody else belongs here with us.'

She gave herself up to the joy of the moment, trying to believe that only this mattered and she could make it last for ever. But that hope was doomed. Even in the midst of her happiness she knew that.

It was the sound of a church bell that forced them back to reality, making them draw apart, both shaking with desire and confusion.

'Do you hear that?' she murmured.

'It's only the clock. Ignore it.'

'I can't. It's striking midnight. Time for Cinderella to go.'

'Why are you laughing?' he asked, feeling her shaking in his arms.

'I'm laughing at myself,' she said with a touch of hysteria.

'Oh, heavens! I should have remembered that midnight always comes. Sensible Polly isn't always so sensible after all.'

'I'm glad of that,' he said huskily.

He turned her face up and looked at it in the moonlight, seeing its clean, perfect lines as never before. The sight entranced him, and he would have kissed her again, but she pressed her hands against his chest.

'It's time we went home,' she whispered. 'The ball's over.'

'But you've left me a glass slipper, right?'

She shook her head. 'More like an army trainer. Nurse Bossy-Boots is back in charge.'

His smile was as sad as her own as they walked together back through the small, winding streets.

# CHAPTER ELEVEN

*'DULL, dreary, prosaic. That's what I am, and I shouldn't have let myself forget it.'*

It was typical of the hand life had dealt Polly that after claiming her freedom by dramatically shearing off her hair she should find that it backfired on her with a feverish cold.

'Can you take Matti?' she croaked to Hope next day. 'I don't want to get too close to him.'

The cot was promptly whisked out of her room, and she herself was banished back to bed, where she was nursed royally. Everyone looked in to wish her well—including Ruggiero, who stayed well back in response to her urgently flapping hands.

For three days she could do little but suffer. Her meals were brought upstairs, and in between eating she slept. At last she felt better, and began to make forays out of bed.

On one of these days she sat by the window, watching as Ruggiero, below, played with Matti, showing every sign of pride in his mental alertness, while his son, as always, strutted his stuff to an admiring audience.

They're both fine without me, she thought.

At that moment Hope pointed up to the window, and they all looked up, waving and smiling to her. For a strange moment it looked as if they were waving goodbye.

When she was sure she presented no threat to anyone, she went downstairs again.

'You were away too long,' Ruggiero told her.

'Or just long enough. You and Matti get on better when I'm not hovering over you.'

'I've taught him three new words. And Toni swears he's learning to call me Poppa, although it sounds more like *patata*.' He grinned. 'But I don't mind being called a potato by my son. He'll probably call me worse when he's older.'

'Brilliant. So now you and he have established a connection, you're not going to be taking any risks, are you?'

'Risks?'

'I can assume that you're enough of a father to abandon this mad idea of the rodeo?'

'It's tomorrow.'

'And you're riding?' she demanded, aghast.

'There's no reason why I shouldn't.'

'There's every reason. You're not fit yet. You'll have another accident and maybe this time you'll be killed. That child has lost his mother—he doesn't deserve to lose his father too. Especially when he's only just met him.'

'It's no more than I've done before. I wasn't killed in the past, and what happened the day we met was a freak accident, and you know it. I have a duty to our workers to prove that the bike is good. They depend on us for a living.'

'So get another rider. You say there'll be others, so I expect any one of them would be glad of the chance.'

His mouth set in stubborn lines.

'It has to be me,' he said. 'Because I was the one riding when things went wrong.'

'And if things go wrong again—?'

Hope, approaching, overheard this and joined in the conversation with horror.

'I knew you were having this party, but I didn't know you were actually riding,' she said, appalled. 'You're not nearly well enough. Get one of the others to do it.'

'Don't give me orders, Mamma,' he said quietly. 'That goes for both of you.'

He walked away before either of them could reply.

Hope groaned and cursed herself.

'I'm sorry, *cara*. I shouldn't have spoken. You would have done much better.'

'But I wasn't doing any better,' Polly sighed. 'He's completely pig-headed. I don't understand that. I thought we were getting through to him—that *Matti* was getting through. Then suddenly everything goes into reverse. He plays with his son, he teaches him words, and he smiles in the right places, but he won't give up his pleasure to protect him. Oooh, I could—'

She made a strangling motion with her hands.

'Do it for both of us,' Hope snapped.

Secretly Polly knew that it was disappointment as much as anger that was driving her. The softened mood between herself and Ruggiero had seemed full of promise for his future with his son. Suddenly his image had darkened into that of a man concerned only with himself and his own wishes, without care for his child.

None of Ruggiero's siblings happened to be in Naples at that moment, so there was only Toni, Hope and Polly who might have attended the rodeo. Hope flatly refused to do so.

'No, you'll just be shopping nearby,' Ruggiero said. 'As always.'

'Not this time,' his mother declared. 'I'm going to stay here and look after your son. If you break your neck, you break your neck. That's your business.'

But when he'd left the house she turned to Polly and said

fearfully, 'You'll be there, won't you? If anything happens you'll look after him.'

'Of course. But he's probably right. Nothing will happen.'

She tried to sound reassuring, but she couldn't voice her real fear—that what had happened before would happen again and he would see something that wasn't there.

*If* it wasn't there.

'Leave him alone,' she whispered. 'You can't have him. Do you hear me?'

There was no answer. Either Sapphire had admitted defeat, or she was too sure of victory to bother arguing.

A privileged crowd had been allowed into the stands that surrounded the track. Potential buyers, a few journalists, everyone from the factory, plus friends and family from the biking fraternity.

In their company Ruggiero relaxed. He spoke the same language as these people—the language of speed and danger, the language of 'to hell with everything!' He'd been away from them too long, among people who didn't understand that risking your life was the most life-enhancing experience in the world. You had to toss it onto the flames to really enjoy the moment when you seized it back. What did they know?

There were ten riders, including Enrico, who had won more races than anyone else that season, and was eyeing the new bike hungrily.

'It's a bit soon for you to be riding again,' he said coaxingly. 'Take a longer rest.'

'I have to prove that bike. Not me, but the bike.'

It wasn't true. It was himself he had to prove again, but he couldn't admit that to anyone else.

The leather suit he'd worn before was now clean and

perfect. When he put it on he felt he become himself again: his real self, the one he wanted to be, who'd almost been lost.

There was applause as five riders walked out for the first race. He knew they were all watching him, willing him to streak ahead on the new bike and leave the rest standing. Either that or get killed. One or the other. That was just how he liked it.

He stood for a moment, looking around through his visor, knowing the others were awaiting his move. From here he could just make out the place where she'd been before. It had been different then, with speed creating half the illusion, but now he needed no speed to conjure up the woman who stood before him.

Suddenly he became quite still, watching, understanding everything for the first time.

Then he began to move.

Toni drove Polly down to the track, left her there, and returned home on his wife's strict instructions. Polly was able to slip in and go to the same place in the stands where she had stood before.

The five bikes were already on the track, each with its own mechanic, waiting for the first race. Around her the crowd was abuzz with expectation. She couldn't understand the words, but she could guess their meaning.

She clenched her hands, waiting for things to start. But before anything could happen she heard the shrill of her cellphone. Pulling it out quickly, she found herself talking to Kyra Davis, a nurse she'd become friendly with two years earlier. Kyra was older, well on the road to promotion, and she had been there when Freda had died.

'I just called to say I've got my own ward at St Luke's,' she said, 'and I have two vacancies. I'd love you to fill one of them. Where are you now?'

'I'm in Italy.'

'But you'll come home soon, won't you? Pop over and we'll have a chat.'

'Can I call you back about that?' Her eyes were fixed on the track.

'Sure, just remember there's a job for you any time.'

She hung up.

There was a cheer. The bikers were coming out now. They all looked alike in their black leather and visors, but Polly would have known Ruggiero's tall, lean body anywhere.

*Don't do it! Don't do it!*

She saw him walk towards the bikes with the others, saw him stop and look around. His gaze seemed fixed on the place where she stood. He seemed transfixed, rooted to the spot, as though something was there that was revealed only to him.

*What can you see?*

Then a murmur went through the crowd as Ruggiero pulled off his helmet and turned to the man beside him, saying something. The murmur turned to a groan of disappointment as Ruggiero made a gesture indicating his bike. The other man let out a yell of delight and punched the air, but Ruggiero never saw it. He was already walking away.

He went on walking across the track until he came to the place where Polly stood, her eyes glistening, her heart overflowing.

'Enrico will ride for me,' he said. 'That's it. *Basta!*'

'What made you change your mind?' she asked, hardly able to get the words out. 'Did you see her?'

'No.' He shook his head. 'I saw you. And Matti was in your arms.'

'It's what you tried to tell me, isn't it?' he asked.

They were sitting in a small restaurant. After speaking to her Ruggiero had gone back to change out of his leather gear, giving her time to call Hope and tell her all was well.

Then they had left the track, finding the first place where they could sit together and talk quietly.

'I tried to find the words, but there aren't any,' Polly said.

'I had to learn it for myself,' he agreed. 'And now I have—just in that moment. I saw you holding Matti in your arms. The two of you were looking at me. But he wasn't really there, was he?'

'He's at home with your parents. But, yes—he *was* with me.'

He nodded slowly. 'And with me. For the first time I feel that he's mine.'

'And you are his,' she reminded him. 'Or it doesn't work.'

He took her hand. 'Let's go home.'

Hope and Toni were watching for them, standing on the steps with Matti between them, each holding one hand. They came down slowly, releasing him when they reached the ground, so that he had only to waddle two steps before clinging onto his father's leg for support.

Ruggiero dropped down to one knee to put his arms about his son.

'We got there,' he said huskily.

Polly stood back, watching them with pleasure, then exchanged glances with Hope and Toni. A decision was forming inside her.

She waited a few more hours, studying Ruggiero and Matti, but in her heart she was sure. These two had a road to travel yet, but they had found the start and placed their feet on it together.

She was even more certain when Ruggiero tried to assist his son in walking, holding his hand, and Matti impatiently thrust him away.

'There's a chip off the old block,' Toni said, and Ruggiero nodded.

'You used to fall over more often than not,' Hope reminded him.

'But he doesn't fall over,' Ruggiero said, regarding his child with pride.

At that moment Matti sat down hard.

'That was my fault,' Ruggiero hastened to say, speaking loud to be heard through his son's bawled indignation. 'He fell over my foot.'

At last Hope said, 'It's time this little one was in bed. Polly, shall we put him back in your room?'

'No, let him stay with you,' she replied quickly.

She joined the procession upstairs, but remained in the background during the ceremony as the last pieces of her resolution fell into place. Afterwards Ruggiero found her brooding on the terrace, and sat down, smiling contentedly.

She took a deep breath.

'I'm glad this has happened now,' she said. 'It makes it easy for me.'

'There's something in the way you say that that makes me nervous.'

'I have to go home for a while.'

'For a while? Are you coming back?'

She hesitated. 'I don't know. I need to be away from here, and you need to be alone with Matti. I'm starting to be in the way.'

'That's nonsense. I couldn't have got this far without you.'

'But you *have* reached this far, and you'll manage the next stage better if you let go of your nurse's hand.' She smiled. 'If you should need a hand to hold onto, take Matti's. You're both going in the same direction.'

'Matti needs you,' he insisted.

She waited, daring to hope. But Ruggiero didn't say that *he* needed her, and her heart sank again.

'I think Matti will be fine without me. This is his home now, and he loves it. He loves Hope and Toni and you.'

'He's getting used to me—'

'No, you're winning his heart. He's as bright as a button, and he's just like his poppa. Everyone can see that. That's the bond. All you have to do is use it. You managed the big first step today.'

He didn't look at her as he said, in a strange voice, 'You're not doing this very well, Polly.'

'What do you mean?' she asked in alarm.

'You're doing what you once accused me of—just reciting the words. Why don't you tell me the real reason?'

For a moment she thought he'd guessed her feelings and was challenging her to speak them. And, if so, would it be so terrible to say that she loved him?

But then he added, 'I suppose Brian's cutting up rough, and you feel you have to get back to him?'

'Yes,' she said, letting out her breath slowly. 'It's Brian.'

'I wish I knew what you see in him. Isn't he worried about you?'

'I told you, he's a doctor.'

'Ah, yes—a man so busy serving humanity that he has no time for you. To hell with him! If he loved you, he'd be hammering on your door.'

'Not every man shows his feelings by tearing the walls down.'

'Just Neanderthals like me, huh?'

'I didn't—'

'Well, you're right. I told you how I went crazy in London when Sapphire vanished—roaming the streets, starving, half mad, knocking at doors. Why isn't *he* pounding doors for *you*?'

'Because for one thing he knows exactly where I am,' she replied in her most common sense voice.

'But does he know who you're with?'

'He knows I'm with a patient.'

'Does he know about this patient? How close we are? Does

he know how I depend on you? That I've kissed you. Does he know that you've kissed me?'

'I didn't,' she said quickly. 'I didn't push you away because your ribs—'

'So that was a nurse's concern, was it? What about your other patients? Do you—?'

'Stop it,' she flashed, her eyes daring him to say any more. *'Stop right there.'*

He flushed.

'I'm sorry,' he muttered. 'I didn't mean to say that.'

'Never speak of this again. The sooner I go the better.'

She left quickly, before he could answer. Her breath was coming sharply, and every nerve in her seemed alive with conflicting emotions—anguish, temptation and desire contending with fear.

The fear was because she knew how close she'd come to yielding to what she must resist. Ruggiero wanted her to stay for Matti's sake, but also because his own nature needed her. It wasn't love, but for a woman who was passionately in love with him it might have been a bearable substitute.

Except for Sapphire.

He could say what he liked about being over her. It wasn't that simple. Her body might be dead, but still she would always be alive in the son they shared, in the memories that would live as long as his heart and soul lived.

And while that was true he could never really be hers.

What tormented her most was the knowledge that if she'd pushed matters, said the right words, she could probably have manoeuvred him into a proposal. But hell would freeze over before she did so. No half measures. He must be hers completely or not at all. Anything else would mean years of misery.

So the answer was not at all. And now she would flee this place, while she could still bear it.

Hope took the news of her impending departure calmly.

'Yes, you need to return for a while,' she said. 'Everything will still be here when you get back.'

'I'm not sure if I— I don't know how things will work out.' Hope kissed her.

'We'll meet again,' she said placidly.

Her goodbye to Matti was tearful on her side but not on his. He'd perfected the art of putting shapes into the right holes and was eager to demonstrate.

'And he knows you'll be back soon,' Ruggiero said quietly.

'Perhaps. Are my things in the car?'

'Yes, I'm all ready to drive you to the airport, if you still want to go.'

I don't want to go, she told him silently. I want to stay with you always. I want to love you and have you love me. But you don't love me, and perhaps you never will. Maybe this is the only way I can find out.

'Yes,' she said, 'I still want to go.'

At the airport he carried her bags to Check-In, and walked with her towards the departure lounge.

'Stay,' he said suddenly. 'Don't go. You belong here.'

If he'd said, *Stay with me*, she would have done so, even then. But 'Stay' wasn't enough.

'I'm not sure where I belong,' she told him. 'I have to find out.'

'Will he meet you at the other end?'

'No, he's—'

'I know—he's busy,' Ruggiero interrupted her, exasperated. 'Then he has only himself to blame for anything that happens.'

He pulled her close and laid his lips on hers. Polly closed her eyes and gave herself up to the feeling for perhaps the last time. In this public place she couldn't embrace him as she wanted to, but she tried to let him know silently that her heart would remain here, although the rest of her might never return.

'Polly…' he said softly.

'I must go now. Goodbye.'

'We'll see each other again soon.' He was still holding her hand.

'Goodbye—goodbye—'

The little flat seemed to echo around her. The year spent there with her cousin and Matti had been terrible in many ways, but now that they were gone it was somehow worse. The emptiness struck her more fiercely for its contrast with the last few weeks in the cheerful villa, with members of the huge Rinucci clan wandering in and out.

She had nobody, she realised. Her only relative was Matti, and she'd parted with him for his own sake. She would visit him in Naples, and know herself to be welcome, but then she would come back here and the family doors would close behind her.

Why, that's it! she told herself. It's all of them I'm missing. Not only Ruggiero. I just loved being part of a big jolly family. I'm not in love with him. Not really.

With that settled it was easier to concentrate on settling in. She whisked around with a duster, bought herself some fish and chips from across the road, made a huge pot of tea and settled down to read the post that had arrived while she was away.

It was very silent. The scream of the phone was a relief.

'Did you have a safe journey?' Ruggiero asked from the other end.

'Yes, I'm fine, thank you.'

'Matti has been waiting for you to call and say you'd arrived. When you didn't, I told him I'd call you.'

Something caught in her throat, half-laughter, half tears.

'So the two of you had a nice little talk?' she asked.

'He did most of the talking. He wants to know how you are.'

'I'm just fine.'

'Was it a good flight? He knows you don't like flying, and he's worried about that.'

'Tell him it was a nice smooth flight.'

His voice became muffled as he turned away to say, 'She says it was a nice smooth flight.'

Matti answered, 'Aaaah!'

'He says he's very pleased,' Ruggiero passed on.

'Give him my love.'

'Why don't you tell him yourself? Here, Matti. Put it to your ear—like that.'

'Aaaah!' he said.

'Is that you, darling?' she asked.

'*Si, si, si, si, si.*'

'You've learned another word. How clever you are.'

'Aaaah!'

'He says he loves you,' came Ruggiero's voice. 'He wants you to say it too. Here, Matti.'

'I love you,' she said softly. 'Matti?'

'He slid off my lap and went to Mamma,' Ruggiero said.

'It's time he was in bed.'

'She's just about to take him.'

'And you?'

'I'll be there, too.'

'Good. I must go now. Goodnight.'

'*Ciao!*'

'*Ciao!*'

She put down the phone and sat quietly in the dusk, until there was no light left.

# CHAPTER TWELVE

THERE'S a letter for you,' Hope said, putting it in Ruggiero's hand. 'From England.'

Conscious of his parent's eyes fixed eagerly on him, he pulled open the envelope. Inside was a letter and a photograph, showing a small headstone in a graveyard. Beneath it was the name of the church and the village.

> *I found this when I got home. One day Matti might like to have it. Talk to him about her. Remember what I told you—that she was a good mother and she loved him with all her heart, until the last moment of her life. Think of her like that, and try to forgive her the rest.*

It was signed, *'Your affectionate Bossy-Boots.'*

'She talks as though she wasn't coming back,' Hope observed.

'I don't think she is,' Ruggiero said heavily.

'And you're just going to accept that?' Hope demanded, outraged. 'Why didn't you ask her to marry you?'

'Have you forgotten that she's engaged?'

'Poof! Don't tell me you're going to let yourself be put off by a trifle like that?'

'Mamma,' he said with a faint grin, 'sometimes I think you're completely immoral.'

'I can remember when, if you wanted a woman, you'd have elbowed a whole army of fiancés out of your way.'

'Well, perhaps it's time I stopped doing such things. Other people have rights.' He gave a grunt. 'I guess I finally learned that.'

'Not from me. I tried but I failed there.'

'No—from her. It's odd,' he said softly, 'but when I think of all the things I learned from her it really makes her seem like Nurse Bossy-Boots. And yet…' He paused and smiled faintly, as though he barely realised he was doing so. 'She wasn't a bit like that.'

'What was she like?' Hope asked, her gaze fixed fondly on him.

He shook his head. 'I can't tell. Even to me she's—I don't know.'

'But what does she say on the phone? You call her every night.'

'Matti calls her every night,' he corrected fondly. 'They talk and I put in the odd word. I'm not sure she'd talk to me as easily. Now she's with her fiancé again…' Ruggiero sighed. 'Heaven knows what kind of man he is, but she seems very set on him.'

'She told you that?'

'No, she gave me only bare details. If I ventured onto that territory I got ordered off.'

'Hmm!'

'Mamma, you can put more meaning into that one little sound than anyone I know.'

'Has it ever occurred to you that this man may not exist? That he may be simply a device she has found useful?'

He nodded. 'At the start I wanted her to keep Matti, but I had to give up when she mentioned the fiancé, and it did cross my mind that she'd invented him to silence me. But when she returned from England with you he called her.'

'She said so?' Hope demanded sceptically.

'No, but I heard her say something about a hospital. And since he works in one—'

'That could have meant anything. Her friends had to return Matti early because their daughter had been rushed to hospital. Perhaps she was talking to them?'

'But you told me she went out to see him while you were there.'

'I said she went out for a couple of hours. I don't know who she saw.'

'But he was there when I called her the other night.'

Hope turned, thoroughly startled now. 'She actually told you that?'

'No, but I heard him in the background, asking where she kept the glasses.'

She breathed again.

'And it didn't occur to you that if he were her fiancé he'd have known that without asking?'

'You think—? No, there could be many things to account for it.'

'You won't know unless you go to find out.'

Unwittingly, she'd touched a nerve. Suddenly he was back in London, searching uselessly for someone who wasn't there, turning corner after corner, always hoping that he would find his dream around the next one. An icy dread went through him at the thought of doing it again.

He didn't call her that night, hoping she would call him. But the phone was silent. And when the next night came he found that he couldn't force himself to call. The silence of the evening before held him in a grip of dread. The next night he admitted to himself that he was afraid, and the admission was a kind of release, so that he snatched up the receiver and dialled her home number.

The phone was dead.

There was still her cellphone, but that had been switched off. He called it repeatedly over the next twenty-four hours, but it was always off.

She had vanished into thin air.

Hope had given Ruggiero the address. All he had to do was take a taxi from London Airport to the building where her tiny apartment was situated. He arrived in the late afternoon. As he got out he looked up at the window on the second floor, which Hope had said was hers. He couldn't be sure, but he thought he saw the curtain twitch.

Seeing someone come out of the front door, he took the chance to slip inside, and began to climb the stairs. There was only one door on the second floor and he knocked at it.

It was opened by the most handsome young man Ruggiero had ever seen.

He was in his late twenties, with tousled hair and a cheerful face. He was also wearing a towelling robe, as if he'd just got out of the bath.

'Hi, can I help you?' he asked.

Ruggiero felt himself engulfed by hell. It was the voice he'd overheard on the telephone, and this young man was built like a god.

'No, thank you,' he said hurriedly. 'I think I've come to the wrong place.'

'Maybe not. I've only just moved in, so perhaps you're thinking of— Coming, darling.'

He called this over his shoulder. Ruggiero knew he had to get away fast.

'Who is it, darling?' A female voice floated from within.

But it wasn't *her* voice. Suddenly his legs were paralysed with relief.

A young woman, also in a bathrobe, appeared. She was nothing like Polly.

'I'm looking for Polly Hanson,' he managed to say.

'Oh, you mean the woman who lived here before?' the girl said. 'She moved out a few days ago.'

'It was very sudden,' the young man said. 'She wanted to move, and we needed somewhere quickly, so we dropped in one evening to look the place over.'

'You mean—you're not Brian?'

'Brian? No, my name's Peter. I don't think I've heard of Brian. Polly didn't mention a Brian, did she, Nora?'

'Not that I heard.'

The hell that had engulfed Ruggiero retreated very slightly.

'Did she leave a forwarding address?'

'She only mentioned a hotel,' Nora said. 'The Hunting Horn, I think it was. Not far away.'

A taxi took him to the hotel. He sat in the back, telling himself not to be fanciful. Just because she'd vanished and he was looking for her at a hotel, like last time, that didn't mean—

She was no longer at the Hunting Horn.

'She stayed just three days,' the pretty receptionist explained. 'No, I'm afraid she didn't say where she'd be after that.'

Now his forehead was damp, and desperation was growing inside him. History was repeating itself, drowning him again.

'Try St Luke's Hospital,' the receptionist. 'She said she worked there once, and she might be going back.'

'Thank you,' he said frantically.

Another taxi. Another desperate journey. Trying to tell himself that this time it would be different. There was the hospital, a huge building, just up ahead. He leapt out and almost ran inside.

For a moment he thought he was in luck. The man on the desk remembered Polly.

'She was here a few days ago. You might try—' He named a ward and directed him to it.

As he approached the ward a nurse in her mid-thirties emerged and halted him.

'I'm afraid visiting isn't until this evening,' she said, in a voice that was pleasant but firm.

'Please, I'm not visiting. I'm looking for Polly Hanson.'

'She's not here.'

Darkness again, blanking out everything except the road ahead that wound around endless corners, leading to nothing.

'I was told she worked here,' he said, his mouth dry.

'I hope she soon will be. I called her in Italy and tried to persuade her to come back here—because we really need nurses like her—but she said she had something urgent to do before she finally made up her mind.'

'You know her, then?'

'I'm an old friend. My name's Kyra Davis, and I got to know her very well the last time she was here.'

'She worked in this part of the hospital?'

'Yes, but I meant when her cousin was dying. Oh, dear—maybe I shouldn't be telling you all this. I don't know who you are.'

'I'm the father of her cousin's child.'

'You mean Matthew? She used to bring him in to see his mother in the last days. We managed to find a little side ward for her, so that they could all be together in peace.'

'It's here?' he asked, looking around.

'Yes, It's empty just now, so you can see it if you like.'

As she opened the door to the side ward her beeper went.

'I think someone wants me,' she said, and bustled away, leaving him alone in the room.

It was small, plain and bare, except for the sunshine streaming onto the empty bed. Ruggiero stared at it, trying to understand that this was the place where Sapphire had died.

Only a few weeks ago she had lain in that bed, looking at this room. He tried to picture her, but there was nothing.

Nothing!

But Polly was present, sitting on the chair, pushed up close to the bed so that she could place Matti in his mother's arms while still holding him for safety. She'd sat there hour after hour, her arms around both of them, growing tired, her body aching, her heart grieving, enduring it all so that mother and child could have those last precious moments together.

How did he know that? She'd never told him. But he knew it was true because he knew her. In those last hours and moments every fibre of her being had been concentrated on helping the people in her care, with never a thought for herself.

*'Polly—are you still there? I can't see you.'*

*'Yes, darling. I'm always here. Feel my hand.'*

*'You won't forget—you'll find him—and tell him about the baby—'*

*'I'll find him—I'll make sure they know each other—'*

*'Where are you? Don't let me go.'*

*'I'm here—hold onto me—feel my arms around you—hold on—'*

Dazed, he looked around. How could he hear them when they weren't there?

Not true.

Sapphire had never existed.

But Polly was there. She would be there in his heart for ever, her arms outstretched in generous giving, the only way she knew to live.

The winding road had finally reached its destination—this little room, where one journey had ended and another had begun, like a torch being passed from hand to hand.

'Are you all right?' the nurse asked from the doorway.

'Yes, I'm fine,' he said joyfully. 'I've never been better. But I have to talk to her.'

'She said she was going away for a few days.'

'With Brian?' he asked, scarcely breathing.

'Who?'

'Her fiancé.'

'Polly doesn't have a fiancé. She's in love with a man who doesn't feel the same way. That's all she'd tell me.' She eyed Ruggiero curiously, but was too tactful to say more. She only added, 'I think she's gone to Yorkshire—back to her old village.'

'Thank you. I can find her now.'

At the station he caught a train north. From there it was a bus ride to the little village, and by good fortune the bus stopped close to the church.

It was dark, but it was a tiny place, and, using the picture Polly had given him, he managed to locate the right corner of the graveyard. There was the little slab, with Freda's name and the dates of her life. He glanced at them only briefly. He was looking for something else.

But he was alone. There was no sign of Polly. Only some flowers on the grave suggested that she'd been there.

He was back on the endless road, seeking something that was always out of sight around the next corner, until there were no more corners left.

'No,' he muttered. 'Not this time.'

He looked around the graveyard, searching in the poor light until he finally found what he was looking for. By now he was at the edge of the ground, with a clear view across the road, where a flower shop was just closing. Ruggiero sprinted across, just managed to get his hand in the door, and engaged in the most desperately important negotiation of his life.

\* \* \*

It had taken a couple of days for Polly go around the old places—the home where she'd lived as a child, the second home when her aunt and uncle had taken her in, the school where she'd done so well, passing her exams with flying colours and helping Freda, whose skills had lain in another direction.

She would have liked to avoid Ranley Manor, but her route had happened to lie that way, so she'd hurried past. Even so she had been unlucky enough to see George handing a young woman into his chauffeured car.

She'd gone to see Freda within an hour of her arrival. She'd wanted to tell her cousin that she'd kept her promise. When she'd laid the violets on the grave she'd said, 'I'll be back tomorrow.'

Next day she'd brought lilies to replace the violets. She had stayed for a while, talking about Matti.

'He'll be all right, I promise,' she'd said. 'You were right to send him to Ruggiero. He's going to be a great father. I'm going tomorrow, but I'll be back here before I go—just once more.'

She was keeping her promise, bearing more flowers, but as she ran the last few steps to lay them down she stopped suddenly and stared.

The grave was covered in buttercups, glorious brilliant yellow and gold buttercups, flaunting their rich, extravagant beauty to the world.

Looking around her, she saw that not a buttercup was left growing in the grass. Someone had determinedly plucked every last one to lay them here in a silent message.

Then she saw that the yellow flowers were not alone. A corner of the grave was given up to tea roses.

And she was back again in the little restaurant in Naples, talking about flowers and their meaning.

Tea roses—in peaceful memory. All passion spent. All forgiven and only the best remembered.

But it was the buttercups that lay in joyous profusion,

carrying their message of love, acceptance, freedom to go on living and loving.

Ruggiero appeared so suddenly that she guessed he'd been waiting for her. He was unshaven and his suit was creased, as though he'd been sleeping on the ground, and his eyes were full of a troubled question.

But before he could ask the question she answered it, opening her arms so that he ran to her at once, his own arms flung wide to seize her and draw her close.

'*Why did you leave me?*' he asked hoarsely. '*Where have you been?*'

'I had to go,' she cried, holding onto him. 'I had to find out if what I was afraid of was true.'

He silenced her mouth with his own, and it was a long time before he could breathe enough to say, 'You should have trusted me.'

'It's not that—I didn't know how you really felt. I thought you might let me go and realise that it was for the best.'

'How could it be best for me to lose you?' he demanded passionately. But then a change came over him. He grew calmer and shook his head. 'But you didn't really think I'd let you go,' he said. 'You couldn't have. In your heart you know everything there is between us. Don't you?'

He was right, she realised. Some part of her had known that he would come after her because he loved her. Hearing it said now, she recognised the truth. He knew her better than she knew herself.

'Everything,' he repeated. 'Now and always. It took us both a little time to see it, but it was always there.'

He drew her close again, not in a kiss, but in a whole-hearted embrace, arms tight about each other, totally committed, nothing held back. For a long time neither of them moved or spoke

There was a small commotion as a crowd of schoolchildren appeared and headed in their direction.

'Come away,' he said, drawing her towards the ancient little church.

They found privacy in the old wooden porch, where they could sit apart from the world, yet still able to see the flowers with their glowing promise of hope.

'You look terrible,' she said, touching his unshaven chin

'I spent the night here. I couldn't risk missing you. I only left for a few minutes, to get the roses I'd ordered from a shop across the road, but I got back fast. I've been waiting here, watching. I was so afraid you wouldn't come back at all.'

'I had to say a proper goodbye to her before I finally decided where I was going next.'

'Back to Brian?' he asked belligerently.

'There's no Brian, and you know that perfectly well.'

'I just wanted to hear you say it,' he growled, holding her tight, almost as if he was afraid 'Brian' would appear and snatch her away.

'He was just a device to make you concentrate on Matti,' she admitted. 'But then I found him useful, helping me to keep everything impersonal. I didn't want you to think of me as a woman. Or,' she added, seeing his raised eyebrows and hint of a smile, 'maybe I wanted it too much. One of the two. I couldn't decide which. I thought he'd fade into the background, but you kept on about him.'

'I was jealous as hell. I could have throttled him because you loved him. All the time I could feel us getting closer, and I didn't know what to believe. When you left I thought you'd gone back to him.'

'I didn't just want to be a substitute for Freda, and I was

afraid I'd never know if I was or not. I couldn't live with second best. It has to be all or nothing.'

He nodded.

'I thought we'd both have time to think, but when I reached England—' she gave a shaky laugh '—a terrible thing happened. I had an attack of common sense.'

'You should have known better. What has common sense to do with us?'

'Everything seemed so clear. You had Matti, and you didn't need me any more. I wanted to break completely with the past, so I gave up my flat and got out so that the new people could move in quickly. I've got a job offer at the hospital.'

'I know. I was there.'

'You went to the hospital?'

'I saw the room where she died. I stood there and looked around, and all I could see was you. Wherever I am I see only you, and that's how it will be—all my life. But I didn't understand at first. The way we met—she was always between us. I lived in confusion for so long. If you hadn't come I don't know what would have happened to me. I was caught up in a kind of madness, and you released me. Now I'm free—truly free at last. It feels like starting life again.

'Sapphire—'

'Freda,' he said at once. 'There was no Sapphire.' He saw her looking at him, and said, 'But now I can be grateful to her. I can even love her memory for Matti's sake.'

'I'm glad of that,' she said fervently. 'Because one day you'll bring him here—'

'We'll bring him together, and tell him about her.'

They were silent, thinking of that moment.

'We might even bring our own children as well,' he mused.

'You've got it planned?'

'Matti has. He wants brothers and sisters. He's a Rinucci; he likes being part of a big family.'

She smiled tenderly and leaned her head against him.

'He told you that, did he?' she asked.

'Sure he did. We understand each other perfectly these days. He also says that if I don't bring you back with me I needn't bother coming home. He was very plain about that—threw his cereal bowl against the wall.'

They laughed together for a moment, but then he took her hand and carried it to his lips.

'Promise that this hand will always be in mine,' he whispered.

'Keeping you safe?'

'No, leading me to the best of life. Even when you stopped me riding the bike you weren't restraining me, just showing me a different way forward. We'll go wherever the road winds, and as long as it's you that takes me there I know it'll be a good place.'

They walked back to the grave and stood for a moment, looking at the flowers—tea roses and buttercups—side by side in perfect harmony.

'You understand, don't you?' he asked softly. 'Please say that you do?'

She nodded. 'Thank you. Not just for my flowers, but for hers.'

'They had to come first. I know that now.' He smiled suddenly. 'You're wearing yours,' he said, indicating the gold brooch on her shoulder.

'I always wear it.'

'Promise me that you always will?'

'I promise—for ever.'

She leaned down and took two of the flowers, one of each, putting them away to be kept, also for ever. All done now. All answered. All forgiven.

He kissed her gently, knowing that everything else must wait a little. But they could afford to wait.

Nor did they look back as they walked away. There was no need. They knew the flowers were blooming brightly in the morning sun.

# THE MILLIONAIRE
# TYCOON'S
# ENGLISH ROSE

BY
LUCY GORDON

# CHAPTER ONE

'*SLIGHTLY to your left...bit more...bit more...reach out now... can you feel it?*'

'Yes,' Celia called in delight.

Her fingers made their way through the water until they touched the rock, eased around it, up, down, exploring in all directions, while the man's voice on the radio spoke in her ear.

'*Try a little farther along. Feel the shape of it.*'

'I've got it,' she said into her own radio. 'Now I want to go down farther.'

Ken, controlling her lightly from on land, asked into the microphone, 'Sure you haven't had enough for the day?'

'I've barely started. I want to do *lots* more yet.'

From the radio in her ear she heard Ken's chuckle as he recognised her familiar cry of 'lots more yet.' It was the mantra by which she lived, her shout of defiance in the face of her blindness. She'd learned it from her blind parents whose motto had been, 'Who needs eyes?'

'I want to go down much deeper,' she said.

He groaned. 'Your boyfriend will murder me.'

'Don't call him my boyfriend as though we were a couple of kids.'

'What, then?'

Good question. What should she call Francesco Rinucci? Her fiancé? No, for they'd never talked about marriage. Her live-in companion? Yes, but that didn't begin to explain it. Her lover? That was true, she thought, shivering pleasurably with the thought. Yes, definitely her lover. But also so much more.

'Don't worry about Francesco,' she said. 'I didn't tell him I was coming here. If he finds out, he'll be too busy murdering me to bother with you. C'mon, let me down. You know I'll be all right.'

'If it's OK with Fiona,' Ken said, naming her diving partner.

'Fine with me,' Fiona sang out on the same frequency. 'Let's go.'

She took Celia's hand and the two of them sank lower and lower into the water of Mount's Bay, just off the coast of Cornwall in England. They, Ken and his crew had set out from Penzance an hour ago, stopping about a mile from the coast in a place that reputedly concealed a sunken pirate galleon.

'Went down in a fierce battle with the British Navy,' he'd told them as they made their way out to sea. 'And they never recovered the treasure, so you may be lucky.'

'You don't need to give me your professional spiel.' Celia had laughed. 'Just having the experience is treasure enough for me.'

She'd forced herself to be patient while they strapped the cylinders onto her back and demonstrated how everything worked. She was wearing a full-face mask, which she had at first resisted.

'I thought it would just be goggles and a mouthpiece connecting me to the oxygen cylinders,' she'd protested.

'Yes, but I want to keep radio contact with you, so you need a full-face mask,' he had said firmly.

She'd yielded under pressure. Then Fiona had taken her hand and the two of them had gone into the water together.

Now Celia could feel her whole body deliciously chilly from the water encasing her outside the rubber suit.

There were more rocks to be felt, plants, sometimes even the exquisite sense of a large fish flapping past, which made her laugh with delight. But the real pleasure lay in the sensation of being free of the world and its tensions.

Free of Francesco Rinucci?

Reluctantly, she admitted that the answer was yes. She adored him, but she'd run away from him as far as she could go. She'd planned this dive a week ago, and kept it a secret from him, saddened by the need, but determined not to yield. If you were blind it was hard enough to keep control of your own life without having to deal with a man who loved you so much that he tried to muffle you in cotton wool.

'All right?' came Fiona's voice over the radio.

'Yes, it's so beautiful,' she said eagerly.

Nobody who knew Celia would be surprised at her saying *beautiful*. She had her own notion of beauty that had nothing to do with eyes. Everything that reached her through the pressure of the water—the coolness and the freedom—all this was beauty.

'You can let me go,' she said, and felt Fiona's hand slip away.

With Ken still holding the other end of the line she wasn't completely free, but she could rely on him to back off as much as possible, and give her the illusion. Francesco could learn so much from him. But Francesco would never face how much he didn't know.

She kicked out with her flippers and powered through the water, relishing the sensation of it streaming past her. Suddenly she was at one with the water, part of it, glorying in it.

'Wheeeeeeee!' she cried.

'Celia?' Ken sounded nervous.

'It's all right,' she said, laughing. 'It's just me going crazy.'

'No change there, then.'

'Nope. Wheeeeeeee!'

'Do you mind?' he complained. 'That was my eardrum.'

She chuckled. 'How far down am I?'

'About a hundred feet.'

'Let me have another forty.'

'Twenty. That's the limit of safety.'

'Twenty-five,' she begged.

'Twenty,' he declared implacably.

The line loosened and she sank farther, reaching out at plants and rocks, anything and everything in this marvellous world.

There had been another time when she'd thought the world was marvellous, when she'd just met Francesco. He'd walked into her workplace and stood talking to the receptionist. Celia had been alerted by a soft, 'Wow!' from Sally, her young assistant, who was sighted.

'Wow?' she queried.

'Wow!'

'That's a lot of wow.' Celia chuckled. 'Tell me about him.'

'He's tall and dark with deep blue eyes. Probably late thirties, black hair, waves a bit. I like the way he moves—sort of easy and graceful—and he knows how to wear an expensive suit.'

'You've priced his suit?' Celia'd demanded, amused.

'I've seen it on sale and it costs a fortune. In fact, from the way it fits, I'll bet he had it specially made for him. He's got that sort of something about him. An "air"—like the world is his, he'll take it when it suits him, and in the meantime it can wait until he is ready.'

'You're really studying the subject, aren't you?' Celia'd said, chuckling.

'Naturally I want to give you an accurate description. Oh, yes, and he's got a brooding look that you only see in film stars— Oh, gosh, I forgot you haven't seen any film stars. I'm really sorry.'

'Don't apologise,' Celia'd said warmly. 'I work hard to make people forget that I can't see. You just told me I've succeeded. But I've always been blind, so I can't imagine anything. I don't know what colours look like, or shapes and sizes. I have to discover them by touch.'

'Well, his shape and size would really be worth discovering by touch,' Sally'd said frankly, and Celia'd burst into a peal of laughter.

'He's looking this way,' Sally'd hissed. 'Now he's coming over.'

Next thing Celia heard a quiet, deep voice with the hint of an Italian accent. 'Good morning. My name is Francesco Rinucci. I'm looking for Celia Ryland.'

The moment she heard his voice she could 'see' him—not in the kind of detail Sally had explained, but in her own way. Easy and graceful, an air as though the world was his; those she had understood at once.

Now, making her way through the water and remembering, she thought that the world really had been his. And when she was in his arms, the world had been hers.

But that had been five months ago. In five short months she'd loved him passionately, fought with him furiously, and learned that she must escape him at all costs.

Five months, and so much had happened in between. So much joy, so much bitterness, so much regret that they had ever met, so much thankfulness that she had known him even for a brief time.

She remembered everything of their meeting. Details

reached her differently from other people, but more intensely. As was her way, she had been the first to offer her hand, and had felt him clasp it in return. His hand felt strong and good, with long fingers and a feeling of suppressed power. It had made her wonder about the rest of him.

'Worth discovering by touch,' Sally had said.

Celia had tried to put the thought out of her mind but without success. She'd been vividly aware of him moving carefully in the confined space near her desk, where much of the room had been taken up by Wicksy, her golden Labrador guide dog.

Wicksy's manners were beautiful but reticent. He had accepted Francesco's admiration as his due, returned it to the extent of briefly resting his snout in Francesco's hand, then returned to curling up beneath Celia's desk, apparently relaxed but actually on guard.

The newcomer had sat down close to her, and she'd been able to sense his height, the breadth of him, and something else, a pleasing aroma that shifted between spice and wood-smoke, borne by the breeze. It had spoken of warmth and life, and it had told her that she was living in a shell and should try to reach outside, where he might be waiting.

Only might?

It would be a chance worth taking.

'Why were you looking for me?' she asked.

He explained that he was part of Tallis Inc., a firm famous for the manufacture of luxury furniture. Its wares were excellent and it was expanding all over Europe.

'We need a good PR firm,' he said. 'The one we're using has gone downhill. I was advised to come here, and to ask for you personally. They say you're the best.'

Being a gentleman, he made a valiant effort to keep the surprise out of his voice, without quite managing it.

'And now you're wondering why someone didn't warn you that I was blind?' she said impishly.

That threw him; she could tell. She burst out laughing.

'No—I wasn't—' he said hastily.

'Oh, yes, you were. Don't deny it to me. I've been here too often. I know what people think when they meet me unawares.'

'Am I that easy to read?' His tone suggested a hesitant smile.

'Right this minute you're thinking, How the hell did I get into this, and how am I going to get out without being rude?'

It was a favourite joke of hers—to read their minds, trip them up, make them feel a little uneasy.

But he wasn't uneasy. He took her hand and held it tightly, speaking seriously.

'No, I'm not thinking that. I don't think you could guess what I'm thinking.'

He was wrong. She could guess exactly. Because she was thinking the same thing.

It was unnerving to find such thoughts possessing her about a man she'd only just met, but she couldn't help herself. And a part of her, the part that rushed to meet adventure, wasn't sorry at all. True, another part of her counselled caution, but she was used to ignoring it.

But for the moment she must act with propriety, so she showed him the array of equipment that helped her to function.

'I talk to the computer and it talks back to me,' Celia said. 'Plus I have a special phone, and various other things.'

He took her to lunch at a small restaurant next door, and he talked about his firm while she tapped information into a small terminal. Afterwards he began to walk her back to the office, but she stopped, saying, 'I have to take Wicksy to the park.'

He went with her, watching, fascinated, as she plunged into her bag and brought out a ball.

'If I throw it now, I won't hit anyone, will I?' she asked anxiously.

He assured her she wouldn't, then wished he'd been more cautious. Instead of the ladylike gesture he'd expected, she put all her force into hurling the ball a great distance, so that a man contentedly munching sandwiches had to jump out of the way with an angry yell.

'You told me it was safe,' she said in mock complaint.

'I'm sorry. I didn't realise you could throw that far.'

With a bark of joy, Wicksy bounded after the ball, retrieved it and charged back to drop it at her feet. After another couple of throws he came to sit before her, his head cocked to one side, gazing up at her with a significant expression.

'All right, let's go,' she said, taking the ball from his mouth and putting it away. 'This next bit is rather indelicate, so you may want to go away.'

'I'll be brave,' he said, grinning.

She found a spot under the trees, said, 'OK, go on,' and Wicksy obeyed while she reached into her bag for the scoop and plastic bag.

'Would you like me to do that for you?' he asked through gritted teeth.

'That's being gallant above and beyond the call of duty,' she said, liking him for it. 'But he's my responsibility and I'll wield the pooper-scooper.'

'Well, I offered,' he said, and something in the sound of the words told her he was grinning with relief.

When the business was complete they made their way back across the park.

At the door of her building he said, 'I meant to tell you a lot more about my firm and our requirements, but there wasn't time. Can I take you to dinner tonight and we can talk some more?'

'I would like that.'

She spent the rest of the afternoon hard at work, for she wanted to impress him. Then she went home, showered, and put on a gold dress that she'd been told looked stunning with her red hair.

In the apartment next door lived Angela, a good friend who worked in a wholesale fashion house, and one of the few people Celia trusted enough to ask for help. Having called her in, she twisted and turned before her.

'Will I do?'

'Oh, yes, you'll do, and then some. You look gorgeous. I was right to make you get that dress. And those sandals. Lord, but I envy you your long legs and your ankles. If you knew how rare it is for a woman to have ankles as slender as yours, and yet have perfect balance so that you can walk on them without wobbling! I could murder you for that alone.'

Celia chuckled. She owed Angela a lot, for it was she who'd taught her how to win the admiring glances that she knew followed her even without seeing them. Angela had decreed the colours that went with Celia's red hair.

'But what does it mean—red hair?' Celia had asked.

'It means you've got to be very careful what you wear with it. You're lucky in your complexion, pale and delicate, the perfect English-rose style.'

'What's an English rose?' Celia had asked at once.

'Let's just say men go for it. That's what you're hoping for, isn't it?'

'Certainly not. This is a business meeting to discuss strategy and forward planning.'

'Boy, you really have got it bad.'

Celia laughed, but inwardly she could feel herself blushing. Her friend's words were true. She had got it bad already.

When she opened the door to Francesco that evening she heard what she'd been hoping for—a brief hesitation that said he was taken aback by her appearance. She smiled at his wolf whistle and inclined her head in mock acceptance.

There was the tiniest hint of their future disagreements when he wanted her to leave Wicksy behind.

'He goes with me everywhere,' she said firmly

'Surely he doesn't have to? I'll keep you safe.'

'But I don't want to be kept safe,' she said, still smiling. 'Wicksy treats me as an equal in ways that nobody else does.'

'But you don't need him if you've got me,' he insisted. 'Besides, restaurants don't like dogs.'

'There's one two streets away that knows Wicksy and always welcomes him. Let's not argue about it. Wicksy belongs with me and I belong with him.'

She kept her tone pleasant, but he must have sensed her determination because he yielded. She knew a twinge of disappointment. Understanding her need for independence was one of her silent 'tests' and he'd failed it. But there was time yet, and she was determined to enjoy her evening with him.

They walked the short distance to the restaurant, and settled down at their table to talk.

'Did you have to bring that great folder in with you?' he asked.

'Of course. How else could I make my pitch? This is a working dinner, remember? I have several ideas that I think you'll like.'

She talked for several minutes, illustrating her points by pushing various pages towards him. She'd earlier marked them with nail scissors, so that she could tell by feel which was which.

'You seem to know everything about everything we've ever made,' he said, awed.

'I've been working hard.'

'I can tell, but how on earth—' he asked.

'I accessed a lot of information about your firm on line this afternoon.'

'And your computer delivers it vocally?' he hazarded.

'There is software that does that,' she said vaguely.

In truth she'd got Sally to read it out to her, a method she sometimes used when she was short of time. But she wasn't going to tell him that.

There were two conversations going on here, she realised. On the surface she sold her abilities, while he admired her work. It was pleasant, restrained, but beneath the surface they were sizing each other up.

Celia listened closely to every nuance of his voice. Without being deep, it had a resonance that excited her and made her want to touch him.

She'd chosen this restaurant and insisted on taking Wicksy because in that way she could keep some sort of control. The trouble was that she increasingly wanted to abandon control and hurl herself headlong into the unknown.

She sensed that he, too, was putting a brake on himself, but his caution was greater than hers. Francesco eased her away from the subject of work, and made her talk about herself.

'How did your parents cope with you being blind?' he asked.

'Easily. They were both blind, too,' she explained.

'*Mio Dio!* How terrible!' he said instinctively.

'Not really. You'd be amazed how little you miss what you've never had. Since they couldn't see, either, and I'm an only child, I had almost no point of comparison. The three of us formed a kind of secret society. It was us against the world because we thought everyone else was crazy. They thought we were crazy, too, because we wouldn't conform to their ideas about how blind people ought to behave.

'They met at university, where he was a young professor and she was one of his students. He writes books now, and she does his secretarial work. He says she's more efficient than any sighted secretary because she knows what to watch out for. They used to say they fell in love because they understood things that nobody else did. So I grew up accepting the way we lived as normal, and I still do.'

There was a slight warning in her voice as she said the last words, but she didn't make much of the point.

She managed to turn the conversation towards him. He told her about his family in Italy, his parents and his five brothers, the villa perched on the hill with the view over the Bay of Naples. Then he caught himself up, embarrassed.

'It's all right,' she told him. 'I don't expect people to censor their speech because I've never seen the things they describe. If I did that I wouldn't have any friends.'

'And you've never seen anything of the world at all,' he said in wonder. 'That's what I can't get my head round.'

'Yes, I suppose it is hard,' she mused. 'This morning my friend told me you had deep blue eyes, but I had to tell her I couldn't picture them.'

In the brief silence she could sense him looking around, and strove not to smile.

'Why—did she tell you that?' he asked, almost nervously.

She assumed a wicked, breathy innocence. 'You mean, it's not true? Your eyes are really deep red?'

'Only when I've had too much to drink.'

She laughed so much that Wicksy, dozing at her feet, pushed his snout against her, asking if all was well.

Something other than laughter was happening that evening.

It was in the air between them. Another woman might have read it in his eyes. Celia sensed it with the whole of her being.

The talk drifted back to his family.

'My mother's English, but you'd never know it. At heart Signora Rinucci is a real Italian *mamma*, determined to marry all her sons off.'

'Six sons? That's quite an undertaking. How's she doing?'

'Four married, two left. But my brother Ruggiero has just got engaged. He'll marry Polly fairly soon, and then Mamma will turn her firepower on me.'

So now he'd contrived to let her know that he wasn't married, she thought, appreciating his tactics.

'Don't your parents do the same with you?' he asked casually.

'It's the one thing they've never given me advice about,' she said. 'Except when Dad's been at work in the kitchen Mum will say, "Never marry a man who cooks squid." And she's right.'

After a brief silence he said, 'We have squid in the Bay of Naples. Best in the world, so the fishermen say.'

'But you don't cook it, do you?'

'No, I don't cook it,' he assured her.

And then a strange silence fell, slightly touched by embarrassment, as though they'd both strayed closer to danger than they'd meant.

Celia found that she couldn't be the one to break the silence, because she was so conscious of what had caused it, but his manner of breaking it brought no comfort. He offered her coffee and another glass of wine, his manner polite and impeccable. Earlier he'd been warm and pleasant. Suddenly only courtesy was left, and it had a hollow feel.

The truth began to creep over her, and with it a chill.

At her front door he said, 'I'll take your folder with me. I like your ideas, and I think we've got a deal, but I'll know more when I've read it again.'

'You've got my number?'

'I made sure I got it. Good night.'

He didn't even try to kiss her.

Now she knew the truth.

When he didn't call her, she understood why. As though she was inside his head, she followed his thoughts, his dread of getting too close to a blind woman, his common sense advice to himself to back off now, before it was too late.

'They all do it,' she mused to Wicksy as they took their final walk one evening. She sat on a bench beneath the trees and felt him press against her. 'We've both known it to happen before. Remember Joe? You never liked him, did you? You tried to tell me that he wouldn't last, and you were right.'

His nose was cold and comforting in her hand.

'Men are scared to become involved with me in case it disrupts their pleasant lives, their successful careers.'

The nose nudged gently.

'I know,' she said sadly. 'We can't blame them, can we? And maybe it's better for him to be honest and retreat now rather than later.'

Another soft nudge.

'It's just that I thought this time it might have been different. I thought *he* was different. But he isn't.'

There was a whine from beside her knee, with a distant air of urgency.

'What's that? Oh, the biscuit. I'm sorry. I forgot. Here.'

She felt it vanish from her hand.

'What would I do without you, my darling? You've got more sense than the rest of us put together. As long as I've got you, I don't need anyone else.'

Celia leaned down and rested her cheek against his head, trying to take comfort from their loving companionship.

But the truth was that her heart was aching. Something about Francesco had reached out to her, and she had reached back because it had felt so right. It was crazy to feel like this about a man she'd only just met, but with all her heart and soul she wanted him.

Now, floating in the blessed anonymity of the ocean, she wondered how she could have loved him so agonisingly then, and five months later be running away from him?

The question tortured her as she sank deeper into the water, reliving the events of yesterday, when she'd slipped out of the home they shared without telling him where she was going. She'd left him a note that she'd managed to write on a large pad:

I'LL CALL YOU LATER TODAY, CELIA.

She'd hated the deception, hated herself for doing it, but she'd had no choice. She loved him now as much as she'd done on that evening, five months ago, when she'd wondered, sadly, if she would ever see him again. If anything, she loved him more.

And yet she'd escaped him, knowing that if she didn't she would go mad.

# CHAPTER TWO

THE PR contract had been arranged the next day, and over the following week there had been a good deal of coming and going between the two firms. But it had never been Francesco who arrived. Celia had resigned herself to not meeting him again when there was a knock on her front door in the evening.

She'd gone to the door, switching on the light as she went, so that the visitor should have some illumination. She lived without lights.

'Who is it?' she called.

'It's me,' came his voice from behind the door.

He didn't need to identify himself further. They both understood that there was only one 'me.' She opened the door and put out her hand, feeling it enfolded in his.

'I came because—' He stopped. 'There are things we need to— Will you let me in—*please?*'

She stood back. 'Come in.'

She heard the click as the door closed behind him. He was still holding her hand, but for a moment he didn't move, as if he was unsure what would come next.

'I didn't think you'd come back,' she said. 'The contract—'

'The hell with the contract,' he said with soft violence. 'Do you really think that's why I'm here?'

'I don't know what to think,' she whispered. 'I haven't known all week.'

'I'll tell you what to think of me—that I'm a coward who runs away from a woman who's different, more challenging than other women. I run away because secretly I'm afraid I can't match up to her. I just know I'll let her down and she'll be better off without me—'

'Isn't that for her to decide?' she asked joyfully.

His hand tightened on hers and she felt him raise it, then his lips against her palm.

'I couldn't keep away from you,' he said huskily. 'I tried, but I can't. And I never will be able to.'

'I'll never want you to,' she said in passionate gratitude.

His lips were burning her hand, igniting her whole body so that she longed for him to touch her everywhere. She drew his face towards her and felt the urgency of his mouth at the first touch of hers. It was as though she'd given him the signal he'd been waiting for.

Now she knew that she'd wanted this since she'd sat with him in the restaurant, listening to his words and trying to picture the mouth that shaped them. His lips on hers, coaxing, inciting, urging, pleading, had been the temptation that teased and taunted her.

And all this week, after he'd gone, she'd been haunted by dreams of the impossible, of his body lying naked against her in the equality that darkness would bring. Now he was here, and joy and excitement possessed her body and soul.

'Celia,' he said huskily. 'Celia—'

She stepped back, drawing him after her towards the bedroom, reaching up to turn out the hall light, so that the place was dark again and only she knew the way.

It might be madness to rush helter-skelter into love.

Caution was indicated. But her circumstances and a combative nature had always made her despise caution. Besides, Francesco had tried it and it didn't work. It was a relief, setting her free.

She touched his face, letting her fingers gently explore its planes and angles, the wide mouth and sharply defined jaw, the slightly crooked nose. He was just as she wanted him to be.

She remembered everything. Floating now on the cushion of water, cut off from the world, she recalled details that she'd barely noticed at the time. They'd been obscured by the sweet fire flaming through her, engulfing all in its path, yet they'd endured in some corner of her consciousness, to be relived later.

Now they made her heart ache for their cruel contrast with the present. Francesco was still the same man who'd won her love by his gentleness and his open adoration of her. He was still the man who'd taken her to bed and loved her with slow, reverent gestures that had brought her flesh to eager life.

The pressure of the water on every part of her body was bringing back those memories. With his very first touch she had felt that he was touching her everywhere. As his lips had lain gently against her breast the reaction had flowed up from her loins and out to every part.

She had been eager to welcome him in, reaching for him, drawing him close, moving with his rhythm. Everything had felt natural because it was with him. His skin, touching hers, had been warm, growing more heated as his passion mounted.

To make love in blindness was an act of trust, but hadn't failed her. He had been a tender lover, gentle, considerate even in the intensity of his ardour, and above all, generous. Looking back, she often said that her passion had started the day they'd met. Her love dated from that first night together.

When the first explosion of delight had been over and they

had fallen apart, stunned and joyful, she'd propped herself up on one elbow and begun to explore him.

'After all, I can't see you,' she teased. 'I have to find out in my own way.'

'I guess you were going to discover my feeble muscles and pot-belly some time or other.' He laughed.

'Yup. Let's see, now, is this your shoulder?'

'It's at the top of my arm, so I guess it must be.'

'Nothing feeble about that muscle,' she murmured. 'And it continues very nicely along here.'

'You've left my arm behind. That's my chest.'

'Mmm,' she whispered, kissing the pectoral muscles one by one. 'You don't have any hair on your chest. I prefer that.'

'Are you saying you're an expert?'

'Blind teaching is very modern these days,' she said in a serious voice. 'We take lessons in everything.'

There was the briefest pause before he said cautiously, 'Everything?'

'Almost everything.'

'Are you making fun of me?'

Her lips twitched. 'Do you think I am?'

'I wish I could be sure.'

'Well, you can decide about that later. Where was I?'

'Exploring my chest.'

'Let's leave that for the moment. I don't want to rush this.'

'I don't want to rush it, either,' he said huskily, letting her fingers roam over his thighs, relishing every moment.

'You have very long legs,' she murmured in a considering voice. 'At least, I suppose they are. I don't have many points of comparison.'

'I wish you didn't have any—unless, of course, you learned that in the leg class?'

She stifled her laughter against his chest, and at last she felt him relax enough to laugh, as well.

Francesco didn't relax easily, she could tell. It had been a real shock to him when she'd made a joke about her blindness, but he'd soon get the hang of that. She would teach him. In the meantime, they had other business.

'Now, about that pot-belly of yours,' she murmured, letting her fingers continue their work. 'It doesn't feel very pot to me.'

'I don't keep it precisely there,' he said in a tense voice.

'You want me to move?'

'No, just…keep doing…what you're doing.'

She did as he wished, realising that their previous loving had barely taken the edge off his passion and he was once more in a state of heated arousal. He was hard and hot in her palm, and she indulged herself in pleasure until, at the precise moment she intended, he lost control and tossed her onto her back.

Her own control was fast vanishing. She was eager for him to move over her and repeat the experience that had been so thrilling the first time. She reached for him, barely able to contain herself, clasping him so firmly that they were united in an instant.

At the feel of him inside her she gave a shout of pleasure that mingled with his and began to move strongly, urgently, wrapping her legs around him and holding him close. She wanted to keep him like that always.

Afterwards they slept in each other's arms for a couple of hours and awoke hungry. She went into the kitchen, refusing his offer to make the food himself.

'I know where everything is,' she assured him.

'Yes, you just proved that,' he murmured.

'Don't be vulgar.' She chuckled, aiming a mock punch at him.

But she misjudged the distance and caught him across the face, making him yell more in surprise than pain.

'Darling, darling, I'm sorry,' she cried, kissing him fiercely. 'I didn't mean that.'

'You're a violent woman,' he complained.

'No, just a blind one. You'll be covered in bruises in no time.'

'How can you talk like that?'

'Because it's true. You should escape me now, while you still can!'

'I didn't mean that. I meant the other thing.'

'About being blind?'

'Yes. Never mind that now. Let's have something to eat.'

She made sandwiches and coffee and they picnicked in the bedroom.

'It upsets you when I make jokes about being blind, doesn't it?' she mused, munching.

'It confuses me. It's like invading sacred ground.'

'It's not sacred to me. Anyway, it's my ground and I'll invade it if I want to. And if I can, you can. So hush!'

They had laughed, and loved again, laughed again and loved again. That was how it had been in the beginning.

And even then the first danger signs had been there, but they'd both been too much in love to heed them. If only...

*'Time to come in,'* came the voice over the radio.

'Just a few more minutes,' Celia begged.

*'Your air will be running out soon. Did you find any pirate treasure?'*

'Not this time, but I always live in hope,' she said, determinedly cheerful.

It was time to go back and face the world. Fiona was close by, calling her, and together they made their way to the boat, where hands came down to welcome them aboard.

'How was it?' Ken asked.

'Wonderful!' Celia exclaimed. 'The most glorious

feeling—being weightless, and so free—such freedom—as though the rest of the world didn't exist.'

'Is that your idea of freedom?' Fiona asked. 'Escaping the rest of the world?'

'Escaping the world's prejudices, yes,' Celia murmured thoughtfully.

'Ah,' Ken said in a significant voice. 'I'm afraid that the world has followed you here. I've just heard on the radio that when we get back to land you'll find Francesco waiting for you.'

'How did he find me here? I just said I was going. I didn't say where.'

'I guess he's got a very good surveillance team working on it,' Ken suggested lightly.

He meant it as a joke, but Celia's face tightened and her voice was hard as she said, 'Evidently.'

'What do you want to do?' Ken asked. 'You've paid for the whole day, and there's two hours left, so we don't have to go back before then.'

It was on the tip of her tongue to tell him to head out to sea for a long as possible. But she mastered the impulse and said in a resigned voice, 'No, let's go back now. I've got to face him sooner or later.'

'Why have you got to face him?' Fiona asked indignantly. 'This is the twenty-first century. A woman doesn't have to put up with an abusive man.'

'But he isn't abusive.' Celia sighed. 'He's gentle and loving and protective. He wants to shield me from every wind that blows.'

'Oh, Lord!' Fiona said in sympathy. As they neared land she said, 'I can see his face now. He doesn't look loving and protective. He looks mad as hell.'

'Good!' Celia said. 'Then can I be as mad as hell and throw something at him?'

'What would you do about aiming?' Fiona wanted to know.

'I wouldn't need to,' Celia said despairingly. 'If he saw me lifting a heavy vase he'd get in front of me and let it hit him. *Ooooh, what am I going to do with a man like that?*'

'Leave him,' Fiona said at once. 'Or you won't survive.'

'I know, I *know,* but it's so drastic.'

'Yes, but I know what it's like. I broke my leg once, and my boyfriend drove me crazy fussing round me—do this, don't do that, let me get this for you, don't strain yourself. In the end I thumped him with my crutch. It was the only way.'

'What happened to him?' Celia asked, fascinated.

'Don't know. I never saw him again.'

Celia laughed, but the laughter soon faded and she leaned on the rail, her head bent down in the direction of the water that she could hear foaming beneath.

When they reached their destination Francesco was the first on board, coming straight to her and taking her hand.

'I'll take you ashore,' he said. 'And we'll go home.'

'No, thank you,' she replied firmly. 'As part of my day out I get a meal with the crew. And I'm hungry.'

'I'll get you a meal on the way home,' he persisted.

His hands were on her arms, urging her so firmly that her anger began to grow.

'Let go of me, Francesco,' she said in a low voice.

'I only want to guide you—'

'So you say. But you're that close to dragging me. Please let go, because I'm going to eat here.'

'If it makes it any easier we'll give you a refund for that part of the fee,' Ken offered.

It actually made things harder for her, by cutting the ground out from under her feet, making her sound childishly stubborn for the sake of it. But he meant well, so she smiled and yielded.

She was forced to let Francesco help her off the boat and escort her towards the changing rooms. But she knew he was waiting for her outside. She must face him. And then what?

She knew him so well. She could feel his moods tearing apart the darkness around her, and could sense that behind his courteous charm he was in a furious temper that he was determined to conceal. She, too, was in a temper, but less sure about the virtue of concealing it.

Celia said her goodbyes and thanked Ken for a wonderful day.

'And I don't want a refund,' she said. 'I had a great time.'

'Er—actually, I've already given the refund to your friend.'

'*What?* I never said I was going to agree.'

'He thought he was doing what would please you,' Ken said placatingly.

'You mean, he took it for granted that he knew best,' Celia snapped. 'How much did you give him?'

He told her, and she immediately plunged into her bag and produced the amount.

'I do not want a refund,' she said.

'Celia, c'mon—'

'*Take it!*'

One look at her set face was enough to make him accept the notes.

'Good,' she said. 'Now, where's the driver I hired for the day? He should be here to take me home.'

'I'm here,' said the voice of a middle-aged man beside her. 'But there's a feller over there keeps trying to make me go away. He says he'll drive you. But I can't just go off unless you say so. What should I do?'

For a moment she was on the verge of getting into the car

and leaving Francesco standing there, looking foolish. But the impulse died. This wasn't the time nor the place for the coming battle.

'Tell him you'll do what he wants,' she said. 'But only in return for a huge tip.'

'How huge?'

'Take him for all you can,' she said crossly.

'Yes, *ma'am!*'

'Remind me never to get on your wrong side,' Ken said with feeling.

She laughed reluctantly. 'Yes, I'm told I scare strong men.'

'I believe it. But here's Fiona with Wicksy. He isn't scared of you.'

Her guide dog came forward, relieved at recovering her after an absence of several hours. For a few moments they nuzzled each other.

'Sorry to leave you alone, my darling,' she murmured. 'I couldn't take you onto the boat—'

'I think he'd have jumped into the water after you,' Ken said.

'Yes, he would,' he said fondly.

'Are you ready?' That was Francesco's voice. 'I'm driving you home.'

'What about the driver I hired?' Celia asked, contriving to sound innocent.

'I persuaded him to go.'

'You had no right to do that.'

'Then no doubt you'll be pleased to know that he exacted a hefty price,' Francesco said grimly.

'Really? Shocking!'

'And don't try to sound surprised, because I saw him talking to you, and it wouldn't surprise me to learn that you put him up to that bit of blackmail.'

'Who? Me?'

'Here's the car. In you go, boy.'

When Wicksy was safely installed on the backseat Celia got into the front, immediately feeling his cold nose against her neck—his way of reminding her that he was still here. She put her hand behind her to touch him, silently saying, Message received, and after that they were both able to relax.

She needed all Wicksy's calming influence to silence her inner rage at what Francesco had done. It was a long drive home, and she didn't want to fight in the car.

At first it seemed he didn't want to, either, but after a while he said through gritted teeth, 'How could you? How could you do it?'

'I did it because I had to. Because I wanted to find out if I *could*.'

'And now you know. Is anything better?'

'It might have been if you hadn't spoiled it. I could just as easily ask, How could *you?* No, no, don't answer that. We mustn't fight about this now. We've said it all so often. Let's just get home.'

Nobody spoke for the rest of the drive, but it didn't feel like silence because the air was jagged with anger and with all the words being suppressed. By the time they reached their destination she was exhausted.

Home was still the flat she'd lived in before, which had been adapted for her in so many ways that it had made sense for him to move in with her five months earlier. After that one sweet loving there had been no question about their living together. Neither of them could have borne to do anything else.

'I'll take Wicksy for his walk,' she said as she got out of the car.

'I'll come with you.'

'*No!*' The word came out in a flash, before she could stop it, and she was instantly contrite. 'I'm sorry—it's just that I need to be alone. I'm all tensed up.'

'I'll be waiting at home, then,' he said in a colourless voice.

She was out for a long time, deliberately delaying her return home because of the fearful voice in her mind that warned her they were approaching a crisis, and the wrong words could destroy them both.

Part of her knew the problem had to be faced, and she wanted to go forward and deal with it. Part of her shrank away, arguing that things could be smoothed over with more time, and perhaps everything would be better in future. He might even be asleep when she returned.

But he wasn't asleep, and she knew that the evil moment couldn't be postponed any longer.

'You were gone a long time,' he said edgily. 'I was—'

'Don't!' she told him quickly. 'Don't say you were worried about me. Just don't say that.'

'Is it wrong for me to be worried about you?'

'You overdo it. That's all I meant.'

'I know what a tough day you've had, and when you vanish into the darkness like that—'

'Francesco, for pity's sake,' she groaned. 'Why do you say things like that?'

'Like what?'

'Vanish into the darkness. I'm always in the darkness. It's where I'm at home. I'm not lost in it, as you would be. Why can't I make you understand that?'

'I do understand it in one way—'

'It's not enough,' she cried. 'I'm not helpless, I'm not an invalid, but in your mind I'm always slightly less than a whole person.'

'No—not really. But—you do have a disadvantage that other people don't have—'

'I also have advantages that other people don't have. My memory is twice as good as yours, because I've trained it. I can hear things in people's voices that you'd miss. I saved you a lot of money once by warning you that the man you were planning to do business with was untrustworthy. I could hear it in his voice. You were very lofty about that at the time. "You and your intuition!" you said. But at least you had the sense to listen to me and throw him out. He's just started a two-year stretch for fraud, in case you didn't know.'

'Yes, I did. I was going to tell you, and say thank you. But I might have known you'd hear it first.'

'Yes, you might. Perhaps I'm not as much at a disadvantage as you think.'

He sighed, and she could hear him pacing the room.

'How did you know where to find me?' she asked.

'I remembered Ken from when we met him at that party. You talked to him for so long that I got jealous—until I realised it was his diving that fascinated you. You've called him several times since then, haven't you?'

'Yes, I have. It took time to set up today.'

'I'm sure there must have been a lot of planning,' he said in a bleak voice. 'Booking the day, hiring the car to drive you down there, leaving the flat secretly, not telling me where you were going—that took some organising. When I found your note I checked up on Ken's firm and discovered that you had a booking.'

'So you jumped into your car and came down to tell me that I mustn't dive because I didn't have your permission?' she said through gritted teeth.

'Because it isn't safe for you.'

'It's as safe for me as for anyone. I was on a line. Ken could have hauled me in at any time.'

'You went behind my back,' he said harshly.

The bitterness in his voice dulled the edge of her anger, reminding her how easy it was to hurt him. She didn't want to hurt him, She wanted to love him as she'd done in their first carefree days; days that she knew would never come again.

'You don't give me any choice,' she cried. 'I had to do it without telling you because you'd have made such a fuss. You always do that if I try to do anything a little bit unusual.'

'A little bit?' he echoed. 'You were scuba diving.'

'Yes, and I managed perfectly well. As I knew I would. But you can't bring yourself to believe that, can you? Sometimes I think you actually hate it when I manage to do something without you.'

'For God's sake, do you know what you're saying?'

'Yes, I'm saying I want to live my life as an adult, without having to apply to you for permission to take every breath.'

'I'm only trying to keep you safe.'

'I don't *want* to be safe. I want the freedom to take the same risks as other people, and before I met you I had it. I loved it. But you set yourself to take it away from me, wrap me in cotton wool and lock me in a cocoon. I can't live in there, Francesco, not even if you're there with me. It's like a prison, and I have to break out.'

'Aren't you being a bit melodramatic?' he demanded

'Not from where I'm standing.'

'Meaning that I'm a gaoler?'

'The kindest, most loving gaoler in the world,' she said, trying to soften it. 'I know that you love me, and it's your love that makes you overprotective, but I can't live that way. I've got to get as far out on the edge as I can without you trying to drag me back.'

'Drag you— Now you're talking nonsense.'

'Anything you disagree with is nonsense, according to you. I can't live my life wondering if you're standing there behind me, trying to bring everything to a halt.'

'You don't—'

'Francesco, listen to me, please. The really sad thing about today is that I would have loved to share it with you. It would have been wonderful to go into the water together and sink down, hand in hand. I even came to the edge of telling you. But I backed off at the last minute because I knew you'd do everything to stop me.'

'Because I don't want to lose you,' he growled.

'But you *are* losing me,' she said piteously. 'Oh, why can't you see that?'

'By trying to protect you? Isn't that my job? We're practically husband and wife, and a man looks after his wife—'

'That shouldn't mean putting a ball and chain on her.'

She heard his sharp intake of breath. 'That's a lousy thing to say.'

'I'm sorry. I didn't mean it like that.'

'I'd sure as hell like to know how you did mean it,' he said bitterly.

'It's just that to you life is one big word—*no*.'

'All right, maybe I take things a little too far,' he grated, 'but I don't just ask *you* to say no to things you want. I wouldn't do that without being prepared to do the same.'

'What do you mean by that?' she asked, with a sudden keen edge to her voice.

He failed to hear its significance,

'My firm asked me to start an Italian branch, in Naples—'

'Your home town,' she gasped in delight. 'That's great. When do we leave?'

'We don't. I turned it down.'

*'You did what?'*

'How could I possibly ask you to come to Italy with me? You manage well enough in England, but what would you do in a strange country?'

'Meaning that I'm too stupid to find the way? Are you forgetting that I've already learned Italian?'

'We've done some together, *cara,* and it's been delightful—'

'A delightful game, you mean?' she said in a hard voice. 'Humouring me. You made a big decision like that without consulting me because you didn't think I was up to the task?'

'I only meant—'

'How dare you? *How dare you?*'

'I was only thinking of you,' he retorted.

'Did I ask you to think of me? I'm not a child, Francesco, and I'm not an idiot. And I've had enough of you treating me that way.'

'Look, we'll talk about it when you've calmed down.'

'I'm not worked up. Inside I'm as cold as ice, and I'm telling you that I want you to go.'

'Go where? I live here.'

'Not any longer. It doesn't work between us. I think perhaps it never could. Please go quickly. I don't want to see you here again.'

'You don't want to *what?*'

'Go!'

'Celia, for pity's sake, stop this before it's too late.'

'It's been too late for a long time,' she whispered.

'Look, I'm sorry if I went too far. But after all we've been to each other you can't just—'

'It's over,' she said, feeling that she would start to scream in a minute. 'Please go, Francesco. Just pack a bag and go tonight. You can get the rest of your things later. But go now.'

In the silence she could sense that he was totally stunned. He knew she meant it.

Suddenly she broke.

'*Get out!*' she screamed. '*Just get out!*'

# CHAPTER THREE

'GET out. Just get out.'

He heard the words before he awoke. They echoed in the darkness behind his eyes, screaming around his head like curses.

Then his eyes were open and he was sitting up in bed, trying to understand the world around him. He didn't know where he was. Surely this was his home back in London, but where was she? Why not in bed with him?

Then the haze cleared, the walls fell into place. He was back at his parents' home, the Villa Rinucci in southern Italy, a place where he hadn't lived for years.

Now he was using it as a refuge until he could clear his head. Nothing had been straight in his mind since the day Celia had thrown him out. Somehow he'd organised himself, agreed to return to Naples to set up the Italian branch of his firm, and left England. There had been one brief meeting with Celia when he'd collected his things, but they had spoken to each other like strangers, and he hadn't seen her again. She was behind him. Finished. Over and done with.

Except that her cry of *'Get out!'* still echoed with him, day and night. And the worst thing, the thing that actually scared him, was that it wasn't only her voice he heard. It was as though someone had cast a malign spell, triggered by those words and those alone. And he couldn't escape.

Francesco got out of bed and went to the window, seeing the dawn beginning to break over the Bay of Naples. As he sat there, unwilling to return to bed and risk a repetition of the nightmare, he heard a soft footstep in the corridor outside and knew that it was Hope, refusing to accept that a man in his late-thirties didn't need to be hovered over protectively by his mother.

He heard her stop outside his door and waited with dread for the knock. He loved his mother, but he shrank from the questions he couldn't answer because he didn't want to face them.

After a while she went away, leaving him alone with the brightening dawn that had no power over the darkness inside him.

'Are you looking at those again?' Toni Rinucci asked his wife warmly.

Hope smiled, looking up from the book of wedding photographs she was studying.

'I can't help it,' she said. 'They are so beautiful.'

'But Ruggiero has been married for three months now,' he said, naming one of their twin sons.

'The pictures are still beautiful after three months,' Hope said. 'Look at little Matti.'

Ruggiero's toddler son stood just in front of his father and Polly, his new stepmother. Although only two years old, he'd already managed to steal the limelight.

'He looks like a little angel in that pageboy suit,' Hope said sentimentally.

'Yes—you'd never know that he'd covered it with mud ten minutes later,' Toni observed with grandfatherly cynicism.

'He's real boy,' Hope declared happily. 'Oh, look!'

She'd reached the picture showing all six of her sons.

'It's so good to see them all together.' She sighed. 'Francesco has been away so much—first America, then England—but this time he was here. Oh, it's so good to have him finally back where he belongs.'

Toni was silent as they went down the stairs together, and Hope, who could read his silences, glanced at him.

'You don't think so?' she asked.

'I'm not sure he's home to stay. He's not a boy any more.'

'But of course he won't stay with us for ever,' Hope conceded. 'He'll find his own place and move out. But we'll still see him far more often than when he was living abroad.'

Hope made some coffee for the two of them, and took it out onto the terrace with its view over the bay. They both loved these moments when they had the house to themselves and could indulge in gossip about everyday matters—their household, their sons, their growing army of grandchildren, their upcoming thirty-fifth wedding anniversary—or just about nothing in particular.

'That isn't really what I meant,' said Toni as she set his coffee before him, just as he liked it. 'I sense something strange about his coming home now.'

'He came home for the wedding,' Hope pointed out.

'Yes, but we thought he'd be here a few days, and bring Celia with him. Instead, he came without her, and stayed. Why did he suddenly leave England? He had a good career there, in a successful firm. He owns shares in it and was making a fortune.'

'But he'll do even better by setting up here,' Hope pointed out. 'It made sense for them to send him to his own country.'

'I don't like things that are too sensible,' her husband complained. 'There's something else behind it.'

Hope nodded. 'I think so, too,' she conceded. 'I just hope it isn't—'

'What?' Toni asked, laying his hand over hers.

'He used to tell us so much about Celia. Every phone call, every letter was all about her. I was surprised when he said she was blind, because he's not a man who— Well—'

'Yes, I can't imagine him living with a woman he has to care for all the time,' Toni agreed. 'But I thought we were wrong. I was proud of him. He even sent us photographs of her, and called her his English rose. I'd never known him to be so committed to a woman before.'

'Then suddenly it's all over,' Hope said, 'and he comes home without her. He's been back for three months now, and he never speaks of her. Why?'

'What are you afraid of?'

'That he left her because his love wasn't great enough for him to cope. I should be sorry to think that was true of any son of mine.'

'But you didn't like him living with her at the start,' Toni pointed out. 'You said her blindness would hold him back.'

She made a face.

'All right, I admit I'm not consistent,' she conceded. 'Is anyone?'

'Never, in all the years I've known you, have you been consistent,' her husband said fondly.

'I wanted him to be sensible.' she said, 'But I suppose I don't like him to be too sensible. I wanted to believe that my son is better than myself, kinder and more generous.'

'Nobody is more generous than you,' Toni protested. 'But for the generosity of your love my life would be nothing.'

'You praise me too much,' she said with a little smile. 'It isn't generous to love a man who gives you everything you want.'

He returned the smile, and she kissed him, but they both knew that it wasn't really true. Despite his love, he didn't give her everything she wanted. Only one man could have done that, and Toni was not that man. It would have been too much to say that he knew it, but he'd always had a suspicion, which he proved by determinedly refusing to ask questions.

Thirty-five years ago he had met Hope, an Englishwoman visiting Italy, a divorcee with three sons: Luke, adopted; Francesco, born during her marriage, but not by her husband; and Primo, the stepson she'd come to love. Toni had loved her from the first moment, and had been overjoyed when she'd agreed to marry him. Only his own children could increase his happiness, and that had come about the following year, with the birth of twin sons, Carlo and Ruggiero.

Since then he had sometimes wondered if Francesco was her secret favourite, but her adoration of each one of her sons was so all-encompassing that it was hard for Toni to be sure of his suspicions. Nor did he ever allow himself to brood about them.

Hope had missed Francesco badly since he'd left home to work in America, later moving to England, but she would have missed any of them who vanished for years, making only brief visits home.

But suddenly, three months ago, he'd returned to Naples from England, ostensibly for his brother's wedding, and full of plans for setting up a branch of his firm and increasing his already healthy fortune. While he looked for somewhere to live he'd moved back into the Villa Rinucci, in the room that had always been kept for him, even when it had seemed he would never occupy it again.

But he had come without the woman he'd once seemed to love, and he would never speak of her.

'You're afraid he just dumped her because she was a burden, aren't you?' Toni asked his wife gently. 'But I don't believe that. Not our Francesco.'

'I've told myself that many times.' Hope sighed. 'But how well do we know him these days?'

'Maybe she dumped him?' Toni suggested mildly.

'Toni, *caro,* you're talking nonsense. A girl with a disability dumping a man who could look after her? No, it's something else—something that gives him bad dreams.'

'He tells you this?' Toni asked, startled.

'No, but sometimes he mutters in his sleep. I've heard him through the door. Last night I heard him cry, "Get out!" At other times he gets up and walks the floor for hours, as though he was afraid to go back to sleep.'

'Now it is you who are talking nonsense,' he told her firmly. 'If he walks the floor, surely it's because he's making plans for the factory? Why should he be afraid to sleep?'

'I wish he would tell me,' Hope said sadly. 'There is something about this situation that he's keeping a secret, and it hurts him.'

'Does he know that you heard him last night?'

'No, I meant to knock on his door, but I lacked the courage.'

'Don't tell me that you're afraid of your own son?' he said in a rallying voice.

'Not exactly. But there's a distant place inside himself, where nobody else is allowed.'

'That's always been there,' Toni pointed out. 'As long as I've known Francesco he's protected that inner place—sometimes fiercely. I remember the very first day we met. He was three years old, and the wary look was already in his eyes.'

'Perhaps he was just nervous at meeting a stranger?' Hope mused.

'Francesco has never been nervous of anyone in his life. People are nervous of him. He's always kept himself to himself. That way he doesn't have to bother with anyone who doesn't interest him.'

'*Caro,* what a cruel thing to say!' Hope protested.

'I don't mean to be cruel, but he's the man he is. He isn't wide-open to people, and his heart is difficult to reach. He prefers it like that. It saves having to make small talk. He's impatient with small talk. It's a waste of time. He told me so.'

'You make him sound so grim,' Hope objected.

'He is grim in many ways. He lacks charm, and that's another thing he's glad of.'

'I've always found him very charming,' Hope said, offended.

'So have I. Inside this family he can be delightful. To those he loves he shows warmth and generosity, but to them only. Generally he's indifferent to the world and its opinions, and nothing's going to change him. That's why if this young woman really was the right one, breaking up with her was a greater tragedy than it would be with other men.'

'But *he* dismissed *her.*'

'Did he? I wonder. What a pity you didn't manage to talk to him when you heard him call out in his sleep. He might have opened up at that moment.'

'You're right.' She sighed. 'I'm afraid I've missed the chance. This morning he rose early and left before the rest of us were up.'

'Careful to avoid us,' Toni murmured.

'No, no, I'm sure we're making too much of this, and all is well with him,' she said, as lightly as she could manage.

Toni rested his hand fondly on her shoulder.

'If you say so, *carissima,*' he said.

For the rest of the day Hope was inwardly disturbed. The

conversation of the morning haunted her, and she found herself repeatedly going out onto the terrace to look down the path to where a car would climb the hill, hoping that Francesco would return early.

But there was no sign of him, and at last the light began to fade.

Despondently, she was about to go inside but stopped at the sight of something moving on the road below. A vehicle was climbing the hill, and for a moment she allowed herself to hope. But then she saw that it was a taxi. It stopped at the steps and the driver got out to open the rear passenger door.

The first creature out was a dog, a beautiful black Labrador, wearing the harness of a guide dog. A strange feeling came over Hope, and she began to understand even before she saw the other occupant unfold her long, graceful legs and step out. It was the young woman in the pictures Francesco had sent her.

'Good afternoon,' Hope called, speaking her native English. 'You must be Signorina Ryland.'

Celia paid the driver, who set a bag beside her, offering to take it into the house. She declined, gracefully, and he drove away. Her face, turned to Hope's, was bright and smiling.

'*Buongiorno,*' she said. '*Si, sono la Signorina Ryland. E penso che siate la Signora Rinucci.*'

Hope was both charmed and impressed by this young woman who confirmed her own identity and guessed that of her hostess in excellent Italian. Then Celia added, 'But if you are Francesco's mother, you're as English as I am, or so he's told me.'

'Indeed, I am,' Hope confirmed.

She reached out to shake Celia's hand, taking the opportunity to assess her, and had the disconcerting impression that she was being assessed in return.

She knew it was false. Celia's eyes were sightless, but it

was impossible to tell—not merely because they were large and beautiful, of an incredibly clear blue, but also because they were full of life. Mysteriously, they contrived to be both guileless and shrewd.

'I'm glad we've met at last,' Hope said. 'It was time. Come inside. Can I take your bag?'

'Thank you, but I can carry it.'

'Then let's go in. There are five broad steps just in front of you.'

'If you walk ahead, Jacko will follow you.'

The Labrador did so, finding the way after Hope until they were in the large living room and Celia was sitting. Then he curled up unobtrusively close to her chair.

'Perhaps he would like some water?' Hope suggested.

'He'd love some,' Celia said quickly. 'He works so hard.'

In a few moments Jacko was gulping down water, making so much noise that Celia smiled, reaching down to touch him lightly.

Hope took the chance to study her, and was astonished by what she saw. Unconsciously she'd fallen victim to the assumption that blind meant dowdy. Now she saw how wrong she'd been. This self-assured young woman made no concessions to her disability. She was dressed with a combination of elegance and daring that actually suggested hours in front of a mirror, getting every detail right.

Her hair was a flamboyant red, just muted enough to be natural, just adventurous enough to be a statement. For the life of her Hope couldn't decide which.

Her make-up was discreetly flawless, her pale complexion offset by a delicate rose tint in her cheeks. Her figure was magnificent, encased in a deep blue trouser suit whose close fit and superb tailoring managed to be both demure and revealing.

The thought flitted across Hope's mind: *If my son threw her away, he's a fool.*

'Francesco didn't tell me that you were coming,' Hope said. 'If he had, I would have looked forward to it.'

'He doesn't know I'm in Naples. I came to return some of his property. When he left our apartment in London he was in a hurry, and he left things behind.'

'And you've come all the way to Naples to return them to him?' Hope asked.

'No, I was coming, anyway. I work here now. It seemed a good idea to bring them myself.'

A thousand questions rose to Hope's lips. She wanted to ask Celia all about herself and Francesco, and what had happened between them, but she found that something forced the questions back. This young woman had a simple dignity that was impressive.

At Hope's request she talked about the work that had brought her here. She spoke with enthusiasm but no self-pity, and laughter seemed to come naturally to her.

Hope's first thought had been that Celia wanted to reclaim Francesco. Now she wasn't so sure. This was a strong, independent girl, and Hope couldn't believe she'd come to get her claws into him. She didn't need him. She didn't need anyone.

'Let's have some fresh coffee,' she said at last, rising. 'I'll just go into the kitchen and tell Rosa. She's the best cook in Naples—but you'll discover that for yourself when you come to dinner.'

'Thank you. I'd love to.'

Hope was gone a few minutes. Just as she prepared to return she heard the sound of a car drawing up outside, and a glance out of the window showed her Francesco arriving. She was about to call him when she realised Celia would be bound to hear her. Instead, she returned to the main room, and arrived just a second too late.

Francesco had started to walk through the doorway when he saw Celia. He stopped dead, silent and motionless. Hope, watching his face from the other side of the room, saw in it all she wanted to know.

The sight of her had astounded him, penetrating his armour that was so strong against the rest of the world, leaving him exposed and defenceless. He just stood there, staring at Celia, paler than his mother had ever seen him before. He actually seemed unable to speak, and his breathing was shallow, as though he'd received a blow over the heart.

'Hallo, Francesco,' Celia said calmly.

Of course she recognised him, Hope thought. She knew his step. Of the two of them, she was the one in command of this situation.

Although she had spoken to Francesco, Celia's face was half turned away from him, so that Hope had a good view of her expression and saw the soft, eager smile that touched her mouth. Her eyes danced with pure joy.

'I had no idea that you were coming to Italy,' Francesco said slowly, and there was a slight hesitation in his voice that would have been a stammer in any other man.

'I thought it was time I changed my life,' she said cheerfully. 'Found new horizons, learned new skills.'

'But—why Italy?'

'Because you may recall that I spent some time learning Italian in case you and I ever came here together. It seemed a shame to waste it. So if you had any idea that I'd come trotting after you, you can just think again, oh, conceited one!'

'That wasn't what I—'

'Yes, it was. It's the first thing that came into your head.'

'Well, I didn't expect to find you sitting in my mother's front room. Does she know who you are?'

'I think she guessed as soon as she saw Jacko.'

'Who the hell is Jacko? Your latest romance?'

'You might say we're constantly in each other's company. He takes me everywhere.'

'I'll bet he never gets told to keep his hands to himself because you're better off without him,' Francesco said bitterly.

Celia's voice rose slightly in indignation.

'For pity's sake, Jacko is my *dog!*'

He swore under his breath.

'Don't be vulgar, my son,' Hope said.

'I didn't see you there, Mamma. This is—yes—well…' His voice trailed off as he realised the incongruity of what he was saying.

'I've been here over an hour,' Celia said merrily. 'Your mother knows who I am by now. I came to return some things that belong to you. They're in that bag by my feet, next to Jacko.'

'He's black,' Francesco said, regarding Jacko. 'I didn't see him in the shadow.'

'Come and say hallo to him,' Celia offered.

He came forward uneasily and reached out to stroke the dog, who stretched up his head for a moment, then settled down again. Francesco seated himself close enough to Celia to talk quietly.

'I don't believe this is happening. What the devil are you doing here?'

'I've told you. But well done for being honest! None of that stuff about pretending to be glad to see me.'

He bit his lip. So often in the past he'd snagged himself on her sharp wits, and clearly nothing had changed.

'Is there any reason why I should be glad to see you?' he growled.

'None that I can think of.'

'Good. Then, as you say, honesty is the best policy.'

'I expect you've got someone else by now,' she said casually. 'Don't worry, I'm not here to make trouble.'

'There's no—' He checked himself but it was too late. Now she would know.

'Then I'm not causing you any problems by being here?' she said.

'No problem at all,' he agreed briskly. 'I'm glad to see that you seem to be on top of the world.'

'Right on top,' she agreed. 'I love your country.'

She repeated the last words in Italian, for the benefit of Hope, whose footsteps she could hear. Delighted, Hope explained in Italian that her husband was here, too, and introduced him.

Celia responded with a few more words in Italian, which made Toni tease, 'Ah, but can you speak our dialect?'

He proceeded to teach her a few words of Neapolitan, which she mastered at once, and demanded to learn more.

'You learn very fast,' Toni said admiringly. 'I expect you're good at that?'

'Yes, I depend on my mind a lot more than sighted people have to,' Celia said calmly. 'My parents, who are blind, too, used to teach me all sorts of memory tricks when I was a child. I'm still proud of my memory, but, of course, now there are all sorts of gadgets to make life easy.'

'Easy?' Toni echoed, smiling at her kindly. 'Well, perhaps.'

Hope drew Francesco aside.

'I think she's marvellous,' she said. 'What possessed you to leave her?'

'I didn't leave her, Mamma. She threw me out. She actually said, 'I don't want to see you here again.' She *talks* like that—like a sighted person—because she almost doesn't realise that she's any different to anyone else. And I can't make her realise it.'

'Perhaps you're wrong to try,' Hope says thoughtfully. 'Why do you want to force her to realise something she doesn't want to know?'

'Because she can't live for ever in a fantasy. I only wanted her to be a little realistic—'

'Realistic?' Hope echoed, aghast. 'Do you think you have anything to teach that girl about realism? I don't wonder she threw you out. I'd like to do the same.'

'You'll probably get around to it,' he said with a wry grin.

Before she could say any more there was a small buzz from Celia's wrist.

'It's my watch,' she explained. 'I set the alarm to go for six o'clock. I have to get back to town and meet a customer.'

'But I want you to have supper with us,' Hope mourned.

'I'm sorry, I'd have loved to, but I'm still making my mark in a new job, so I have to try to impress people.'

'But you will come another night?' Hope asked anxiously.

'I'll look forward to it. Can you call me a taxi?'

'I'll take you,' Francesco said at once. 'I'll be home later, Mamma.'

'Thank you,' Celia said. 'Jacko?'

Hope saw Francesco lean forward, as though about to take her arm, then check himself and pull his hand back quickly. Something told Hope that Celia was fully aware of this, although she showed no sign of awareness.

'Until we meet again, *signora,*' she said to Hope, before following Jacko out of the door.

# CHAPTER FOUR

'WHERE are we going?' he asked as he started up the car.

'It's a little café called the Three Bells.'

'I know it.'

Silence. This was the first time they'd been alone together since the split, and suddenly there was nothing to say. Francesco, taken totally by surprise, was full of confusion.

When he first arrived in Italy he'd been sure she would contact him, but as the silence had stretched out he'd begun to realise that she'd really meant their parting to be permanent.

But *parting* was too light a word for it. Celia hadn't left him, she'd cruelly dismissed him, tossing him out of her home as though desperate to rid herself of all traces of his presence.

Even then he hadn't believed in the finality of what had happened. How could he when their love had been so total, so overwhelming? For him it had been unlike any other love. Transient affairs had come and gone. Women had spoken to him of love and he had repeated the words with, he now knew, only the vaguest understanding of their meaning.

Real love had caught him off-guard, with a young woman who was awkward, provocative, annoying, difficult for the sake of it—it had often seemed to him—unreasonable, stubborn and full of laughter.

Perhaps it was her laughter that had won him. He wasn't a man who laughed often. He understood a good joke, but amusement hadn't formed a major part of his life.

She, on the other hand, would never stop. With so much stacked against her she would collapse with delight at the slightest thing. Often her laughter was aimed at himself, for reasons he could not divine. At first it had been an aggravation, then a delight. Let her laugh at him if she pleased. He was her happy slave. Nothing would have made him admit that to anyone else, but within his heart he had known a flowering.

In her arms he'd become a different man, shedding the tough outer shell like unwanted armour and being passionately grateful to her for making it happen.

He'd known what had happened to him, and had assumed it was the same for her. He'd tried to take reassurance from this, reasoning that the sheer violence of her feelings meant that she was bound to change her mind about their parting. She would calm down, understand that their love was worth fighting for, forgive him whatever he'd done wrong—for he still wasn't quite sure—even, perhaps, apologise.

But none of it had happened. She'd been there when he'd cleared out his things from the apartment, had made him a coffee and told him she was sorry it had ended this way. But that was all. The long, heartfelt discussion that should have marked the end of their relationship had simply never happened. Night after night he'd sat by the phone, waiting for her to call and say they must meet just once more, to clear the air. But the phone hadn't rung. He'd sat there for hours, until the silence had eaten into him and he'd been close to despair.

He hadn't called her after that. Not even when he was leaving for Naples. Why bother? It was over.

And now, when he'd just about taught himself to believe that they would never meet again, here she was, tearing up his preconceptions, stranding him in new territory, as awkward and unpredictable as ever. He wanted to bang his head against the steering wheel.

Sitting next to him in the car, Celia tuned in to his agitation and distress. That was easy—because she shared it. She had come to his home knowing she might meet him, thinking herself prepared. She had even congratulated herself on her well-laid plans, but they had all vanished the moment she'd heard his voice. In the surge of joy at being near him again she'd almost forgotten how carefully she had arranged everything, and for a wild moment had almost thrown herself into his arms.

But that would have been a disaster—as she'd recognised when she'd forced herself to calm down. In his arms, in his bed, she would forget the things that had driven them apart— but only for a little while. Soon it would all happen again, and the second parting would be final. At all costs she must prevent that.

She had come to Italy with a set purpose. She would reclaim him, and this time it would be for ever—or never.

*Per sempre,* she mused, practising her Italian. For ever. *Per sempre e eternità.* And if not—*finita.*

'We're just entering Naples now,' he said at last. 'Have you been to the Three Bells before?'

'Yes, several times. I've got a favourite table in the garden, under the trees.'

As he drew up she said, 'Thank you for the lift. There's no need for me to trouble you any further.'

'Don't speak to me as though I was a stranger,' he growled.

'Let me escort you to the table. I won't try to take your arm. That's a promise.'

He spoke roughly, but she knew him well enough to hear the pain that would have escaped anybody else.

'Don't be silly,' she said, also speaking roughly, to cover the fact that his unhappiness wounded her. 'I'd like you to escort me. Then,' she added, hastily recovering her self-possession, 'I can buy you a drink and show off my Italian.'

'It's a deal.'

He opened the door for her, and there followed an awkward moment when she reached out for his hand, but it wasn't there. Swearing, he lunged forward, trying to put things right, and stumbled over Jacko, who'd got himself into position. Celia instinctively tightened her hand on his, almost saving him from falling.

He swore again, louder this time, and with real fury.

'I'm sorry,' he snapped. 'The hell with everything. I'm sorry.'

'Let's go and sit down,' she said hastily.

He went ahead, followed by Jacko, with Celia walking afterwards. When they were seated at the table under the trees she was as good as her word, speaking to the waiter in Italian and ordering drinks for them both.

'You did that very well,' he conceded when they'd been served.

'You're a good teacher. I took your lessons to heart.'

'Some of them,' he remembered. 'Some you tossed back in my face.'

'Not about Italian.'

'No, just everything else. It got so that everything I said was wrong—'

'Only because you started every sentence with, "I'll do that for you," or "You shouldn't be doing that."'

'And you ended up wanting to kill me,' he remembered. 'I suppose I'm lucky to still be alive.'

'Yes, we were going downhill fairly fast,' she said.

'I'm sorry about what happened at the car. I thought I knew what you wanted, so I didn't reach out my hand to you—'

'But why not? You'd have assisted a sighted woman as a matter of courtesy, wouldn't you? So why not me?'

He drew a slow breath of frustration.

'Excuse me while I bang my head on the tree,' he said at last.

Celia gave a sudden chuckle. 'It's like old times to hear you take that long breath. It always meant that you were clenching and unclenching your hands.'

Goaded, he spoke without thinking. 'I don't know what you'd do with eyes if you had them. You see everything without them.'

She beamed. 'That's the nicest thing you've ever said to me.'

'Now you're confusing me again.'

'It's the first time you've ever made a joke about my eyes,' she explained.

'It wasn't exactly a joke.'

'Pity. I thought you were improving. Anyway, don't apologise about what happened at the car. If we'd both fallen it would have been my fault.'

'Or your new friend's, for moving when I wasn't expecting him to.'

'Don't blame poor Jacko,' Celia protested, instinctively reaching down to caress the dog's head. 'He was only doing his job.'

'But who is he? Last time I saw you, you had Wicksy.'

'Poor Wicksy was getting old, and it wouldn't have been fair to bring him to a strange country. He'd earned a comfortable retirement, and that's what he has. Remember how he liked children? There are three in his new home to make a fuss of him. I went to say goodbye before I came to Italy, and I could tell that he was happy.'

She stopped suddenly.

'What is it?' he asked gently.

'As I left I could hear him playing with the children, barking with excitement, as though he'd forgotten me already. I'm glad of that, truly. I'd hate to think of him pining for me, but he was the best friend I had.'

'And now you're pining for him?' Francesco supplied.

'Yes, I am. We were such a perfect team.'

'Aren't you a perfect team with Jacko?'

'It's too soon to say. His name is short for Giacomo, and he's a real Italian dog. He's always lived in Naples, so he knows it well and I can trust him completely. He even understands the Neapolitan dialect.'

'But how long will you have him? He looks quite elderly, too.'

'He's nine, and he might have retired when his previous owner regained his sight. But I needed a really experienced dog, so they assigned him to me for a while.'

'Then what? Will they give you a younger one?' Francesco asked casually.

Celia shrugged. 'Maybe.'

He understood. Maybe then she would go home. He wished she would go home now.

He wished she would stay for ever.

He wished she had never come here.

The waiter served their drinks, and they sipped in silence for a while.

'You're very quiet,' she said. 'Did I offend you by turning up?'

'Of course not. I'm just a little surprised.'

'You told me so much about Naples I wanted to find out for myself. I used to look forward to coming here with you, and visiting all the places you told me about, seeing if it had all the lovely smells. You were right about that. I walk through the streets here and I can smell the cooking. Mmm!'

'But how did you get here?'

'I went home to my parents for a while, and they said it was time I explored the world a little. Dad gave me a large cheque and told me to blow it on enjoying myself.'

'But you said you have a job here. Aren't you supposed to be just a tourist?'

'I've invested the money. I fancy myself as an entrepreneur. That's how I'm going to enjoy myself. You taught me that.'

'I did?'

'You used to talk a lot about finance. It was your great interest in life. I listened and learned at the master's feet.'

'Is that a way of telling me that money is all I know?'

'Don't be so touchy. You showed me that making money could be fun, so now I'm going to double mine. Or treble it.'

'Or lose it?' he suggested lightly.

'Oh, no, that won't happen,' she assured him.

'How can you be so sure?'

Celia turned her head so that her clear blue eyes were facing him, so full of expression that he could almost swear she saw him.

'Because I never lose,' she said simply. 'When I want something, I make sure I get it.'

'And when you've finished with it you throw it out, marked "No longer needed,"' he said quietly.

'Francesco, do you know how bitter you sound? I wish you wouldn't. We promised each other that we wouldn't be bitter.'

'Did we? I don't remember.'

'The day you came to collect your things,' she reminded him. 'We had a chat then.'

'Oh, yes, it was all very civilised, wasn't it? But I don't remember that we talked things over. Five minutes over coffee and that was that.'

'Well, there wasn't much to talk about, was there?'

'Except you throwing me out.'

'I asked you not to be bitter because I didn't want you to hate me. Still, I guess that wasn't very realistic of me.'

'I don't hate you,' he said gruffly. 'But neither can I pretend that it didn't happen.'

'I don't want to pretend that, either,' she said with a touch of eagerness. 'It did happen, and I'm glad of it. You left me with some of the most wonderful memories I'll ever have, and I want to keep them. Don't you want to?'

'No,' he said with sudden violence. 'I don't want to remember any of it. What use are memories when the reality has gone?'

She gave a little sigh. 'I suppose you're right. We're agreed, then. No memories. We never met before.'

'Why did you come here?' he growled. 'To have a laugh at my expense?'

'No. Why should you say that? Why should I laugh? I can tell you're doing very well without me.'

He shot her a look so fierce that he was actually glad she couldn't see. It was on the tip of his tongue to tell her that she didn't know what she was talking about. Unless, he thought, she'd been trying to provoke him. He only wished he knew.

'Who's your customer?' he asked, for something to say. It was strange how the silences troubled him more than her.

'He's not really a customer. I said that so as not to bore your parents with involved explanations. We work together. His name is Sandro Danzi. He owns a firm organising trips for blind people.'

'Is he blind himself?' he couldn't stop himself asking.

'Does it matter?' she flashed back instinctively.

'For pity's sake! Aren't I even allowed to ask?'

'Why is it always the first thing you ask?'

'It isn't.'

'One of the first. As though nothing else mattered in comparison.'

It mattered, but not in the way she thought. Another blind person understood things that she understood, was potentially closer to her than he could ever be, and that excluded him.

'I didn't mean it like that,' he said, wishing he could find the words to say that he was jealous. Why couldn't she simply understand?

Celia clenched her hands, hating herself. How often had she lashed out at him, wounding him for something that she knew he couldn't help? But she couldn't let down her guard. She didn't dare. It was part of her fight not to be swallowed alive by her blindness, and it seemed the cruelest trick of fate that he should be ranged on the other side.

She sat listening. Even in the bustle of the café she could sense the silence that belonged only to him. She had never seen him, but she knew what he looked like—not the details of his face and body, but the tension of his attitude that told of misery.

'Don't look like that,' she begged.

'How do you know how I look?' he demanded.

'I know your silences,' she said sadly. 'I can always tell.'

Why was she here? she wondered. In a moment of madness she'd thrown up everything and followed him to Naples, hoping to teach him that he could love her and still let her be free. But within a few hours they were enmeshed in the old quarrel. Nothing had changed. However much it hurt, perhaps they were better apart. In a moment she would find the courage to tell him finally.

'Are you hoping for a PR contract from Sandro Danzi?' he asked, in the tone of a man determined to find a more pleasant subject.

'No, I already have that. I've invested my money in his business, and I might go in a bit deeper.'

At Celia's feet Jacko gave a small grunt and became alert.

'What is it, boy?' she asked, touching him gently.

'He's seen another guide dog,' Francesco said.

The strange dog was leading a young man towards them.

'Hey, there!' he called.

'Sandro!' Celia's face lit up. 'This way,' she called.

The newcomer was in his early thirties, tall and strikingly handsome, with a brilliant smile that appeared as soon as he heard her voice.

'Go for it, boy,' he instructed his guide, and the dog came forward confidently until he reached the table, gave Francesco an appraising look, and nudged Celia with his nose.

Francesco rose and stood back while Celia said the stranger's name again, reaching out a hand to him.

'Meet my friend Francesco,' she said. 'Can we talk English? My Italian isn't up to a three-way conversation.'

Sandro put out a hand, which Francesco shook briefly. Sandro's returning clasp was firm and confident, and although he had to reach behind him to find a chair he did so in the easy way of a man with no real doubts.

'Francesco, this is Sandro,' Celia said.

'I'm her boss,' Sandro said at once. 'She does as I tell her.'

'No way!' Celia instantly riposted. 'I'm his associate. I give advice, and he listens if he knows what's good for him.'

Sandro laughed. 'Well, it was worth a try. I'm always trying to get the better of her, but I haven't managed it yet. Awkward, prickly, argumentative, difficult, contrary—did I miss anything?'

'If you did, I'll remind you later,' Celia said through her laughter.

'Tell me, Francesco,' Sandro continued, 'have you found her awkward?'

'Don't get him started on that subject,' Celia said. 'He becomes so annoyed with me that he may go off pop.'

'You have my sympathy,' Sandro observed to Francesco.

'Thank you, but I don't need sympathy,' Francesco said, hearing himself sound pompous and stuffy, hating it, but unable to stop.

'Really? I'd have thought anyone who'd experienced Celia's more maddening ways had earned all the sympathy he could get.'

'Oi!' Celia cried indignantly.

'The world should know the truth.' Sandro sighed. 'I'm black and blue from the bruises. At least, they tell me I'm black-and-blue. For all I'd know I could be pink-and-green.'

'Red-and-yellow,' Celia supplied.

'Polka dot!' Sandro declared triumphantly.

Celia loved that, Francesco noted grimly. She laughed and laughed, reaching out to Sandro, touching his arm until he took her hand, and they sat there shaking, united in mirth.

Francesco watched them, feeling lonelier and more excluded than ever in his life.

'I'd better be going,' he said politely. Part of him wanted to escape, but part wanted to say here and watch them.

'Don't let me drive you away,' Sandro said politely. 'Stay for a coffee.'

'Just one, thank you,' Francesco said.

Then he would go, leaving them with each other, and he would never see or think of her again. Meantime, he must make polite conversation.

'So you're in business together?' he said. 'Is it going well?'

'It's getting off the ground,' Celia said.

To Francesco's surprise this remark was greeted with a deep groan. 'You promised…you promised,' Sandro moaned.

'Oh, dear—yes, I did.' She looked overwhelmed with guilt. '*Mea culpa, mea culpa, mea maxima culpa*,' she intoned, beating her breast.

'You're frightening the dogs,' Sandro told her sternly.

'Sorry! Sorry!'

'She swore she wouldn't make any more terrible puns,' Sandro explained to Francesco. 'And that one was *truly* terrible. It was the worst pun I've ever heard. And I've heard them all.'

'Quit boasting!' Celia ordered him.

'Yes, ma'am.'

'But I don't understand,' Francesco said. 'Where was the pun?'

'We've got a little firm called Follia Per Sempre,' Sandro told him. 'Madness For Ever. It used to be mine until my friend here mounted a hostile takeover bid—'

'I bought half,' Celia put in quickly.

'It exists to help blind people,' Sandro resumed.

'You mean, visual aids?' Francesco asked.

'Good Lord, no way. None of that sensible stuff. *Madness* means exactly that—helping the blind do crazy things.'

'The crazier the better,' Celia supplied.

'Like deep-sea diving,' Francesco muttered.

'That, too, and parachuting,' Sandro said cheerfully.

'Parachuting?' Despite his good resolutions Francesco couldn't keep the outrage out of his voice. 'You don't seriously mean jumping out of aircraft and falling thousands of feet?'

'And why not?' Celia asked in a challenging voice.

'Because—' Francesco tried to control himself and failed.

'Because you're *blind,* that's why not. Because it's madness. Because you could be killed.'

'Anyone can be killed,' Celia riposted. 'Why shouldn't we be as free to take the risks as sighted people?'

'You could say that we're acting like a pair of damned fools,' Sandro said, seeming to consider the matter seriously. 'And you'd probably be right. But why not? There are as many sighted fools as blind fools, but we're supposed to keep quiet about our foolishness.'

'We're supposed to keep quiet about a lot of things.' Celia sighed.

'That's true,' Sandro said at once. 'But no more. The days of silence are over. We stand up for our right to act like idiots.'

'Indeed, we do,' added Celia sonorously.

'Plenty of people think like you,' Sandro said, in a voice so reasonable that Francesco wanted to commit murder. 'They feel that blind people should know their place as semi-invalids, and be grateful that the world allows them to emerge into the light at all. Our firm exists to combat that view. The dafter it is, the more we want to do it.'

'You could say,' Celia added, 'that stupidity is a human right, and it ought to be enshrined in law somewhere.'

'Why bother?' Francesco said crossly. 'You're doing fine without the law.'

'Celia, I think your friend is afflicted with a severe case of common sense,' Sandro said, shaking his head.

'I know,' she replied mournfully. 'I've been trying to cure him, but I'm afraid it's too late.'

'But our fight continues?'

'Indeed, it does. Never let it be said that we were deterred by common sense!'

'Will you two stop?' Francesco said, goaded beyond endurance. 'People are looking at you.'

'That's all right,' Sandro said cheerily. 'We can't see them, so it doesn't bother us.'

It was the way they both said *we* that pierced Francesco like a knife. *We*—we who live in a world from which you are excluded.

'I'll leave you two to talk business,' he said, rising.

'Actually, we're leaving, too,' Celia said. 'Did you bring the stuff?' This was to Sandro.

'All of it.'

'Then we'll listen to it on my machine at home.'

'Let me drive you there,' Francesco said.

Courtesy demanded that he make the offer, but it tore him apart. On the one hand it would tell him where she lived. On the other it would force him to deliver her there with another man, and then drive away while they went in together.

When they were in the car Celia said, 'I live in the Via Santa Lucia. That's near the shore.'

'The quickest way from here—' Sandro began, and proceeded to give every turning accurately.

'You know the way very well,' Francesco said through gritted teeth.

'That's because I used to live there. I designed the interior to suit my needs, and when Celia needed somewhere, and I'd already moved out—'

'Yes, I understand,' Francesco said hastily.

Before long he was drawing up outside a tall apartment block.

'Thanks, we'll manage from here,' Sandro said. 'It's only on the lowest floor. Good evening.'

Francesco replied politely and stayed in the car, watching them go in. He could see the apartment. The only one in the building that was dark. He sat for a moment, waiting for the lights to go on, until it dawned on him that this wouldn't happen. The two inside had no need of lights. United in confidence and laughter, they were also united in their indifference to darkness.

He pictured them going inside, turning on the computer, listening together, deep in their private world

Sandro would say, *Who on earth was that?*

And she would reply, *Oh, that's just Francesco. He's nobody. I thought he was getting a bit tense.*

*He's always tense about something. Forget him!*

And they would.

After a while he drove away.

## CHAPTER FIVE

'I'VE decided to invite Celia to have dinner with the family,' Hope declared three days later. 'I would like to know her better.'

Francesco forced himself to smile.

'That's nice of you, Mamma, but I don't think she'll accept.'

'Why ever not? She likes going out. She told me so. Anyway, she's already accepted. I noted her cellphone number when she was here, and called her last night.'

Francesco had the feeling that a tank was rolling over him. It was a sensation familiar to all Hope's sons, but for once he tried to rebel.

'Mamma—'

'She agreed in principle, but we still have to set a date. Kindly ask her if Saturday would suit, or if she would prefer another date.'

'Why don't you do that yourself, since you get on so well?'

'Because I want her to understand that the invitation comes from you also. Besides, surely you know her better than I?'

'I'm not sure,' he said wryly.

'Oh, you're being difficult today. Very well, I'll send her an e-mail.'

'You have her e-mail address?'

'Oh, yes, and she told me how it works. When she opens her e-mails the computer turns them to speech. She listens, then replies into the microphone, and it reaches me in the normal way. Didn't you know that?'

'Yes, I knew that. I just didn't realise you and she had exchanged so much information.'

'You'd be amazed at how much I know, my son.' Then, seeing his darkened eyes, she added gently, 'But Celia was also discreet about many things.'

He relaxed slightly.

His first thought had been to rebel against this dinner invitation. He'd had no sign of Celia since the day she'd visited the villa. He hadn't contacted her, and although he braced himself whenever the phone rang it was never her.

Now he was becoming used to the situation, and he told himself that his mother's idea might be a good one, establishing for both of them that they could still be friends, in a civilised manner.

Besides, he missed her damnably.

Celia accepted for Saturday, and the word went out to as many of the family as could make it. Primo and Olympia accepted at once, so did Carlo and his wife, Della, and also Ruggiero, whose marriage to Polly three months earlier had provided Francesco with his excuse for a sudden return. Luke and his wife, Minnie, made a special trip from Rome.

Only Justin was missing—Hope's eldest son, who lived in England with his wife and three children. But in a phone call he promised to bring his whole family 'for the wedding.' Francesco had spent so much time abroad that his love-life had been a closed book to them for too long. Now everyone was curious about his lady.

'Giulio and Teresa are coming,' Toni informed Hope,

mentioning his elder brother and his wife, who lived just outside Naples.

'Excellent.'

'Also Teresa's sister, Angelica,' Toni said, in the tone of one making a confession. '*Cara,* I know you don't like her—'

'I don't dislike her. I just wish she'd shut up sometimes and let someone else speak,' Hope said frankly. 'And she's horribly tactless.'

'I know, but she's visiting them just now, so she had to be included.'

'You'll have to take care of her, Poppa,' said Carlo, who happened to be there at that moment. 'Keep her attention occupied.'

'How?' Toni demanded plaintively.

'You must flirt with her,' Hope declared calmly. 'She's quite attractive for her age, so you should have no trouble.'

'You wouldn't mind my flirting with her?' Toni asked his wife faintly.

'We must all do whatever is necessary, *caro.*'

She kissed him and departed from the breakfast table, humming, leaving her menfolk aghast.

'You'll have to take firm action, Poppa,' Francesco said, grinning.

'How?' his much-tried father repeated.

'Strike a blow for all men. *Really* flirt with Aunt Angelica. Make Mamma so jealous that she'll be careful what she tells you to do in future.'

'But my heart wouldn't be in it.' Toni sighed. 'And your mother knows that.'

'Of course, or she'd never have suggested it,' Carlo said. 'She knows she's got you on a string.'

Toni nodded. 'Always,' he said. 'Right from the moment I first set eyes on her.'

On Friday Hope informed Francesco that he was to collect Celia the next day and bring her to the villa.

'Perhaps she'd rather get here without my help,' he observed.

'No, she's fine about that,' Hope informed him. 'She said she'd prefer you to a taxi.'

'I see that the two of you have decided everything,' he observed.

'Of course. No point in waiting for you. Make sure you look your best tomorrow.'

'Any minute you'll be telling me to wash behind my ears,' he said wrathfully.

'Don't forget to do that, either,' Hope instructed him.

He might complain that his mother still treated him like a kid, but the next day he was on the road to Celia's apartment, elegantly turned out and wondering what kind of reception he would receive. Whatever it was, he decided that his best course was to keep back emotionally and stay safe. Somehow he would endure the evening, although he couldn't think how.

Celia was sitting by the window as he drew the car up, her head turned slightly in an attitude of listening. By the time he reached the door she was already opening it.

She was beautiful, in a long dress of honey-coloured silk which brought out the soft glow of her skin and the blue of her eyes. Diamonds sparkled in her ears and about her neck. They were tiny. It was Celia's way never to overdo things. But they announced that she was putting the flags out tonight.

'You're lovely,' he said, instantly forgetting his resolution to be distant.

'Will I do you credit?'

'You don't need to ask that. You know exactly what you look like. Don't ask me how, but you do know.'

She laughed delightedly. 'Yes, I do. I chose this colour because I know you like it.'

'Well, I guess you know my tastes well enough by now to be able to pick the colours in the— *Hell!*' He caught himself up, horrified at what he'd nearly said.

Had there ever been another woman like this one? he wondered. Celia laughed and laughed until he thought she would collapse.

'In the dark!' she choked. 'You were going to say in the *dark*.'

'All right, I'm sorry,' he growled. 'I forgot—'

'Of course you did. Oh, darling, that's wonderful. I begin to think you're human after all.'

He stared at her, feeling all at sea—not for the first time.

'You're not upset? I didn't mean to—'

'I know. You didn't mean to make a joke about my blindness but you did—well, you almost did. It's a start. I'll teach you yet.'

'Will I ever understand you?'

'Probably not. Never mind. Give me a kiss.'

He opened his arms and would have drawn her against him, but she brushed her lips faintly against his and slipped away at once. He followed into her front room, where a dark gold velvet jacket lay over a chair. Beside it sat Jacko, wearing his harness.

'Ready?' she asked him, reaching for the jacket.

'We don't need to take him, surely?' Francesco asked, taking the jacket and holding it up to receive her arms. 'I'll be with you all the time.'

'I can't leave him behind,' she said firmly. 'It would be like telling him he's useless when he needs reassurance. He hasn't quite settled with me yet. Jacko!'

The dog came to stand obediently in front of her.

'*Andiamo!*' she said.

As soon as he heard the Italian for *let's go!* Jacko turned so that she could take hold of the long handle.

'We're ready,' Celia said. 'If you'll just open the door and lead the way?'

He did so, escorting them to the car, showing Jacko into the back and Celia into the front.

'I'd better warn you that there's going to be a big crowd tonight,' he said. 'My family all want to meet you. Including,' he added in a hollow voice, 'Aunt Angelica.'

'Is she the one who puts her foot in it?'

'Good grief, you mean, I've told you about her before?'

'Not at all,' Celia reassured him. 'But every family has one.'

'Well, you're right—she's ours.'

She gave a chuckle. 'I'll remember.'

Everyone was waiting when the car pulled up at the villa. They stood on the terrace, watching as Celia climbed the steps, guided by Jacko, but holding Francesco's arm on the other side. One of the men—nobody was ever quite sure which—gave an appreciative wolf whistle, and Celia beamed in equal appreciation.

Uncle Giulio and Aunt Teresa were introduced. Then came Aunt Angelica, full of words, most of them inappropriate.

'I've heard so much about you—all exaggerated, I'm sure. But there, that can't be helped, can it?'

'Can't it?' Celia asked.

'Well, people don't understand, do they? But I pride myself on realising things that are hidden from the rest of the world.'

'Let's start the evening with a glass of wine,' Hope said quickly, appearing with a tray of glasses. 'Celia, *cara,* what would you like to drink?' She named two excellent wines, one white, one red.

'Oh, do have the white!' Angelica exclaimed at once. 'Then if you should spill it on that lovely dress it won't stain. These things happen so easily, but I assure you we'll all understand. You and I must have a nice little talk—'

There was a swift intake of breath from the family, and Francesco cast a horrified glance at Celia. She had pressed her lips tightly together, as though controlling some response or other, but exactly what it was impossible to say.

'But you promised to talk to *me*,' Toni hurried to tell Angelica. 'I'd counted on having all your attention.'

He put an arm firmly around her waist, swept her off as gallantly as a young man, pressed a glass of wine into her hand, and everyone breathed again.

'What's happening now?' Celia asked Francesco.

'Poppa's flirting madly with Aunt Angelica, gazing deep into her eyes until she forgets everything but him, so she won't drop any clangers—for a while, anyway.'

'Doesn't your mother mind him doing that?'

'Mind? She told him to.'

Celia chuckled. 'I knew I was going to like your mother.'

'It's mutual,' Hope assured her. 'What wine would you like?'

'White,' Celia said at once. 'Just in case I have an accident, you know.'

'Nonsense!' Hope said robustly. 'I don't suppose you can remember the last time you had an accident.'

'I do believe you're right,' Celia replied impishly, and everyone relaxed.

From the first moment she was a great success. Her beauty, her merry laugh, her complete ease with who and what she was won everyone over. Standing back a little, Francesco knew a glow of pride in her accomplishments and her courage. They were regarding him with envy, he realised: the man who had won the prize.

If only they knew how far away from the prize he really was!

At his mother's command he had racked his brain to recall Celia's favourite dishes, and now they were served up with a flourish that made it clear she was the guest of honour. She obviously understood and enjoyed this, for she tried everything set before her and was unstinting in her praise.

They admired her for her proficiency in Italian, and competed to teach her words from the Neapolitan dialect.

'All the best words come from Napoli,' Primo told her. 'Take *sfizio*!' Only Naples could have produced that word.'

'But I thought that was Italian,' Celia objected. 'It's one of my favourite words.'

'You know what it means, then?' Primo asked with a grin.

'It's the pleasure you get from doing something for the sheer, beautiful, stupid sake of it,' Celia replied, in a voice that held a touch of ecstasy.

Francesco saw his family exchange glances of pleasure, sharing the same thought. If she knew that, she belonged among them.

'It's not really Italian,' Carlo explained. 'It's a Neapolitan word that the rest of the country hijacked because they don't have a word that describes that feeling. You have to be one of us to understand.'

Primo said, 'Francesco must have taught you well for you know about *sfizio*.'

Now they were all regarding Francesco with approval, and he felt awkward—for he hadn't taught her that word. He hadn't even known she knew it. She must have concealed her discovery, knowing that, of all things, it was her love of *sfizio* that he feared most. It had driven her to dive in deep water. It had driven her to cast him out of her life.

But Celia was mistress of the situation.

'I think the English hijacked it, as well,' she said. 'Think of the English word *fizzy*. It means bubbling and sparkling, and if you were *sfizio* you'd probably feel fizzy.' She reached for her wineglass, located it at once and raised it in salute.

'All the best words started in Naples,' she cried.

'*Si*,' they all answered with one voice.

'So here's to being fizzy. May life have an endless supply of fizz.'

They all raised their glasses and joined the toast. Francesco did the same, but only so that they wouldn't notice how uneasy he was.

The meal over, they went into the next room, which led onto the terrace. With the doors wide-open and the huge windows pulled back, the party could spill out into the night air.

Celia was enthroned on the sofa, and it seemed to Francesco that people were queuing up to speak to her.

'She's touting for business,' Primo said with a grin. He owned a factory in Naples which Olympia, his wife, ran for him. It was Olympia who sat head to head with Celia now.

'They're discussing modifications to be made so that we can employ more partially sighted people,' Primo said. 'I only overheard a little. I fled when it began to sound expensive.'

As they neared, Olympia hailed them.

'Celia's agreed to come to the factory and suggest some improvements so that we can draw our employees from a wider source,' she said. 'I thought tomorrow would be a good day.'

'That's—that's excellent,' Primo said.

Celia laughed. 'Don't worry. It won't cost as much as

you're afraid of. And you can tell everyone that I'm efficient and not expensive, so I'll get plenty more business.'

'You can have mine,' Francesco said suddenly. 'The factory's just starting up, so we ought to begin as we mean to go on. When you've finished with Olympia perhaps you'd fit me into your diary somewhere?'

'Certainly,' she said, and immediately dictated a brief message into a small recording machine.

'That's what I call style,' Carlo observed. He'd been watching the whole performance with admiration. 'You've been keeping her a secret, Francesco,' he said, in a low voice so that only the two of them could hear.

'You've all got the wrong end of the stick,' Francesco replied in the same voice. 'We're friends, no more. Until recently we hadn't seen each other for months.'

'But you're back together now? Hmm!'

'*Mio dio!* You're as bad as Mamma.'

'Nobody's as bad as Mamma,' Carlo said with feeling.

'Some more wine?' Hope asked, tapping him on the shoulder.

'Mamma—fancy you being there!' Carlo exclaimed, the picture of innocence. 'I had no idea.'

'Indeed! Well, the last time I believed anything you said you were six. Or was it five?'

'Four?' Carlo said helpfully.

'Anyway, don't start planning the wedding, either of you,' Francesco said firmly.

Carlo gave him a humorously jeering look, but it faded when he saw his brother's set expression.

'*Like he'd woken up to find himself in a dungeon,*' he told his brothers later.

From somewhere behind them they heard Angelica's shrill

laugh—only now it had an extra unfortunate edge. Toni was making his way nervously towards them.

'How much wine has she drunk?' Hope asked him.

'It was the only way I could obey you and keep her occupied,' Toni pleaded.

'I said flirt with her, not ply her with drink.' Then a sweet reminiscent smile came over Hope's face. 'You didn't always need wine to turn a woman's head.'

'That was different, *carissima,*' he said. 'That was you.'

The others watched them fondly, delighted by this sudden flicker of late romance as only a family could be. But the spell was soon broken.

'Angelica's coming this way!' Francesco said, aghast.

Clearly emergency action was called for. Carlo dived for the music centre, and in another moment music filled the air.

'Let's dance,' he said, seeing Della, his wife, nearby, and taking her in his arms.

'Let's dance,' Toni said, turning to his wife.

'Is anyone dancing with me?' Celia asked.

'Yes, I am,' Francesco said, drawing her to her feet. 'Before anyone else gets near you.'

'What was going on there?' she demanded, smiling as they moved slowly around the floor. 'The air was thrumming.'

'How much did you hear?' he asked, wondering if she'd heard the remarks about weddings.

'It started with a laugh in the background that could have cracked glass.'

'Aunt Angelica. She's a bit squiffy because Poppa's been plying her with wine.'

'Did your mother tell him to do that, as well as flirt?'

'No, I think he was just running out of ideas. He doesn't

care about anyone but Mamma, so making eyes at another woman comes very hard to him.'

'She must be very sure of him.'

'Totally sure. I don't think he even knows other women exist.'

'How charming!'

'Yes, it's lovely to see a couple so devoted at their age. They'll be celebrating their thirty-fifth wedding anniversary soon.'

'Let me try to get this straight. You're not Toni's son, are you?'

'No, Mamma already had me before she met him.'

'So your father was her first husband?'

'It's a bit complicated. Hold on to me tight, because I'm going to move fast. Angelica's headed for us.'

He turned sharply and managed to spin her the length of the room, out of danger. Celia clung to him, loving every minute and distracted from the way he'd changed the subject—as he had meant her to be.

'Safe now?' she teased as they slowed.

'Quite safe,' he said.

It wasn't really true. He'd spun out of one kind of danger right into another. This had been a mistake. His resolve to hold himself aloof was being set at naught by the closeness of her body and the warm perfume wafting from her.

Memories of a hundred nights came back to him: pure, vigorous sex for the sake of it, love spiced with exquisite tenderness, sometimes one followed by the other. The silk dress might not have been there for all the protection it gave her from his fevered thoughts.

'Am I a credit to you?' she asked lightly. 'I did my best.'

'You look glorious, but—'

'What is it?' She'd felt him stiffen.

*'Are you wearing anything under this dress?'*

'Of course not. It's tight-fitting satin. I wouldn't want any awkward lines showing.'

He took a deep, ragged breath. 'I'd forgotten what a shocking flirt you are.'

'You don't really mean *flirt*. You mean something much more extreme.'

'Whatever I meant, you're driving me crazy.'

'Of course. It's one of the great pleasures of life. You wouldn't expect me to give it up, would you?'

'You'll never give up any chance to torment me,' he growled. 'I know that.'

'I never tormented you—not on purpose.'

'Are you saying you didn't realise you were doing it? I find that hard to believe.'

'Does that mean you're doubting my word?' she asked lightly.

'It means I know you. You could always tell what was going on, whether you seemed to or not. That was the joke you always had at my expense.'

'But I couldn't always tell,' she mused. 'When we were together there were times when you might have been exchanging lingering glances with every girl in the room. How would I have known?'

'You'd have known,' he said softly. 'Because my attention was always on you, every second of every minute of every day, and you'd have sensed the moment it was taken away. But you knew it never would be. Didn't you?'

'Yes.' She sighed. 'I did know.'

'It was one of the things about me that you found unendurable, wasn't it?'

'Don't say that,' she urged quickly. '*Unendurable* is a terrible word.'

He wanted to say that it described his life without her, but he controlled himself, refusing to admit the truth. He still had his dignity.

But it was hard to think of dignity—or at least to think that it mattered—when the feel of her body gliding against him reminded him of a hundred lovings. Why had she come here to torture him?

'What do you look like?' she whispered. 'If I could see, what would I find in your eyes?'

'The same look that's always been there,' he said softly. 'You never really doubted that, did you?'

'I don't know. Everything became so confused. You gave me so much. It's just that—'

'I gave the wrong things.' With a sudden rush of sadness he added, 'And I always would, wouldn't I? A man can't change himself that much—'

'Don't, Francesco. I didn't mean—'

*'Celia, my dear girl!'*

Angelica was descending on them, full of a booming bonhomie that would not be denied. She enveloped Celia in a vast bear hug, while Francesco gave an inner groan, knowing how she would hate this.

'I've been searching for you all evening for our get-together,' Angelica informed the world. 'I've been watching you, and I want to tell you how much I admire you. I just can't believe how well you manage to cope with life.'

There was a brief silence. Francesco clenched his hands, knowing that this was the worst thing to say to Celia. Even the others, who didn't know her so well, picked up the tension.

'But what is there to cope with?' Celia asked, smiling. 'I live life just as you do.'

'Not exactly, surely?' Angelica cooed. 'There must be so many things you don't know about—'

'And many things she knows about that we don't,' Francesco said. 'Celia's world is different to ours, but not worse.'

'But surely,' Angelica persisted, 'it must make life very difficult, having so much less than other people—'

Hope and Toni exchanged alarmed glances, but it was Celia who saved the situation by bursting into laughter. Someone suggested more coffee and there was a cheer. Toni took over Angelica again, demanding that she come out and see the stars with him.

'Phew!' Francesco breathed close to Celia's ear.

'She didn't mean any harm,' Celia said, still laughing.

'If I'd said anything like that you'd have hung me out to dry,' he said wryly.

'But you don't say things like that any more. And thank you for what you did say.'

'Well, as you said earlier, I guess I'm learning,' he said lightly.

She turned her face to him with an odd expression, as though she was thinking something important. Suddenly his heart was beating with hope.

But before she could speak they heard the sound of her cellphone coming from inside her bag.

'I'm sorry. I should have turned it off,' she said, hastily reaching for it.

'No problem. We'll leave you in peace,' Hope said.

She shooed everyone away, including Francesco, although he lingered long enough to hear Celia say, '*Ciao,* Sandro.'

He could have cursed. Just when things were going well that *buffone* had to intrude.

'Come away,' Hope said, chivvying him. 'Let her be private.'

'There's no need,' Celia said quickly. 'I'll just tell him I can't talk now.'

She did so, shutting off the phone almost at once, but, still,

Hope drew Francesco away some distance to ask furiously, 'What were you thinking of to let that wonderful creature slip through your fingers?'

'It wasn't quite like that, Mamma.'

'That's a matter of opinion. And who is Sandro?'

'A vulgar nobody,' Francesco snapped, 'who pushes in where he isn't wanted.'

'I see,' Hope mused. 'As dangerous as that?'

# CHAPTER SIX

IT WAS A fine evening, and they were both feeling cheerful as they drove away. Francesco's good humour had been restored by Celia's refusal to talk to Sandro for more than a moment.

'Oh, I like your family so much,' she enthused now.

'They just love you. My brothers are particularly impressed with the way you combine pleasure with business.'

'Not just your brothers. I had a most interesting conversation with Olympia who, I gather, is the real power in that factory.'

'Yes, I think Primo has only just discovered that. Jacko was a big success, too. Everyone wanted to make a fuss of him.'

'I know,' Celia said. 'They were all very nice, and asked me first if it was all right to pet him while he was "on duty". I said it was, but I don't think he enjoyed it much. He didn't seem to respond.'

'Not like Wicksy,' Francesco recalled. 'He was a real party animal. But Jacko's always a bit quiet.'

'He and I need a little more time to get used to each other,' Celia said. 'I'm going to give him lots of extra love until he feels better.'

Suddenly she began to chuckle.

'What is it?' he asked, grinning with delight in her pleasure.

'There was one moment tonight when I really wished I had

eyes. It was when Toni announced that he wanted a divorce so that he could marry Angelica.'

Francesco shouted with laughter.

'But he made sure Angelica was safely off the premises before he said it,' he recalled.

'I'd have given anything to see Hope's face,' Celia said longingly. 'Still, I expect she got the joke.'

'I think even she was a bit taken aback by that one. Toni said it would make her think carefully about what commands she gave him in future.'

'Does he always obey her commands?' Celia asked with interest.

'More or less. But don't think he's henpecked. Being devoted to her is what makes him happy.'

'Then he's the one who loves?'

'They love each other,' Francesco declared.

'No, I mean, that old saying about there's always one who loves and one who lets themselves be loved. He's the one who loves.'

'I suppose that's true,' Francesco said thoughtfully. 'I'd never realised it before, but I often see his eyes follow her around the room. With her it happens less.'

She didn't answer this, and when he stole a brief glance at her he saw that she was leaning back with her eyes closed, perhaps dozing.

At her apartment he opened the car door, handed her out, then did the same for Jacko, and watched as the dog took her to the front door.

'Can I come in for a moment?' he asked.

'Yes, of course.'

He forced himself to stay back as she allowed Jacko to take

her inside and knelt down to remove his harness. He immediately went to drink from his bowl, then flopped onto his bed.

'He looks a bit dispirited,' Francesco observed, 'not lively as Wicksy used to.'

'I know,' she said. 'I sense it. He works hard, but he's not happy.'

'You said he was with his last owner a long time?'

'That's true.'

'And then he got told to go?' Francesco mused.

'Well, not quite like that.'

'It probably felt like that to him. He doesn't understand the reasons. Everything he thought was secure was suddenly snatched away.'

'But the same thing happened to Wicksy, and he adjusted to his new owners,' Celia pointed out. 'When he was playing with those children he had that special note in his bark that means a dog's having the time of his life.'

'I suppose dogs have different personalities, like people. Wicksy got lucky, but it hasn't worked out so well with Jacko. How does he come to terms with his loss if nobody can explain it to him?'

Celia turned her head towards him, frowning at something she'd heard in his voice.

'What did you mean by that?' she asked.

'Nothing,' he said hastily. 'Nothing special.'

'Yes, you did. Tell me. Francesco, please, it's important. Tell me what you meant.'

'I'm not sure that I know. Just that it's something I seem to sense in my bones: being safe, and then not being safe and not understanding—'

'Tell me,' she said again, urgently.

'I can't. I don't know the words.'

Even as he spoke he felt the mood drain away from him, leaving him empty inside.

'I only meant—about Jacko,' he said heavily.

'Yes, of course.' Celia dropped to her knees and fondled Jacko, kissing and caressing his ears. 'Poor old boy,' she crooned. 'It's hard for you, isn't it?'

The animal responded by gazing up at her from gentle, yearning eyes. Francesco watched her hands moving over him, offering comfort, and suddenly he was back in another time.

The details were vague, but he recalled that he'd missed a contract he'd badly wanted and come home in a foul mood. She'd come up behind him as he'd sat glowering into a whisky, slipped her arms about him from behind, and dropped a kiss on top of his head.

'Don't let it get you down,' she'd murmured. 'It's not the end of the world.'

'Right now it feels like it,' he'd growled.

'Nonsense. Other things matter far more.'

'Like what?'

'Like this,' she'd said, proceeding to demonstrate.

In a few minutes they'd been in bed and the contract had been forgotten.

Now her caresses were wasted on a dog.

'Is Jacko looking any happier?' she asked.

'Yes, he only wanted you to show you love him. You can leave him now. He's all right.'

To his relief she did so, rising to her feet and turning in his direction. He reached out his hand and took hold of hers gently.

'You're beautiful,' he said. 'All evening I couldn't take my—my eyes off you.'

She smiled and moved closer to him. 'That's good,' she said. 'At one time you'd never have said that. You're learning fast.'

'You once said I'd never learn.'

'I underestimated you.'

'Sure, I'm a quick learner. If you bash me over the head a few times I get the point—even if it's too late.'

'Yes,' she echoed. 'That can be the worst of all. You look back and think—'

'If only,' he murmured.

'Yes—if only. If only I'd known then what I know now I'd have made better use of it. If only I was wiser and cleverer than I am—'

'I thought I was the one who wasn't wise or clever,' he said wryly.

'I wasn't so bright. I could have handled a lot of things better than I did.'

There was a melancholy in her voice that made his heart ache. So much between them. So much anger and misunderstanding, resentment, grief, yet so much warmth, so much joy and love. Where had it gone?

'Could you have done anything differently?' he asked. 'Could I? We are as we are. I think we were made to hurt each other—'

'And miss each other in the dark,' she said wistfully.

'But you're not afraid of the dark,' he reminded her.

Celia was standing very close to him, and it was natural to lay his hands on her bare shoulders, so that she turned her head up, almost as if she were looking at him, and spoke softly.

'No, but there are other things to be afraid of.'

'Not you,' he said at once. 'You were never afraid of anything.'

'I don't do so well with people, though, do I?' she whispered.

'Some people are beyond help,' he said heavily.

'Nobody is beyond help, if only—'

'Yes?' he murmured. 'If only—but it's a big "if only."'

'Francesco—'

She shook her head in a way that was almost helpless. It was so rare for her to be at a loss that it hurt him obscurely. His head seemed to lower itself without his will, until his cheek lay against hers.

He felt her tremble, but she didn't push him away, and he was emboldened to turn so that his lips brushed her face. She raised her hands and laid them on his shoulders, letting them drift inwards until they touched his neck. He drew back an inch so that he could look down into her face, trying to read her expression.

There was a gentleness in her face that he hadn't seen since she'd arrived in Naples, but more than that, a sort of wonder, as though she hadn't believed that this could still happen.

Francesco held his breath while she began to run her fingers over his face, tracing the shape of his jaw, his lean cheeks, the outline of his lips, making it hard for him to keep his rising feelings under control. If he'd dared yield to them he would have seized her up in his arms, kissed her until they were half out of their minds, then carried her to bed. It was what he'd done many times before. But now he forced himself to stay still, waiting to see if she would move so that her lips could meet his, and at last she did.

It was as though time had vanished. The kiss she gave him now was the kiss she had always given him, the one he wanted from her all his life.

He should be strong and resist it, but he had no strength where she was concerned.

Her lips teased his seductively, reminding him of things best forgotten. A man could lose his sanity with a woman like this. But while his mind worked his mouth was caressing hers in return, taking over the kiss, becoming the tender aggressor.

All was well again. They had never been apart, and never would be, because this was the only thing that mattered.

The shrill of the phone startled them. Francesco muttered a curse.

'I thought you turned it off.'

'That's the landline,' she said reluctantly. 'I'll have to answer it.'

She was shaking, but not as much as he was. Through her hands and her whole body she could sense the disturbance that racked him. She didn't want to answer the phone, but it would just ring until she did.

Francesco pulled away and snatched up the phone, barking, 'Hallo? No, she can't come to the phone right now…I don't care how urgent it is, you'll have to try later—'

'Who is it?' she asked.

'Sandro. Here!' He handed her the receiver. 'Get rid of him.'

His curt command acted like a burst of cold water cascading over her. He was trying to control her again.

'Sandro? I told you I'd call you back. Can't it wait?'

'No, we're about to lose our best chance of a really big customer,' came the voice down the phone, naming a man they'd been cultivating for days. 'He's about to leave town, but he wants to talk to you before he goes. Please, Celia, we really need this one.'

'Yes, we do,' she admitted. 'All right, I'll call him at once. I've got his number. Good night.' She hung up.

'So that's that?' Francesco said coldly. 'He says jump and you do.'

'I jump when the business needs me,' she said, equally coldly. 'Not Sandro.'

'To hell with business!'

'There's a thing I never thought to hear you say.'

'Couldn't you have put us first and work second?'

'I was going to,' she cried. 'Can't you understand that? I was going to put him off, but then you had to charge in like a steamroller, giving your orders, telling me what I could and couldn't do. Haven't you learned by now that I won't stand for that?'

'I'd better leave,' he snapped. 'You have a phone call to make.'

'You're right. Good night.'

As he departed she was already lifting the phone.

The conversation that followed was long, complex, and took all her skill to bring to a successful conclusion. She was left with a sense of triumph in her achievement, but also a sad awareness of the price she'd paid.

When she'd hung up the apartment seemed suddenly empty. It wasn't just the fact that she was alone. She was used to that. But there was a special quality to this aloneness, as though Francesco's anger was still imprinted on the air, still reproaching her with his absence.

It might have been so different, she thought despondently.

She undressed, settled Jacko down and got into bed, still aching with the yearning for what had nearly happened. She lay for a long time, wondering if nothing was truly all there would ever be.

A sound from the floor reminded her that she wasn't truly alone after all.

'Are you all right?' she asked Jacko, reaching down to touch him. 'You sound sad, poor old boy. Come up and join me, and we can be sad together.'

He nuzzled her hand, but otherwise didn't move.

'Come on,' she urged. 'Jump up on the bed with me. Never mind what they said at Guide Dog School about not getting on the furniture. I want you up here, where I can cuddle you.'

His mind relieved, he hopped onto the bed and snuggled against her. Celia buried her face against his warm fur.

'What would I do without you?' she murmured. 'You're the only real friend I have. You don't talk nonsense like him—or like me. You don't give me orders or try to control me and you understand everything without being told.'

His tongue flickered against her cheek and she smiled.

'Mmm! Do that again! That's nice. Thank you. You're beautiful. Everyone says so, and I know you are.'

They lay awhile in companionable silence while she stroked him.

'Shall I tell you a secret?' she asked after a while. 'I couldn't do it without my dogs. First Max, when I was a little girl, then Wicksy, now you. I go on a lot about my independence, but the truth is that it all depends on my furry friends. Don't tell on me, will you?'

He nudged her with his nose.

'Thanks. I knew I could rely on you. You see, without you I'd fall into the hands of a control freak like Francesco. I can only fight him by being as awkward as possible—and if there's one thing I do know about it's being awkward—but I can't do that without you there to prop up the illusion.'

She sighed despondently.

'Listen to me, talking about fighting him. I don't want to fight him. I want to love him. I call him a control freak, but he isn't really. It's just something that makes him act that way. I don't understand it, and I don't think he does. I still love him. I wish I didn't, but you can't just turn it off, can you?'

He gave a sad whine of agreement.

'Was I very stupid to come here?' she asked him. 'It seemed so easy when I planned it. If I could only meet him on his own ground we might start again and get it right this time. Now I wonder if that can ever happen. Tonight I even hoped— It was going so well. I was remembering how much I love him, and why. When he kissed me it was just like before, and I wanted him so much. Suddenly it seemed a hundred years since we last made love, and I couldn't wait for it to happen again. All the things that came between us didn't matter any more, as long as I could belong to him and know that he belonged to me. Oh, Jacko, we were that close— that close— If only—'

She sighed, forcing herself down to earth.

'But then Sandro phoned and it was like time had rolled back. Francesco became the man I hate, taking control, barking orders. Everything has to be done his way, and I can't bear that. And then I was glad that the call came in time to stop us making love. Yes, I was. I was glad—really, really glad.'

Jacko pressed closer, giving her cheek a soft nudge of sympathy. He knew a lie when he heard one.

Francesco didn't contact Celia next day, but Olympia did. She spent the afternoon being escorted around the factory, making verbal notes, and was then swept off to the apartment where Olympia lived with her husband, Primo Rinucci.

As she was working on the evening meal and chatting to Celia in the kitchen, the phone rang.

'*Ciao?*' she sang into the receiver. 'Yes, everything went well.' To Celia she said, 'It's Francesco. He wants to know how your visit went.' She turned back to the receiver. 'We've got lots of ideas to talk about.'

'Tell him to come over here,' Primo said from the doorway. 'We'll mull the ideas over together.'

Then Olympia, talking into the phone, 'Come and join us for supper— Oh, nonsense! You can't have that much to do—'

Celia deciphered this without trouble. After last night, Francesco didn't want to come where he would meet her. And he was right, she told herself firmly. Everything was falling apart again and he was wise to avoid her.

'Besides,' Olympia was saying, 'you introduced us to Celia, so you must come and hear how your protégée is doing. I'll lay another place. No argument. Get moving.'

She hung up.

'Does your brother ever stop working?' she complained to Primo.

'He took yesterday evening off for the party,' Celia said lightly. 'You can't expect him to rest for two evenings in a row. You know how driven he is about business.'

'Not really,' Primo said. 'He went abroad ten years ago, and stayed there until recently. None of us knows him really well.'

'Why did he go?' Celia asked.

'I'm not sure, but he was never at home much even before that. He travelled all over Italy, working a year here, a year there, always making money. He has the devil's touch about that. Then he'd get fed up and come back, only to leave again. At last he went to America, stayed there until three years ago, then went to England. I don't know why he wanders so much—what he's looking for. But maybe you can tell. You must know him better than anyone.'

'No,' Celia said, shaking her head. 'I don't really know him at all.'

Half an hour later there was a ring on the bell and Primo went to answer, returning with Francesco and Carlo.

'We met in the street,' Francesco announced.

'I just came to say hallo,' Carlo said, giving Celia a peck on the cheek.

'Stay for supper,' Olympia said.

'I can't. Della will be home soon,' Carlo explained, naming his wife, a television producer, who'd been forced to take a long rest owing to poor health.

'She's trying to take up the reins again,' he said, 'and she's gone to look at a place with a history that's given her an idea for a programme. She'll be expecting to find me at home.'

'Call her,' Primo said. 'Tell her to come here instead.'

While they argued about it Francesco sat beside Celia and said quietly, 'I gather things went well today?'

'Yes, I drummed up lots of business. There was a man there who'd come to sign a contract from another firm. He's booked me for an assessment visit, too, and he says he knows several other people who'd be interested. I'm going great guns.'

'I'm glad you're a success. Is Sandro pleased?'

'This has nothing to do with Sandro. Giving advice in the workplace is exclusively mine. Follia Per Sempre is another firm. I told you, Sandro and I don't do sensible.'

'Ah, yes, Sandro and you!' he said wryly.

'What does that mean?'

'It means what it sounds as though it means. It means that when he called last night you abandoned everything else. *Mio Dio,* you forgot me easily.'

'Some men are easy to forget.'

'*Thank you.*'

'And some are impossible to forget,' she murmured.

Silence. Hell would freeze over before he asked her into which category she had assigned him.

Now they could clearly hear Carlo talking to Della, explaining the change of plan.

'But only if you're not too tired,' he added quickly. 'You've been working hard all day, and now you've got the journey back—you should have let me come, too, and drive you home—all right, all right—don't be mad at me. I know what we said, but—'

'You see, I'm not the only one,' Francesco said wryly to Celia. 'He annoys Della as much as I annoy you.'

'Why?' she asked, refusing to rise to the bait. 'Is she really as ill as all that?'

'She was in a plane crash, and had a heart attack immediately afterwards. She'll always be frail, plus she's seven years older than Carlo, and he's very protective of her.'

'Yes, I can hear. Poor Carlo, he sounds desperate. The sad thing is that he's probably infuriating her and he doesn't know it.'

'Oh, he knows it all right,' Francesco said wryly. 'He just doesn't know how to stop.'

It became clear that this was true. Carlo wouldn't let it go, and the conversation ended so abruptly that Celia wondered if Della had hung up. After that Carlo was on hot coals until she arrived half an hour later, full of eagerness and enthusiasm for the day she had spent, and then he became happier.

## CHAPTER SEVEN

OVER dinner the six of them plunged into a professional discussion in which everything was forgotten but the exchange of ideas. Celia came to vivid life, in command of her subject, thoroughly enjoying her expertise and the admiration that it won for her.

Carlo listened to her with particular interest. He was an archaeologist whose life had been spent on the move until he married. Then he'd taken a job running one of the Naples museums, enabling him to stay in one place for Della's sake.

It had been the sacrifice of a brilliant career, but he'd set himself to transform the museum, and had done it so well that he was becoming an authority in his new sphere.

'It's a pity there's so little scope for visual aids in a museum,' he mused. 'I'm not talking about employees, though. I'm putting some things in place to help them, and I'd be glad if you'd come and give me your opinion, Celia.'

'I'd love to. But if you're not talking about employees you must mean visitors?'

'That's right. How can I help them? They can listen to audio descriptions, but how much does that help? It doesn't tell you what a picture really looks like, or an ancient vase. I did try letting people run their hands over things, but the trustees went ballistic in case of breakages. Mind you, the only person who broke anything was the son of a trustee who had perfect eyesight—or would have done if he'd been sober at the time.'

Everybody laughed, but suddenly Francesco said, 'Why don't you make replicas?'

'They're no use,' Carlo said. 'I had a crowd of students in last week all trying to copy a Greek statue. Some of the results were good, but they couldn't have passed for the original.'

'I don't mean that,' Francesco said. 'There's some computer software that'll take a thousand photos from every angle. You can use these to make a three-dimensional virtual model, which the computer then turns into a real model by giving instructions to another machine. The result is an exact likeness, except that it's made of resin. Every little scratch and dent is duplicated. If it's a statue, you can even see the chisel marks. People can pick it up to study it. If it gets damaged, no problem. You just tell the computer to make another. You could copy every artifact in the place and make them available to everyone—not just the people who can't see.'

'That's right,' Celia said. 'Why should we have all the privileges? Francesco, it's a marvellous idea.'

'Yes, it is,' Carlo agreed. 'You're a dark horse, brother.'

'He hides his light under a bushel,' Celia said, smiling.

She was suddenly very happy, as though Francesco had reached out to her in a new way. And the next moment she felt his hand seeking hers under the table.

She hadn't been wrong about him, she thought joyfully. Everything was still possible.

As they were all leaving to go she said to him, 'I hope you're going to offer me a lift home.'

'Of course. I'll fetch your jacket.'

On the way he passed Carlo and Della, who had resumed their argument.

'Be careful,' he said, laying his hand on his brother's shoulder. 'The belief that you're doing the right thing can be the biggest trap there is, and the most destructive.'

'Did you fall into it?' Della asked.

'Big-time. Celia and I—well—'

Briefly he explained the circumstances of their parting.

'I thought I was taking care of her,' he finished, 'but I was simply making her want to bang her head against the wall.'

He saw the other two give each other a quick glance, then Carlo's arm went around his wife's shoulders and he dropped a kiss onto her head.

'Just don't let it happen to you two, that's all,' Francesco said. 'Good night.'

When he'd gone Della looked up at her husband, holding him tightly.

'I don't know why you said Francesco was a hard man,' she said. 'I think he's lovely, kind and sensitive. I hadn't expected him to have such insight.'

'Me, neither,' Carlo said. 'I'm beginning to wonder if any of us have ever understood the first thing about him.'

As he drove home to Celia's apartment Francesco said, 'How's this for a plan? I'll collect you tomorrow and we'll go to my factory so that you can give it the once-over and tell me what needs doing.'

'That sounds lovely, but I'm booked tomorrow,' she said regretfully.

'Sure—I was forgetting that your diary's getting crowded. What is it? A rival factory?'

'No, I'm working with Sandro. We're investigating new activities to offer people.'

'Mad activities?' he asked lightly.

'The madder the better.'

'I'll be there to give you a lift.'

'Without even asking me where we're going and why?'

'Does it matter?'

'It might be something you disapprove of.'

'I have no right to disapprove,' he said expansively. 'You are your own mistress, and you make your own decisions.' He was full of goodwill towards the world, and for once it was easy to say the right thing.

'Excuse me? Can I have that in writing?' she asked sceptically.

'It's none of my business,' he declared, warming to his theme and enjoying her astonishment. 'I have no opinions, and if I had I wouldn't dream of inflicting them on you.'

'You're an impostor,' she said firmly. 'Where have you hidden the real Francesco Rinucci? He would never have said anything like that.'

'I'm a reformed character. Now, what time shall I collect you tomorrow?'

She gave him the time, and he dropped her outside the apartment building. His last view was of her following Jacko inside. He drove away, remembering the previous night and wondering how things could have changed so quickly for the better.

Francesco was there on time the next afternoon, smiling with pleasure at the sight of her, beautiful in white linen pants and blue shirt. But his smile faded as they were driving away and she gave him their destination.

'That's an airfield,' he said.

'That's right. A small, private airfield about five miles outside Naples.'

'To do what?' he asked ominously.

'Skydiving. It's all the rage among people who want a new experience.'

'Skydiving? You're going to do a parachute jump?' he demanded, so appalled that he had to swerve to avoid an accident.

'No, just Sandro. He's jumping out of a plane, but I have to be there to talk to the people on the ground—negotiations, sponsorship, etcetera.'

'The two of you are as insane as each other.'

'Well, we told you that,' she said patiently. 'It's the whole point. Anyway, like you said, you have no opinions one way or the other.'

'I never said anything as daft as that.'

'Yes, you did. You also said it was none of your business.'

After a moment he managed to say, 'On second thoughts, I can bear, with fortitude, the sight of Sandro risking his neck.'

She chuckled, understanding perfectly.

'Never mind about Sandro,' she said.

'I don't. I don't think about him from one hour to the next.' Then he added thoughtlessly, 'Mind you, I might wish he were less good-looking.'

'*Is* he good-looking?' she demanded with suspicious eagerness. 'Oh, do tell me, because I've always wondered. Is he really, *really* handsome?'

Francesco ground his teeth. 'I walked right into that, didn't I?' he asked.

'Well, you were a little incautious,' she teased. 'Go on, tell me.'

'No way. You know exactly what he looks like, because you got someone to tell you with the first meeting.'

'You don't know that.'

'Yes, I do, because it's what you did with me.'

There was a slight pause before she said, 'What I did with you, and what I do with other people—well, they're not the same thing at all.'

'Are you going to tell me what that means?' he asked cautiously.

'With you, it mattered. Is it far to this place?'

'Not long now,' he said, accepting her change of subject. He needed time to think. Things were moving with dizzying speed.

After an hour's drive they reached the little airfield, already busy with several private planes. At the offices they were met by a small crowd. Amid the introductions Francesco gained an impression of a local journalist, a businessman considering becoming a backer and several charities who stood to gain from sponsorship.

'Did you fix all this?' Francesco asked.

'Of course. This is my side of things.'

'I'm impressed. But I always knew you were efficient.'

He concealed his relief that she had no thoughts of flying, and even allowed himself a moment of complacency at his own tact.

The pilot appeared with Sandro, already dressed up and strapped into his parachute. Behind him came another man, similarly dressed. This was Sandro's skydiving partner.

'We take off,' Sandro said, 'climb to about thirteen thousand feet and circle the airport twice before jumping.'

'How far do you fall before opening the parachute?' Celia wanted to know.

'Down to about two and a half thousand feet,' Sandro replied.

'As low as that?' Francesco queried in surprise.

'Well, the whole point is to freefall as far as possible,' the pilot said. 'The parachute is just to break the fall at the last minute.'

'Otherwise you'd be killed,' Sandro observed cheerfully.

'Which would seriously spoil your enjoyment of the next jump,' Celia supplied, and they punched the air together.

The journalists thoroughly enjoyed this exchange, Francesco noted sourly.

'Will you look after my dog for me?' Sandro asked Celia.

'Sure.' She took the harness, but then found herself rather encumbered with two animals and her bag.

'Give Jacko to me,' Francesco said.

'Good idea. You and he seem to be on each other's wavelength.'

'Now you're just being fanciful,' he said, half fondly, half in exasperation.

'No, I'm not. He heard what you said about having his security snatched away, and he knows you understand him.'

Outwardly he dismissed her words. And yet it seemed to him that Jacko moved towards him willingly and sat close to his leg, as though contented.

I'm getting over-imaginative, he thought.

'What's happening now?' Celia asked.

'They're walking away towards the aircraft. It's just a tiny one, barely enough for the three of them—nearly there— someone's taking a last look at the parachutes—the pilot's climbing aboard and reaching back to help Sandro.'

Then he heard something that froze his blood. It was the softest possible sound, but it raised ghastly spectres, howling death and despair at him.

It was a sigh of envy.

He gave a sharp glance at Celia, hoping he'd imagined it, but there was no mistaking the way her head was thrown back, as though she could see up into the sky, or the look of ecstasy on her face.

Envy. Delight. Determination. All the things that would make a rational man bang his head against the nearest brick wall. And when he'd done that he would shoot himself, or jump off a cliff, whichever seemed most likely to promote health, happiness and sanity.

What he would *not* do was involve himself with this woman a second time. He would never again put it in her power to break his heart with her outrageous, wilful, insane, dotty-headed enthusiasms. That was out, finished, done with.

'Are you all right?' Celia asked, reaching for him in alarm.

'Of course I am,' he snapped. 'Why?'

'You're trembling.'

'No, just a bit chilly.'

'It's windy. They should have a good flight. What are they doing now?'

'They've just closed the plane door—now they're starting to move—gathering speed.'

'I can hear the engine. They've left the ground, haven't they?'

'Yes, the plane is climbing—climbing—almost out of sight—'

'But it's coming back soon?' she asked anxiously, almost like a child fearful of being denied a treat.

'It's coming back now, circling the airfield—it's almost out of sight—lucky it's a clear day—I can just make it out…'

His voice trailed off. When she could bear the silence no longer Celia squealed, *'Well?'*

'I think Sandro and his partner are jumping now—yes, there they go!'

Way above him in the blue he could just make out the two men, leaving the aircraft together and going into freefall.

'What are they doing?' she cried, in the anguish of unbearable tension. 'Have they opened their parachutes yet?'

'No, they're still holding on to each other—coming lower—lower—I can see them clearly now—they're going to have to open up any minute—aren't they?'

The hair-raising possibility of a last-minute disaster was there in his voice, and in the gasps from the crowd that turned to cheers as the men released each other and two parachutes opened, letting them glide gracefully earthwards.

'They've landed,' Francesco said. 'They're both safe.'

'Wonderful!' Celia rejoiced. 'Now we've really got something spectacular to offer.'

Francesco pulled himself together. There would be time for his misgivings later. Just now he would concentrate on saying and doing the right things to get the business over with quickly. So he assumed a bright smile and prepared to say something suitable. But before he could do so Celia was surrounded by journalists, all hurling questions at her. She replied eagerly, leaving Francesco and Jacko to retire discreetly into the background.

'That's put us in our place,' he commiserated with the dog. 'We're definitely not needed just now.' He scratched the silky head. 'I guess we both know how that feels.'

A soft grunt was his answer.

'I wonder what your folks were like,' he mused. 'I guess you loved them, and then they said, "Get out!" And that was that. You're coping somehow but—'

He stopped himself in alarm.

'Listen to me, talking to you as if you understood. But maybe you do. She thinks so. I expect she talks to you, doesn't she? She used to talk to Wicksy a lot. I wonder what she says about me.'

But he was only trying to distract his own attention from what had happened inside his head. As often before, the words, *Get out!* had acted like a malign spell, causing the universe to spin with terrifying speed before settling down into a bleak place.

'What the devil's the matter with me?' he muttered. 'Why does it happen? *Why?*'

They weren't the only words Celia had hurled at him, nor the cruelest. So why? He asked himself that again and again, but there was no answer. If he could have discovered one, he felt he might have begun to find his way out of the maze.

'Francesco?' It was Celia's voice, calling him back from a trance, and her hand shaking his shoulder. 'Are you all right?'

'Yes, of course. Where shall I take you now? Are you having dinner with your new contacts? With Sandro?'

'No, we've set up meetings for next week. Let's go home.'

There was a shout. Sandro was approaching, hailing them.

'What a day! So many new opportunities. Not just jumping from planes, but from balloons.'

'That'll really be something to try!' Celia exclaimed. 'Just wait until we get talking next week.'

'Fine, I'll see you then,' Sandro said, using the word *see* in the casual fashion that always startled Francesco. 'Goodbye, *cara.*'

He put an arm around Celia's shoulder, drew her close and gave her a hearty kiss. She kissed him back. To Francesco it seemed an age before they could get away, and even then she had to dash back to Sandro to say something she'd forgotten. But at last they were in the car on the way home.

'Let's do some shopping and I'll cook you supper.'

The next hour was pure pleasure. This was how they'd been at their happiest—planning meals, shopping together. She would let him choose the vegetables, and sometimes the meat, although she really preferred her own judgement for meat.

'You were always a good cook,' he recalled as they worked out the menu, walking around the grocer's. 'You made a list of all my favourite dishes and practised until you could do them perfectly.'

'But some of the Italian ones I'd never heard of,' she remembered.

'And you wanted me to show you how to make them. As though I knew a potato from a bean! My expertise stopped at eating them.' He laughed suddenly. 'Do you remember how shocked you were?'

'Yes, I thought all Italian men were great cooks.'

'I'm part English,' he reminded her defensively. 'That's the part of me that's useless. And you actually went out and took a course in Italian cookery—'

'What is it?' she asked, for he had fallen silent abruptly.

'Nothing. I just suddenly remembered how determined you are. That cooking school said you were their best pupil.'

'When I want something I stop at nothing,' she said lightly. 'Ruthless and unprincipled, that's me.'

'I guess. Only it didn't feel like ruthless and unprincipled. It felt like being spoiled rotten. I loved it.'

'So did I,' she said softly.

'Only…' he hesitated, then said, 'Only I wanted to look after you, too.'

'I know.'

'I can't just sit there with my feet up, being waited on by the little woman.'

'Not unless you want the little woman to thump you over the head with a saucepan,' she chuckled.

'As you say. Sometimes I wanted you to put *your* feet up.'

'Only sometimes?'

'Just sometimes,' he said hastily. 'I'm enough of a chauvinist porker for that.'

This time they laughed together, and reached the checkout in perfect accord.

The goodwill lasted as they returned to her home and unpacked in her kitchen. In an ecstasy of helpfulness he volunteered to take Jacko out for the necessary walk.

'Don't worry,' he assured his canine friend. 'I used to do this for Wicksy. I know the drill.'

Celia was just getting ready to serve the first course when her menfolk returned.

'The first course is cold,' she said, 'So that's all right, but I wanted to wait until you were here before I put the light under the pans.'

'Why? Is there something you want me to do?' he asked, missing the note in her voice that would have warned him she was about to make some outrageous joke.

'Just keep an eye on the lighted gas,' she informed him solemnly. 'Because—' she moved closer and lowered her voice melodramatically '—I can't see. I thought you knew that.'

For a moment her innocent manner almost fooled him, then he gave a gasp of shock.

'Celia, you little wretch!' he exploded. 'When will you stop doing that?'

'Never,' she cried, rejoicing as his hands clasped her shoulders and gave them a little shake. 'If anyone else said it, it would be vulgar and insensitive, but I can say what I like. Oh, darling, your face!'

'You don't know what my face looks like.'

'Oh, yes, I do,' she crowed. 'I know exactly what it looks like. You're thinking, How can she *say* a thing like that?'

'That's putting it very mildly. Oh, *you*—'

His grip tightened, pulling her against him, and the next moment she felt what she had been scheming for the last few minutes—his mouth on hers, urgent and frustrated, just as she wanted it. His whole body was shaking with the desire he'd been controlling, and she rejoiced in the sensation of having him in her hands, in her arms, almost under her control.

'You,' he muttered, between raining fierce kisses on her face. 'You—you—'

'What about me?' she asked, kissing and laughing together.

'Just that you're— Come here!'

This time there was no way she could talk against the caressing pressure of his mouth. For too long she'd lived without the fulfilment that only he could give her, and now her body clamoured for him as achingly as her heart had done for months.

Two nights ago they had come so close to finding each other again, but Sandro's call had interrupted them. Now nothing would get in the way. Just before leaving the airfield she'd warned Sandro not to call her tonight, just as she'd previously warned—or perhaps promised—Francesco, she was ruthless and unprincipled in getting what she wanted.

He was hers, and the time had come to make that clear. Her determination infused every movement of her swift fingers, finding buttons to undo, pulling his shirt out of his trousers, caressing his skin, inciting him with every skilful movement at her command while keeping her mouth against his and her tongue teasing him wickedly.

'Celia,' he gasped, 'do you know what you're doing?'

'I do— Do you?' she managed to gasp.

'It's too late to change your mind.'

*'Who's changing her mind?'*

That was it. Now nothing could have stopped him. Scooping her up with more vigour than gallantry, he strode into her room and collapsed onto the bed with her in his arms. Undressing each other was difficult while they were so intricately entangled, but they managed somehow, working through the layers, getting in each other's way, laughing exultantly, getting it wrong, getting it right, trying to control the mounting pleasure long enough to reach their goal, and finally reaching it with long sighs of satisfaction.

'Oh, yes,' she murmured, half out of her mind with what she had wanted for so long and so hopelessly.

The feel of having him inside her again was so good that she wondered how she'd survived so long without it. She moved strongly against him, seeking to repeat the first, unrepeatable sensation. She wanted to touch him all over at the same time—his arms, his neck, his wide shoulders and muscular torso. Then she wanted to slide her hands down the length of him to the narrow hips and long muscular thighs. In their frenzy of action all she could manage was to wrap her own thighs around him, enclosing him, drawing him deep into her body as she wanted him deep in her heart.

They climaxed together almost at once, and continued without a pause, their desire barely touched, far from slaked. Other lovings had taught them that they could inspire each other for a long time before they were satisfied. But there had never been a loving like this.

As he lay over her afterwards, looking down into her face, Celia had one of her rare moments of wishing for sight. She longed to see his face and find in it the tenderness she'd felt in his touch. But then he kissed her gently, and she knew that she had all she needed. He moved off her while still holding her in his arms, so that she was pulled over against him, heart to heart.

'Are you all right?' he asked softly, as he had always done before.

Her answer was the same as then, a little sound of blissful content, for there were some emotions that no words could express. He responded by holding her closer and burying his face in her hair.

'I was afraid I'd lost you for good,' he said.

'You couldn't lose me,' she murmured against his skin.

She went on whispering incoherent words, wondering how it was possible to be so happy.

Somewhere above her head he gave a brief laugh.

'What is it?' she asked at once.

'I was remembering our first night together. I'd been trying to imagine what you wore underneath, and I'd decided it must be something practical, because you were so fiercely efficient.'

'But it wasn't practical at all, was it?'

'No way. A satin thong that practically didn't exist, and a satin and lace bra, all in brilliant scarlet.'

'Did you disapprove?'

'No, I loved it. I knew then that I'd underestimated you.'

'You always did.'

'And you're wearing them again today.'

'You mean, I *was* wearing them, don't you?' she teased.

'Yes, I guess I do.'

She smiled to herself. She'd never told him that she'd bought the sexy underwear after their first evening together, when she'd spent that lonely week, longing for him to return, determined to be ready for anything if he did. And when she'd set out for Naples, determined to reclaim him, it was the first thing she'd packed.

For the moment she'd triumphed. Whatever their problems were they had faded to nothing. Perhaps she would remember them one day. Or perhaps not. It hardly seemed to matter.

# CHAPTER EIGHT

'Do YOU know what we need now?' Francesco asked sleepily.

'What?'

'Champagne. I don't suppose you keep any?'

'I might just have some,' she said, carefully casual.

In fact, she'd laid in a store of that, too, but there was no need for him to know that.

They rose from the bed and stood for a moment leaning against each other, like two people who'd come to the end of a long and exhausting race and needed time to recover before enjoying the prize.

Afterwards she donned a satin robe, while he pulled on his trousers and followed her into the kitchen where she produced the champagne and two glasses. He poured them both a glass, and they clinked.

'I've just discovered I'm tired,' he said.

'That's a pity, because I've got plans for you later.'

'Have mercy, woman.'

'Slacker,' she jeered.

'Not at all. But let's stretch out on the sofa first.'

They did so, with her sitting and him lying with his head on her leg.

'I could stay like this for ever,' he said blissfully.

'Me, too.'

'It's how we used to be.'

'And now we've got it back,' she murmured. 'How could we have been so careless?'

'We never will be again. In future we'll—' he made a vague gesture '—discuss things rationally.'

She chuckled. 'Shall I give you lessons in that?'

'Oi, cheeky!'

'Rationally!' she mocked. 'You wouldn't recognise rational discussion if it bopped you on the nose.'

'OK, you may have to give me a few lessons, but we'll get there. I'm not going to lose you a second time just because— *Oh, hell!*'

The last remark was jerked from him by the ringing of the telephone.

'If that's Sandro, just let me speak to him for five seconds,' Francesco begged.

'It won't be, I promise.' Celia reached for the phone, which was on a small table at the end of the sofa. 'Hallo? *Ciao,* Mario.'

Suddenly she sounded pleased, and Francesco's head rose from her leg in query.

'Journalist,' she mouthed. 'He was there this afternoon.'

'Then he should have talked to you this afternoon.'

'He did. Mario, it's not a good time…oh, I see…when's your deadline? All right, just five minutes, as long as you promise me a great story. And Sandro, of course…he had a great time, so he told me afterwards…oh, yes, green with envy…my turn soon. But I may jump from a helicopter, or a balloon. That way we cover the whole range…yes, you can say that. And there's one other thing—'

After a few moments she hung up, aware that something had

changed. It wasn't just that Francesco's head had vanished from her leg. The atmosphere was suddenly spiky and dangerous.

'What is it?' she asked, feeling for him.

'You just said that to make a good story, right? About jumping? You're not going to do that.'

After a brief silence she said, 'Are you asking me or telling me?' Her voice was quiet, but suddenly it had an edge.

'*Cara*, please! Let's not go into this again. We said it would be different this time. You've had your fun. You've turned me white haired with fear often enough—'

'Had my fun?' she echoed, aghast. 'Is that how you see it?'

'I've heard you call it fun.'

'Among other things. Sure, it's fun, but that's not why I live as I do. It's because I won't be pigeonholed as "disabled"— by you or anyone else.'

'All right,' he said, making a belated attempt to stop the world disintegrating a second time. 'But you've done those things, and I've put up with—*accepted* it. Surely it's time to—that is, we've talked and I thought you understood—'

'You mean, you thought I'd given in,' she said slowly.

'I thought you'd seen reason— No, I didn't mean that—'

'Why not? It's honest. I don't mind you saying things like that. What I mind is your assumption that if I dare to disagree with you I'm off my head. Well, I do disagree, and it's time *you* saw reason.'

With disaster looming on the road ahead Francesco tried— he really tried—to avoid it. But stark terror was taking him over again, as so often in the past, making him forget everything he'd learned.

'It *isn't* reasonable for you to carry on like this,' he snapped. 'One day you'll get killed. Am I supposed to just shrug and say, "Oh, well, it doesn't matter?" If I protest it's because I love you.'

'But with you love becomes control,' Celia cried. 'It's not just dangerous things, it's everything. You never felt that I had the right to my own life.

I won't be treated as someone who can't do what other people take for granted. Above all I won't have you telling me what I can and can't do. Oh, God, why are we talking like this—*again?*'

Her voice rose to a shriek as the truth hit her. It struck him, too, in the same moment. Aghast, they regarded the ruin that had come upon them so suddenly.

'Look,' he said at last, 'let's forget this. We don't know what we're saying. Before the phone rang—'

'We were living in a fool's paradise,' she exclaimed in despair. 'But it couldn't have lasted. This was always going to happen.'

'I won't admit that loving each other is a fool's paradise,' he said stubbornly.

She gave a bleak little laugh. 'It could be—for some people. Shouldn't we just admit it?'

'That's a terrible thing to say. It's like saying there's no such thing as love.'

'Perhaps it's just one of those things I can't do the way other people do,' she said bitterly. 'Maybe you were right about that, and it's time I listened. Diving in water or out of planes—fine! But a normal human relationship is beyond me—because it has to be on the terms I lay down, and they're too harsh for other people. Or maybe just too selfish. After all, what have I said? That you've got to let me do what I want all the time? Even I can hear the selfishness in that, but anything else suffocates me.'

'Don't talk like that,' he said violently. 'You're not selfish. It's just that I— Oh, let's just forget it.'

'How can we when it's always there?'

She turned away to hide the fact that she was beginning to cry, and he immediately reached out, trying to hold on to her.

'*Cara*, please—'

'Let me go.'

She pulled herself out of his grasp and turned away, not heeding where she was going. The next moment she'd collided with the doorjamb and reeled back.

'Celia—'

'No, no. I'm all right.'

'You're not all right. Your lip's bleeding. Come here.'

She seemed ready to fight him, but then she gave up and let him lead her to the sofa and make her sit down.

'It's nothing,' she said. 'I often bump into things.'

He shook his head. 'No, you don't,' he said in despair. 'I've never seen it happen before. It was my fault. I'm so sorry—'

'It wasn't your fault. You didn't push me. It was an accident. Francesco, please, *please*—why must you take every little thing to heart?'

'I don't know. It's just that—' He shook his head, as though by this means he could clear his confusion. 'I've always been that way, but suddenly I became worse, and it's grown out of control and made a monster of me.'

'You're not a monster,' she hastened to say.

'No, just a man it suffocates you to live with. And perhaps even I am beginning to see why. I guess I've turned into a bully again, haven't I?'

'Francesco, please, I never said you were a bully—'

'Not tonight. But the last time—when we broke up.'

'You remember that?'

'I remember every word. I'm even glad now that you said it.'

'It was cruel and untrue—'

'No, it was cruel and true. Which means it wasn't cruel at all. It needed saying. You'd been thinking it for a long time and biting it back—'

'No—'

'Celia, *carissima,* you've always been honest to the point of brutality, and I mean that as compliment. Don't weaken now. That night—when we came home after your dive and we quarrelled—you didn't say *bully* like someone who'd just thought of it. You said it like someone who'd been suppressing it for ages. If there's anything to regret, it's that you didn't say it before. We might have—'

He broke off. The thought was too painful to put into words.

'Yes,' she said huskily. 'We might have managed better. Who knows?'

In the silence he reached out his hand and touched her hair very gently. She turned her head at once, so that her cheek brushed his palm, and for a moment they stayed like that, aching with memory.

He was almost sure that he felt a touch of moisture on his hand, but he didn't ask if she were crying. He was afraid of breaking the spell.

'Celia…' was as much as he dared to say, in a voice no louder than a murmur.

She raised her head so that she was facing him, and he couldn't believe that she was blind. It was all there in her eyes—everything they'd had, everything they'd lost. And he knew that it must be in his own eyes, as well. She couldn't see it, but surely she would know? Because she knew everything.

He longed to comfort her, to promise that he'd make everything all right for her. But how could he when what was wrong was himself?

He'd dreamed of finding a miracle, but now, reluctantly,

he had to recognise that there were no miracles. The time had come to free her for the better life she would find without him.

'*Carissima,*' he said softly, 'let us talk.'

'Not yet,' she said in a muffled voice. 'Please, not yet.'

So she knew. Of course she did. Perhaps she'd come to Naples for him, hoping that they might have a second chance. She'd never told him that, but a thousand things had made him hope. Now he knew hope was futile, and so did she.

'Not yet,' she repeated.

'No,' he murmured. 'Not yet. We can have a little more time.'

A little time to hope for the miracle that would never happen. A little time before the pain would have to be faced. Finally.

He went into the bathroom and came out with a damp flannel to clean the graze on her lip. A tiny bruise was just beginning. Now it didn't seem right that they were almost naked.

'I'll get dressed,' he said.

But then he dropped his head and lay his lips against her breast. She drew a shuddering breath and tried to clasp her hands about his head, but he rose quickly and left her. After a moment she, too, moved into the bedroom to get dressed.

'Perhaps I should go now,' he said heavily.

Before she could reply the doorbell shrilled.

'I'm not expecting anyone,' she said. 'Would you go?'

Outside her front door he found a man in his fifties with an eager, nervous look.

'Does Signorina Ryland live here?' he asked. 'I was told she did.'

At the sound of his voice something happened to Jacko. He'd been curled up peacefully, but suddenly his head lifted and he was alert with his whole body. A soft 'Wuff!' escaped him.

Francesco ushered him in. Celia emerged to face the newcomer, frowning slightly.

'*Signorina,*' the man said earnestly, 'I am Antonio Feltona, and I have come to beg you to grant me a favour.'

'Feltona,' she murmured, then her brow cleared. 'Jacko was yours, wasn't he?'

'That's true. Then my sight came back and I no longer needed a guide dog.'

'And they gave him to me because I need someone with his experience in this city,' she recalled. 'Have you come to make sure he's all right? Here he is.'

As she spoke Jacko leapt up, yelping with delight, and hurled himself on his old master. Antonio dropped to his knees and embraced the eager dog, cooing affection into his ears.

'That's what's been wrong with Jacko all this time,' Francesco murmured.

'Something has been wrong?' the man asked.

'Only that he's seemed a bit listless, and not very happy,' Francesco explained.

'Yes,' Signor Feltona said, rising. 'My family loves him, and he loves us. When I regained my sight it seemed natural for him to be given to someone who needed him, but I think he was too old to make this move. And so I have come to ask you—to plead with you—to let us have him back.'

'What?' Celia was thunderstruck.

'I know it will be hard for you, but there are other dogs.'

'Not for me,' she said, agitated. 'It's his years of experience that make him valuable to me in the way a young dog couldn't be. No, I'm sorry. I can't do without him.'

'Please, *signorina,* won't you even think about it for a while?'

'No, there's nothing to think about. I'm sorry. It's out of the question.'

Celia turned and fled towards the kitchen door, her hands outstretched to prevent another collision. She just managed to avoid the wall, but it was a near thing.

It distressed her that Francesco should have seen this happen. After all she'd said about independence. How he would gloat!

But then his hands were on her gently, his voice in her ear.

'Steady, *carissima*. Just a little to your left. Just here.'

He edged her through the door into the kitchen and towards a chair.

'Sit down and I'll pour you a drink.'

She sat, trying to understand what was happening to her. She'd always been proud of her own confident efficiency, but suddenly she was swamped by fear. It swept over her in waves, making coherent thought impossible. Instead of giving calm consideration to the proposal, she'd blurted out her terrified resistance.

She felt a glass pushed into her hand and drank it without asking what it was. It was brandy.

'Thanks. I needed that,' she said huskily. 'Poor man. I didn't mean to shout at him.'

'It's not like you to lose it,' he said gently.

'I don't know what came over me. It's just that—I rely on Jacko so much. He's my lifeline. Another dog wouldn't be the same.'

'He could be trained to be as good. After a while it would be exactly the same.'

'But that would take time. This place is still new to me— Oh, I know I'm being selfish. You're right about Jacko. He's done his duty faithfully, but I've always sensed something not quite right, and now I know what it is. His heart's breaking. I ought to let him go, but how can I? I'd be lost without him.'

It passed across Fransesco's mind that she hadn't been lost without *him,* but he banished the jealous thought quickly, overtaken by another thought, one so startling that he pulled away from her to walk the room lest his eagerness show too clearly in his manner.

It was impossible, and yet...

'He's not the only dog in the world,' he began carefully. 'You'd have had to have another one eventually.'

'But if he goes now, what can I do?'

He drew a slow breath. Now was his last chance to draw back from the colossal risk he was about to take. But there would be no drawing back. It was the biggest gamble of his life, but he must take it or lose her. And she was worth everything.

'You can use me,' he said.

She turned her head sharply, as if staring at him.

'What did you say?'

'Let me be your dog. Make use of me.'

'Francesco, be serious.'

'I am serious,' he said, walking back and dropping down on his knees beside her. 'Listen to me, Celia. I know I sound crazy, but you're the one who's always talking about the virtues of craziness.'

'For me, not for you,' she protested.

'You think I'm not good enough to be crazy, huh? Let me show you.'

'*Caro,* this is madness. You don't know what you're suggesting. You'd have to be with me constantly. What about your own work?'

'That can manage without me for a while. What is it, Celia? Can't you trust me? I can do the job as well as a dog, I swear it. I know all the commands—stop, start, stand, sit. I'll even wear a harness.'

His clowning made her laugh, but there was still a serious doubt in her heart.

'I know you mean it,' she said, 'and it's a wonderful offer. But it would be so much harder than you think.'

'I'll do everything your way. When you don't need me, you won't even know I'm there. Isn't that enough?'

She hesitated, not knowing how to put it into words, and at last he came to her rescue.

'Once a bully, always a bully,' he said softly.

'No—*no*—'

'The dog is your independence, but that means independence from me. I should have understood that.'

'I don't always want to be independent from you,' she said in despair.

'I know, but we can't—*I* can't seem to stop blurring the lines. Knowing when to back off is something I never learned. I could try but– well, you know me. The man who shuts his ears.'

'Don't—please don't,' she whispered.

'I'm not saying that to be unkind, just reminding you that you got it right about me. You made your decision for us to part and it was a good one.'

'A good one for you?' she whispered.

He sighed and leaned his forehead against hers.

'It'll never be good for me without you. But I'm not good for you. It took me too long to see that, and if I'd had any sense I'd never have suggested taking Jacko's place. You keep him as long as you need him. Trusty friends are hard to replace.'

'Yes, I'd better go back and tell them.' She reached for his arm. 'It's all right,' she said. 'I can find my way, but I'm clinging to you for moral support.'

'I do have some uses,' he said lightly. 'Let's go.'

He stopped, silenced by the sight that met him as they entered the other room. Signor Feltona was sitting on the sofa with Jacko at his feet. The dog's head was turned up to him in an attitude of adoration.

'What is it?' she asked in a hurried under-voice.

'It's them—the way they're sitting together.'

Signor Feltona heard them and looked up quickly, his face full of hope that died when he saw their faces.

'Please—' he said.

'I can't—just yet,' Celia told him. 'But I'll get in touch with the society and ask for another dog very quickly. So you might get him back soon. That really is the best I can do.'

The man's shoulders sagged, and so did Jacko's, it seemed to Francesco. He told himself to stop being sentimental, but there was an air of misery about the dog that suggested he'd followed what was happening.

'I see,' Signor Feltona said heavily. 'I had hoped—my children love him so much—but I may tell them that they can still hope?'

'I'll do it as soon as I can,' Celia assured him. 'I'm sorry. It's just—'

'I understand,' he said in a husky voice. 'I'll leave you now.'

He rose and prepared to be gone. A soft whine broke from Jacko.

'It's all right, boy,' he said. 'Stay. Maybe later. Now, say goodbye to me.'

He dropped to one knee and embraced Jacko, who whined again in misery.

'All right, now. We'll be together again soon, I promise. No, no—you mustn't do that. Get down, boy.'

'What is it?' Celia asked.

'He's trying to go, too,' Francesco said.

'It's nothing,' Signor Feltona said hurriedly. 'He's just a little distressed. Please don't be angry with him. He's a good boy.'

'Of course he is,' Celia said. 'Come here, Jacko.'

She held out her hand. For a moment it seemed that Jacko would defy her, but then he seemed to abandon hope and moved slowly forward until he was in front of her.

'Goodbye,' said Signor Feltona, turning towards the door.

Jacko didn't move, but a wail of such anguish broke from him that it froze everyone who heard it. He laid his snout in Celia's hand while wave upon wave of despair came from his throat as a lifetime's discipline struggled with heartbreak.

'*Wait!*' Celia called. 'Don't go. Francesco, stop him.'

'No need,' Francesco said, going to where their visitor was standing frozen, joy and disbelief warring on his face. 'Come back, *signore.*'

'Go on,' Celia said, giving Jacko a little push.

Nothing would have stopped him then. The dog bounded across the room to hurl himself into his old owner's arms so fiercely that the two of them landed on the sofa.

'Forgive me,' Antonio said, recovering some poise but still clinging to Jacko. 'Do you mean—'

'Jacko belongs with you,' Celia said. 'He can't bear to be parted from you. I won't force him to stay.'

'You mean it?' he asked incredulously. 'You really mean it?'

'I mean every word. Take him with you now, and I'll make it all right with the society.'

'But what will you do before you get a new dog?' Having got what he wanted, Antonio was suddenly assailed by conscience.

'Don't worry about me,' Celia said. 'I have a friend who will look after me. Now, take Jacko quickly.'

'First we say thank you,' Feltona said. He touched Jacko gently, whispering, 'Go.'

She dropped to her knees for one last embrace and the dog came into her arms—willingly this time. Francesco watched as he nuzzled her and she buried her face against him. When she released him he put up a paw as if to have one last contact.

He understands, Francesco thought. He's a dog, but he knows she's made a sacrifice for him.

'Goodbye,' she said at last, huskily. 'Be happy. Good dog.'

Celia came with them to the door. Francesco came, too, watching her closely, seeing how close she was to weeping. She controlled herself until the door had closed, then she leaned against it, making no effort to hide the tears that now streamed down her face.

'That was a very brave and generous thing you did,' he said gently.

'No, it wasn't. I should have let him go at once. How could I be so cruel as to keep the poor creature here against his will?'

'But you didn't.'

'I was going to be so practical. But I could feel his misery and I couldn't bear it.'

'I'm glad,' he said.

'But just think of the ramifications of this,' she cried.

'It's actually very simple. Tomorrow you contact the society, explain what happened and ask them to find you another dog. In the meantime, just call me Jacko.'

'You know what you've let yourself in for, don't you?'

'And you know that I am willing.'

'I must be crazy.'

'Hey, play fair! Don't keep all the craziness to yourself. I've earned some, too.'

'What are you talking about?' she asked, laughing weakly.

'Well, I know that for you only crazy people count, and I'm doing my best.'

'Oh, *caro,* will I ever understand you?' She sighed.

'Probably not. But you could make me a coffee.'

As they sat in the kitchen he said, 'So, tell me about my duties. Shall I wear a harness?'

Her lips twitched. 'I think I can let you off the harness. But you have to obey my every command. Sit when I say *sit.*'

'Curl up under your chair when you don't need me?'

'I'd love to tell you to do just that,' she mused. 'I think I might just enjoy this. Whether you will is another matter.'

'I've told you—I'm a slave to your every whim. Well, except for one thing. I draw the line at the pooper-scooper.'

She gave a little choke of laughter that enchanted him. 'Hmm! So much for being my slave.'

'I'll be Jacko's substitute in every other way,' he promised. 'I'll even sleep at the foot of your bed.'

'You'll sleep in the spare room like a good doggie,' she told him firmly.

'Wuff!' he said.

## CHAPTER NINE

THE next day they drove to the Villa Rinucci to collect his things. Knowing his mother, Francesco took the precaution of telephoning her first, to explain that this was strictly a practical arrangement, and would she kindly refrain from asking Celia when the wedding was going to be?

'*Please,* Mamma—unless you want me to die of embarrassment.'

Hope promised to be good, and contented herself with loading Celia with gifts of home-baked treats, which she received with delight. Then it was back to the apartment for him to unpack and settle into the spare room, where they made the bed together.

As they were preparing a meal she said, 'I called the society. They were very understanding and said they'll find me another dog, but it may take a couple of months. I hope you won't find that awkward.'

'I hope *you* won't,' he said. 'I know you don't want me around that long.'

'We'll just have to try to endure each other,' she said lightly.

The exchange was pleasant enough, but behind it they were each assessing a situation that had taken them by surprise.

They spent the evening working in their various ways.

Francesco had brought his laptop so that he could direct the firm as far as possible.

'Is this going to damage you?' she asked worriedly. 'Your business is only just starting and the boss is deserting it.'

'I can still go in for a few hours. You can come with me. It'll help you assess our progress for your report.'

At last he said, 'Isn't it time for the evening walk? We both need some fresh air.'

Francesco found that he was nervous. Earlier in the day he'd taken her arm for a few moments when they'd visited the villa, but that had been too brief to count. And in the apartment she knew her way around. But this would be the real test—the first time she would be completely reliant on him.

She took his arm as they left the building and went down the three stone steps together.

'Let's head for the docks,' she said. 'Or shall we go the other way and wander around the shops?'

'You're the boss. Isn't that what Jacko would have said?'

'No, he wouldn't, and nor would Wicksy. In many ways they were the boss. Let's head for the port.'

As they walked he asked, 'How was Jacko the boss?'

'If I wanted to cross the road and he could see that it wasn't safe he'd refuse. I'd say, Go forward, and he'd just sit there, sometimes actually on my foot so that I knew he meant business. He could see the danger, so I had to take his advice.'

'Yes, I saw that once or twice,' he recalled. 'I thought he was being awkward.'

'No, he was doing his job. And sometimes he'd obey me in a roundabout way. If I said, Forward, and the way was blocked, he'd go sideways and find a way to negotiate the problem.' She squeezed his arm. 'He was a clever dog. He knew there was more than one way forward.'

'Yes, I guess he did,' Francesco murmured.

They wandered the short distance towards the sea, and she stood breathing in the odours of a busy port.

'That's good,' she said. 'I love the sea.'

He made a non-committal reply and she let it drop, remembering that the sea conjured up unfortunate memories for him.

'Do you want to go in any particular direction?' he asked.

'No, I don't know any details. Jacko was a good guide, but he never told me how things looked.'

After a moment he realised that she had made a joke, but by then it was too late to respond.

'What do you want to know?'

'Tell me about the boats.'

He did so, describing the ferries that came and went while she leaned on the wall that overlooked the water, an expression of total absorption on her face. At last she sighed and reached out for him.

'Let's go,' she said. 'Francesco?'

For a moment she touched only empty air, and she was suddenly full of tension.

'I'm here,' he said, quickly taking her hand. 'Sorry—my mind wandered for a moment.'

'I didn't know where you were,' she said quietly. 'I didn't know where *I* was.'

'I'm sorry,' he said urgently. 'I'm sorry.'

'Don't take it so much to heart,' she told him, smiling faintly.

'You're shivering.'

'I guess it's getting cold. Shall we go?'

He gave a groan.

'I'm useless at this. I thought it would be simple but it isn't. I keep wanting to tell you everything, then backing off in case I overdo it and annoy you.'

For a moment Celia was silent, too shocked to speak. The words, *He's afraid,* flashed through her brain.

From the beginning she'd known him as a forceful, domineering man, easily annoyed with people who wouldn't agree with him, including herself. But with her he'd suppressed his exasperation, always loving and tender, except in their quarrels. Even then she'd sensed him controlling himself, and it had had the perverse effect of increasing her anger because she'd felt she was being patronised. With a sighted woman he'd have felt free to let his anger explode. She'd always been certain of that.

Now she wasn't so sure.

She'd thrown him out, but was that the only reason for his hesitation? Hadn't it always been there, if she'd had the wit to sense it?

He's afraid, she thought again. And hard on the heels of that came the worst thought of all. Afraid of *me.*

'Let's try again,' he said. 'I'm holding out my arm close to you.'

'If you were a gentleman you'd take my hand and tuck it into place,' she said, in a voice that sounded strangely shaky.

'Sure—if that's all right with you.'

She felt him fit her hand into the crook of his elbow, and waited for him to give it a small pat before withdrawing his own hand. But he didn't, and a thousand thoughts clashed in her mind.

Forceful? Domineering? *Him?*

He's on hot coals for fear of offending me. Is that what I've done to him?

'Let's get back,' she said. 'I'm very tired.'

A moment ago she could have walked for ever. Suddenly

she was nervous. A sense of failure was creeping over her. She wasn't used to it and didn't know how to cope.

They walked home in silence.

Sharing an apartment, which had seemed so simple, turned out to be a minefield. Before, they had lived together with the casual intimacy of lovers, free to walk in on each other half dressed, without thinking.

Now he was a cross between an upper servant and a guide dog, with no privileges, only a duty to keep a respectful distance and obey his owner at all times. He had persuaded her on the solemn promise of respecting that duty.

Francesco's first inkling of just how tough this was going to be came on the second evening. Searching for his favourite pen, he recalled that it had been in his jacket pocket the night they had made love. He'd torn the jacket off, tossing it onto the floor. Now the pen was missing, so it had probably fallen onto the floor and might be there still.

Thinking Celia was in the bathroom, he went into her room. But she was sitting on the bed, naked except for a tiny pair of pink satin briefs.

'I'm sorry,' he said hastily, backing off. 'I thought you were— I'll go.'

'Did you want something?'

'I was looking for my—' Maddeningly, he found that his mind was blank. 'Never mind. Another time.'

He got out fast, shocked by what was happening to him. He'd seen her wearing less before—many times—but always with her willing consent. Now he felt like a Peeping Tom, intruding on her vulnerability. Most stunning of all was the undignified thrill of seeing something that should have been off-limits. Illicit pleasure, forbidden enchantment. It was like watching *What The Butler Saw,* utterly disgraceful and un-bearably exciting.

He fled to his own room while he still had some self-control, and lay all night without sleeping.

They found a kind of routine. Within the apartment she needed no help, because she knew where everything was. She would cook, and even clean the place, although she employed help for this. Not because she was blind, but be-cause the success of her work left her little time to spare.

Francesco insisted on looking after himself, including making his own bed, despite Celia's mischievous insistence that she had never required this from Jacko.

If she worked at her projects at home he would be free to leave her for a few hours, to put some time in at his own job. If she was working with Sandro he would deliver her to Sandro's office and leave her in his care, collecting her at the end of the day.

The parachute jump had caused a lot of interest, and Francesco waited for Celia to announce her own jump. He was well prepared, his self-control primed and ready for the worst. When the blow fell he would not protest. He would accept her decision, drive her to the airfield and muffle his terror.

But days passed with no announcement, and he allowed himself a sigh of relief.

Last thing at night they would take a walk together through the streets of Naples, while he described the sights to her. These were their happiest times. Sometimes they would stand by the water's edge, listening to the cry of sea-gulls and the sounds coming from the boats, before walking back to the apartment.

It wasn't exciting, but it was comfortable. He could sense her relaxing with him, and knew that this was a new phase for them.

One night she said, 'Why do we always branch left here?

Isn't there a right branch that would get us home just as well? Or have I got that wrong?'

'It would take longer,' he prevaricated.

'I don't care. Let's take the other way.'

'I'll bet you didn't argue with Jacko like this.'

'I wasn't suspicious of Jacko.'

'I'll sit on your foot in a minute,' he threatened.

They laughed together, making their way slowly along the street until they came to the moment when his dark secret was revealed.

'Who's that calling us overhead?' she asked.

'That's my brother, Ruggiero,' Francesco said in a resigned voice. 'He and Polly live in this block, and right now they're leaning out, enjoying the sight of me being a good dog.'

'But how do they know that's what you're doing?'

'How long do you think it took to go around the family?' he asked through gritted teeth. 'No, don't stop—let's get on.'

'We can't go without talking to your relatives if they've seen us. It wouldn't be polite.'

From above them came riotous cries of, 'Woof, woof!'

'Take a running jump,' Francesco called back. 'Preferably out of that window.'

'Celia, tell your hound to lead you in this direction,' Ruggiero called down.

'Well, go on,' she told him. 'Good doggie. Obey!'

'I'll get my own back,' he vowed as they went up. But he was grinning.

'You've been avoiding us,' Ruggiero said when they were each settled with cake and a glass of white sparkling *prosecco*.

'And you've been looking out for us,' Francesco said. 'Don't tell me you haven't leaned out of the window every night, hoping for a good laugh at me.'

'All right, I won't say it,' Ruggiero agreed.

Newly married, they had just finished visiting the more far-flung family members. Justin and Evie had welcomed them in England; Luke and Minnie had given them a riotous party in Rome.

'Mind you, most of the riot came from Minnie's previous in-laws,' Polly recalled. 'Heavens, they know how to give a party! We were exhausted when we went on to Uncle Franco and Aunt Lisa the next day. Luckily they're much more sedate, because I don't think we had enough energy for another mad evening.'

'How are they?' Francesco asked.

There was nothing in his voice to suggest that the subject particularly concerned him, and Celia wondered if she only imagined that the casual note was just a little contrived.

'They seem fine,' Ruggiero replied. 'Of course, they're getting old. Aunt Lisa has had bronchitis recently, but she's over it now. And Uncle Franco—well, you know him.'

'Not really,' Francesco said quietly. 'I've seen very little of him.'

Now Celia was sure she heard something strange in his voice. It seemed a good moment to discover that she had a headache, and in a few minutes they were heading home.

For a while she chatted casually, but at last it got through to her that he wasn't responding.

'What is it?' she asked.

'Nothing.'

'It's not like you to be so silent. Has something upset you.'

'You're not the only one with a headache,' he said abruptly. 'Let's get home.'

When the apartment door was locked behind them he bade her good-night as quickly as possible, and she did the same. It wasn't what she wanted. Painful as it was, she had to accept that.

She longed to reach out to him and take his troubles on herself—for that he was in some kind of trouble there could be no doubt.

In the old days she would have enfolded him in her arms and her heart, giving him all her love. But now things had changed, and suddenly she knew she had to be cautious. Like him, she went to bed without delay.

She fell asleep quickly, then awoke in the early hours, certain that some noise had disturbed her, but there was only silence. Sitting up in bed, she listened, and at last heard a muffled sound that seemed to come from next door. Slipping out of bed, she opened her door and went to stand outside Francesco's room. Now she could clearly hear the desperate, gasping mutters from inside.

Turning the handle quietly, she slipped inside and went to the bed. Sitting down on it, she discovered that Francesco was lying on his back, his eyes closed, muttering in his sleep. At first she couldn't make out the words, but then she realised that he was saying the same thing, over and over.

'Get out—get out—get out—'

'Francesco—' She shook him, but he didn't wake. It was as though he was trapped inside his nightmare, with no escape.

*'Francesco!'*

She shook his shoulders again, but he only began to toss and turn. Moving her hands gently across his face, she discovered that his cheeks were wet, as though he was weeping in his sleep.

She hesitated. They had set rules for sharing the apartment—rules that kept them firmly on different sides of a line. But this situation wasn't covered by any rule that she acknowledged, and if it had been she would have broken it.

She was about to lean down and kiss him when he let out

a cry and shot up in bed, colliding with her so that she almost fell off, and had to hold on to him.

'Francesco, what's the matter? Are you awake?'

'What? What? *Who are you?*' He was shaking her.

'Francesco—it's me—Celia.'

One of the hands holding her disappeared, and she heard the light being switched on. Dismayed, she wondered if his confusion was really so far gone that he had to see her to be sure.

'For pity's sake, what's the matter?' she begged.

'Nothing, I— What are you doing in here?'

'I heard you cry out in your sleep. Then you were muttering over and over to yourself— It sounded like *Get out.*'

She heard his sharp intake of breath.

'You imagined that,' he said in a cold voice. 'It could have been anything.'

'No, it was definitely *Get out* but—'

'*You imagined that.*'

'All right. Maybe I did.'

'Who knows what people say when they have a bad dream? Don't you ever have them?'

'No,' she said simply. 'But if I did I'd come to you and ask you to put your arms around me. Especially if it was bad enough to make me cry.'

She put her hand up to touch his face, but felt him seize it, holding her away from him.

'Don't be absurd,' he snapped. 'I'm not crying.'

She knew better than to argue, but she was full of confusion. She'd never known him in this mood before.

'Go back to bed,' he said. The anger had gone from his voice, but instead there was a quiet implacability that was more daunting.

'Good night,' she said.

If he'd softened for the briefest moment she would have kissed him. But all her senses told her that he was hard as iron, and she left the room.

She lay awake for a long time, listening for any sound from his room, but there was nothing. Everything had changed, she realised. In their old quarrels it had always been him trying to reach out to her, while she withdrew from what she considered his interference. Now it was he shutting her out.

She had not the slightest inkling why it had happened. But she was suddenly afraid.

The following day Celia chose to stay at home, freeing Francesco to leave and concentrate on his factory.

'But if you need me, just call and I'll come home,' he said.

'Don't worry. I shan't be going out,' she replied, as scrupulously polite as he.

'I expect you have your day's work all planned?' he observed.

'Actually, I thought I'd do some cooking.'

She could tell he was surprised, but he said no more, only lay a hand on her shoulder and departed.

Left alone, she didn't immediately get out any ingredients, but pondered for a while, then called Hope.

'I'm practising being a good housewife today,' she told her cheerfully. 'I know some of Francesco's favourite dishes, but only the English ones. I thought you could advise me about the Italian ones.'

'An excellent idea,' Hope said at once. 'Shall I come over?'

'Lovely.'

Hope arrived an hour later to find the coffee already perking. She'd come prepared with home-made cream cakes, and they plunged into a delicious session without delay.

'You don't need Francesco today?' Hope asked, looking around.

'Not while I'm here. I know this place so well that he's only in the way.'

They laughed together.

'Poor Francesco.' Hope sighed. 'He's trying so hard to be useful to you.'

'I wish…' Celia paused. 'I wish I knew what he was really like.'

'You can't tell from being with him?'

'I know how he is with me, but—in a way, we fell in love too soon. We really knew how we felt the first evening. It took us a week to admit the truth, but it was there from the start. I sometimes wish it had taken longer, so that I could have become acquainted with the man he was before.'

'Before love changed him?' Hope said, understanding 'I'm not sure that I can be much help. I saw little of him for the past ten years.'

'And you don't know what his demons are?'

'Ah, you've discovered those. Do they trouble him at night?'

'Only recently. He has nightmares, and he won't tell me.'

'Nor me,' Hope said sadly. 'I know it's happened since he returned, but as for before that—you probably know better than me.'

'It never happened in England.'

'He is a strange man,' Hope mused. 'Our family life has been full of upheaval. Justin, my eldest son, was the most affected. After him, I think it troubled Francesco most, but in a way I find hard to understand.'

'I've heard Francesco mention Justin. You only found each other a few years ago, didn't you?'

'Yes, he was born when I was only fifteen, and stolen from

me. Luke and Primo were part of my marriage, but Francesco—well.'

'I'm not trying to pry,' Celia said hurriedly. 'It's none of my business.'

'But I think I would like to tell you. I've known you only a short while, yet I feel I can trust you—as I know Francesco trusts you.'

'You *can* trust me,' Celia assured her.

'When I married my first husband in England, years ago, he already had a son—Primo—by his first wife, Elsa. She'd been a Rinucci—Toni's sister. She died, I married Primo's father, and we adopted Luke. It wasn't a happy marriage, and that was my fault. I married him for safety, but safety wasn't enough. Then I met Franco Rinucci. He was Elsa's and Toni's brother, and he came from Italy to visit Primo. And so we met.'

She paused, and a heavy silence filled the room.

'And so we met…' she repeated.

Then there was another silence.

'And it happened?' Celia asked softly.

Hope turned to her, smiling through her tears.

'Yes, it happened. We knew in the first moment. We tried to fight it, for we were both married with children. He stayed with us for a week, and when he left I was pregnant. We knew we couldn't be together. I would never have asked him to leave his wife and children, and he wouldn't have done so. We had that one week—the most glorious of my life. But glory doesn't last. It can't. It shouldn't. Nobody could live on that pinnacle for ever. I shall always have that week, and I shall always have the child who took his life from that lovely time.'

'Francesco?'

'Yes, Francesco. For a long time my husband thought the baby was his. He even made a favourite of him. But then he discovered the truth and threw us out. I got custody of Luke, but he kept Primo.

'Soon after that my husband died, and Primo came to Italy to live with the Rinuccis. I came out here to see him, and that was how I met the rest of the family.'

'Including Toni?'

'Oh, yes. He was a fine young man in his thirties—very strong, but very gentle.'

'Did you see Franco on that visit?' Celia asked.

'Briefly. His home was in Rome. He and his wife came down for a short while. I think we had five minutes alone. That was all either of us could have endured. The following day I told Toni that I would marry him.'

'Does he know about you and Franco?'

'I tried to tell him but he silenced me. He said that our lives would begin from that moment, and that nothing that happened before was any of his business.'

'So he suspects but doesn't want to know?' Celia hazarded.

'I think so. He has never asked questions. It's almost deafening, the way he doesn't ask anything.'

'Did you marry him for safety?' Celia asked cautiously.

'I thought I did,' Hope said. 'But then a strange thing happened. I found that I had married a man who was kind and loveable—who gave everything, asked little in return, and always put my happiness before his own. I ask you, what is to be done with such a man?'

'There is only one thing to do with him,' Celia replied at once. 'And that is to love him.'

'That's how I feel, too.'

Warmed by Hope's trust, Celia ventured say, 'But it's not the same as being *in* love, is it?'

Hope didn't answer for a moment, and when she did her eyes were focused on a distant place and her voice was soft.

'As I said, I had my pinnacle and it was glorious.' She was silent a moment. 'Perhaps there is more to life than being in love.'

Perhaps, Celia thought. But at this moment she couldn't believe it.

# CHAPTER TEN

FRANCESCO got home late that night. Celia was already in her room, and she heard him moving about quietly, so not to wake her. Once he looked in, but she pretended to be asleep. Anything was better than forcing him to talk to her when he clearly didn't want to.

For the first time she faced the possibility of defeat—something she'd never done in her life before. Right from the start—the child of two blind parents who'd conquered the world, she'd known that failure wasn't an option. Aided by a sharp brain and a natural talent, she'd mastered everything that came her way. It also helped to have a bolshie nature, she acknowledged.

Whatever she wanted, she went out and fought for—sometimes with blunt weapons. All those months ago, when she'd first met Francesco, if he hadn't come to her after the first week she would have sought him out and *made* him understand that they belonged together.

Throwing him out had been an act of recklessness that she'd soon regretted. So she'd made her plans—travelling to a strange country with a smile on her face, challenging all comers. The one she'd challenged the most was Francesco himself. And she'd been winning; her heart and her singing flesh told her that.

Then something had gone wrong, but exactly what it was still mystified her. It had started with his nightmare—No, before that, earlier in the evening, when Minnie had mentioned Aunt Lisa and Uncle Franco, his secret father.

On the pretext of cooking instructions she'd sought help from Francesco's mother, who hadn't been fooled for a moment. The two women had understood each other perfectly, and Celia had learned a good deal. But it didn't explain the dark mood that had suddenly come down over Francesco's mind.

At breakfast the next day she said, 'I had a call from the society yesterday. They think they'll have a dog for me soon. I'll have to go and live there for a month, so that we can get used to each other, but then I'll be all right.'

'Good. You'll feel happier. Let's hope he's as good as Jacko.'

This was how it would be from now on. His manner to her was pleasant and helpful, but no longer charged with something that made the air vibrate.

He performed his guide-dog duties perfectly, but time was moving on. Those duties would soon be over, and their best chance would be lost. She'd thrown the dice and she had failed.

Worst of all was the knowledge that she'd failed in understanding. He wasn't sufficiently at ease with her to open up. That was the truth of it.

It's always been about me, she thought, dismayed. I talk about being exactly like everyone else, but I talk about it too much. When did I ever let the poor man get a word in edgeways? Now it's too late. No, it mustn't be. *It mustn't be!*

But she didn't know what to do.

Every two weeks Hope arranged a family gathering at the villa for anyone who happened to be in Naples at the time. Usually this simply meant those who lived there, but occasionally a distant relative passed through and was scooped up for a dinner party. When Toni's second cousin once removed came to visit, he and his wife were feasted like royalty.

The younger members of the family thought them pleasant, but dull, and were politely relieved when a car arrived to collect them. But Hope and Toni followed them out to say more goodbyes by the car.

'You should go and join them,' Della scolded Carlo. 'Where are your manners?'

'They died a death when he told that story about the boar for the fifth time,' he said faintly.

She aimed a playful swipe at him, but she did him an injustice. A slight family resemblance had made Carlo the object of the old man's attention most of the evening. He'd done his duty with great charm. Now he'd earned a breather.

'You're driving us home tonight, aren't you?' he checked with his wife.

'Promise.'

'In that case I'll have a large whisky,' he said with relief.

When they were all sitting around, relaxing, Celia said, 'Why don't you tell us the rest of *your* story?'

This raised a laugh. For most of the evening Carlo had been trying to tell an anecdote of his own, constantly interrupted by their guest, who had led everything back to his own tale of the boar.

'Right—I'll tell it fast,' Carlo said. 'This man came to the door, and when he—'

He plunged into the story. Francesco watched him, and also Della, who laughed at her husband's story as freely as if she hadn't heard it a dozen times already. They were clearly happy and at ease with each other, he thought, remembering how stressed he'd seen them before.

'I see that you've got it sussed,' Francesco said as Carlo finished the story and came in search of his wife. 'I wish you'd tell me the secret.'

'The strange thing,' Carlo mused, 'is that it was you who told me the secret. Since your warning I've been watching myself—backing off, in case I smother Della with my love. I could end up depriving her of any meaningful life, which would be easier for me but would destroy her.'

'So why can't I practise what I preach?' Francesco sighed in frustration. 'I can't seem to find the way.'

'You won't,' Carlo told him. 'It'll find you. One day you'll just see the path at your feet, and that's when you have to decide whether to walk it. If you walk forward it'll be hard, but she'll be there, waiting. Until then you just have to keep watching for the moment.'

The phone rang in the hall, just outside.

'I'll get it,' Carlo said. 'I'm nearest.'

He vanished into the hall, and they heard him say, '*Ciao,* Minnie.'

Celia appeared at Francesco's side, asking, 'Is she the one who lives in Rome, with Luke? Ruggiero and Polly visited them recently?'

'That's right. Minnie's a lawyer and Luke owns an apartment block. They met because she was fighting him on behalf of his tenants. They started by going at it hammer and tongs and ended up married.'

'Hammer and tongs can make a very good beginning,' Celia said. 'You discover the worst of the other person, and if you can fall in love after that you have real hope.'

There was a general laugh at this, then Primo said, 'Just a minute— I think something's wrong. Carlo's voice has changed.'

They all grew alert, and heard Carlo say, 'All right. I'll get Poppa.'

By this time Toni and Hope had finished their goodbyes and were returning to the house, just as Carlo appeared, saying urgently, 'Luke's on the phone. Aunt Lisa is very ill.'

Toni and Hope hurried to the phone at once.

'It's bad, then?' Primo asked.

'She's dying,' Carlo said. 'She had a massive heart attack, and the doctors say there's very little hope. Uncle Franco asked Luke to call us, because he can't leave her for a moment.'

There were murmurs of consternation. Most of the others rose and surrounded Carlo, asking him questions, but Della remained with Celia, saying, 'They live in Rome, so Luke and Minnie have seen more of them than the rest of us. It's strange, really. Rome isn't so far away, but they never seem to join us here for family celebrations.'

Remembering what Hope had told her, Celia realised this wasn't surprising. The love between her and Franco had been so strong that they had to avoid each other—even years later. Now Franco's wife would soon be dead. His children were grown, and he would a free man. How would this make her feel? And Toni? Would he be afraid lest this changed everything?

At last Hope and Toni returned.

'How bad is it?' everyone asked.

'She's going,' Toni said heavily. 'My brother wants his family there.'

There were murmurs of agreement from the others, but Francesco said, 'I can't come, Mamma. I can't leave Celia alone.'

He spoke in a low voice, but Celia heard him—and Hope's immediate response. 'I hope Celia will come with us. I regard her as one of the family.'

'Thank you,' she said. 'I'll be glad to come.'

Inwardly she thought that there was more here than met the eye, but she, who had no eyes, might see more clearly than the others. Concern for her was chiefly an excuse. Francesco had his own reasons for not wanting to visit his true father.

It was decided that they would all leave by train the next day. An invitation to stay at Franco's home was politely refused.

'He will have enough on his mind without playing host to all of us,' Hope declared. 'There are several good hotels.'

After that the party broke up, and they made arrangements to meet at the railway station in the morning. For once Celia wished she could see. Hope had trusted her with her feelings, and now she would have liked to seek her out and speak to her. But it would attract too much attention.

She had to settle for asking Francesco to take her to his mother and giving her a hug. Through the pressure of the older woman's arms she sensed the feelings Hope could not express.

Francesco didn't speak until they were home, and then he said awkwardly, 'I'm afraid you were rather corralled into that, whether you like it or not.'

'I'm happy to come. If only I thought you wanted me there.'

'Nonsense—why shouldn't I?' He sounded edgy.

'Because there's something about this that you're keeping to yourself. There are warning signs all around you, telling me to keep off.'

'You're imagining that,' he said impatiently. 'If I'm a little awkward it's because of something I have to tell you. Della booked the hotel rooms, and she automatically booked each couple into a double room. I couldn't think of a way to tell her that we didn't want that, but when we get there I'll change it.'

'No, don't do that. In strange surroundings I'll be safer in the same room with you. Leave things as they are.'

'That's fine, then.' He stopped, as though words suddenly came hard to him.

She turned her head in his direction, trying to read the silence. She'd always been able to do so before, but this time he was blocking her out. The nothingness that resulted was the most frightening thing that had ever happened to her.

But she had to know the truth. If he'd turned against her she needed to feel that, too, by touching him, experiencing his bitterness through her fingers.

Celia began to walk in his direction, moving slowly and quietly, not to alert him. That was how she discovered that he was sitting down, his head sunk low, as though he'd come to the end of something and didn't know what to do next. Aghast at her own stupidity, she realised that there was no hostility here, only a dismal despair, bleak and all-engulfing.

'Tell me what it is,' she begged, leaning over him from behind and putting her arms around him.

'I can't,' he said in a stony voice. 'I don't know.'

'How can you not know what's troubling you? You didn't have these dark moods before.'

'Sometimes I did—they've always come over me without warning, all my life. But not very often, so it wasn't a problem. They'd come and then they'd go, sometimes for years. I thought I'd got the better of them for good. But suddenly they came back, all in a rush, a few months ago.'

'Because of me?'

'It's connected with you,' he said reluctantly, 'but not only you. There's something else—like a huge shadow looming over me, blotting out everything else.'

'I know about Franco,' she said softly. 'Your mother told me.'

'That he's my father? Yes, it's one of those things that everyone knows and nobody mentions, for Toni's sake. But

.t isn't a big deal, funnily enough. We've only met a few times. When we do, we look each other over, exchange the time of day, and that's that. I don't look like him, luckily, and he has another son and two daughters. I've always been content to leave it like that. Toni's been a great father to me, and I wouldn't hurt him for the world.'

Before she could say any more he added quickly, 'It's getting late, and we need to make an early start tomorrow.'

They went to their separate rooms for the night. Celia lay listening carefully for any sound from Francesco. But all was quiet, which meant that either the nightmare hadn't returned or he, too, was lying awake, determined not to sleep and give himself away.

Celia was a little reluctant when they set out for Naples Central Railway Station next morning. This was a family occasion, and she didn't really belong, yet a part of her wanted to be with Francesco—to be ready for whatever might happen. Perhaps she could be of no help to him. Perhaps he would shut her out. But he was going to need her in some way, of that she was certain.

In less than two hours they were drawing into Rome Central, where cars waited to take them to the hotel. The room she shared with Francesco overlooked the Via Veneto. It was large, and had two double beds, and through the windows came sounds from the luxurious heart of the city.

Celia declined the chance to go to the hospital with the rest.

'I've got a headache,' she said untruthfully to Francesco. 'We'll meet up later.'

Alone, she unpacked and walked the room to get a mental picture of it. She'd taken the precaution of bringing some work with her, and spent the next hour listening to tapes and dictating messages. But it was a relief when her cellphone rang and she found herself talking to Sandro.

'How long will you be away?' he asked. 'Things are beginning to happen here.'

She explained the position and he sighed.

'I guess you'll do what you have to do. But why you're taking the trouble for that prickly, awkward so-and-so I'll never know.'

'That's easy,' she said. 'It's *because* he's a prickly, awkward so-and-so. He needs me.'

'*I* need you.'

'No, you don't. You've got your life together in a way he'll never have.'

Sandro chuckled. 'Well, don't tell *him* that. He'd never forgive either of us. He hates my guts. The two times we met, the air was full of it.'

'He's afraid you're going to talk me into doing a jump.'

'Talk you— You're the one who found that place, remember? And we had a fight about who was going to make the first jump. You were ready to murder me when I won.'

'Well, there's no need to go into that,' she said hastily. 'It's best forgotten.'

'That's a pity, because the press are dead keen for you to do it. Simon wants you to call him. He writes for *L'Esperienza*.'

Her heart gave a leap before she had time to think. But then—

'I can't even think of it just now.'

'Of course. Just make the call and say you'll do it when you can. The number is—'

'I've got his number. I have to go now.'

She hung up and lay back on the bed, thoughtful. After a moment she switched her cellphone off.

There was a knock on the door.

'It's me,' Della called. 'And I've got goodies—tea and cakes.'

'I could kill for a cup of tea,' Celia said, opening the door.

When they were seated, and enjoying the first cup, Della gave a long sigh and said, 'I took the chance to get away. It's really the sons who belong with Franco, not us. Francesco really needs to be there. I think he's feeling a bit edgy.'

'What's Uncle Franco like? He said there was no resemblance.'

'There isn't. They're both tall, but that's about it. Uncle Franco is hefty and muscular, like a football player, and he's managed to keep his figure without putting on weight.'

'I wonder what Hope thinks of him now,' Celia mused.

'She's not giving anything away. I was watching her, so elegant and proper, everything in its place, the perfect picture of a respectable, virtuous, elderly matron. And I suddenly realised what an eventful life she's had. Her first child at fifteen, then a husband, a lover, another child, then another husband. The rest of us are quite dull by comparison. Even now, Hope is still beautiful, but I've seen pictures of her as a young woman, and in those days she was more than beautiful. She had a sort of wild quality that makes it clear why all the men fell for her.

'There's a wedding picture of her and Toni. She's smiling at the camera, but he's looking at her with his heart in his eyes. It's been there ever since, according to Carlo. He says all the time they were growing up they knew that if Toni said, "That's how Mamma wants it," then that was how it was going to be.'

'But aren't we making too much of this?' Celia asked. 'Maybe Franco *was* the great love of her life, but that was years ago. She's not going to leave Toni now.'

'No, but if he senses that the old feeling is still there between them it will hurt him terribly. She's everything to him. He's such a dear, I'd hate him to be hurt.'

'So would I,' Celia said. 'Even though I don't know wha he looks like, every time he's there I get a feeling of kindness and gentle strength.'

'That's Toni,' Della agreed.

Everyone returned from the hospital that evening. They had seen Franco, who'd thanked them for coming, but Lisa had failed to regain consciousness, against all their hopes.

Francesco said little, but as they all sat at dinner that evening Celia felt him touch her gently now and then, as though seeking reassurance. She looked forward to the moment when they would be alone together later that night, and she could ask him to confide in her.

But before that there was a phone call that changed everything.

It came just as the meal was ending. Hope answered her cellphone, listened for a moment, then said tersely, 'Very well. I'm coming.'

'What's happened?' Toni asked her.

'Lisa is awake and wants to see us.'

'All of us?' Toni asked softly.

'Me—and Francesco.'

Nobody could have told from Toni's face that this meant anything unusual to him.

'Come with me,' Hope begged.

'No, *cara*. I have no place in this. I'll wait for you here.'

'But—'

'Go,' he said, with sudden intensity.

Hope didn't reply, but she put her arms about her husband and kissed him.

'Francesco,' Toni said in a low voice, 'go with your mother.'

'Yes, Poppa.'

His hand was tight on Celia's. He didn't ask her to accompany him, but neither did he release his grip. They went out to the car together.

Franco met them in the corridor outside his wife's room.

'Lisa is conscious,' he told Hope, 'and she has something she wishes to say—to ask you. All these years it's been on her mind. I've tried to—' He lapsed into the helpless silence of confusion.

'What have you told her?' Hope asked.

'I've denied it,' he said heavily. 'But nothing I say seems to bring her peace.'

'And that's the only thing that matters. Say whatever you have to, Mamma.'

It was Francesco who had spoken, making the others stare at him.

'What do you mean?' Hope asked.

'You know exactly what I mean. Aunt Lisa is dying. Help her.'

Celia heard the click as the door opened, and the faint sound of Hope's footsteps, then a faint, husky voice from within the room. She waited, expecting either that Francesco would lead her forward or that the door would close, shutting her out. Neither happened. By accident or design Hope had forgotten to shut the door.

Lisa's eyes were open as Hope moved quietly towards the bed, and she managed a faint smile.

'Thank you for coming,' she said. 'There's something I need to know. I always lacked the courage before.'

'I understand,' Hope said softly.

'It's about Francesco— Is he—is he Franco's son?'

Francesco, standing in the doorway, saw his mother raise her head and look directly at Franco on the other side of the bed.

'Tell me,' Lisa said weakly. 'I must know before I die.'

At last Hope spoke.

'My dear, I wish you'd asked me years ago, then I could

have told you that it's not true. Francesco isn't his son. I never told anyone his father's identity, but I never meant t cause you a moment's unease. You should never have doubted Franco. You are everything to him, just as my Toni is everything to me. Now I will leave you.'

She gave Lisa a brief kiss on the cheek and backed out of the room. Her last view was of Franco in his wife's arms. This time she closed the door.

'Mamma,' Francesco said, putting his arm around her, 'was it very hard?'

'I said what had to be said,' Hope told him. 'Giving her peace was all that mattered. You were right about that.'

'It was a good lie,' Francesco said.

Hope gave a little smile.

'Not everything I said was a lie. All those years ago he stayed with her because she was his true love. *She* was. Not me.'

'And the other thing?' he wanted to know. 'About Toni?'

Hope didn't answer in words, but her gaze went over Francesco's shoulder, so that he turned and saw what she had seen. The next moment Hope had gone.

'What's happening?' Celia asked.

'It's Toni,' Francesco told her. 'He came after all. He's been sitting at the end of the corridor.'

'Where he could be there for Hope but not intrude on her,' she said.

'Yes, I think so. But now she's walking towards him. He's seen her—he's got to his feet—she's started to run—he's opened his arms to her and—'

'Let's go,' Celia said softly. 'There are some things that nobody's eyes should see.'

# CHAPTER ELEVEN

IT WAS the early hours of the morning when they arrived back at the hotel. Francesco had been silent since they'd left the hospital, but Celia sensed that it wasn't the same silence as before. She no longer felt shut out from his thoughts. Rather he was immersed in them, struggling to find a way out, but his continual clasp on her hand told her that she was part of everything going on inside him.

Since the beds were so large she hoped he might be tempted to join her, but he slipped quietly into his own. She came to sit by him and said a soft, 'Good night.' He didn't answer, and actually turned away, but before doing so he raised her hand to his lips.

They had slept barely an hour when she was woken by the sound of his voice. She was alert in an instant, slipping out of bed and going to sit beside him, listening for the old cry of, 'Get out.'

But it didn't come. Instead, he was muttering feverishly, 'What did I do? What did I do?' Over and over again the words poured out, intense, anguished.

'*Caro,*' she said, shaking him gently. 'Wake up. It's me.'

She reached out, touching him, running her fingers over his

face. He seized her hands, holding them tight against him, b
still he seemed unable to wake.

'Why?' he cried. 'Tell me why? What did I do?'

Driven by desperation, she moved until she was close to
his ear and said firmly, 'You didn't do anything. It's not your
fault—not your fault.'

She repeated the words like a mantra, with no idea of their
meaning, desperately hoping that she'd found the key to
whatever tormented him. At first she thought it was hopeless,
but gradually his voice slowed, the words became less frantic,
but imbued with a kind of despairing resignation.

'It's not your fault,' Celia repeated.

'Yes, it is—it was something I did—or why did he throw
us out? Why? *Why?*'

Briefly she wondered if it was their own quarrel and its
aftermath that tormented him, but he'd spoken of 'he' and 'us.'

She gave him a shake, determined to wake him because she
didn't think he could bear this any longer. But instead of
waking he began to mutter, 'Get out, get out, get out—'

'Wake up!' she cried. 'Francesco, please wake up.'

Suddenly he went still in her hands, and the sound of his
gasp told her that he was awake.

'What are you doing here?' he whispered.

'I'm always here. Whenever you want me. Francesco, tell
me what happened. You kept saying, *What did I do?* And then
you started saying "Get out" again. What was your dream?'

'It was more than a dream,' he groaned. 'It was all happening again, just like last time.'

'Tell me quickly, while you can still remember. Why do
you say, "Get out"? Did I give you the nightmare, by saying
that when we quarrelled?'

'Not really. You triggered it with those words, but it goes

...ack long before you. Only I couldn't remember. That's what was so terrible. It was always there, waiting to come back, but I couldn't see it or confront it.'

'But tonight—'

'Yes, tonight he came back. As he's been waiting to do for years.'

'He? Who is he? Is he a real man, or did you imagine him?'

'He was real once. He's been dead for years, but to me he'll always be real.'

'What happens in the dream?'

'He towers over me,' Francesco said hoarsely. 'So high he seems almost to reach the ceiling. He looks like a giant because I'm only three years old. I'm terrified of him, and I want to run away, but I don't because only cowards run. He taught me that. He taught me lots of things—we were so close. I learned everything he had to teach. I thought he was wonderful.'

'But who was he?'

'His name was Jack Cayman—Mamma's first husband, the man I once thought was my father. I can see him, leaning down to me—I couldn't take my eyes off him—and screaming, "*Get out! And take this little bastard with you.*"'

Celia held him tightly. 'Go on,' she urged.

'He just screamed, "*Get out, get out!*" again and again. I didn't know what he meant, or what had happened, but I know we left the same day. He must have found out the truth—that he wasn't my father.'

'You said you were close?'

'Yes, he made a favourite of me. The joke is that he used to say that of us three boys I was the one most like him. Luke was adopted, Primo was his own son, but for some reason he latched on to me as the kind of son he truly wanted. I loved that. The best thing in the world was when he swept me up his arms, tossed me the air, then caught me, grinning all ov his face. I guess I was a bit of a chauvinist, like boys of three tend to be. Mamma came in handy at feeding time, but the one who mattered was my dad. His love, his approval—they were what made the sun come out.

'Then suddenly, in one hour, it was all taken away. And I didn't know what I'd done wrong. I just knew that warmth and safety had vanished without warning, leaving a terrible emptiness.'

'Poor little boy,' she mourned.

'Of course, I learned the details later. He was livid because he'd found out that he wasn't my father, and it wasn't anything *I'd* done, but it was too late to make any difference, and what happened that night got blotted out. All I knew was that the words *Get out* always had a strange impression on me. If I heard them, it was as though a switch had been thrown.'

'But surely you didn't hear them often? How many people would dare tell *you* to get out?'

He gave a faint bark of laughter. 'One or two have tried. There was one lady who was so determined to be rid of me that my feet barely touched the floor.'

'She sounds like a very stupid woman to me,' Celia said, lying down beside him, her face close to his.

'No, she was a very clever one. I realised that she was right when I got over my shock enough to do some thinking. I've always been a bit forceful, and nobody had really stood up to me before, you see. But it wasn't just real people. If I was watching television and one character told another to get out the words triggered something in my mind. And I'd be in a black mood for hours, without understanding why. But it passed, and I'd forget again.'

'But then I screamed the words at you, just like him?'

'Yes, and that's when it really began to haunt me. Because it was actually aimed at me. But it was more than that. It was losing you. Everything that I treasured—warmth, safety, love—had vanished again, leaving me stranded in a desert. And then tonight—coming here, seeing Franco, everything they talked about—it came back. Suddenly I could remember everything that happened that night, and the last brick slipped into place.'

'What happens now?' she asked anxiously.

'It'll be all right now. I can cope because I can confront it.' He turned his face to her on the pillow. 'Mind you, I'm never going to be sweetness and light.'

'Well, I guess I knew that,' she said, snuggling contentedly against him. 'But you know me—I like to live dangerously.'

'You don't want sweetness and light?'

'Bor—ing!' she sang out. 'Bor—ing!'

He felt for her. 'Why are you lying outside the duvet?' he asked.

She scrambled under the covers. 'Is that better?'

'You're still overdressed.'

'So are you.'

They solved the problem at once, not disrobing slowly, to tease, but quickly, like people who couldn't wait to get to their destination. They urgently wanted to be naked together, and when they were they lost no time seeking the moment of complete fulfilment. There would be time for tenderness later. This was important.

For Celia it was almost like making love to a different man. He didn't need to tell her that his shadows had begun to fall away; she could sense it in every movement. But she knew, too, that he needed her presence to escape them completely.

Afterwards they lay together in sleepy contentment, u. she said, 'How lovely that Toni came to the hospital.'

'He was bound to. It was always there in the way his eye. followed Mamma around.'

After a moment, he said, speaking hesitantly, 'To be honest, that's the only thing I mind about you being blind. I'll never know if your eyes would have followed me.'

'Then you haven't been looking properly,' she said. 'Because they do—all the time.'

They went to the hospital next day, to hear the news that they had expected.

'She fell asleep finally about an hour ago,' Franco said in a slightly unsteady voice. 'She was conscious almost until the end, and I was able to tell her how much I loved her.'

'She had no real cause to doubt your love,' Hope said gently. 'And in her heart I think she really knew that. You were together for such a long time—nearly forty years.'

Long ago, when they were young and their passion had been at its height, they could have been together. But he had chosen to stay with his wife. The truth behind that choice was there now, as they stood there in the hospital corridor, the slanted sunbeams from the windows falling on their white hair.

As they walked away afterwards Della fell in beside Celia, taking her arm so that Francesco could give his attention to his parents.

'For a man in his sixties Franco's incredibly handsome,' she said in low voice, not to attract attention. 'He must have been dazzling when he was young. Toni's delightful, but I doubt if he was ever dazzling.'

'It's got nothing to do with a man's looks,' Celia told her. 'If it had, I could never fall in love.'

'And you are in love, aren't you?'

'Oh, yes,' Celia murmured. 'Yes, I am.'

'Is everything all right with you and Francesco?'

'It's getting better, but we've a way to go yet.'

Toni had remained behind to talk to his brother, and Francesco took the chance to draw his mother's arm through his and say, 'Is it all right, Mamma? You know what I mean.'

'Yes, all is well, my son. I knew years ago that he loved Lisa more than he loved me. So when he offered to stay with me I told him no.'

'He did offer?'

'Oh, yes. But I knew I must not accept. If he'd left Lisa for me he wouldn't have forgiven me in the long run. Not just because of his children, but also because she was his true love.'

She gave his arm a slight pressure.

'Sometimes the only way you can show how much you love someone is to let them go.'

Lisa's funeral was held three days later. The whole family was there to see her coffin, covered with flowers, being laid to rest. Despite what Celia had said, Della couldn't help wondering what Hope was feeling now. Had the past come back to her, making her heart ache with its loss? Had Franco, too, become sharply aware of what had come and gone?

But Franco's eyes were fixed unwaveringly on the coffin, and his expression was heart-rending. Della stole a glance at Hope, but Hope was looking at Toni.

On the surface life went on as before. The society apologised that Celia's new dog would not be ready as soon as hoped, but Francesco seemed untroubled by the delay.

Things had reached a strange pass between them. Th_
were lovers again, spending nights in each other's arms, jus_
as in the past, yet they never spoke of the future, and an air of
impermanence hung over them. There were still decisions to
be made, but neither of them wanted to face them for a while.

'We're cowards,' she murmured dozily one night, from the
shelter of his arms.

'What's wrong with that?' he wanted to know. 'We've tried
being brave, and nuts to it.'

She giggled and blissfully snuggled down farther. The big
problems still lurked outside the tent, but in the meantime
there was a lot to be said for cowardice.

She supposed it was a sign of losing her nerve that she often
kept her cellphone turned off, lest the call come from
*L'Esperienza,* demanding that she make her dive from a helicopter. She owed it to the firm that she'd promised to support,
but she didn't want to face that decision yet. Eventually she
would feel guilty and turn it on again.

In the end the decision was taken out of her hands, when
she slipped up to the flat above to return a CD, assuring
Francesco that she could manage that little distance alone. It
was half an hour before she returned, having got caught up in
cheerful gossip.

'There was a phone call for you,' Francesco informed her.
'A journalist wanting to know when you'd be ready to go skydiving. He says he has a space in the paper all ready, and it
can be a good story, but it has to be you, not Sandro.'

'What did you tell him?' she asked.

'I told him I thought you were free any time, and you'd call
back tonight to fix the date.'

Astonishment held her silent, staring.

'*You* told him I'd go skydiving?' she echoed in disbelief.

'Yes—and could you call him back quickly? Because he's going out, and he wants to get it settled.'

He left the room abruptly, before his resolve weakened and he said what he really thought—that she must commit herself quickly before he broke down and begged her not to do it.

It was his mother who had given him the clue, saying, 'Sometimes the only way you can show how much you love someone is to let them go.'

He'd heard the words without truly realising what they meant. Now he discovered the reality for himself, and it was terrible. Sweat stood out on his brow, and he had to call on all his stubbornness.

Stubbornness had never failed him before, he thought wryly.

After a while she came to find him.

'Is it all settled?' he asked with forced brightness.

'Yes, I'm going tomorrow. But, Francesco, did you mean it?'

He managed a laugh. 'It's a bit late if I didn't.'

'But why?'

'Does it matter why? I won't fight you any more about anything you want to do. I give in. Do what you feel you must. I'll see things your way.' He added with light irony, 'You'll observe that I make better jokes about it these days.'

She wanted to cry out a protest at the pain she could sense beneath the wit. She didn't want him to give in. That wasn't his way. But neither did she know how she *did* want it to happen.

He increased her discomfiture a moment later when he said, 'All those years of watching Toni with Hope have taught me a few things about graceful yielding.'

'No,' she said at once. 'Not like that. You're not Toni. He's happy that way, but you never could be.'

'You know your trouble?' he said. 'You don't know how to accept winning.'

'But—'

'I'm hungry. How about something to eat?'

Francesco made it impossible for her to pursue the subject. Only when they were getting ready for bed did he say, 'You can send your driver for tomorrow away. I'll take you to the airfield myself.'

'Is that really a good idea?'

'You mean, you don't trust me?' he asked, as lightly as he could manage. 'You think I'll back off at the last minute?'

She had briefly wondered. But while she sought for an answer, he said softly, 'I think I've earned better than that by now.'

'Oh, darling!' She reached for him. 'I'm sorry. I didn't really mean to suggest—'

'Yes, you did,' he said without resentment. 'You always do. And maybe I deserved it once. But I've learned a lot. The trouble is, I don't think you've noticed.'

'Yes, I—' She stopped as the truth of this hit her. She *had* noticed how much easier it was to relax with him these days, but only in a vague way. Preoccupied with herself, she had missed much that she should have seen.

'Never mind,' he said, drawing her close. 'I'll drive you down there tomorrow—if I may?'

'I'd love you to come—if you're sure you won't get too upset.'

'I won't make any trouble,' he said, interpreting her correctly.

Celia kissed him again and again, full of contrition and love and something that was more than either. She didn't under-stand it at first, but then she sensed his heart beating against hers, so close together that it was one beat. And suddenly she felt everything that he was feeling—sadness, dread, the fear of losing her, but most of all the fear of offending her.

Pain for him was so intense that it almost deprived her of the power of speech. She could only murmur, 'Darling, darling…'

But words weren't enough. Only actions could express the depth of her love, and she tried to show him with ardour and tenderness.

That night their lovemaking was like never before. It was as though they were open to each other in new ways, speaking silently of secrets never shared.

The first time they had loved had been a night of discovery as they'd explored each other's bodies and hearts. Now it was as though they were discovering each other again, with new intensity and sweetness, but also with a new knowledge that cast doubt over the future. The time was coming when a final decision must be made, and the thought of what that decision might be made every movement and caress mean a thousand times more.

When at last they lay quietly together, he whispered, 'Promise to come back to me—until the next time.'

So he understood about the next time, and recognised that it was inevitable, she thought. That should be a help, but mysteriously it was a new source of pain.

'Of course I'll come back,' she said. 'I always do.'

He didn't answer, and she reached out to caress his face, relishing the details, the high forehead and the strong jaw, the mouth with its unexpected sensitivity.

'Darling?' she murmured. 'Darling?'

Then she realised that he had gone to sleep, his arms still about her, and she felt a curious sense of delight.

'It's all right,' she whispered. 'Just stay there. I'll take care of you.'

She stroked his hair, relishing its springy feel in her hands, wondering at the surge of protectiveness that went through her.

Blind in one way, blind in another, she thought, condemning herself. If you can't see other people it's easy to forget their needs.

It would have been so easy to do the dramatic thing and tell him that she had changed her mind and would stay safely on the ground. But she knew she couldn't do that. All her life she'd fought for her precious independence, wounding herself in the process, but never until now seeing the wounds of others. Even now something that was essential to her true self wouldn't let her yield, though he'd generously shown her the way by yielding first. That was the truth of it.

And yet something had changed. Now she understood how much he was in her hands, how cruelly she could make him suffer—far more than he could ever inflict on her.

She leaned down, kissing him gently, not to awaken him.

'Forgive me,' she whispered. 'Forgive me for what I can't help.'

## CHAPTER TWELVE

As THEY drove to the airfield next morning Francesco asked lightly, 'Why are you and Mamma thick as thieves these days?'

'Not just us. Olympia and Polly, too, and Della, when she's here instead of hunting backgrounds for her series. There's a big party to be planned for the wedding anniversary.'

'I'd forgotten. How many years is it?'

'Thirty-five. Hope says she and Toni always celebrate in style, but this year it's going to be special. It's all being planned well in advance, so that everyone has time to get here, wherever in the world they live. It's going to be the party to end all parties.'

He thought, but didn't say, Let's hope you're still alive to be there.

But she could read his thoughts. 'And I'm going to be there, too. I've promised Hope that when this jump is over I'll concentrate on the party. You know, it's lovely the way she's welcomed me into the family. In fact, they all have.'

'Maybe they're trying to tell you something.'

'Maybe. I know they've turned this jump into a family occasion. Hope and Toni are going to be there, also Carlo and Della, and maybe some of the others.'

When they reached the airfield Francesco dropped Celia

by the steps into the main building and gave her into the hands of a young woman who would help her change. When she had gone inside he turned to find Carlo and Della approaching him. With his new sharp eyes Francesco saw how Carlo had his arm protectively around Della's shoulders, but so lightly that she wouldn't feel it as a constraint.

'Are you all right?' Carlo asked, giving him a meaningful glance.

Francesco grimaced. 'Surviving.'

'She'll be fine,' Della told him. 'Women are a lot tougher than men allow for. In fact, the truth is that we're a lot tougher than men, full-stop. Isn't that so, *caro?*'

'Yes, dear,' Carlo said in a comically robotic voice. 'No, dear. Anything you say, dear.'

'You two are turning into Mamma and Poppa,' Francesco observed.

Carlo grinned, not in the least offended by the comparison. He drew his wife closer and dropped a swift kiss on the top of her head.

'I've got him well trained.' Della chuckled. 'You'd better watch out. Celia will have you in line in no time.'

'She already has, or we wouldn't be here,' Carlo said. 'Francesco, we'll see you later.'

They wandered off, arms entwined.

Francesco watched them, wondering if he and Celia would ever reach such a pitch of perfect understanding. Or would today be the end of everything, one way or another?

Then he saw the door open and Sandro come out, led by his dog, with Celia's hand tucked in his arm. He brought her over, followed by a man dressed in the same kind of gear Celia was wearing. Relieved, Francesco recognised Sandro's skydiving partner from the previous occasion.

'Just dropped by to tell you not to worry,' he told Francesco. 'Celia and I will jump out together, and I won't let her go until I know she's safe.'

'Who's worried?' Francesco said cheerfully. 'But, thanks.'

'We'll be back for you in a few minutes,' Sandro told Celia, and the two men departed discreetly.

'Everything all right?' Francesco asked. He did his best to sound cheerful, but he could hear the strain in his own voice and doubted he was enough of an actor to hide it.

'Everything's fine,' she said, sounding too polite, too cautious. She was making allowances in case he backed off.

He grew frantic. He *must* convince her that he was really behind her in this. It had never been as important as now.

'That huge thing on your back is your parachute?' he said, putting as much interest in his voice as possible. 'How do you open it?'

'This ring, here—in the front. I just pull it and the parachute opens.'

*Suppose it didn't open? It might not and then she'd crash to earth and die. He must stop this madness, for her sake.*

But the desperate thoughts that screamed through his head stayed silent on the outside. Instead, he asked brightly, 'What about the other bits and pieces? There are too many to count.'

'This is my two-way radio, so that someone on the ground can warn me if I look like I'm coming down in the wrong place. I can guide the parachute in different directions using these rings. And don't worry—I know exactly where they are and can find them easily.'

'I'm sure of it,' he managed to say.

She laughed then in delight, putting her hand up against his face.

'I love you,' she said.

He took her hand and kissed the palm. 'Come back me, Celia.'

'But I did,' she said.

'No, I mean—'

'Oh, you can be so stupid sometimes,' she breathed. 'I *did* come back to you. Didn't you notice?'

'You mean—when you came to Naples—it was really— All that stuff you said— You returned to *me?*'

'At last the truth gets through,' she said fondly. 'It took long enough.'

'I've always wondered, but you never exactly—'

'I have to be going now,' she said. 'I love you.'

He kissed her palm again, horribly conscious of Sandro, who had reappeared nearby.

'I love you,' he said quietly. 'Now you must come back to me again—or what shall I do?'

'Time to be going,' Sandro called.

She drew back from Francesco, letting Sandro take her away in the direction of the light plane.

'Come back to me,' Francesco called. *'Come back to me.'*

He waited for her to respond to the sound by turning her head, but she didn't. It was as though everything in her was focused on what would happen next. The last few moments might never have been. He wondered now if she even remembered that he existed.

In fact, he did her an injustice. In her usual methodical way Celia was trying to order him out of her mind, so that she could concentrate on what was about to happen. But his ghost, so tractable before, had become rebellious. It insisted on staying with her every step across the tarmac, reminding her that he existed, and that if she died he still had to find a way to go on existing, however empty it might be.

Now she was at the helicopter, and a hand was reaching out to pull her aboard.

'Good luck!' Sandro said from the ground.

'Thanks,' she replied mechanically.

She heard the door slam, cutting off all sound from outside. Now the only sound was the crackling of the radio and a disembodied voice that came from some mysterious other place.

*Come back to me.*

Her diving partner touched her shoulder to check all was OK.

She'd met him before, a strong hearty type called Silvio, whose geniality made him pleasant company. She nodded, strapping herself in.

He did a quick check to make sure she'd done it right, and pronounced himself satisfied.

'Check your radio,' he said.

She exchanged a few words with her guide on the ground, and found that everything was working perfectly.

Silvio clapped the pilot on the shoulder to indicate that they were ready.

The whine of the engine that had been in the background now grew higher. Above them the blades whirred, and suddenly they were whisked up into the air, going higher and higher at an incredible speed.

At first her stomach seemed to be falling away from her, but then it steadied itself and she was calm again.

Now Silvio's voice reached her on the radio.

'It'll take us a few minutes to reach our height, then we'll circle a couple of times and return in this direction, so that we can make the jump and land on the airfield, where all your friends can see you.'

'See me make a fool of myself, you mean,' she said lightly. 'With my luck I'll land on the control tower.'

'Nah, that hasn't happened for ages—at least six w◄ he clowned.

She chuckled. This was how she liked her adventures be—light-hearted and relaxed.

But the silent companion in her head was reproachful, reminding her that it was *his* life she was dicing with, as well as her own.

'Getting near,' Silvio said. 'I'm about to touch the button that will slide the door back, then I'll jump, taking you with me. When we've jumped, we'll hold on to each other with both hands as we start the fall. Then we'll release hands and pull the rings to release our parachutes.'

'Nearly ready,' said her guide from the ground. 'Helicopter just coming into sight. All set?'

'All set?' Silvio asked her.

'All set,' Celia confirmed.

She felt Silvio's hand tighten on hers, drawing her to the open door.

'Now,' he said.

A sudden pull and they were both free in the air. He seized her other hand and they began to float down, both at full stretch, supported on a blanket of air.

This was when it should happen—the feeling of glorious escape that always came as she launched herself into the unknown. This was her freedom.

But it didn't happen.

'All right?' Silvio asked through the radio.

'Wonderful!'

Silvio released her hands. Now—now it would come. The exhilarating sense of liberation, the thing she lived for. *Now!*

But no rush of joy possessed her. Instead, she realised that

ind was roaring past her, and it was time to pull the ring
. would open her parachute.

She yanked, and felt the tug at her back as the parachute
streamed up behind her.

'Yeee-haaah!' she cried up into the void.

It was good to be floating down through the fierce, bluster-
ing air, and perhaps if she shouted her joy aloud she would re-
capture the joyous freedom that had always possessed her before.

But then she had an alarming sensation, as though someone
had seized her and was throwing her around the sky.

'What's happened?' she cried.

'The wind has changed course,' Silvio told her. 'Don't
worry. Pull the upper left ring and you'll turn.'

She scrabbled for the ring, but the wind was fierce on her
fingers, making it hard to take hold. She managed it at last,
and felt her body swing in the other direction.

'Pull the lower left ring,' Silvio told her. 'It'll help you
navigate.'

This time she managed better, and felt the parachute respond. Even so, she wasn't safe yet. She knew that. It was going
to take all her cool head to avoid a crash—perhaps a fatal one.

But that mustn't happen. Because she'd promised. She'd
given Francesco her solemn word, and she *must* keep it.

For herself she wasn't afraid, but she was swept with a
terrible fear for him. She'd promised him, and she was about
to betray him.

And then something happened that she could never afterwards explain.

She *saw* him—not as others would understand seeing, but
in a way that had never happened to her before. He was there
behind her eyes, a presence so intense that he was visible as
nothing else had ever been. She didn't know what his face was

like, but she did know the expression it wore at this mo‚
terrified, tortured with the effort of concealing his fear f‚
sake, facing a desolate future without her.

The desolation was there inside her head, too, all around h
a life that was empty because the only person who counted ha‚
gone. She had done this to him, and the knowledge of what she'd
done was there, howling, shrieking at her, making her understand things to which she'd wilfully blinded herself before.

*Come back to me.*

Silvio's voice through the radio made her calmer.

'Lower left a bit more. You're nearly there— A bit
lower—lower—'

And then there was the blessed feel of the ground as she
landed heavily, going down on to her knees at once and rolling
over. When she stopped she could hear the sound of distant
cheering. The whole family had been watching her, their
hearts in their mouths. But there was only one who mattered.

Francesco. She must get to him.

Silvio, too, had landed. Now he pulled her to her feet, got
her free of the parachute and drew off her mask, freeing her face.

'They're heading this way across the airfield,' he said. 'But
it's some distance.'

'Can you see Francesco?'

'He's way out in front. Here.' He took her shoulders and
turned her slightly. 'He's right ahead, and there are no obsta-
cles between you.'

*'Thanks.'*

She began walking, carefully at first, then faster, faster,
running at top speed, running with total abandon, as she'd
never dared to run before.

And now it was there—the rush of intoxicating joy, the
glorious freedom that she'd awaited in vain during the dive.

come at last, possessing her as she hurtled confidently
ds the arms that waited to enfold her.

ou really mean it?' he said, later that night.

They were curled up in their own bed, warm with satiated
desire, and warmer still with the comfort of opening their
minds and hearts to each other in a way that was new.

'I mean every word,' she assured him. 'I'm finished with
all that. No more diving, jumping and suchlike.'

'You don't have to give it up now if you're not sure. I'll
wait until you're ready.'

'I *am* ready. I knew that today.'

'I guess that would be about the time you were blown off
course?' he said, trying to make a joke of it.

'No, it was when I landed and ran to you. I couldn't see
you, but I knew you were running to me, and we'd find each
other. And then I knew I didn't need anything more.'

After that there was a long silence as they held each other,
not even kissing but absorbing warmth and comfort from
each other's presence

'Always?' he murmured.

'Always.'

After a while he ventured to ask,

'Does that mean—no more craziness?'

'I didn't actually say that,' she said hastily. 'But there's
more than one way of being crazy.'

'Well, I guess if you were sensible all the time I wouldn't
know you.'

'Mum and Dad used to take risks,' she remembered. 'But
they stopped when I was born. After that Dad took up sending
messages into other galaxies.'

'Does he get anything back?' he asked, startled.

'Only stuff he can't understand. He'll tell you all ⸂
when he comes for the wedding.'

He kissed her. 'What did your mother take up?'

'Me. She said I was mad enough for both of us. I'll prc
ably find the same.'

'Are you telling me—'

'Be patient.'

Just as she thought he'd gone to sleep he murmured, 'I'm
glad it happened this way.'

'Glad we quarrelled?' she asked.

'Glad we quarrelled, parted and found each other again.'

'Could it actually have been a *good* thing that I told you
to get out?' she wondered, and held her breath, for the answer
was important.

'Yes, or I might never have learned to confront it. You dis-
pelled that darkness as nobody else could. And since then
we've learned things about each other, and ourselves, that we
needed to know.'

And solving problems was what would keep them together,
she thought, glad of his wisdom.

But there was one more step before his darkness was finally
banished, she thought. One more thing that only she could do.

'So now the door's open for us,' she said. 'The one that
leads to the rest of our lives. Come in, my darling. *Come in.*'

Della had said that Hope's life was colourful enough to throw
the other women into the shade, and it was true. She'd loved
and been loved by several men, and had mothered six sons—
four of them her own, two by other women. All of them
looked to her as their mother.

It had been her dream to surround herself with daughters-
in-law, and although the wedding of Francesco and Celia was

the future she considered the dream fulfilled. On this
that she would share with her husband—the man who had
ays been her true love, even while she herself had only half
own it—they would be surrounded by the children and the
grandchildren they considered theirs.

Every member of the family who could manage it had
travelled to Naples. Some stayed at the villa; some took rooms
in nearby hotels. The celebrations had already lasted several
days, as Hope had given a series of small parties so that she
and Toni could spend time with everyone.

'The big party, with everyone, will be a crush,' she had told
her husband. 'So packed that there will be no time for words
except for speeches, which aren't the same.'

She had been right, but now the time had come she found
that no words were needed. As she stood looking around the
garden, where dinner was being served under coloured lamps,
she saw that all her sons were there, and all the women who
loved them. Beside them were their children—some fast-
growing, some babies, but all providing the promise of plen-
tiful activity, the wellspring of her life.

By now everyone knew what had happened at the hospital,
and they looked at the couple walking among them with new
eyes. Both were in their late sixties, together for thirty-five
years, yet now they had the glow of young lovers.

There they stood, arms entwined, while the speeches proceeded and the toasts were drunk.

'And I'll swear, they never heard a word of it,' Carlo said
later. 'They were in their own world and nobody else existed.'

'Did you see Franco there at all?' Della asked.

'No, he was the only person who didn't accept.'

Later that night, in the privacy of their room, Toni read
again the letter his brother had written.

I know you will understand why I cannot be ther
rejoice with you, but I'm still learning to cope with ι.
own loss. I'm going away for a while, to Switzerlanɗ
where Lisa and I went on our honeymoon. I shall revisit
the places of our first happiness, and I like to think she
will be there with me, as she will always be in my heart.

Toni looked up, smiling, as his wife came and rested an arm
about his shoulder.

'Do you remember how we planned our honeymoon?' she
asked, glancing at the letter which, like Toni, she had read
many times before.

'Yes, and we never took that trip,' he remembered. 'Luke
got the flu, and then Francesco caught it from him—'

'And then I caught it, and you nursed me so tenderly,' she
recalled with a smile.

She put her other arm about him and kissed him.

'I think it's time we took that trip, *carissimo*,' she said.
'We've waited far too long.'

\* \* \* \* \*

*A sneaky peek at next month...*

# By Request

**RELIVE THE ROMANCE WITH THE BEST OF THE BEST**

*My wish list for next month's titles...*

In stores from 20th January 2012:

❑ His Mistress Proposal? – Susan Napier,
   Trish Wylie & Kimberly Lang

❑ The Australians' Brides
   – Lilian Darcy

*3 stories in each book - only £5.99!*

In stores from 3rd February 2012:

❑ Matchless Millionaires – Anna DePalo,
   Elizabeth Bevarly & Susan Mallery

**Available at WHSmith, Tesco, Asda, Eason, Amazon and Apple**

*Just can't wait?*

*Visit us Online*

You can buy our books online a month before
they hit the shops! **www.millsandboon.co.uk**

*Don't miss Pink Tuesday*
*One day. 10 hours. 10 deals.*

# PINK TUESDAY IS COMING!

*10 hours...10 unmissable deals!*

This Valentine's Day we will be bringing you fantastic offers across a range of our titles—each hour, on the hour!

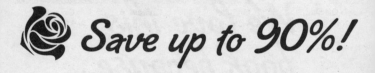

*Save up to 90%!*

*Pink Tuesday starts*
*9am Tuesday 14th February*

# Special Off

Every month we put together collections and longer reads written by your favourite authors.

Here are some of next month's highlights— and don't miss our fabulous discount online!

**On sale
20th January**

**On sale
20th January**

**On sale
3rd February**

**On sale
3rd February**

# Save 20%
## on all Special Releases

# *Have Your Say*

*You've just finished your book.*
*So what did you think?*

We'd love to hear your thoughts on our
'Have your say' online panel
**www.millsandboon.co.uk/haveyoursay**

- 🌹 Easy to use
- 🌹 Short questionnaire
- 🌹 Chance to win Mills & Boon®
  goodies

*Visit us*
*Online*

Tell us what you thought of this book now at
**www.millsandboon.co.uk/haveyoursay**